EXIT 312

The Detour Series Part I

By: Leonard Sharp

First print 2017 December

This is a work of fiction. Make no mistake about it. While it is laced with elements of the truth, more often times than not I exaggerate, embellish, and flat-out fabricate in an effort to further sensationalize the tale being told. My objective is to deliver a "gratifying" read while simultaneously conveying an urgent message. I would hope that no one takes these words as factual and acts or responds accordingly in fear of starting a chain reaction that could become a detriment to yourself, as well as others.

This includes, but is certainly not limited to, any and all law enforcement agencies, children, parents, husbands, wives or significant others in general. It is not my intent to expose, reveal, frame, cause discomfort or break up any home that may otherwise be happy. Nor do I wish to see anyone whisked off to jail. This is simply a story being narrated. I hope you enjoy reading it as much as I enjoyed writing it.

ISBN-13:978-1981635955
ISBN-10: 1981635955

Printed in the USA

DEDICATION

This body of work is dedicated to the past and to the future. To my brother, Tawayne, and to my children Londyn, Braylon, Laneir and Kamarion (Sharp). My step-children Janiyah and Bobby Riley. To my nieces, Khalia Sharp and Taianna Graves. And, of course, to my nephew, Nhazir Sharp. You guys are my source of strength.

It's been said "when you ignore history that's when it has the greatest chance of repeating itself." Smart people learn from their own mistakes, but brilliant people learn from the mistakes of others. Don't be like me. Aspire to be better. Do better. Be brilliant!

ACKNOWLEDGMENTS

I would like to acknowledge my parents. It's virtually impossible to know where you're going without acknowledging and accepting where you came from first. I came from T.C. Britton, by way of Susan Sharp. I'd like to not only acknowledge, but thank you both for giving me life amongst so much more. Without "you" there could have never been a "me."

I love you unconditionally.
Your "baby" boy, Bookie.

Acting as surrogates during different stages in my life... I would like to first acknowledge Benny Smith. Early on in life when me and Tawayne "couldn't" you always "could". I want to say thanks (from both of us).

We love you, "Smurf."

If Benny represented the male category of this particular section or the "dad" segment of this episode, then the female, or "mom" title would have to be attributed to Fay Kirby Coleman. The motherly affection, which you've expressed over the years is hard to put into words. What I can honestly say is in all the years, no matter how many times our personal relationship changed (e.g. from despising to dislike to like and ultimately love), your mission statement has always remained the same. And for that I am eternally grateful.

Love you, "Your Son"

To My Baby Sister, Martha Jean Sharp
YOU WAS THERE!

for as long as I can remember you've been an inspiration to me in more
ways than one. when I was ignorant, immature and didn't quite realize
what I had become ..
YOU WAS THERE!

not just tell me but more so to show me, better.
less conversation and more demonstration
when I was flying first-class from state to state,
scraping Pyrexes to put food on my plate,
living the life, driving old schools and foreign cars
with different girls alike...
at the club *B*lowing *M*oney *F*ast long into the night...
YOU WAS THERE!

as the streets applauded me and referred to me as "the man"
waiting in long lines eager to shake my hand,
I stood erect, feet planted firmly in quicksand
offering up paper as opposed to water,
failing to cultivate my own seeds, what a great father,
stagnation of growth, I made the process that much harder.
YOU WAS THERE!

it was you who made yourself emotionally available
and physically present
with little to no time on hand, all I had to offer was more presents,
in my mind money was always the solution.
you led by example, proving to me that that same money was just
another form of pollution.
later when tragedy befell the family, and I started to become unglued...
YOU WAS STILL THERE

the adhesive that kept us together, and for this,
I personally commend you.
more often than not I received credit and many called me brave.
truth is... that credit belongs to you, cause without you,
I too would have been in a grave.
parts of what's being said may be a bit confusing right now
but in due time made abundantly clear.
every year on your birthday you should read this aloud twice,
be sure to "listen" too - don't just "*hear*."
sincerely from me to you, Thanks for always being there.
LOVE YOU, GIRL

FAM AND FRIENDS

When I say family, I don't mean those related necessarily by blood. This could be a number of people. Many I've nevereven met. Instead, I'm referring to those related by comraderie, by loyalty.

My "La familia"

The term friend has been consistently watered down for generations. When I say it, the term is not used loosely. Like so many others nowadays, I don't speak of a buddy, an acquaintance, a person I met only yesterday or a female I'm creeping with.

Much like "family" when I say friend I mean someone I'm willing to go the distance for or with. A true friend is the single most precious commodity this world has to offer. Being worthy of his/her weight in gold would be an inadequate statement. Believe me, there are not many. So, to my friends, the very few of you who do fall into this category, *THANK YOU!*

When I was surrounded by darkness, you represented a spark that caught fire. That flame flickered, ultimately igniting and illuminating a path through your countless acts of affection, your increased levels of tolerance, and your generous sprinkles of love. Through these actions I was eventually guided along this path *out* of the way of life I so liberally describe (not glorify) in the following pages of this book. A path that, had I not been shown another route, would have surely led to my demise.

As for anyone who is involved in this way of life, or anything even remotely similiar, I strongly urge you to refrain from it and get out now! Especially the youth. Change your course ASAP! Unless you want a long prison sentence or an early departure to the afterlife. The odds are not in your favor. Take it from me, I've run with the best of them & got money with the rest of them. I've seen it, done it, lived it! Been behind Juvenile, State, and Federal bars. Had front row seats to live murder shows. On both sides of the fence. It's all a facade, a mirage if you will. With catastrophic results on the other side of the oasis. In layman's terms, it's a trick, a gimmick, one big game designed for you to lose in some way, shape, or form. The system, THEIR SYSTEM, is not playing with you, so why play with it? It wasn't designed for play.

Life Ain't No Joke.

In the end, the means are never justified. Simple math: the risks do not equal the rewards. Unfortunately, it took me years to realize this. A billion bumps and bruises later it finally dawned on me. Sad to say, but even after coming to such a realization I was still in denial. To accept all that you've been taught thus far is BS, or everything that has been indoctrinated into your genetic makeup is wrong … well, let's just say it's a hard pill to swallow. No one likes to play the fool. It's a pill that most never even put in their mouth, let alone swallow. Don't wait as long as I did. *In order to receive wise advice, you yourself must be wise.* If you're not wise, you won't be able to discern whether the advice (that you're actually receiving) is wise or not. I wasn't wise; the proof is in the pudding. Look at the results I got. A wise man said, *"Ignorance does a man more harm than a cancer in the body."* That's a profound statement when you think of how many people cancer kills annually. Don't be ignorant. And if you have been, don't continue to be. It's never too late. All it takes is one time. One wrong move and Game Over!

Table of Contents

PROLOGUE

*Sometimes you have to get your hands dirty in order to
clean things up. – Author*

Loose gravel that had somehow found its way onto the
uneven pavement made the only sound as the two
unmasked gunmen approached their destination. The
chorus the rocks sang was a symphony of death. Their
strides were brisk, their movements swift and expertly
executed. The shortest of the pair assumed the lead,
ultimately dictating the pace of the assault.

An idling Ford Taurus with New Jersey tags waited
patiently, its driver listening to Gucci Mane rap about how
he was So Icy. Any second his passengers would return,
albeit in a rush. He positioned the rental car to make their
getaway as uncomplicated as possible.

The shooters walked to the edge of the parking lot in
front of thirty or so preoccupied witnesses. Without a hint
of hesitation, they both took aim. Bang! Bang! Out the
corner of his eye, the intended target saw fire escape a
chrome barrel. He saw the flash, hearing a simultaneous
explosion even before he felt the bullet. The fitted cap fell
to the ground. Another blast, another victim crashing to
concrete like an unsupported sack of potatoes, his white tee
now splattered a violent red. A series of shots followed in
rapid succession.

Plaza was more than just an alcohol dispensary. It was a

meeting ground for all walks of life that shared a common goal. On weekends, particularly at night, the liquor store became a scene from a conventional rap video.

Flashy cars, guys behind the wheels in their Sunday best. Girls half naked. Everyone either on their way, or just leaving the club. Hordes of people fraternizing. Tonight, however, that fun had been interrupted. A hail of bullets had rained on their parade. There was a stampede underway. Complete chaos. Panic. Men and women screamed. Bodies dropped, cars collided in a rush to flee, horns sounded off, car alarms came to life.

In the wake of the melee, there were three gunshot victims, seven reported injuries, and five fender benders.

The Dalai Lama, when asked what surprised him most about humanity, answered, "Man. Because he sacrifices his health in order to make money. Then he sacrifices his money to recuperate his health. And then he is so anxious about the future that he does not enjoy the present; the result being that he does not live in the present or the future; he lives as if he is never going to die, and then dies having never really lived."

-Story of our life-

CHAPTER 1 – SQUARE ONE

When a soul is left in darkness sin will be committed. However, the guilty one is not he who commits the sin but rather he who creates the darkness. – Victor Hugo

It was like looking at a complete stranger. Baffled was an understatement. Bookie was taken aback. Mentally, the transition was not yet fully complete. How could it be? Looking around, the once wise guy with quick comebacks and a grocery list of slick sayings thought how in the hell did he go from boarding commercial flights weekly, staying in three- or four-star suites with A-list amenities, to this. From flying first class, or "business class" as the airlines liked to call it, across the country, turning up in every major city in the U.S., to squalor. Bookie lost his bankroll, lifetime partner in crime, and his freedom. In that order. A once-annual membership to a chain of exclusive spa franchises where he enjoyed facials, pedicures, manicures, hour-long massages...the pampered lifestyle of the affluent...to not even having access to bar soap.

Of all the places in the world, how in the hell did he find himself in the Timothy McVeigh suite? The last known address where the 1993 OKC bomber had resided prior to his 2001 execution.

The breathtaking panoramic views were replaced by rolling barbed wire and metal fences. Whirlpools traded for a gnat-infested shower from the early nineteenth century, where inside a copper-toned rust met with a hideous manure green, making for a dazzling display of a perverted rainbow. Room service paled in comparison to that of the Crowne Plaza.

Roaches could be found stuck to every other food tray served; if you were lucky, they'd still be breathing. Mouse droppings accompanied each meal. Almost as if they were condiments. Pillowtop Sealys had been substituted for pancake-thin cots about as soft as a frozen t-bone.

The bunk, toilet, and shower...all within a few feet of the next. Noise levels rivaled a sold-out Cubs game at Wrigley field during playoff season. It was too loud to think. Yelling, screaming, kicking on doors, toilet water coming in your cell because some idiot didn't get a letter from his wife and he decided to flood the deck. Pure Hell! No fresh air, and you never left your cell.

Just a short period ago, it had all been so promising. So full of potential. Now this. The surreality compelled him to shake his dreads, in disbelief. Just like that, in the blink of an eye, it had all come tumbling down. Now far away from home, somewhere in rural Terre Haute, Indiana, the realization of his future began to set in. It was as bright as the 5x9 cage that he now occupied.

The late Mickey Blue Eyes was once quoted as saying, "If you lived my life, one time was enough." As strange as it may seem, while Bookie hadn't lived much of his life yet, he empathized with old Blue Eyes to the point where he felt that his life's journey had epitomized those words.

It was the last day of Ramadan, the holy month, which he had observed with the community. But from a distance.

This was the first time he had endured the fast in almost ten years. It was also the day prior to his beautiful princess Londyn's birthday. He missed his baby dearly. However, survival in here meant he had to check his emotions. Exiled to federal prison while further isolated in the Special Housing Unit ("the hole") as FBOP Inmate #18096-026 meant that survival was a must for Bookie. And survival ultimately depended on his mental fortitude, his ability to detach from happenings beyond the barbed wire fences. His SHU cell was dimly lit, albeit due to the retiring of the sun approximately an hour ago outside and the dungeon-like lighting inside. Nevertheless, he stood immobilized by the reflection of what so long ago used to be him – a baby-faced jovial being with an optimistic viewpoint on life. There was just enough light cast on the sad excuse for a mirror to reflect the image of the alien-like features that made up his being.

Bookie's facial hair resembled that of the most devout Muslim, particularly of the Orthodox sector. He counted fourteen gray strands in the beard that Prophet Muhammed (May Peace Be Upon Him) would have been so proud of. The grays atop his head that haphazardly intertwined with his abundance of shoulder-length dreadlocks were countless.

The once-smooth caramel complexion was now riddled with pus-filled bumps, mostly on his forehead. Remnants of a nasty staph infection had left a repulsive rash blanketing his upper torso that was now threatening an invasion of his back. Inflammation and excessive itching resulted in constant scratching. His eyes went from the blood and skin under his fingernails to the mirror, back to his hand, and then to the mirror again. The study gaze rested there. Bookie shook his head again, this time in disgust.

His once radiant brown eyes had been drained of their life force and were now almost zombified. In a matter of months, it seemed, he had aged a decade. Things, specifically his condition, seemed to go from bad to worse with each day. All the money, gone. The girls and foreign cars, adios. Designer clothes, no more. In addition to countless other losses. His trademark diamond watches and other jewels, over with. His 165-pound frame was rapidly diminishing as well.

Despite his outward appearance, there was something else. Something not so easily recognizable. Something that hadn't just changed with the recent circumstances – a fire! A fire that resonated from deep within and emitted a source of heat like no other. Over time and with each incident, this fire had grown. Now it was on the cusp of becoming a raging inferno, and he knew it had to be extinguished. Nothing good would come from this fire.

It took years to get to this point. Years of leaving tiny bits and pieces of himself – now scattered behind. People, places, and things taking parts of his existence. He didn't know if he would ever be whole again. This was what burned the most. Perpetually searching for completeness. Nothing near a walk in the park, but he knew he had to fight the flames lest they engulf him.

To those unfamiliar with Bookie or who didn't truly know him, the fire might go unnoticed. Most likely it'd be accepted as the norm without the proper instrument to gauge or get an accurate reading (on him). But Bookie noticed. He noticed the look now. He was that instrument. His looks now and then were like oil and water. On the totally opposite end of the spectrum, allowing the first and final meal of the day to properly digest, Bookie sat on his bunk thinking about the direction his life had taken. He thought about one time, just one life .. being enough.

Barely into his thirties, was he really saying the same thing as Frank Sinatra? In retrospect, he'd had only a nine-year run and all of them weren't exactly good. Was that really sufficient in a pragmatic sense?

Lying back, he took a deep breath. Instinctively, his eyes shut. Bookie was twenty-two years old again, peering into another mirror, in another cell, housed in another segregated unit, in another prison. Only moments before his release after serving eighty-four months behind bars.

By all accounts he was just a kid. Bright-eyed and ambitious, yet timid. Outspoken and candid, but conservative and reserved. Present and in abundance was the false bravado that came with youthhood. But Bookie was humble enough to not always act on it. Like the majority of mankind, he was most comfortable in his own comfort zone. That zone, figuratively speaking, was the Illinois Department of Corrections, where he had resided since the age of fifteen.

During Bookie's stint in the Big House, the first thirty months had been in juvenile before he was transferred to the adult prison. No matter where he served time, there seemed to be a common thread. An inherent lack of regard for authority. A blatant thumbing of the nose to any and all institutions of authority. Coincidently, this didn't sit well with those delegated to be in control or "correct" him.

The end result was he spent more than half of the seven years in solitary confinement, isolated from general population inmates. Plenty of time to discover his inner self.

Despite his many idiotic actions, Bookie couldn't easily be pinned as an idiot. Therefore, when it came to pass that the gates were open to emancipate him, he would proceed with caution. Prudent enough to know certain parts of life were uncharted territory for him. He readily admitted his growing discomfort, yet accepted the challenge head-on.

After surviving some of the worst juvenile facilities this country has to offer and later achieving the exact same results in adult penal institutions throughout central and southern Illinois, one did not have to ponder long to determine Leonard "Bookie" Sharp had developed a modus operandi (that obviously worked). Physically, he was small. At the time of his 1997 arrest, his booking sheet listed him at 5'1" and a hundred pounds even steven. Seven inches and thirty-nine more pounds would come during his tenure inside the belly of the beast.

Although he had grown physically during his hiatus, in the mental department, the area that mattered most, he'd surpassed his peers with relative ease. The tools Bookie relied on throughout the years were not so much physical as mental. When others had resorted to their fists, he had relied on his brain.

"Any fool can fight with his hands," he had reminded himself over time. "But to win in this world, you have to fight with your mind." People said only the strong survive. Sure, the strong ruled the weak, physically. However, it was the mentally strong who were truly crowned King of the Hill. To them, whether you were Incredible Hulk or PeeWee Herman, you were all in the same boat. They saw no distinction between the two. When factoring strength, they looked at your brain not your biceps. And this was what Bookie lived by. In the end, he had made it through eight different facilities and a staggering 113 cellmates practically unscathed. Well, physically at least.

Adopting the same disposition while approaching the free world, Bookie prided himself on being a "thinking man." The world was quite like chess. As long as you thought out your next move and stayed a step ahead, you would be okay. He had learned from MJ himself that you can't win them all, and he was the absolute best whoever did it. Another Mike, however, taught him that you damn sure can put up a good fight in the process of trying.

Part of good fighting is predicting your opponent's next action prior to his execution so that you may counter. In the likely event that you make an error, as long as you're a move or two ahead, there is ample time to recover. Thus, you remain in the fight. Chess, never checkers.

Long ago the *Old Man* had instructed Bookie that proper preparation prevents poor performance. So that's what he did. Prepared properly so as to avoid performing poorly upon his release. What he failed to factor into the equation upon his release, though, was that unknown variable... the X-factor. How can you counter the unknown? After being adamant about doing the right thing – like Spike Lee – for years, Bookie wasn't free an entire week before his equilibrium was molested. The armor he had so carefully put into place over the years chinked. After a month, his epicenter was penetrated.

There was no way of knowing then, of course. But in hindsight, the path to perfection that he had so meticulously planned for, his careful calculated road to riches he would navigate, was suddenly blocked. He was made to detour. Where that route ended and the construction/detour sign had been erected, another route began. That route would eventually lead Bookie here. Back to square one!

CHAPTER 2 – LIBERATION

Give me liberty or give me death. – Patrick Henry

Adrenaline increased his heart rate a few palpitations as the recently paroled young man took in his surroundings. Nausea threatened to overcome him. The roller coaster of emotions he was currently experiencing had the inside of his clenched fists moist. Commuting from Danville Correctional Center to Champaign had seemed to take an eternity, in addition to a toll on his nerves. Unsupervised, with no leg restraints or handcuffs, the surreality was at its peak.

Bookie watched a cadre of passengers exit their arriving Greyhound and scurry to various destinations. Oblivious to the ex-con dressed in his cheap black attire, two teenagers rushed into awaiting arms of parents. The family, overcome with joy, embraced a full sixty seconds. Something about the encounter sent a chill down Bookie's spine. He wasn't much older than the teenagers. Where were his family? Where were his open arms?

No one present, no family around to greet him after a harrowing journey didn't sit right with him, after the better part of a decade in bondage. Clutching his ticket, Bookie pushed the thought to the back of his mind before it had time to fully take form. Suspiciously, he looked around the bus depot. He half expected armed guards to appear, force him into an IDOC vehicle, and haul him back to state prison. The more time passed, the more he realized it wasn't a dream, this wasn't a hoax. It was real! This was it! He was finally liberated.

Seven years had passed since Bookie had been this free. Seven years and seven million memories. A few of which he would rather forget. All the racism, the rapes, riots, fights, stabbings, even suicides. So much violence. A controlled environment where homosexuality was considered the norm. No place for any human, especially a teenager, to spend his formative years.

The journey leading to this point had been a difficult one, at times seeming impossible. An unbearable burden. But here he was, free. Finally emancipated. Against all odds. Sometimes he thought he was never meant to make it out. The system had written him off, early on sentenced him to a (psychological) death sentence. Yet through perseverance and prayer, he got the case overturned, the sentence vacated and walked off death row a free man. Despite the newfound freedom, being raised in an atmosphere such as this came with a hefty price. *A price that society would soon pay.*

Spending the years of your life that really determine who or what you'll be as an adult in a jungle, amongst savages, doesn't give you many options. In fact, there are only two: predator or prey. From such a perspective, the former was a lot more appealing than the latter.

******

Home to the fighting Illini, Champaign, Illinois, was a typical midwestern college town. On this particular

Wednesday in early October, there wasn't a lot going on. As if Bookie would notice if there was. The optimistic twenty-two-year-old seemed to be suffering, for lack of better words, from some form of temporary shock. Possibly on the verge of a mental breakdown. Perspiration formed at the hairline, above each partially connected brow, despite the cool breeze that had others turning up their collars.

Although the area was crowded, Bookie felt all alone. Unfamiliar were the sounds of life. Traffic, voices, birds... even the wind blowing made a sound that now seemed strange or peculiar. So many people milled about, coming and going; he tried to watch them all, but it was a daunting task. A lump trespassed amid his esophagus, rendering it difficult to swallow. His mouth was dry all of a sudden, the roof stale. Anxiety. Nervousness. Maybe even fear.

No stranger to fear, Bookie had surmised up until this point in life that he and fear had an understanding. An agreement of sorts. Clearly that was not the case. If so, fear had reneged on its end of the bargain. Thus the current invasion. It's been said that the unknown is one of humanity's greatest fears. And boy was he human!

What could have passed as acute resperatory failure compelled the young man to seek a place to sit. Several benches saturated the immediate area. Many were enclosed, protecting one from the elements of Mother Nature while a few remained exposed. Taking up shelter on the nearest available bench with a cover, Bookie flopped down in the only empty seat and began to count backward from ten.

Inhaling deeply, he forced himself to relax. This was the known, contrary to the unknown, so why the fear? Where did it come from? Was it divine? A warning from above? Should he be afraid? Death around the corner like Pac had prophesized? Something or someone out there, an unknown force awaiting his arrival?

Had he not properly prepared for this day? Plan after intricate plan explored? Plot after plot, strategy after strategy? All of the above to ensure the highest success rate possible? Yesterday, he had been so sure of this moment, so confident. But not today. That was then; this was now. Bookie had put a lot of time and energy into this moment, not knowing when or even *if* it would ever come. Now, here, something was terribly wrong.

You didn't have to be Tom Skilling to see rain was on the Doppler. He unzipped the state-issue khaki jacket in the hopes the cool air would bring some much-needed relief. The bold presence of cotton mouth offered the precise opposite.

A fancy new soda machine unlike any he had ever seen, with neon lights, complete with a life-size mural of Kobe Bryant gracing the front, exuded thirst-quenching promises, just a few feet away. The sun was now completely hidden by the clouds, resulting in a darker-than-average afternoon, coinciding with the convicted felon's mood. According to his ticket, the bus north to Chicago would depart in two hours. What the hell.

Bookie fed the machine a Lincoln. A parade of whirling sounds preceded a mechanical clank and the rattling of loose coins. The soda machine spat out a dirty Country Time Lemonade with the label partially torn and the change for the $5 simultaneously. Soda machines taking $5 bills?

Wow, that was something new. Must have something to do with this new millennium Y2k thing or that thing they call the internet. His soft drink was surprisingly refreshing despite its appearance. Aside from making him spit excessively, the rich yellow liquid served its purpose. Just as the butterflies in his stomach came to life, presenting another dilemma. The onset of "bubble guts."

Change still in hand, he headed back to the bench. Would-be passengers either didn't notice or didn't care; no one acknowledged the young baby-faced being who felt so out of place. Slowly twisting the top counterclockwise on the twenty-ounce recyclable bottle, Bookie began to inspect those individual coins he still held in his hand. Absentmindedly, he patted his pocket where a blank white envelope contained another Lincoln the great state of Illinois was so gracious to provide to all its parolees. This was his entire life savings. He had to keep it close.

The coins all seemed much smaller than Bookie remembered. Quarters were like nickels and dimes. Maybe he was bigger. Sure he was. Inspecting the date on each coin, the lad racked his brain, attempting to remember whether or not anything of significance had occurred during that era, or specifically that year. He loved history, and the need to divert his attention was immense. It didn't work.

He couldn't take his mind off the issue at hand. He couldn't figure it out. Why the mental malfunctioning? What was happening? Agitated, he tossed the change into the pocket of his jacket, wiped his sweaty palms on his pants leg and took another sip of the sweet lemonade. All of the preparation, he thought. The dedication, determination and discipline. Bookie couldn't understand it now, but he would a lot sooner than later. The rain came down.

CHAPTER 3 – EMANCIPATION

Prison is like a drug, only with a lot more severe side effects. If you are able to conquer said side effects, then upon your release, your journey to greatness will merely be a walk in the park .– Author

Approximately ninety minutes of traveling north on highway 57, just forty miles south of Chicago, the Greyhound got off on exit 308. It was the first of Kankakee's three exits. The destination was a rundown motel called Nights Inn that doubled as a bus stop. What a dump. This was not the same Kankakee Bookie remembered. He gathered his meager possessions and headed to the front of the bus. He would now put what he had learned to use.

******

The transition back into society didn't go as smoothly for Bookie as he had hoped. After all, how can one prepare for the unexpected? How can you factor into the equation the X-factor when you don't have all of the components? Immediately, his momentum was offset by the news of several requirements he must meet. First, there was the electronic monitoring device. An ankle bracelet!

He hadn't known he had to be under house arrest. Then he had several mandatory assessment classes and reentry programs to attend. This was all new to Bookie. The first time he heard of such was when he finally sat down to review the bundle of release paperwork handed to him as he exited the prison. His last six months incarcerated were spent in segregation where no counselor had spoken with him. No one bothered to convey details associated with re-entry. It wasn't that Danville CC didn't have designated employees for this task, but the administration was just as glad to rid themselves of him as he was of them.

As Illinois Department Of Corrections (IDOC) Inmate #K90717, Bookie was listed as an unsavory character and a nuisance. Internal Affairs had him listed as a Gangster Disciple (GD), his religion Nation of Islam (N.O.I.) At various stages during his sentence, he had held leadership roles in both factions, despite his youthful appearance, height, age or size. His sworn enemy was the administration, whom he often referred to as "the oppressor." From the time he got off the bus with his #DeathToAllOppressors tattoo, "segregation-to-segregtion" transfer, straight to the hole on disciplinary, it was clear he would be a pain in the ass. Anti-authority, anti-administration, anti-*everything*. Most of the correctional officers (C/Os) and staff being white, suffice it to say Bookie was anti-white. He'd blatantly refused to conform and routinely achieved success in encouraging others to follow him down this rebellious path. During his stay at Danville Correctional Center, the medium-maximum security facility, Sharp kicked up more dust than the start of the Kentucky Derby. Therefore, when it came to his release, the warden did away with protocol.

CHAPTER 4 – HOMECOMING

No one exits prison the same as when they entered. Absolutely no one!
It's virtually impossible. Put simply: you're either better or worse.
SoftER or hardER. Not soft or hard per se, but softer or harder. Those
soft as medicated cotton will be in some ways hardened. People hard
as a rock will begin to soften in areas. Many already hard will become
even harder and vice versa. Prison has that effect, that ability to
change the otherwise unchangeable. Prison can, when society couldn't.
                                                                – Author

Family was no longer the same. Kids weren't kids anymore. Innocence had somehow been transformed into guilt. There were different trends and new fads. The dialect was gone, replaced by a new form of ebonics. Those first were now last, and last were first. The economy was down while the cost of living was up. Followed closely by the recidivism rate.

The world Bookie left behind was no more. Where or when it departed, he hadn't the slightest idea. After the new millennium? Y2K? After 9/11? He'd been locked up during the twentieth century and released into this mystery of the twenty-first. Without a proper manual. How was he expected to operate? Bookie didn't even know what the World Wide Web was. Google first went live in 1998, revolutionizing the industry and the way people found information. Bookie was locked up for all of this.

Twelve months prior to the projected release date, IDOC requires potential parolees to submit possible residency addresses or host sites. Bookie complied. However, soon after the submission, he had landed in the hole for 304 – Insolence – and 403 – Disobeying Direct Orders – from Lt. Brown. During those thirty days, the administration again failed to follow standard procedure. Instead of keeping Inmate #K90717 in the loop or consulting him, someone from records randomly picked an address for him from the listed options. That someone also doctored his paperwork, seeing to it that Bookie got extra classes, house arrest, and whatever else they could make stick.

Of all the possible residences that were submitted, Bookie's first cousin Cherry's was the one approved. As a kid, Bookie had spent a considerable amount of time with or in the presence of his older cousin. There was a mutual fondness between them. Being paroled under her roof would give them plenty of time to catch up. Already, it seemed like her home served as headquarters for family and friends alike. But with her favorite little cousin back on the scene, foot traffic would increase threefold.

His parents came, Top Cat and Sue. His only two siblings were also present, Tawayne and Martha. At the time of his arrest, Martha was a mere ten years old. Here she was today at seventeen, almost bigger than her big brother, like a lil woman, on track to graduate high school soon. Bookie was elated. He would witness her walk the stage, so proud of his kid sister.

Tawayne, three years older than Bookie, kept pulling him to the side, checking on him as if there was a zero behind that three and he was thirty years older instead of three. He bent over backwards to protect his little brother, though; that's just what big brothers did. On parole himself, Tawayne hadn't been free much longer than Bookie, but no one could tell.

Within the first twenty-four hours, waves of people poured in to see him. He felt like a rare artifact on display at a museum. Nobody slept much when night fell. Bookie would stay up late into the wee hours, asking about holidays he'd missed, arguments and fights. About Mama and Snow, his maternal grandparents, who'd both passed during his time away. About Streetwalker, his uncle who succumbed to cancer, Phillip Brown and how he died of a heart attack in Mary's basement. The adults would give one version, but kids would always see the picture from another angle. Bookie found this intriguing. But not as intriguing as when they found that their cousin talked funny, didn't eat certain foods, drink soda or smoke. It's like he was from mars when compared to everyone else around him.

Domonisha and Royce were both teenagers who remembered Bookie, but while he was gone, Cherry had given birth to their baby sister Vinisha. Vinisha was so little and so funny. The spitting image of her daddy, Tip. It had been so long since Bookie interacted with children, he immediately took a liking to Vinisha and vice versa.

Visitors offered hugs, kisses, and good wishes in addition to words of encouragement. Many a female straggled along thirsty, with hopes and aspirations geared toward being the "first." Each one offering a little more than the next, but all sexual advancements were declined. Some flat-out ignored. Indeed, it had been ages since his few encounters with experimental sex, but his mind was elsewhere. There was a time back in the can, when he was sixteen, seventeen, even eighteen years old, and he would jack off four times a day.

Nowadays, his mind was more focused on the mission ahead, doing the right thing like Spike Lee. Well aware of the disease epidemic plaguing communities such as Kankakee, to be frank, he was afraid to have sex. Being as pure as holy water was a rarity. It gave Bookie the upper hand. He intended on keeping it that way.

In the midst of the multitude coming to pay homage or simply to be nosy, there were others who came with more noble intentions. To ensure he was making the necessary adjustments. To hit "his hand". Tawayne was the foreman of this crew. Whenever the influx of people subsided, the more seedier characters would pop up, showing their faces.

Under the cover of darkness, they came bearing gifts. Cocaine, crack, and heroin. Weed and cash too were included occasionally. Each generous gesture was individually acknowledged and accepted. In the event that there was some alone time, which wasn't often, immediately his imagination would run wildly in the direction of Danville Correctional Center where he'd left behind Papito, JB, and Lil C.

For at least thirty days straight, friends and family descended upon the small residential dwelling located at 1975 E. Oak in Mary Crest. Neighbors hadn't a clue why there was a sudden surge in activity at the little black and white house directly behind the old Days Inn.

Nonstop, like bees in a hive, they never seem to let up. Girls, kids, boys, old people. Each person Bookie knew seemed to bring two people he didn't know from a can of paint. The end result was a constant flow of traffic, causing a continuous clusterfuck.

******

Kankakee, Illinois, or K3, was just twenty-five miles from Chicago's Cook County line. K3, a three-prong geographical location, also known as a tri-city area, consisted of Bradley, Bourbonnais, and Kankakee. Many residents had no clue where one began and the other ended. Of the three, Kankakee was the more prominent when it came to citizens of color, and certain factors came with that, factors with negative connotations attached.

In the 80s and 90s, there were Kmarts, Wal-Marts, eateries and dives everywhere throughout the tiny community. Then, all of a sudden, the land was barren. Everyone packed it up and headed to Bourbonnais and/or Bradley. Kankakee was sometimes referred to as "The Kees" or "Killa Kees," and many residents liked to refer to it as "Little Chicago." "Little" was an understatement considering the big city that was only an hour's drive had a population in the millions and Sears Tower, one of the tallest skyscrapers in the world. Compared to the Windy City, the Kees was minuscule, but due to the proximity, the influence of "Chiraq" on the Killa Kees was not that surprising.

While Chicago has close to three million residents, Kankakee is reported to have under thirty thousand. In a way though, for some, Chicago was almost as connected to Kankakee as Bradley or Bourbonnais.

As far back as Bookie could remember, his dad would

get on Exit 312, heading north to the city. With five uncles, six aunties and more cousins than he could keep track of, there was always plenty enough reason to visit Chi-town. A huge percentage of the trips could be attributed to his dad's illicit affairs, but who cared. Back then, Bookie and Tawayne didn't mind as long as they got to see their closest cousins. Spida was growing up in Moe Town, and Roy Boy lived in the notorious Robert Taylor housing projects.

Back in Kankakee, Top Cat would sell the product he scored in Chicago at wholesale prices, bringing in quite a profit. The weed game was a family hustle passed down over generations. Bookie's grandama, "Mama", had migrated from Mississippi north with millions of other poor blacks seeking opportunity. In the late 50s, the destination was originally the Motor City, specifically Black Bottom, Detroit. But when things didn't go right, she ended up in Chicago. She and eighteen of her twenty children, including Top Cat, who later found his way to neighboring Gary, Indiana, then eventually Kankakee.

Mama was into gambling, nu5mbers, prostitution, and whatever else brought in a dollar; Bookie's grandmother lived the street life. She was the Queen in her own right. However, when you wear the crown, there comes a time in life when you have to defend that crown. That time came, and she ended up fleeing south to avoid a life sentence in the Department of Corrections. In tow were Top Cat and half her other children.

She set up shop and didn't look back. For approximately thirty years, she sold marijuana in Kankakee County, mainly in Sun River Terrace, then Hillcrest, a couple hundred feet from District III Junior High School. In the late 80s and early 90s, she was so generous as to pay Bookie $10 to help bag up pounds into dime bags until he got hip to her and started cuffing half and whole ounces of the Red Hair Sensimilla.

"I'm sorry, baby, but Mama gotta search you," she had told him one time in the softest, sweetest voice, with her hand on the .38 she kept in the snuff-stained gown she wore like her uniform.

The stolen ounces were behind the couch, though, so he was good to go. She expertly patted him down. He hated to think what would have happened had she found the missing "reefer".

******

But those days were over. God designed man with two ears and one mouth for a reason. You should listen twice as much as you speak. These early stages of his release, this was exactly what Bookie did.

Tawayne, much the businessman, would pop up unexpectedly at the oddest of times, making sure his "lil bro" was cool. He would always come with his hands full. Money, clothes, shoes, gadgets, etc. He'd show up with Nike socks and blue underwear, then slide Bookie $250 when no one was looking. Later the same day, he was back. This time with a pair of pants and the matching shirt. Handing him a Grant while everyone was looking but whisper that a folded-up Franklin was inside the watch pocket of the jeans. Before he even woke up the very next morning, Tawayne would be back with Reebok socks and red underwear, forking over a couple hundred more bucks all in small bills.

"Just a lil pocket change to hold you over until you can get in traffic," he'd say. Bookie was on house arrest for the time being with little to no movement. The money began to pile up. Collectively, the handouts made for a substantial amount of cash. All drugs he received were sold wholesale or passed out on consignment. Not wanting any part of the business didn't mean he was naive enough to not want the money. Sure he was born at night but not last night.

It wasn't that Bookie wasn't used to having money; in elementary, his pockets had the mumps. In high school, he had sold cocaine, so he kept a bankroll on him as well. This was nothing new to him. However, due to the seven-year lapse, he felt the need *now* to keep his pockets stuffed with dead presidents. With nothing to do and nowhere to go, Bookie hung around Oak Street. That feeling became something of a dependance, pants fitting like he wore thigh pads.

CHAPTER 5 – TRANSITIONING

In prison monsters are created. Consciously and subconsciously. Those conceived subconsciously are by far the worst, for they are released into a sleeping society that unfortunately won't be awakened until it's far too late. – Author

Twenty-five of the hundred grams of heroin and an eighth of the cocaine had been fronted to his cousin Malik.

Malik owed $4,000. Bookie received the news via another cousin. Seventy-two hours after receiving the drugs, Malik was apprehended in Waterloo, Iowa. One-hundred twenty-six grams of cocaine and an ounce of black tar gone down the drain. After begging, promising to be careful, crying how no one ever believed in him to afford him the luxury of "getting on," look what happened. Bookie was more concerned with his cousin's freedom, than the 4k owed. Ten other people were already simultaneously promising that once he was able to get in motion that they would also have a "gappa" or something for Bookie.

Tawayne stopped in to check on Bookie one morning a few days after he'd gotten home. "Aye, what's up? You posed to get some movement today or what?"

Shirtless and rubbing his dented afro, Bookie stifled a yawn. "Man, ion know what the fuck going on."

"What you mean? You ain't talk to yo P.O.? What he say? You ain't got that faggot-ass dude, Winks, do you?"

"I got a female. Her name Karen somethin. She posed to

slid on me damn near three days ago. Why? Waddup, what you on, what's the move?"

"Wanted to take you shopping, at least to the mall or something."

"I'm cool on the gear for right now. Plus it's a million otha mufuckas say they wanna take me shoppin."

"Yea? That's cool, but you my –" Tawayne slapped his chest twice for emphasis – "lil brother. I gotta make sure you cool. I wanted to tell you too," he continued. "It's a few niggas asked for yo number. Since ion know who you want to have it or not have it…" he trailed off. "I gave it to JD, though. I know that was yo man hundred grand before you left. Just growing up together, I know you fucked wit him. He doing aight for his self too. That nigga used to always ask about you when I first got out."

Standing to indicate the conversation was over, Bookie couldn't help but notice the physical resemblance. People had said in the past the brothers looked alike, but Bookie had never seen it until now.

"You talking about Jason? What that nigga got going on?" A couple inches taller and a few pounds heavier, Tawayne was obviously the bigger brother.

"He be fuckin wit the green."

"Aww, yea?"

"Donnie asked for yo number too," Tawayne remembered.

"I heard he was getting a lil money."

"Yea, I be fuckin wit 'em. He runnin up a check. I gave it to Jigga too just now bout an hour ago. He got a bag. He hit me and asked what was the address over here. I told him to hit yo line."

"He already called. Him and Taj posed to slide through later."

"Taj fulla shit, he just told me later on we goin to Gala Lanes to shoot pool. He said he wanted his run back cuz I fucked him up last time at Bada Bing.. he cryin 'bout they tables not bein right."

Tawayne pulled out a Black & Mild, removed the top half of the plastic wrapper that covered the filter part and commenced to rolling the tiny cigar in between both palms. It looked like he was trying to start a fire. While he freaked the Black, he went on. "That nigga Jigga said he got something for you. Him *and* Yodi. I be fucking wit'em every now and then."

"What that nigga Yodi on, where his slick ass at?"

"Man, ain't no tellin like Jack told Helen with that dude." With this, Tawayne showed some teeth and shook his head.

"What happened, why you laughing? What he on?" Bookie asked knowingly, with a smirk of his own.

"Come on, man, you know Y. Ain't shit changed, he still caked up." And Bookie did know Yodi, or 'Y' as some like to call him.

"Ion know. I been hearing bits and pieces."

Y was the King of pulling stunts. He had more gall than the great Evel Knievel when it came to stunt pulling, and just as many, if not more, under his belt. Y was going to get to the money rain, sleet, snow, or sunny. By force or fraud, hook or crook. It didn't matter to him. He had that Malcolm X state of mind...by any means necessary.

His most noteworthy caper to date was the collecting of twenty-three different people's money. His spiel was simple: I'm fina go cop, if y'all want, y'all can send y'all money. Coincidentally, during this time there was a drought. In the hood, finding a "plug" or a person with good cocaine was as rare as a High Point 9mm that didn't jam. The twenty-plus unsuspecting investors were well aware of the short supply of the Schedule II narcotic, and that was all the more reason. Along with the allure of receiving a cheaper price. Many of their last encounters with cocaine had been via Yodi so why not roll the dice with him one time?

The individual investments ranged from three to eighty-one thousand dollars. Per person. It was rumored to be two, three or even four hundred grand total. Needless to say, Yodi was far from just a one-trick pony; he pulled a Houdini. Six months later when he re-surfaced amidst threats on his life, violence perpetrated against those close to him and several other actions on behalf of those demanding a return on their investment, Yodi smoothed things out by yielding a high return to all twenty-three people.

Not only did he give them what they had coming plus extras, he put an end to the drought by turning on a supply that wouldn't shut off for years to come. A mere thirty days later, people had forgotten all about the Ponzi scheme.

Tawayne turned to leave. He never stuck around too long; his services were in high demand, made obvious by the two phones ringing and vibrating non-stop.

As promised, a few hours later, Taj made his debut.

Originally he was Tawayne's best friend, but now the three of them were like brothers. Despite it being early and a weekday, Taj was sloppy drunk and could barely stand. Bookie couldn't believe it. The first time seeing him in seven years and he shows up like this!

Approaching Bookie and his company on the small porch that had become his unofficial headquarters, he and Kmart made quite the spectacle. Normally, Bookie attempted to keep guests restricted to the outside in order to respect Cherry's tranquility. She never griped or complained; it was just a gesture of respect.

The lighter of the two young ladies entertaining Bookie murmured abruptly, "We'll be right back," and made a beeline exit to the Chevy Cavalier they had just pulled up in. The duo was not interested in conversing with anyone except for who they'd come to visit. Especially since one of them had lied about her age. As they were leaving, Taj tried to proposition the taller of the pair. She scrunched up her nose and made a facial expression that translated as: not if you was the last guy on earth, then quickened her pace.

Kmart and an ankle-bracelet-wearing Bookie burst into laughter. Kmart was also a close friend of the family. He, too, was Tawayne's running buddy. "Was that Tangie daughter?" Kmart asked more seriously. "That lil girl.. if it's her, she ain't shit but like fourteen, I think."

Bookie shrugged his shoulders.

"I don't know; I met'em the otha day. They say they eighteen but I can tell they probably young cause they keep coming ova here, and err time anotha mufucka pull up they run."

Taj ignored the issue at hand. "What's up, lil bro?" Taj asked with slurred words and a lopsided grin, after coming up empty-handed in his pursuit. He then rubbed and patted Bookie's mini afro like he was a cute little puppy.

"How does freedom feel, boy? Yo ass was gone forever!" Kmart chimed in. "Lo ain't been through here today?" He was referring to Tawayne.

"Come on, bro, this that man lil bro. If your little brother just did five years and came home yesterday or day before..." he paused as if he had lost his train of thought before going on. " ... wouldn't you go see'em?"

Kmart's only reply was a five-second sympathetic stare, then a pitiful shaking of the head. Bookie, a tad humored, fought back a laugh. He didn't bother to correct Taj, who was way off on his math by two years, but before the inevitable argument ensued, he intervened.

"Kmart, what's up wit you, what you been on?"

Kmart was still looking at Taj like his shoes were on the wrong feet. Hoping to break some of the tension, Bookie spoke up.

"Taj, how you been? Where Pudgie at? Yo mom cool? Where Keisha? Where lil Junior, how old is he now? What's up wit the rest of the fam?"

Just then, another car pulled up. Taj's phone began to ring, then stopped suddenly. "Nobody but Nikki ass. Want me to call her, waste my minutes; I told her she gotta wait til after seven. I don't got unlimited," he mumbled more to himself than anyone else present.

Bookie didn't care about free nights or weekends or incoming calls; as far as he was concerned everything was unlimited. "Here, use my phone," he handed Taj his cell phone.

"C'mere, Bookie. Shit! Wit yo fine ass!" a female yelled from the curb.

Bookie called back from the porch. "Who is that?"

"Come and see wit yo lil sexy ass. I know you ain't scared!" Two women could be heard giggling like schoolgirls.

Kmart and Taj had started their bickering again. Arguing back and forth like intoxicated siblings. What the hell, Bookie thought, hopping off the porch.

Janiyah Williams and Reneka Henderson were his best friends since middle school. They parked and got out. He embraced them both affectionately, and the trio exchanged pleasantries. Over the years, the girls had stayed in touch, Reneka a lot more than Janiyah, but he loved them the same.

Kmart and Taj were Tawayne's friends. Bam, prior to his untimely death, Jigga, Lavann... all these guys were his brother's age, therefore his peers, not Bookie's. Of course, Bookie knew them, hung out from time to time, but it wasn't his crowd. The same month Biggie Smalls was gunned down in L.A., Tawayne had been arrested. In the wake of the arrest, his crew had adopted his kid brother and taken him under their wing.

CHAPTER 6 – REMINISCENT

A soldier don't know if he a soldier until the outbreak of war. – Author

Three cribs on east Merchant Street served as HQ back then. Levann's, his cousin Deon's, and Vodus'em crib on the corner of Orchid. On Merchant Street and throughout the entire area, they became a force to be reckoned with. The reign lasted all of six months. In the first week of October, following in the footsteps of his older brother, Bookie too was jailed. Possession of crack cocaine in school. He hadn't seen the streets again until now. The drug case, along with the two other cases he was already fighting, had robbed him of his adolescent years.

For this new charge, combined with the previous two, Bookie received thirty-one years from Judge Gould. Twelve years for the case in school, twelve years for a home invasion and seven years for a separate burglary. Fortunately, they all ran concurrently, which translated to a twelve-year sentence total. Doing one twelve-year sentence would eat up the other twelve-year sentence, as well as the lesser seven-year sentence. In the State of Illinois, you did fifty percent back then. On top of the fifty percent, you could earn six months good time.

Instead of being a model inmate and doing the minimum, Bookie converted his five and a half years to seven. In fact, at the time of his release, in addition to the last 180 days of his stay spent in the hole, Bookie had another year's loss of good (time) conduct credit in Springfield pending approval. He had ten more months in the hole and three years C-grade, where you could only spend thirty dollars a month at the store among several other restrictions.

That seemed like a century ago. Back on the porch, the five of them congregated. Bookie was amused seeing his childhood friends all grown up. Hours slipped away and the sun disappeared, but no one noticed. What was extremely noticeable, however, was Taj's drunkenness. He and his drinking partner had never stopped turning up their pint of Hennessey. When the first bottle ran dry, they simply retrieved another from the car. By now Taj's pupils were dilated, and the mangled porch railing was the only thing holding him up. Due to a higher BMI or a higher tolerance, Kmart wasn't as affected. But his speech was becoming incomprehensible as well.

Taj's cell phone started playing 50 Cent's "Wankster." The ringtone stopped then started again a few seconds later.

"It's in yo back pocket, man," Bookie directed after watching Taj pat every pocket but the back one with a stupefied look on his face. "That shit sad."

The girls laughed as he barked into the receiver.

"We over here now! ... Aight, bro, waiting on you."

Minutes later, he was motioning Bookie to the side of the house away from the group. At the conclusion of a series of gestures indicative of him being well-endowed – jerking, yanking, and pulling at his crotch – he proceeded to unzip his pants. Turning just slightly out of view, Bookie did an about-face as Taj spread his legs.

"Bro, aye, bro, you listening? Bro?"

"The only thing I hear is the draining of your unwanted fluids. What you think, man, how can I not hear yo drunk ass? Shit don't make no sense." Bookie kept his back turned.

"Bro, did you talk to her yet?" The intended whisper came out more like a shout.

Bookie was beyond annoyed. It was bad enough that Taj was literally pissy drunk, but he was making him a part of a pissy-drunk conversation.

"Man, who the fuck are you talkin bout?" The fact that he had referred to a "her" wasn't lost on Bookie, but he chalked it up to his buddy's current state. "You mean Jigga? Did I talk to Jigga?"

"Nawl, not Jigga. I said her!" This was said as if he was talking to an idiot or if Bookie was the one drunk. "Yo wife. I'm talkin bout yo wife. You talk to her yet, bro?"

Now Bookie was upset. Talking to him like he had learning disabilities or issues with comprehension was one thing, but to get him confused with someone else completely…"Man, I'm outta here. Dude, you drunk. You don't even know who the fuck you talking to. Ion got no fucking wife. I ain't married." Bookie started toward the porch.

"Hold up, bro, hold up real quick."

Bookie heard Taj's pants zip and turned to face him. "Dude, ion know what the fuck you on or what you talking bout, but y'all need to lay off the bottle. You act like you doing drugs and—"

"Kadaisha," Taj cut him off mid-sentence. The name

was pronounced crystal clear. Those three syllables knocked the wind out of Bookie.

Silence.

Bookie was confused.

"Yea, I'm talking bout Kadaisha, bro. That was her calling me."

Now it was Bookie's turn to be drunk. Punch drunk! Just the mention of the name had a soul-stirring effect on him.

"Fuck that bitch!" Confusion, anger, love, and another emotional ingredient caused the words to spew forth without him realizing what he'd said. "She broke bad on me. Ain't no sense in her coming back now trying to show up. That shit over with. I need her like I need a hole in the head."

As if Bookie hadn't said a word, Taj asked, "You talk to her yet? Bro, she loves you. She been on my line, she on yo bumper. She not like all these other girls around here."

It took everything in Bookie not to scream – or worse – but Taj's drunken stupor didn't allow him to catch on to his boy's ill feelings on the situation. Bookie just stared at him in disbelief.

"Bro, she loves you," he went on, unfazed. "Just talk to her. Do it for me," he rambled on. "She really loves you."

"What you mean? She got a pussy, don't she? She was fucking, wasn't she? She wasn't there for me, was she? Man, get the fuck outta here!"

Bookie had had enough. He turned to head back to the porch with Taj on his heels.

"Aye, look, bro; aye, look." He smacked his lips in

frustration.

There wasn't much light on the side of the house or driveway, so Bookie slowed down.

He didn't want Taj to fall or hurt himself. Taj's stride was unsteady, but he managed to stay upright. Taj wiped his mouth with the back of his hand when he made it to the front porch. He looked around, lost, before stopping just out of earshot of the guests.

"Hold on, bro." Again, the whisper was a lot louder than he had intended. He drew his face near Bookie's, alcohol stench and all. A streak of moonlight illuminated one side, and the streetlight lit the other side, casting a ghastly glow. Taj now looked like a storyteller around a campfire.

"Her hair, bro," he proclaimed in a drunken drawl. He gestured with this hand to indicate the length. With wild eyes and a contorted face, he continued, "Real hair, not that fake shit. She look *good*. She ain't been getting ran through either!" Spittle sprayed like a bottle of disinfectant in a filthy bathroom from his lips.

It had been a long time since Bookie looked the word "love" up in the dictionary, but at last check, Kadaisha's pretty face was next to it. Your very first love is one of those people that the unsolved enigma called life will never let you forget. Bookie's had been a scrawny twelve-year-old named Kadaisha with a very smart mouth. As a seventh-grader at Kankakee Junior High School, he'd been introduced to her casually during a sporting event. Tawayne's then-girlfriend, Lavetta, just happened to be Kadaisha's older sister. More interested in gangs and guns than girls, Bookie had only agreed to go out with Kadaisha to appease his older brother, whom he idolized.

She was his first and only girlfriend. Therefore, when it came to the kind of love reserved for the opposite sex, Kadaisha was all he knew. Which, in retrospect, meant little to nothing. Adamant that he did not want to see her, Bookie wished Taj would just change the subject already.

This proved to be equivalent to residents of hell wanting ice water. Taj was still trying to drive his point home. Kmart was far away from the chatter, standing in the street arguing with someone named Nish. The girls were ignoring the guys while they huddled around the latest T-Mobile Sidekick featuring pics of their friend's newborn.

"But..." Taj was mumbling.

"Ain't no ifs, ands, or buts about it. Ion even know why you steady talking bout the shit." Bookie cut him off.

Taj wouldn't let up! Even after everybody else was back on one accord and chilling. Bookie finally agreed to his request just to shut him the hell up and enjoy his company.

Jigga came and went. It wasn't really his crowd, he said. Janiyah had to tend to the three kids she had given birth to during Bookie's stretch. Reneka split with her, leaving Bookie with Cain & Abel. They eventually packed it up while running low on their stash. Bookie said a silent prayer for his old chums upon hearing they were making another liquor run. Then he stopped short, saying aloud, "What's the use of praying?"

"What you say, bro?" Taj yelled from behind the wheel after cranking the engine. "We'll be back, gotta grab some more drank."

"Man, are you serious? You don't need to be driving,

Taj."

He increased the volume of the stereo, allowing 50
Cent's "Many Men" to drown out Bookie's caution. A
broad grin on his face said: I got this! With Kmart bobbing
his head to the beat, Taj yelled over the music, "You *my* lil
bro! This what I do. I *been* doing this, I *do* this, I'm not
new to it. I'm true to it! Let me fuck the cow while you hold
the tail."

Before Bookie could reply, the Wide Track Grand Prix
lurched forward at an accelerated speed. "Turn y'all lights
on!" Bookie yelled after them. It was too late. A block or
so away, he heard burning rubber and prayed that Plaza
Liquors would be closed when they arrived.

His ear felt icky from Taj's saliva. While he was on the
porch alone, his mind drifted back to the inmates he'd left
behind at Danville CC. He missed Papito; he wondered
what JB and Lil C were doing. He was astounded, still not
really believing that he'd made it out and was now free.
Gazing into a far-off place, Bookie unconsciously fingered
his bacteria-filled ear and massaged the lobe between his
thumb and forefinger.

The other hand scratched his leg around the small black
monitoring device that caused quite an itch. A late-model
red Chevy Monte Carlo pulled up, slowing to a crawl,
stopping directly in front of 1975.

Who could this be, he wondered as the horn honked
twice, forcing him back to this realm.

"Who is that?" Bookie was getting used to this now.
Quite a few cars drove past the small residence just to be
nosy, making sure it was on their routes at least twice a

day.

"Who you want it to be?" a female's voice shouted back. He knew it was a female but hadn't the slightest clue as to the precise one. After taking only a few steps, he could make out Kadaisha, even in the dark. Initially just her silhouette, then specific features as he got closer.

There were no hugs or rushing into each other's arms. No fireworks or earth-moving French kisses. This wasn't a movie or a fairy tale greeting from a romance novel. This was real. Bookie gave a very dry, "Wadd up," followed by, "What yo ugly ass want?"

"Boy, don't front."

Bookie had added a touch of humor to his last question that Kadaisha caught, but she also knew he was probably not pleased with her performance over the last couple of years.

"Don't act like you don't wanna see me or you ain't want me to come over here." In a softer voice, she added, "Mary said come see her too. Where Taj?" She looked around, hoping to lighten the mood. "He said he was over here. I know his drunk ass ain't lie to me."

"He was. They just left. Tell Mary I just got my movement. I only get four hours a day though, just for job hunting. I'll probably stop through there tomorrow for a few minutes."

Staring straight ahead, Kadaisha had a nonchalant look about her. Bookie leaned in the window of the passenger side, and for a split second their eyes met when she turned unexpectedly. Her scent was intoxicating. They both looked away uncomfortably, hoping the other didn't notice.

Kadaisha looked the same as when he'd last seen her. Her petite frame, smooth brown skin and long silky black hair had set the standard for Bookie's "type" almost a decade ago when the two first met during halftime in the cafeteria at the junior high school. Bookie could now see what Taj was implying. Put simply, Kadaisha was beautiful. Not just beautiful, but naturally beautiful; she looked clean, pure, innocent. Mary once described the adolescent (puppy) lovers as siblings.

"Y'all kids look like brother and sister," Mary had joked, adding, "Top Cat may have been over there with Fay."

The females Bookie had encountered thus far couldn't hold a candle to the woman before him. They paled in comparison.

Outside the car, Bookie stood for an hour until his legs tired. Kadaisha casually asked if he wanted to sit in the car. Minutes later, she was rubbing his afro affectionately, the way mothers do their kids, or maybe wives do their husbands, it was hard to tell.

"What you gonna do with this? You growing your hair out?" Her tone was so sincere, soothing, loving and caring. Her mouth inquired about his mane, but her heart and body wanted to know his plans for her and the future.

Inside the confines of the coupe, her right arm rested alongside his left arm on the center console. It was just enough contact to cause the bulge in his pants. 107.5 WGCI pumped out R&B tunes for twenty minutes nonstop. Bookie didn't like the feeling of aloofness, but he loved the mood. For two hours he fought it but eventually came to grips with the fact that he had no control over the situation. He was smitten as a kitten. His emotions were similar to a raging bull running wild, not able to be contained. Kadaisha told him she'd been living in Georgia. She'd come back recently and was just getting back on her feet, staying in between her grandma's and her mom's. What she didn't say was she'd come back for him. He knew, though.

Car after car rode past. Some more slowly than others. Then Shawn and Icholis came. Shawn pulled up next to the Monte Carlo and opened his door, "Aye, who is that? Tell that bitch Bookie to come outside!"

"This is me. Fuck you want?" Bookie raised his voice from the passenger side.

"Bitch, I want a hug. C'mere! I got this bitch, Icholis, too; he tryna fuck you."

When the erection evaporated, Bookie got out the car and told Shawn to park right, stop blocking the street. Shawn complied but kept whispering, "Who is that bitch? She decent, G."

Bookie greeted his boys before rushing them on their way. With a flaccid penis and almost a half fluid ounce of precum in his Calvin Kleins, Bookie got back in the passenger seat.

One or two other people came through, but they were all redirected. The lovebirds talked about nothing in particular into the wee hours of the night. As hours passed, the suppressed feelings of old resurfaced with a vengeance. When at last Bookie did go in the house, he felt an emptiness immediately. He wondered was he soft or just lonelier than he'd known? Or maybe it was Kadaisha. If only he didn't have that stupid band on and could go past the curb. Maybe he could have gone with her and talked some more.

He longed for Kadaisha. So much so he dreamed of her as his heavy eyelids fluttered. The Sprint flip phone came to life with B.G.'s "Don't Talk To Me." Due to the years in the penitentiary, he was a very light sleeper. God knows that wasn't the place for deep sleep.

"Hello?" he answered sluggishly.

"I'm home. You told me to call you when I got here. Was you asleep?"

"Unn-unh... nawl, not really."

"Boy, you sound tired. Gone head and go back to sleep. Tomorrow on my break, I'ma call you, k?"

"Aight."

"Love you too. Good night."

Bookie was confused. What should he say?

Kadaisha picked up on the hesitation. "You don't have to say it back. It's cool. I'm just telling you how I feel."

"I hear you."

He dozed again, but suddenly he was wide awake. Kaidaisha had a fifteen- to twenty-minute drive home. Where her mom lived was heavily wooded. He had his doubts about her driving to such a secluded area as Hopkins Park at this hour. Anything could happen. At least the sun was coming up. She said she was already home so….

He wanted to call back and for a brief moment pondered whether to do so. Then Vinisha was there, shaking him from sleep. Had it all been just a dream….

CHAPTER 7 – OPPORTUNITIES

*There is some good in every person, place or thing, but not many
people possess the uncanny ability to extract it . –* Author

"My mama said is you hungry?" Vinisha demanded.

"What?" Bookie croaked, struggling to get his bearings
while vigorously rubbing his eyes.

"And somebody outside for you."

"Who is it?" Sunlight penetrated the bedroom he shared
with Royce, forcing Bookie to squint at Vinisha, who
shrugged her shoulders like a five-year-old who didn't
know the answer to an adult's question. Bookie
remembered Royce showing him something on the internet,
a video on this new phenom called YouTube just prior to
counting sheep. Bookie asked what YouTube was. "Some
shit that just came out this year; you can watch videos
people upload."

"Where Royce at?"

"My brother gone."

"Where Domonisha and Martha?"

Instead of answering, she said, "My mama cooking." It
was no use. He shuffled to his feet.

"Can you turn the game on for me? Please?" she asked
politely.

"Vinisha, I just got out the joint. I don't know how to
work Playstations and Nintendos and all that shit." He gave
his little cousin a few seconds of his time in a vain attempt

to assist before heading for the kitchen, leaving Vinisha behind to separate wires alone.

******

JD was outside waiting on him. He had brought Bookie a half pound of weed and $500 cash. "When you get done with that shit, lemme know. I keep that shit, I'ma make sure you good."

He and Bookie discussed old times.

"All the niggas I seen since I been out, all the niggas who were good in sports or had good parents and shit, they not on nothing."

"That's crazy, ain't it," JD laughed but acknowledged the truth in the statement. "It's the niggas like us that's making it, that came from shit and neva had nothin."

"Yeah, that's crazy, but I can see how. See, for them, once that sports shit don't work out, what do they have? Once their parents take the leash off or cut their supply off, it's ova."

"Hell, yea, you ain't lying, G. Them niggas was sheltered. They can't make it out here."

"Hell yea, after that leash come off then they gotta get it out the mud. Shit like finding a diamond in a rough. It's only so many diamonds though, and we been doin it already five, ten or twenty years before they even get the leash off, our whole life damn near. They can't compete."

"Man, for real, I'm not gon shelter my kids. I want them to know what's what, cause like you say once that shelter gone, they ass'll be grass. Especially in the hood!"

"Yea, see, if they ain't in the hood, they probably could make it, but in the hood, it's over with for them."

"You ain't lyin, G," Bookie agreed. "I ain't sheltering mines either. When I got out, I asked about a few decent lil hoes I remembered from school. All of them were washed up. The star of the football or basketball team gave them babies, and they bodies all fucked up wrinkled and shit, stretch marks. Now them stars, them niggas ain't shit, nobodies. Had all the hoes back then, now they hoes tryna fuck wit niggas like us. They riding mountain bikes, smoking cigarettes and drinking 40s and shit. Clown shit. I just saw that nigga Travis, he all the way in the way. I thought that nigga was going to the league. Shit crazy out here."

Bookie sat in the passenger seat of JD's Olds chopping it up. They reminisced about a couple capers they had pulled. Talked about Romale and how a bitch had killed him. "That nigga used to write me," Bookie told him.

"Aye, you know Mrs. Tate posed to be coming over here to see me later on," Bookie said, clearly enthused.

"Man, she bout to have yo ass in church and some more shit, watch. I saw her in that lil jeep or Rodeo or whatever it was, I think it's gray. Soon as I saw her, she start preaching." He laughed.

The throaty trademark laugh hadn't changed after all those years. In fact, not much had changed. While attending Aroma Park Elementary, JD had towered over Bookie in Mrs. Tate's fourth-grade class. He was still probably seven inches taller than Bookie. Aside from the zigzag French braids and the excess gold and diamonds, he was still JD. A good dude with a huge heart and very extended sense of humor.

"Seems like just yesterday, she was in class trying to whoop us. Me, you, Marco Wilson, Sherman Collins, Tron Claypool. Damnn, lemme see who else... Wasn't nobody worse than Nate Franklin."

"What about Laurie Williams?" Bookie said.

"Hell, yea, I forgot her ass, ol' Punkin. Yea, that was our class. We gave her ass gray hair. We bogus!" he laughed. "On the G, we was bad as hell."

While Bookie and JD were trippin down memory lane, a blue Crown Vic pulled up with rims clearly too large for its chassis. Pounding bass rattled the trunk.

"Who the fuck is that?" Bookie asked, watching the car in awe. "Are those twenty-twos or twenty-foes?"

"Then some foes," JD said matter-of-factly. "That's Cap Ball fat ass."

"Aww, that's Fat Boy," he corrected after the car came to a stop and Shawn got out.

Before his door could even close behind him, he called out, "What you doing with this bitch, JD?"

Laughing, JD said, "Bitch, stop playing with me. That's crazy, G, this bitch gonna get the same necklace I got."

"That's some hating-ass shit, ain't it, G, tell the truth," Fat Boy asked.

Shawn was at the car now, and he shook their hands.

"Get down, bitch, I'm tryna knock you!" Shawn pulled two pairs of dice and commenced to shaking each pair in both his meaty fists like maracas.

"Bitch, I'm already broke. I just bought a couple more of them same necklaces you talking bout you had first. I only wear them muhfuckas for a few months. I ain't like you, keep the same necklace yo whole damn life." Bookie laughed at JD's comeback.

"Bitch, you ain't broke! I'ma knock you. I hope you gave folks something too. Did he hit you, G? That bitch got it, on my mama, on GGGGGD, that bitch on!"

It appeared Shawn went by the name Fat Boy nowadays. He had three solid reputations: Saying "Bitch," shooting dice (mostly cheating with loaded or trick dice), and selling pieces of crack from his phone. He definitely wasn't the guy Bookie remembered. But people did change. For better or worse.

JD had a few moves to make and left. Alone, Shawn updated Bookie on what all he'd missed while doing time. Romale's name came up again.

"Yea, that bitch told me he had got a couple letters from you."

"That's crazy, man, I can't believe that nigga dead. Who you said did it? What's ol' girl name again?"

"Jessica."

"Ion think I know her... Jessica?" Bookie repeated, squinting his eyes and wrinkling up his features in contraction.

"Man, you know that black bitch, Microwave's sister." The way he'd pronounced the bitch word when referring to Romale was totally different than with Jessica. The malice or contempt in Jessica's epithet was evident.

"Yea, I know Jessica. That's my buddy. She did that shit? I swear I aint know y'all was talking bout her."

Shawn broke it all the way down, how they were going together. How she ran him over in a car. The consequences and repercussions of her actions.

Before long, Reneka and Janiyah pulled up. As they got out of the car, Bookie's Sprint rang. Kadaisha phoned to say she missed him and would be over later. Failed attempts to control his emotions plagued the ex-con for hours. The truth is he couldn't keep his mind off her. Her voice alone caused butterflies, the ones Michael Jackson sang about.

"Come on, bitch, let's go to the mall."

"Man, I told yo fat ass I gotta wait till my movement start."

"Bitch, I ain't fat. On my momma, I ain't fat! That's fat right there."

Shawn pointed at an approaching Reneka, who was at least seventy-five pounds heavier than him.

"Fuck you, Shawn! Yo momma fat bitch!" Reneka shot back, unwavering.

"Bitch, my name Fat Boy! I keep telling you and this lil bitch," he said, jerking his head in Bookie's direction.

"Aye, watch yo mufucking mouth, SHAWN!" Bookie yelled.

"Bitch, what you gonna do? You can't fight. I know you, you ain't shit without a pistol." He was laughing now.

"You forgot, bitch, you used to spend the night at my granny crib on weekends. Rememba you used to try and wrestle?"

Shawn went on and on and on. He was feeling himself. Approximately the same height as Bookie, Shawn had over a hundred pounds on him, and his skin was a couple shades darker with French braids to the back. He could have passed for the Penguin from *Batman* if observed from a distance..

Seven years ago, Shawn had been a shy lil chubby boy. Very insecure. He probably was the same Shawn, but now he'd found a way to manage it. Staying in the latest apparel, the newest Mike's (with the hat to match) no less than a few grand in his pocket. Can't forget that word "bitch" that he spread like mayo on a cold-cut sandwich at every opportunity possible.

Bookie just shook his head, with a smirk creeping in from both sides of his lips. He had to overlook his homie.

"Aye, nawl though, G, on GGGGGG'D, which one of these hoes sucking your dick?"

Shawn laughed at his own joke. Bookie laughed too, not at the joke, but the way he dragged out the G in GD, then placing heavy emphasis on the D. For the most part, the explicit remark made Bookie cringe.

Janiyah went ballistic.

"Don't play with me, Shawn, cause you know I don't play with you like that. You need to be in somebody's church some damn where, tha's a crying shame. Got me cussing and I don't even cuss. I'ma pray for you, Bookie. Reneka, let's go before I end up in somebody's jail cell. I can't be around this. This ain't nobody but the devil's work." Rolling her neck and snapping her fingers, Janiyah set Shawn straight.

Bookie thought, wow, she put him in his place. But it was the exact opposite. Shawn didn't flinch.

"Shut up, bitch. You wanna get saved after doing all them dicks? You had some of that head, G?" Shawn asked

Bookie. "On the BOS, she a monster."

Bookie didn't know what was true or false or anything in between. What was indisputable, though, was the level of disrespect in the explicit reply.

Laughing even harder, Shawn reached out and shook Bookie's hand. Every time someone refuted anything Shawn said, it was like adding fuel to the fire. Bookie was bracing himself for what Janiyah might say, but instead of going back and forth, she quit.

"Let's go, Reneka." She looked at Bookie with a look that one of the eleven disciples might have reserved for Judas. He shouldn't have shaken Shawn's hand. To Bookie it was just shaking an outstretched hand, to Janiyah, it was agreeing or siding with Shawn.

"Hello," Shawn answered his Nextel chirp.

Someone was asking, "Where you at" and "Why ain't you grab me before you went ova there?"

"This bitch Icholis want me to come get him, he tryna come over here."

A smiling Bookie replied, "That nigga wrote me a couple times too. And I saw him on the weight pile in Shawnee a day before he left. I had just got there. What that nigga on? Why you hang up on'em?"

"He ain't on shit. Broke. That bitch ain't got nothing for you unless he tryna fuck you."

"Man, stop playing with me, Shawn."

"Did they fuck you in there? On the G, I ain't gonna say nothin. Yo bitch ass was gone for a minute."

He was whispering and looking serious like it was a secret. Reneka and Janiyah was just pulling off from the curb. Bookie waved, trying to ignore his childhood friend on the porch with him. Suddenly Reneka's car made an illegal U-turn at the end of the block.

"While you smiling in his face skinnin' and grinning. Tell him what you did to his brother, Shawn, you snake!" Janiyah yelled from the passenger seat, still hot around the collar from the insults as they drove off.

Bookie took a second to process the bit of information and all expressions of bemusement evaporated. Shawn took notice.

"On my mama, I ain't do that shit, G."

The denial was related to a brutal assault on Tawayne at a hole in the wall called the ATM, a local night spot. Supposedly Tawayne got into a fist fight with a patron who'd accompanied Shawn to the dive. As Tawayne was getting the best of this person, rumor had it that Shawn and/or someone else joined in on the action. Shortly after, Tawayne was on the floor. He was hit with a blunt object, a bottle, gun, club or something consistent. Bookie had asked his brother what happened and never received a definitive answer.

If Tawayne actually knew what happened or could finger Shawn, Bookie was certain his brother would avenge such egregious actions himself, but obviously that wasn't the case. Bookie had been quietly gathering intel on the incident since he landed on Oak Street. Shawn was his friend, so the accusations troubled him naturally, but Tawayne was his brother, so it still warranted an investigation. Due to the sensitivity of the situation, he had to tread light. He would eventually bring it up but had been awaiting the right time. Now it had fallen into his lap.

"On some real shit, G, ask yo brother. He know."

"I already asked him. He said he didn't know for sho, but if he did or even thought it was you, then we wouldn't even be having this conversation right now."

"What you mean?" he asked skeptically, all jokes vanishing.

"You know what I mean. Yo talking days would be over."

Shawn waited for a punchline that never came. Bookie was serious as a heart attack and his "Day One" picked up on it. Family first! Nine times out of ten, Tawayne would've been in jail for murder already. Bookie was leery, especially since days later at an annual Christmas party for Shapiro employees, Shawn and his cohorts sent the place up. It was hosted on Route 50, and some Stones up north were the victims. Shawn was allegedly seen doing the same thing people said he'd done to Tawayne. But with no conformation, Bookie's hands were tied.

Jigga and Yodi rolled up in separate cars, back to back, bumper to bumper. While Bookie engaged them, Shawn said he'd be back; he was going to get Icholis. The shift in his demeanor, the muting of his body language, wasn't lost on the guy who did seven years needing to hear what wasn't always said verbally in order to see another day.

Yodi was glad to see him. "Waddup, fam," he said from the driver's seat. "I just wanted to see which crib you in. When you get a chance, stop in Hobby Hikes; you know I got something for you. You know you family."

He spoke his piece and left, but Jigga hung out for a

while. Half an hour later, the red Monte Carlo was parking.

Everyone worth seeing had been seen by the time November rolled around. Bookie had the latest Sprint phone released, the latest gear, and a bankroll. He'd been showered with gifts and blessings of monetary value. Throughout the greater Kankakee area, the two driving forces in the cocaine trade had both extended their hands.

Donnie's crew, the Entourage, had the top spot, but Jigga and Yodi's faction, The Family, wasn't far behind if you judged off street sales. Donnie had taken him shopping twice and given up cash. Jigga gave up cash also. Yodi decided to take the white beaten path; he forked over some coke and promised more sooner than later. Black came through, Double R, and a handful of other nobodies.

These were all the Kankakee people, or those comprising of the Kees mostly. Connections he'd made in the joint later rendered several gratuities. Two hundred grams of heroin, a crate full of handguns, two assault rifles, and a bulletproof vest. A half brick of hard, and nine ounces soft. All drugs were handed out immediately, either at a wholesale price or on consignment. The guns were sold dirt cheap or given away. There was a Colt .45 no one wanted due to its larger than average size and unattractiveness, so he was stuck with it by default. An SKS, too, was kept along with a flimsy flap jacket. His cousin – eager to make his mark in the game, caught in Iowa with a portion of the work Bookie had fronted him – was the only complete loss Bookie had suffered to date.

CHAPTER 8 – NEW YEAR

A journey of a thousand miles starts with a single step. – Lao Tzu

2004 came to a noisy close. Eighty-five days had passed since his release. The New Year brought new hope, and the fact that he was still free was reason enough to celebrate. Recidivism rates were at an all-time high.

But celebratory actions weren't exactly his forte. Bookie didn't drink, smoke or even have sex. No gambling, no partying or turning up, no nothing. Square as a pool table, but not twice as green. Small increments of movement had afforded him the luxury of spending some cash. And more cash. And more. Making poor financial decisions had his dividends low: all withdrawals, no deposits. Being on house arrest with very limited movement and no particular way to generate revenue outside of the welcome home handouts that were rapidly drying up, Bookie began to contemplate his next move. The dwindling stack of presidents had his frustration growing.

Pressure to get a job mounted. Circumstances, societal norms, his parole officer's nudges and what was expected of him by his now-official girlfriend, Kadaisha, compelled Bookie to quietly seek employment. The Wal-mart and Kmart warehouses in Manteno were the beginning of the job safari, and it ended with Delmonte. A deal was struck with the P.O. during their initial encounter.

"Stay out of my way, and I'll stay out of your way. It's that simple. I don't like to work. Let me get paid for doing nothing and I'll let you be. Make me work, and I'll make you pay." When Bookie had smiled in disbelief, she went on.

"Seriously, I hate paperwork, answering to superiors, submitting reports and the works."

She had eventually told him that if he secured employment, she'd cut the house arrest term of 180 days in half. Possibly even reduce the three years of paper to two. With the ninety-day mark rapidly approaching, what better time, he thought.

By Martin Luther King Jr's birthday, Bookie was off house arrest, working full time and having sex on the regular. Three factors completely unheard of the previous year. He'd been hired at the fruit factory through a local temp service.

Delmonte was the ideal place for those having trouble finding employment. Mexican immigrants represented at least seventy percent of the workforce. The only requirements were two hands and two feet. His job description consisted of working in a garage-size refrigerator for eight hours processing diced fruit. Had it not been for the presence of his Latino co-workers, Bookie would have hated the place. Each day senoritas, mostly mother figures, would assist him to get through his workday. Physically and emotionally, they helped a young Bookie cope with a transition that proved tedious. They were a great group of people with arms as wide as the seven seas.

With the removal of the band from his ankle came a newfound liberty. He'd never experienced such freedom.

Prior to his incarceration, he was still under the rule of parents. In their home abiding by their rules. There were constant boundaries drawn, although most of the time, he ignored them. No more walking on eggshells. Small privileges such as staying out all night or using profanity were now his. Even going into bars or establishments that sold alcohol. No more curfew cops; he was grown.

Did Bookie have the discipline to harness this power source? Could he stay focused, maintain his position and remain grounded? Or would he receive a one-way ticket back to state prison? Would he arrive at his destination or would he be made to detour? That was the seven-figure question.

In most cases people serving five years or more in the penitentiary undergo an evolution. They evolve into a freak or a faggot. Either you reserve it, hold it all in and allow it to build up so when you get out you go crazy, or you let it out while inside. Bookie had heard this many times but believed since he regularly "purged" the system via masturbation that he would be fine & dandy but that wasn't so.. He discovered he was a lot freakier than he'd care to admit.

His girlfriend Kadaisha provided the much- needed (and appreciated) platform to showcase his many premature talents. Turns out the female anatomy was his Achilles' heel. Bookie could perform for hours straight, and enjoy every nanosecond of said performance. The endurance or stamina he possessed was surreal. So passionate, so eager to please. Kadaisha was in heaven. This mass of clay named Bookie was being molded and formed to perfection by her hands, for better or worse.

February rolled around with bad news in hot pursuit. Bookie was fired, and his girlfriend was pregnant. Societal pressures weighing heavier than ever before, Bookie went to the drawing board, contemplating his next course of action.

A series of unfortunate events transpired that left the twenty-two-year-old felon financially screwed. There were people he could call who would assist him in the struggle, but what they offered as a solution to Bookie's problems came with a hefty price tag. He'd have to be a team player, participating in the lifestyles of his sponsors. The streets were calling, but Bookie refused to answer.

Not wanting to indulge in the street life nor wanting to work at a menial gig paying peanuts presented him with a dilemma. A choice had to be made. The proverbial fork in the road. Left or right?

Bookie was somewhere in between, straddling the fence. Hanging in limbo. Every chance he got, Bookie would visit Nation Of Islam headquarters Mosque Maryam on Stony Island in nearby Chicago. He was seeking guidance, hoping to obtain direction conducive to his mission. An associate from the past, Chris, who was a registered member, made access that much easier.

He heard Minister Farrakhan speak for the first time in person at the Harold Washington Cultural Center, located at 47th and King Drive. Amongst many others who would be a godsend, this divine being affectionately referred to as The Minister delivered an electric message. "Man of the cloth", was an understatement when describing one of the –

if not *the* most – well-versed individuals Bookie had ever known to walk Planet Earth.

Under the N.O.I's tutelage and adhering to the life-giving teachings of the most Honorable Elijah Muhammad since the tender age of eighteen, Bookie had read practically every book published by the N.O.I or stemming from this particular school of thought. Therefore, one might surmise he'd know what to expect, but nothing could have prepared him for that first encounter. None of the DVDs or tapes he'd watched or heard behind bars, none of the lessons he studied like a high schooler getting ready for SAT's, nor anything anyone had ever told him.

He was flabbergasted! It's a wonder no one wanted to hear the Minister speak. Farrakhan had such a way with words that listeners were actually convicted by each syllable. Fight or flight. The ones in the audience, for the most part, were staunch supporters, already fighting for the cause. Others, feeling compelled by the truth to act, would rather tuck their tails, cover their ears and flee to higher ground. Easy street. Where the road was crooked but broad as opposed to the straight and narrow.

Bookie knew you had to form an alliance with a force beyond your natural capabilities in order to survive in this world. There wasn't a shadow of a doubt whether or not he would form such an alliance; the only question was with whom? Joining the Nation became a very strong possibility.

From the angle he viewed the picture, there were three options. Work a regular 9-5 and maybe some night school on the side. Climb the social ladder offered to all tax-paying citizens the good old-fashioned way. Due to his background, however, his felon stamp, he knew certain rungs on this ladder that would be essential to his elevation had been removed. Furthermore, the racial caste system America was founded on and still operated with might restrict or limit access to said ladder altogether. And the "American Dream" wasn't guaranteed to be at the top of the ladder once he got there, *if* he even got there. All he had to do was get a little financial stability, secure a decent little nest egg. Everybody else had a seven year head start, if ony he could catch up and even the playing field, then from there, he'd be ok.

What others may have perceived to be a pessimistic outlook, he knew to be an accurate assessment; thus, he was discouraged and discarded that route.

There was the option of joining the N.O.I. A strict way of life that left little-to-no wiggling room for folly. Bookie had been forced to be a man when he was still a boy, which didn't sit well with him. His childhood went up in smoke and his adolescent years were spent in a cage, eating, shitting, and sleeping at the behest of others. He agreed with the Fruit of Islam's M.O., a strict way of life, based upon a spiritual foundation. The Most High, the Creator, was the focal point, Bookie knew. He wasn't one to play with. Being half-cocked wasn't going to cut it. It was wholehearted or nothing, no gray area. Either black or white! So he opted out of this option as well, choosing to support the Nation from a distance.

He wasn't sure if he chose the streets or the streets chose him, but eventually, that's the way the cookie crumbled. No other options were available. The path of least resistance. Being young and having a little "fuck up" room was a plus. "Distorted views," "irrational thinking," and "can't be serious" were just a few of the things his conscience accused him of. His reply: if trouble came or he got in too deep, he could always fix things, smooth it over and get back on track. He wasn't even twenty-three yet, for Pete's sake; surely, he could find his way back to Glory if it ever got ugly. After all, it would only be a temporary deviation. Or would it?

Whichever avenue he traveled, he was one hundred percent sure he wanted to go back to school. Not just wanted but needed to go back. He was huge on empowerment through education. Academic advancement was extremely significant. America was a credential society: this was a truth that never left his mind. Nor did his skin hue. At the very least, he could acquire a formal education by their standards, which would put him up a notch or two on the totem pole.

Whether you knew the sun was ninety-three million miles from earth or not wasn't important. Long as you had a piece of paper stating you know this bit of information, that's what mattered, especially in their books. His educational history wasn't exactly the best. Nothing to boast about.

In eighth grade, Bookie was expelled for possession of gang literature. Despite the expulsion, he was admitted entry to the high school as a freshman the following year. A few months into ninth grade, one of fourteen-year-old's two pagers went off, interrupting a discussion about the

Boston Tea Party. Ordered by the male teacher to hand it over, a ninety-six-pound Bookie vehemently refused. This led to a confrontation that became physical. The 200-pound-plus adult attempted to overpower the freshman.

"Manhandling" wasn't a good approach as the teacher soon learned when the teenager pulled a knife from his pocket and began vigorously swiping at the instructor to protect his personal property. He was expelled again.

Immediately following the latest expulsion, he enrolled in an alternative school, Ombudsmen. The school itself wasn't far from his home on Court Street, a ten-minute walk tops. It consisted of a very small office-like building on the corner of Greenwood that housed approximately twelve students and four teachers at any given time. Kids sent here for disciplinary reasons attended class for three hours a day. Group One met from 7-10 a.m, Group Two 10 a.m-1 p.m., and the last group from 1-4 p.m. Every day, he left home at 12:45 p.m. with noble intentions, but enroute, the distractions were just too much.

One tardy turned into three, the three spiraled into five, and seven isn't far from five. An unexpected visit from a friendly but formal truancy officer inquiring about a record-breaking thirteen unexcused absences in one calender month left Bookie speechless. He was forced to conjure up a fib tailed by a request to switch from Group Three to Group One.

"Man, change that shit to the first group," his big brother, who had also attended Ombudsmen, told him.

"By the time you get outta school, mufuckas still asleep, it's gonna be like you don't even have school. You got yo whole day to yo self." And Tawayne was one hundred percent right. Things picked up quick. He got back on course and excelled, making it to the top of the class.

Performing up to par the remaining of the alternative school year, he was allowed to attend KHS again. This time he shattered records, good ones. Attendance, grades, punctuality and the like. He was happy to be back amongst his peers, but the celebration was short-lived.

Shooting dice with Lincoln Lee, Moe Man John and Manny in the bathroom warranted some unwanted attention. When the smoke cleared, Bookie was in handcuffs. Charged with Possession Of a Controlled Substance with intent to deliver while on school property, crack cocaine. His entire life, he hadn't completed ninety days of high school.

CHAPTER 9 – SCHOOL

Along the journey we commonly forget its goal. – Friedrich Nietzsche

Incarcerated, Bookie took his education to new heights, discovering a wealth of information hidden in books. At sixteen years old while at Illinois Youth Center Harrisburg, Bookie took and passed his G.E.D without any effort whatsoever. The same month he would enroll in four college courses. Days were spent either building houses courtesy of Habitat for Humanity or tending to greenhouses. He took a liking to the horticulture classes. Seeing a finished project brought a certain joy, whereas, in the construction building courses, they'd just build individual sections of homes, later to be transported to various sites. What actually came of them, Bookie never knew. Allegedly they were being added to other parts coming from other prisons to construct a home for the needy, but he never saw it.

Being transferred to the adult division of IDOC afforded him even more opportunities, vocational and academic. For a minimum of ten hours a day, Bookie was inside a classroom of some sort. When the only two options were a makeshift classroom or a dog kennel passed off as a cell, it wasn't hard to decide. On his twenty-first birthday, five years and four institutions later, Bookie had managed to rack up almost a hundred credit hours. He could have and should have had a bachelor's or two associate's, but the administration wrestled with him about the one associate's he had coming. Lord knows they didn't make nothing easy.

Every facility he'd ever spent time in he'd received some type of schooling. Because he was such a "troublemaker" and spent so much time in the hole, many classes he couldn't complete due to "failure to appear". He'd show up 177 days straight to a 180 day class. He may go to the hole that weekend, the following Wednesday classes would be over, instead of receiving accolades he'd get a write-up. Six months gone down the drain. But he was taking so many courses simultaneously that it really didn't matter. This happened several times.

Despite this taking place on the regular, he would go on to obtain eleven certificates, three certifications, and at least one license. He excelled in various fields of study, taking pride in knowing a little about a lot instead of a lot about a little.

Maurice X approached eighteen-year-old Bookie at Graham Correctional Center, introducing him to Islam. Bookie embarked on a personal journey of study and enlightenment that would continue for years. Every single book, pamphlet, packet, or paper the Nation Of Islam was associated with, that he could get his hands on, Bookie read. X was in his twenty-seventh calender year being down, so he had some of the original documents passed on to him by those who'd groomed him. Files and lessons literally a half-century old, teachings of the most Honorable Elijah Muhammad.

This would eventually lead to other areas of study and schools of thought. Many lacked a spiritual foundation but were still helpful in his growth. They were the militant and pro-black propaganda focused more on inciting riots than legitimate causes. From there, the finger pointed to government conspiracy literature or conspiracy theory books. That phase ended with philosophy, only to start another phase with psychology. Each book seemed to refer to another book or author. He couldn't get enough!

Bookie read fiction too, "paper movies" as he liked to call them, while in the hole or on lockdown, where, unfortunately, four of his seven years were spent behind bars. He could knock a 375-page novel out in one day when he was in the mood. Over one thousand books later his fuel gauge was nearing E. He was convinced *knowledge without application was just information.* No need to get all the knowledge or read all the books if you weren't going to put it to good use.

On his own accord, Bookie learned subjects not offered by the Lakeland Community College or South Eastern Illinois College employees contracted to come into the facilities and teach. Without these personal studies, the information provided in class would surely have been a detriment to a young impressionable mind like his. It's been said ninety percent of learning occurs outside of the classroom. In Bookie's experience, this held true.

With each semester came different classes, with the same inexperienced and ill-equipped teachers expounding on a particular subject. During one summer module, two science courses were offered on Mondays, Wednesdays and Fridays. He signed up to take them both. On Tuesdays and Thursdays, his schedule consisted of World Religion and Philosophy of Religion. The entire summer was spent asking question after question, sweating bullets and plucking gray hairs that wouldn't stop popping up.

This religion, that religion. Monotheistic beliefs, polytheistic practices. All the contrary doctrines, the conflicting ideologies. It was just too much. During science classes, the origin of man was a hot topic. There was an occasional insinuation or reference to a higher power, but for the most part evolution and the Big Bang theory ruled. In the religion classes, however, the majority of the time they were teaching the precise opposite. Come finals, he was a lost sheep. As a direct result of these tumultuous times, Bookie set out on a quest. A quest for truth.

He read the Bible in its entirety, cover to cover. Twice. Coming up empty-handed, he moved next to the Holy Quran, which he already had under heavy scrutiny. A copy of a Satanic Bible came into his possession. He thought, "Why not?" and dissected it piece by piece. He purchased a pocket dictionary from the commissary and mastered the tiny Webster in seven days. Spelling and definitions, every word. His sights were then set on other dictionaries, larger, with more content.

During this phase, Bookie would question anything and everything he heard. He evolved into the "great debater." People, even those well grounded in their beliefs, hated to see him coming. He found ways to challenge anyone on any subject. He analyzed, criticized and scrutinized persons, places and things as if his life depended on it. Unless there were "nutritional facts" to be investigated, Bookie refused to consume any hygiene or food product. Not even a stick of deodorant or a piece of penny candy.

In the end, he felt like a K9 chasing his own tail. There were more questions than answers. To get the required answers to the subject matter at hand, or at the least the location of these answers, Bookie knew he needed to go back to school. To obtain the credentials that were such a prerequisite to becoming more decorated, Bookie had to go back to school. He knew that if he could get a hundred credit hours just hanging out, not even trying, if he were to ever to apply himself, the sky was the limit. He could achieve a BA in a matter of months, maybe even a master's or Ph.D. in a few years. Would those degrees guarantee a job or make people color blind? Of course not, but more doors would be open than currently. To beat them at their own game, he had to learn it.

He remembered being in Finish Line buying shoes with Donnie when an old classmate, bending down to check his toe and see if the shoes fit right, told him he'd recently graduated with a four-year degree. Bookie asked, "What the fuck you doing selling shoes?"

"Ain't no jobs in my field; it's ugly right now." He wasn't discouraged, though, and neither would Bookie be. That was the plan. But it never came to fruition. In need of some quick cash, he looked up some old contacts from the joint and called in a few markers. This path led him a couple hours southwest of Kankakee, to Decatur, Illinois. While in the can, he'd done time with two brothers at separate times. One in juvenile, the other in adult. In Harrisburg with TK and in Graham with Bam.

It was these two brothers Bookie reached out to in early 2005. He was received with open arms. Having put the word out that he was "fucked up" and needed a "lick," he got replies from as far south as Memphis all the way up to Minnesota. Only one person had responded positively to the request, in an attempt to deter him.

CHAPTER 10 – JUSTIFIABLE

How narrow the gate and constricted the road that leads to life. And those who find it are few – Matthew 7:14

"Don't do it, G, that shit ain't worth it," Ro-Ro from Joliet had said. They met downtown at the Harrah's Casino, minutes from the Will County Jail where Bookie had served seven months fighting his cases.

"Err mufucka got licks. I got some Eastside niggas, all them YN niggas you can get, even some from the Hill but then what? You'll be right back looking for another lick. Fuck that shit."

His advice went in one ear and out the other. Bookie accepted the wad of cash Ro handed him, complimented him on his gold grille shining like new money, and the two parted ways. He knew his homie meant well, but he was between a rock and a hard place.

Everyone else calling back was either A) too far, or B) their characters too shady to get in bed with them. Spending thirty percent of his life behind bars taught him to read and judge people's character, know who he was dealing with. Whoever said, "There is no honor among thieves" was lying. You had people you could trust when 10K was on the line. Others you could confide in about a stolen car but not a dead body. It just depended on the individual circumstances.

And Bookie knew. He knew the locations were too far

or the characters of the individuals involved not kosher. He didn't mind putting the L on the line to get the W. However, he prided himself a thinking man; thus, his moves had to be calculated. There were two offers on the table from Chicago; they just weren't lucrative. Not lucrative enough anyway.

Decatur made sense due to the distance from Kankakee and the amount of revenue to be generated. Many Kankakeeans never knew Decatur existed and vice versa, so that, too, was a plus.

******

He arrived in Decatur around noon. TK met him at a gas station on Eldorado.

"How long it take you to get here?" he asked after greeting Bookie. "Did it take long?"

"Nawl, it ain't take long, like two hours, I think. We was on 57 for a lil over an hour then we got off the e-way, made a wrong turn by Champaign somewhere and had to get back on the e-way. We here."

TK was shaking his head, showing his mouth full of golds. "Man, how yo ass get lost?"

"I ain't know it was that close to Killa Kees though."

"Wait, where Bam ass at?" Bookie asked while goose necking. "I thought he was picking me up too."

"Will ass ain't even answer the phone when I called. I hit his line though."

He told the female companion thanks, handed her the hundred bucks he'd promised and climbed out of the driver's seat. She took over, pushing the trunk release as instructed. Bookie retrieved her purse, took it to the passenger seat, removed his banger and left the car. Bam told him one would be provided, but his motto was to (completely) trust none and suspect all, ergo he never left home without his own. No exceptions.

An hour and forty-five minutes later, while eating the best hot wings he'd ever tasted at a local mom and pop joint, he was briefed. He learned it would be a "hit," not a robbery. This was all new to him, not that it mattered. He was at the point of no return when he got off the e-way. *Sometimes you had to get yo hands dirty in order to clean shit up.* It sounded oxymoronish, but that's just the way it went.

Bam did most of the talking (and eating) while his younger brother, who was a lot darker and skinnier but still favored him nevertheless, looked nothing like him, co-signed as needed. Brown-skinned, hazel eyes, with a pot belly, Bam had a bright smile that lit up the otherwise darkened dive. TK was the same color as Wesley Snipes, slim with a gold grille to envy. The pair were like night and day, but in so many ways, just alike.

A diagram was outlined on one of those white square napkins these types of places used as coasters. The plot was elementary, almost comical. Bookie was to gain entrance to a residential dwelling that doubled as a gambling house. Once inside, shoot as many people as possible but not kill a single soul.

"Man, now what the fuck sense does that make?" he asked no one in particular, a huge glob of buffalo sauce smeared on his chin.

"Yea, that shit is crazy," TK chimed in.

"Somebody took three hundred racks," Bam spoke up.

"What's racks?" Bookie interrupted, unfamiliar with the term.

"Bands. Three hundred grand, nigga. Stacks! Somebody took three hundred thousand from my man, and he want his shit back. At the same time, he wanna send a message. If this don't work, then… well then, you know what's next."

"I guess it makes sense. Long as he know what he doing or got a plan. Now, how much you say I get again?" he asked for clarification.

"You get seventy-five hundo for err mufucka you hit," Bam replied almost too nonchalantly. "One of them his cousin too. He think that's the nigga who orchestrated the play."

"I wouldn't give a fuck if it was his daddy, I'ma make it happen. But hold on… What the fuck type number is $7,500?" Bookie inquired. "That odd-ass number?"

TK's golds were exposed.

Bookie looked Bam directly in the eye. "Come on, now, how much am I really getting? What yo slick ass up to?" The already existing smile transformed to a genuine laugh.

"Come on, fool, I gotta get something," he came clean. "It's really a sawbuck. Ten racks apiece and it shouldn't be no more than five people."

Now Bookie laughed. "Man, you know I ain't trippin'. Yo slick ass. I ain't superstitious, but ion do that odd shit. We ain't going to seven and I definitely ain't going down to six. So let's just do the eight, and you get a deuce off each lick. That's cool? Two packs… ain't that what you said?"

"Rack, nigga. I said racks," he repeated with a broad smile. "That's why I fuck with you though, on Oso."

They went over the plan some more. Then, out the blue, TK blurted out, "At night they be having a mufucka on security."

"*Will*, you ain't tell me that!" With Bookie calling out his government-issued handle everyone knew he was serious. "What you mean, *security*?" He showed the first sign of concern since he'd arrived in the town.

After hearing what he didn't care to hear, he suggested a revised version of the plan. He would strike in broad daylight as opposed to under the cover of darkness. The gun element and an armed security guard would almost certainly result in him killing or being killed. Killing wasn't a problem, but it was unnecessary heat he'd rather avoid.

"In the daytime, it might don't even be five people. We got a mufucka that will let us know. He told us at night and what time to do it. But now in the day... I don't know." He shrugged his shoulders. "And err mufucka gone see your face."

Bam was adamant about sticking to the original plans; the amendments suggested by the shooter didn't sit well with him.

"Man, what the fuck you think I need, a whole army?"

"The more people, the more money!"

"The more risk too," Bookie pointed out.

"Yea, the more risk of them seeing yo face."

"Fuck them! I ain't from here, they don't know me."

* * * * * * * * *

The following evening, when it was approaching dusk, a

compact rental car in compliance with the stop sign came to an abrupt halt. Clad in a black hoodie, a figure emerged from the vehicle, quietly easing the door shut behind him. The driver quickly drove off. Bookie pulled the hood up onto his head, placed both hands deep inside the front pockets and walked to his destination.

Aside from the occasional kid oblivious to weather, there weren't many people outside in the March coolness. Approaching the driveway, Bookie walked past and spoke to a lil girl with a runny nose getting on a bicycle. "You gotta go in through the back," she told him. Following the driveway to the rear of the home, he found the screened-in patio unlocked. Voices and music could be heard coming from inside.

He entered the back door of the home without preamble. One could have surmised his name was on the lease the way he just walked in. Already having the layout of the place, it wasn't hard to locate his targets. An ongoing argument didn't exactly help them either. Something bout a six-eight or straight six.

The midsized dining room was filled with smoke, impairing his ability to see clearly. The only light was from a broken ceiling fan that shined directly on the dice, making the dice shooters just shadowy figures hovering over the small homemade crap table. Three of the men were still arguing when the muzzle from the millennium 9mm flashed, casting even more shadows. Aiming for their femur bones... Bang Bang! Bookie fired a total of eleven shots from the doorway of the dining room. There was an adjacent room, possibly a bathroom, where one of the victims attempted to escape. Two bullets in the back helped him along his merry way. He cried out in agony, slamming hard into the door.

The thunderous roar of the small but efficient firearm left Bookie's ears ringing. He looked around at the piles of cash strewn about, ignoring the moans and sobs of pain echoing throughout the room. Specific instructions had been given. Nothing was to be taken or stolen. It was a hit, a calling card, not a robbery. At least one person was crying, begging "please"...something about God or to God. Maybe it was two people, but with music still playing it was hard to tell. A couple drinks sat atop a very large house speaker within arm's reach. Bookie yanked out the wires behind it. Immediately, an eerie silence followed.

A house full of people playin' possum, he thought as he left the same way he came in, not bothering to close the door behind him. When they realized he was still in the house, possibly with more bullets, they must have been petrified and thought it better to play dead.

Now, on the porch, he could hear them panicking and shouting frantically. He knew without a shadow of a doubt he shot at least five people. No one should be dead, maybe one paralyzed, but not dead. The little girl was just coming back, and she was in a rush.

She rode up and hopped off the bike, allowing it to hit the ground. She climbed the three steps hurriedly. She and the kid with the oversized black hoodie (as she would later tell the police) spoke to each other. He even held the screen door for her. The following day, expecting to get paid $7,500 x 5 (or 6) people, Bookie was shocked to learn it would only be multiplied times four. Newspaper headlines dubbed the shooting March Madness. No injuries were life-threatening, a job well done. He got paid and went back to the Kees. It was literally that simple.Although many of his victims weren't as fortunate as the dice shooters, this became the norm for Bookie. The money would never last, though. He'd always find himself taking another job. His pockets had holes in them. Bankrolls evaporated into thin air, and he had absolutely nothing to show for it. Not even a vehicle to call his own.

Bookie always said his first car would be a Bentley. He would see people in 5K or 10K cars and laugh at them, knowing he had one or two of their cars in one of his pockets. Then once the money ran out, he'd see those same people in their same cars and say, "I gotta pull it again." It was sad.

CHAPTER 11 – CONSCIENCE

Any man who lives life on the edge will eventually fall off. – Author

The last job he took of this magnitude would become the catalyst. A Chiraq, Drillinois, native residing in the south suburbs was indicted by the feds. "Hood rich" since the 90s, it took two decades, but now the federal government finally had him. And he wasn't alone; his long-time on/off girlfriend was caught in the net also, although later released on pre-trial bond.

There was a child from a previous relationship used as a bargaining chip. They placed her child in DCFS and were now threatening her with a 120-month extended vacation in the Federal Bureau of Prisons. Her only way out: become a star witness for the government. She'd receive custody of her child, immunity from prosecution, and a one-time fee of 25K.

He wouldn't be so lucky. Thirty years to life. His team of six-figure attorneys kept him abreast of every move made by the Assistant United States Attorney (AUSA). Suffice it to say, his days were numbered. An offer came down the pipeline. A hundred thousand to silence the girl. Fifty now and fifty later. The individual acting as liaison, connecting the dots, demanded 10K for securing the contract.

Bookie met with an unidentified black female at Brunswick Bowling Alley on 183rd and Kedzie. Without so much as a hello, she handed him a brown paper bag containing fifty large. This was on a Friday; come Monday, $7,000 was gone already. He was locked in way before he found out the target was female. A female *and* a mother. And the operation could only be performed when the sun was up due to her being on house arrest with restricted movement. Once she was inside her condo, the living quarters made the job virtually impossible to execute.

Bookie was the real victim here. What had he gotten himself into? Time after time, he tried to wiggle out of the agreement, but money kept dissipating. It dragged on a little bit over a month before he finally operated. He only had $11,000 to his name.

Anyone could kill. You had to be special to gun down an innocent woman, cold-blooded, in broad daylight, a young mother with her entire future ahead of her. You had to be numb. Without feelings, lacking a conscience. All the violence he'd experienced in prison, segregated, did something to him long before he even had hair on his face. He discovered an on-off switch he never knew existed.

Jail has a way of desensitizing you. You're in a cell worried about who's having their way with your girl, thinking about your kids, your parents... you will literally go crazy. Sure you could keep busy or try not to think about it, but in isolation, you have no choice. There are no distractions. Cards, weights, T.Vs, interactions with people didn't exist in the hole. You find yourself losing touch with reality each fleeting moment. At this point, it becomes imperative you *do the time and don't let it do you*. The only way to execute this effectively is to relinquish, to let go, to stop giving a rat's ass. You can't worry about what's out of your control. You have to stop caring about your girlfriend, your kids, parents, etc. You have to find that switch and hit it!

Bookie's medial prefrontal cortex, the part of the brain that governs emotions, was severely damaged during this time. It would take double the amount of years to fix or reverse the assault on his psyche. Put simply: he was able to adjust his moral compass as he saw fit, to justify his actions. The system had made him a dangerous person.

Dangerous but not evil. Like Tony said in *Scarface*, woman and children were completely off limits. He could probably do a woman, but the thought of a child would not be entertained under any circumstances whatsoever. He shot her twice in the leg, in the ass and the calf. He kept the Sig Sauer pistol that was provided and sent word the client could stick the remaining fifty racks up his ass.

Bookie was repeatedly warned, later threatened, told he must finish the job or else. That fifty grand, subtract 10K for the middleman, wasn't worth the nightmares and all the gray hairs popping up. While awake, he could do whatever and easily justify it, but when he slept, the nightmares would always catch up with him. They attested to the fact he was human, not some animal. Those nightmares let him know that "switch" was just a coping mechanism, a figment of his imagination that didn't actually exist.

In the beginning, Bookie told them he dropped the ball but would try to follow up when things cooled down. Their threats became more brazen in response, and Bookie's replies more blatant. "Fuck you!" It got to the point the client was so thirsty he called Bookie directly from the Metropolitan Correctional Center (MCC), located in downtown Chicago. He was spiraling out of control; his mental competence had taken a nosedive. Desperate people make mistakes. Under the watchful eye of the AUSA, he was starting to get messy, his judgment clouded, much to his detriment. Bookie wouldn't go down with him.

The girl ended up getting killed anyway, having been used as bait by authorities. The original charge, the drug conspiracy, was weak; now, with no witnesses, it was dismissed due to lack of evidence. The feds introduced another conspiracy at the same hearing, this time a murder conspiracy. It would stick, earning him a life sentence in the Federal Bureau of Prisons.

That was the end for Bookie. Muslims often refer to Jihad, translated as Holy War. The greatest Jihad, however, the most significant, is the one within yourself. Between the lower and higher self, good and evil. At just twenty-three years old, he found himself struggling to keep suppressed his awareness of what he was doing, what he might do. He knew it was wrong. He knew something was wrong with him; he wasn't completely normal.

A system hellbent on rehabilitation had done the complete opposite. Prison was a house of corrections. Aimed at correcting you, slowing you down, stopping you, curbing your behavior – at least that's what they pitch to the public, to the taxpayers. How, then, did it make him worse? An eighteen-year-old in a violent prison, a cellmate who's never going home, surrounded by seasoned vets and career offenders old enough to be his dad and granddad.

How was he to be rehabilitated? Were there no other options?

Bookie remembered a cellmate he'd had in Harrisburg. Strohmeyer. This kid was sentenced to juvenile life. Meaning at twenty-one, he was to be released, records sealed. His adult life/record would start anew. Basically, he got a second chance. But not Bookie. Bookie was sentenced as an adult; thus, his record would follow him the rest of his life. Bookie was fourteen when he caught two of his cases, fifteen for the third one, drug case. He wasn't yet able to buy cigarettes, drink alcohol or even drive a car. So if he can't act like an adult, why or how can he be treated as one by the system? Strohmeyer was fifteen. The only difference was Strohmeyer was white. Least that's all Bookie could see. After all, Strohmeyer had killed his entire family. A total of five people, six if you count the dog, burned alive in a house fire the kid had intentionally set, after making sure they were trapped and couldn't get out.

And then there was "Sick." Sick was Bookie's cellmate for three months. He was a necrophiliac charged with having sex with dead people. An average-looking guy, about twenty-eight years old, fully functional, he had worked at a morgue since age twenty-one. You would never have known.

Mad Dog, one of the board members for the Latin Folks, killed two policemen in the 80s. There was Musah, an elite elder, after finding his girl with another man back in the 70s, cut her head off and went to a bar. He politely ordered a drink for himself, neatly unwrapped what he'd been carrying and carefully put the head on the bar. "Give my wife a drink, too."

Red was smoking crack with a female companion who thought it wise to swipe one of the small white pebbles. Since they were naked and there was nowhere to hide it, she swallowed the crack rock, intending on shitting it out later to smoke it. Bad idea. He first beat an admission out of her, then cut her open, removed the $10 rock and beamed up to Scottie while she lay there bleeding. She died, and he was arrested for murder.

A neighbor Bookie was in segregation with, Rick, had been in the hole for eleven years straight. He was on dialysis. Only two male prisons in Illinois had the equipment to cater to dialysis patients. Menard and Graham. A max and a medium. Long as he was "good," they let him remain in Graham; when he acted up, he went back to Menard for a year or two. He was never allowed a bunkie, and when he went to get his treatment, it was on a dolly, strapped down and wearing a Hannibal Lecter leather mask. Heavy security. According to legend, every chance he got he'd bite, spit on, or attack a nurse or c/o. He became good friends with the eighteen-year-old next door. Bookie found out when Rick came to jail, he was a kid, regular... much like himself... but along his journey, something changed. Now he was diagnosed with ten different diseases including Hepatitis C, which was killing him, so every chance he got, he gave it back to those who had given it to him. He'd been successful seven times thus far. He had no beef with inmates; his fight was only with the system.

These were just a handful of Bookie's peers. People he slept in the room with or next to. Gangbangers, drug dealers, rapists and murderers were all run of the mill. As common in prison as razor-wire fences. You didn't just walk out of prison one day and forget it all or act like it didn't occur. You could, but it would never work. Those memories stick with you. For better or worse, no matter how deep you bury them. Later in life, when you least expect it, they come to the surface.

Before Bookie could be done and out of that line of business, he was furnished with a nickname, Killa, a moniker he shied away from every chance he got. People would go on for years referring to him as such, not even realizing the true origin of the nickname.

******

The streets weren't exactly a walk in the park or a place where he was faring well, so he got yet another job. His objective was to stay out of the way, try to resume some semblance of normalcy and possibly get back on track. He and Kadaisha had moved into an apartment on Sunnyside, the south side of K3. Bookie hated the gig, but it seemed to please Kadaisha and the P.O., so why not?

Gilster-Mary Lee, better known as the "Chocolate Factory," was located in Momence, Illinois, about ten miles east of Kankakee. The pay was not great due to the temp agency that hired him taking out their proper chop, but it was a lot better than nothing.

Kadaisha, beginning her second trimester of pregnancy, was still working, also in Momence, but at Baker & Taylor. They made ends meet. The lifestyle was mediocre at best, but he was free. That had to count for something. He had peace of mind and wasn't living life on the edge. When down on cash, Bookie simply called Tawayne, who'd come through like a freight train every single time Bookie called. So much cash wasted on nothing. He couldn't figure it out. He felt horrible accepting handouts from his big brother, but the pattern, which had become the norm, went on for a couple of months. Outside of the Sharp residence, other actions were being carried out. Actions with a gravitational force so strong that Bookie would soon be sucked in, much to his dismay.

Through the grapevine, he was turned on to a white guy who had an addiction to Schedule II narcotics. He also had a supply of firearms that would rival the N.R.A. In the streets, it was essential to have access to a gun at all times. Bookie had access to quite a few, but his personal thumper was a .45 Colt. He never went anywhere without it.

Back when he'd received the crate of guns as a welcome home gift, the Colt was in it. He tried to sell it, but no one wanted any part of the pistol. Old, big, and unattractive, it didn't shoot as many times as its competitors, but there remained a sense of reliability, and when you pulled it out people paid attention. Then, in mid-2005, he met a mysterious figure resembling the Marlboro Man, though with a crack pipe dangling from his lip as opposed to the proverbial white cancer stick. Bookie didn't know much about him except where he was from, and that was going off the fact that he had Indiana plates on his beat up Ford - 150.

Bookie said to himself, "Wow, this shit gettin out of

hand," regarding the glass dick he was smoking. Upon learning he too had a .45, the Marlboro Man asked Bookie if he could spare "a couple bullets." To Bookie's surprise, the man pulled out a .45 from a bag he carried. His .45 was an ACP Glock, with an extended magazine. Thirty-two shots. Bookie was enamored. Minutes later the Glock had a new owner. For a meager two hundred bucks, Bookie had purchased the firearm. Being impressed that Bookie was impressed, the man boasted of a cache filled to capacity with similar handguns. He said that he could get as many of these as Bookie liked, any and all kinds.

In a matter of days, Bookie was getting guns for all his closest allies. Charging as much as $750 per gun, seeing $500-$600 profit per sale. When there were no more buyers in Killa Kees, he took his show on the road like the Wringling Bros. The first stop was 53rd and Aberdeen, Chicago's Moe town. They sold like hot cakes. Soon the Glock well ran dry, and it was on to the Rugers, P89s, P90s, and P95s — all extended clips.

CHAPTER 12 – RE-ACCLIMATION

When you ain't got nothing, you got nothing to lose. – Bob Dylan

Within Chicago limits where handguns were prohibited, not even sold in pawnshops, he doubled the price. Word spread like an Arizona wildfire.

Out of the blue one day, the crack-smoking gun-runner stopped answering the phone. It would seem he had just dropped off the face of the earth. Back in the Kees, the demand for semi-automatic weapons was high, matter of fact even higher than before. A lot was going on in the streets at this time. Bookie heard bits or pieces here and there, but he was out the way, so it was of little to no importance.

Gilster-Mary Lee was behind him now. After constant insubordination, Bookie was fired. Some racist-ass supervisor named Larry Hoover with a Joe Dirt mullet and a handlebar mustache didn't much care for the ex-con with the baby face and lack of respect for authority. He let it be known. Bookie laughed at his antics and shrugged him off, not really "seeing" or respecting him – a gesture that made Larry's blood boil. His job assignment was eventually terminated. Having approximately 20K at home and a few grand in his pocket from trafficking stolen guns cushioned the blow. Bookie took it in stride.

Now Bookie was back where he started, looking for work, submitting applications and creating resumes that substantially lacked "work history." He was also looking forward to his firstborn while trying to maintain his position as head of the household. Bookie kept the lifestyle from Kadaisha, who was patient, understanding and considerate, so caring, so loving. His focal point was the prize, but it was hard to stay anchored and keep his eyes on the goal with so much going on.

He wasn't really hanging out. He might go on the westside or on Fifth Avenue to Bada Bing, watch Taj and Tawayne shoot pool, talk shit for a second with Kmart, but that was it. Every so often he'd have an episode with Jigga and/or Yodi. Tip was still around, him and his fleet of custom vehicles. Occasionally they'd go up north or to Indiana, turn up with a couple different car clubs. All things considered, Bookie was a homebody now. When or if he did stay out late, Kadaisha would remove his house key from his key ring as he slept. A warning to stay in or be locked out, after he left there was no way to regain entry without going thru her.. Her patience was starting to wear thin, just that quick. Had to be the pregnancy and the hormonal changes, Bookie thought.

Two weeks after the Marlboro Man stopped answering his phone, Bookie was approached by the Chevy Boys on Court Street. He ordered his chicken wing dinner, BBQ sauce on the chicken, and a cup of cheese for the fries. As it was being prepared, Bookie left Poor Boy's diner, walking the few feet to the convenience store to pick up a grape strawberry Mistic. At the halfway point, directly in front of the currency exchange, Bookie was intercepted.

"Aye, Bookie, let us holla at you for a second."

"Waddup?"

He and this group of guys shared a not-so-good history. Ever since middle school when lines had been officially drawn, they were on the opposite side of the ball. They were Vice Lords, which wasn't bad in and of itself seeing as how Tawayne and half of his first cousins were all Vice Lords. Bookie had been groomed to be such, but at the last minute, he went another way. One would have thought he'd go the BPSN way since the other half of his cousins threw up the five too, but hit their chests immediately after balling up a fist. Bookie, now the black sheep, surprised them all by going in a completely different direction than the Black Stones and the Vice Lords.

"We heard you got some heaters for sale."

These idiots must be on drugs, he thought. He remembered fist fights far back as third grade. He had never cared for them, and the feeling was mutual. This would be their first time ever speaking or holding a casual conversation.

"Y'all must be talking bout Bookie D, or that otha Bookie dude that play football or some shit. It's another Bookie too, ain't it?" he said, squinting his eyes and looking to the sky, feigning confusion.

It was three of them and only one of him. Bookie wasn't alone though; he had 32 hollow tipped friends on his hip sticking so far out his shirt he couldn't hide it. Anyone could see it, but everyone overlooked it. Who would be walking around like that? No one that was in his right state of mind or who was a convicted felon with two X's on his back. One more and he could face twenty-five to life.

Bookie, stern in his replies, maintained a straight face. His body language screamed, "I don't fuck with y'all," which he didn't. And never had. The Chevy Boys smiled and smirked extensively, intimidatingly, as if he could be bullied or muscled into compliance. Which was absurd.

"Nawl, we talking bout you. We got some money."

Bookie's unibrow arched. This was a first. Their entire lives they were known to be broke and in bad shape.

They must have read my mind, he thought.

"I aint say you didn't." His expression was one of dramatized hurt (at the notion he would think they would be broke, or as Fat Boy said, "eating out of the garbage").

"I know you heard about your boy Donnie?" They cut the sarcasm short. "We know you don't fuck wit 'em. We need one of them "foe fimps".

Bookie patted his hip. "All I got is this one right here... and this mufucka here for my personal use," he boasted with an unusually broad grin, revealing much-needed orthodontic treatment.

"For real, for real, I can't wait to use this mufucka. I had it a couple months now and still ain't got the chance yet." This last line was delivered with a polite smile, sympathetic almost, which could have been a threat but closer in nature to a warning.

"If I hear somethin', though, I'll let you know," he concluded in a dismissive tone and walked off.

* * * * * * * * * *

He hadn't spoken to Donnie since last year. After he'd taken Bookie shopping, given him a bankroll and offered him a spot on his team, an incident transpired causing him to completely sever ties with the Cocaine Cowboy. His phone rang one early Sunday.

"Homeboy."

"Donnie, waddup?"

"Man, whoa, say it ain't so."

"What? What happen?"

"Man, homeboy…"

"Waddup?"

"Homeboy, my baby mama tellin me some wild shit over here."

"Aww, yea? What she say? What happen? I just seen her the other day, she cool?"

"Homeboy… My baby mama said that you tried to holla at her, homeboy. After I just looked out, extended my hand, you tried to snake me like that?"

"Holla at her? Man, get the fuck outta here! That bitch lying. She was all in my mufuckin face asking for hugs and shit." With the seeds of separation sown, Bookie made sure harvest came early.

Donnie was good at manipulating; this much was obvious. Bookie didn't know if he was blowing smoke up his rectal cavity or if his baby mama had actually told him that; women did things like that from time to time to make their men jealous or to see how they responded, seeing if they cared or not. Either way, Bookie didn't care; he had said all he had to say. Donnie seemed like he was siding with her, so Bookie said, "fuck 'em."

******

Donnie Jackson was a charismatic individual in that his

ability to inspire devotion in the average Joe Blow had no boundaries. A street savvy hustler with as many years in the game as Michael Jordan had in the league, Donnie had been on his own since age thirteen. The following year he'd managed to scheme his way up on a whole kilo of cocaine. In the hood, this was a feat similar to an Olympic contestant winning a gold medal.

The orgin of Bookie and Donnie's relationship dated back to the SunRiver Terrace. Approximately five years his junior, Bookie had borne witness to his meteoric rise just prior to his incarceration. Nowadays, Donnie had reached new heights. In fact, he was the sole ringleader of the number one cocaine distribution ring throughout the Kankakee Metropolitan area, the Entourage.

There were other dealers. Possibly even with more money, but they wasn't as tangible; they weren't as accessible. They didn't sell to certain people for fear of getting robbed; they didn't come out after dark. They kept their wealth a secret and stayed in their lanes.

Donnie was infamous for doing the exact opposite. He flaunted his profession like a badge of honor, told anyone who cared to listen what he did for a living. He wasn't a big man or physically imposing, but the aura he exuded more than compensated for this deficiency. An inch and three quarters shorter than Bookie, the H.N.I.C. of the Entourage outweighed him by fifty-three well-spread pounds. He was an immaculate dresser, preferring urban/casual wear, and saw to it that every single pair of pants were expertly hemmed and creased prior to sticking a leg in them.

His bald fade was cut no less than twice a week, and

manicures were mandatory. There was no day that ended with a "Y" when Donnie didn't look the part of being exactly what he was: a successful drug dealer.

Not long after Bookie's release, Donnie reached out via Tawayne. Bookie gave him a few hours of his time in exchange for a shopping spree and a few grand of his money. During the exchange it was made crystal clear that there was indeed an offer on the table for Bookie to join the Entourage. When lengthy prison sentences are executed flawlessly, it's not uncommon for major players in the game to offer you a job or a spot on their teams. Especially if you didn't start eating cheese, which Bookie was allergic to in this sense!

Typically it is done out of fear or loyalty to the game, a way of paying homage either way. The ex-con gets a bankroll. On the flip side, the dealer has done a good deed, a deed that will keep you off their ass, and they get to bask in your temporary fame. Enjoying part of the spotlight that's on a person from the hood when he first gets out.

Bookie didn't reject the offer, but he didn't accept it either. The fact it was made indirectly left just enough wiggle room to get out of it without giving a direct answer, thus keeping his options open for future contingencies.

After that Sunday morning phone conversation resulting in a "fuck Donnie," that's where Bookie stood. He would ride past him and other Entourage members and deliberately mean-mug them. They didn't want any smoke. Instead of addressing the issue, Donnie reached out to Tawayne. "Tell lil bro that ain't necessary; ion got no beef with him. We tryna get money over here. We ain't on that."

Bookie wasn't trying to hear that peace treaty, white flag talk. He didn't share such sentiments. Due to his older brother, he'd swept it under the rug though.

Since his release, Bookie maintained a relationship with the Family, which basically consisted of a few older dudes that stayed under the radar. Flagship members Yodi and Jigga had been close to him for years, literally like family. Prior to puberty, Bookie was said to have a "lucky hand." Well-established street figures sought him out, asking that he shoot the dice for them while they betted. Whenever Yodi's dad, Joe Lee, used to see Bookie at a dice game, Bookie would end up rolling the square cubes for him. Win or lose, he'd be compensated.

Bookie might come to the game with Lil Harry, then end up shooting against him, Bo Scott, Jayzo, and Lay Lo. Bets could easily surpass a thousand dollars a roll. In Minnesota, Bookie's aunt was even married to Joe Lee's brother Nate. So in more than one way, Bookie was considered "family". Bookie had last seen Joe Lee when he was sentenced to thirty-one years. Joe Lee was at his court date begging him to not "cop-out." During the seven-year bid, Joe Lee had passed.

Yodi was crowned King of Kankakee when it came to making something out of nothing. Back when Juvenile was saying "Ha" and telling hoes to "back tha ass up," Yodi was supplying eighty-five percent of Kankakee's cocaine dealers. He founded the Family at this time. But it didn't stop there. He wasn't limited to Kankakee by any means. Yodi operated in a hundred-mile radius; he didn't mind traveling. Yodi made playgrounds out of other states, and his connections came from as far west as California, but Kankakee was home. There was a time when all roads leading to cocaine ended with Yodi. He put the whole hood on. Every street figure aspired to be him, old and young alike.

Loud, boisterous, obnoxious, arrogant, cocky. Yodi was all of these, and very much conceited. And Donnie was his protege! The most noticeable difference was that Yodi was a die-hard gambler, whereas Donnie usually refrained from such activities unless he could gain the upper hand by cheating. Showing up to crap games with a cool quarter million in twenty-dollar bills wasn't surprising for Yodi, who bet upwards of 50K on a single pool game when either he or Ike Runnles was behind the stick.

And if Yodi was the Bill Gates of Microsoft, then his younger cousin Jigga would be Paul Allen. Donnie always figured he should be second in command. This would eventually lead to a split and the forming of the Entourage. Jigga, roughly the same age as Donnie, barely in his twenties, became the first person in K3 to cop a spankin' new Lincoln Navigator off the showroom floor. Paid for in cash. He then dropped an additional ten racks for an after-market competition sound system, state of the art.

CHAPTER 13 – LOYALTY

A person that's used to less than nothing, even when he receives nothing, to him it's something. – N.O.I

A series of events took place over a period of time, a continental drift in the social structure of Kankakee's underbelly. Yodi's plug was arrested south of the border by the DEA for interstate drug trafficking here within the States. Coincidentally, a joint task force did not one, but three separate sweeps in and around the Killa Kees, casting the dragnet around Bradley, Bourbonnais, Momence, and Hopkins. Everybody who was somebody was going fed. Those who didn't make the "big time" would evenutally settle for state charges.

Yodi and Jigga laid low, taking frequent extended vacations until the heat blew over. With the Family's top brass scrambling for cover, Donnie saw an opportunity, free enterprise! He was already ambitious, but the desire to show Yodi he, not Jigga, should have been his star pupil became the high-octane fuel that kept his engine running at full speed. He could care less about the law or those indictments they were handing out like free lunch trays at Proegler in the 90s. Brave or stupid, Donnie hit the gas.

By the end of 2004, when Bookie was released from prison, Donnie was on top. The Family were still around, doing what they did, but it was only a fraction of what they used to do and even that fraction was done from a distance, with extreme caution. *If you don't plan, you plan to fail.*

Put simply: Bookie didn't plan. Had he planned or made a conscious decision to be in the streets he would have been with the Family. Part of that reasoning was the Entourage's members were not people he'd want to be in a huddle with during halftime. Some of them weren't a hundred; some were suspect.

This proved to be true when the Chevy Boys went on a robbing spree. They stuck up any and everybody, literally. If you had it, they were coming for it. It was only a matter of time before they made it to Donnie's outfit. They robbed one member coming out his baby mama's crib early morning, then two days later poked Donnie's cousin at the car wash. Donnie was furious.

In the streets, respect was the foundation you built on. Disrespect could easily result in death. If disrespect wasn't properly addressed, it would become contagious, ultimately spreading, and lead to your ruin. Donnie promptly went into action. After scouting and recruiting a pair of adolescent amateurs, he handed them a couple grand apiece and pistols, demanding results immediately.

Forty-eight hours later he got what he wished for. The results came in a failed attempt on Chestnut and Wildwood, near the projects. Both sides had exchanged gunfire, but no one was hit. Hours later, with a copy of the *Daily Journal* in his lap, Donnie rode past the scene, trying to pinpoint the exact location of his premeditated midnight shootout. Traveling westbound on Chestnut, he came to a stop sign on Wildwood. Donnie fished his Nextel out of a pocket to chirp Sog.

"Aye, I'm pulling up at Mona house now, come

outside."

Before Sog could reply, four gunshots rang out back to back. He mashed the gas pedal to the floor. Down the street in Mona's driveway, he checked the Dodge Magnum for bullet holes and found two near the driver's side passenger door, only an inch apart.

Nextel already in hand, he came straight through on his righthand man, TG chirp, telling him what just took place. While Sog, Baby Dre, Donnie, and TG was all huddled around the Magnum minutes later discussing their next course of action, Bookie was engaging in a conversation with the Chevy Boys on Court Street in front of a currency exchange about an extended clip .45 semi-automatic.

******

By nightfall, Bookie was in Hillcrest at Tawayne's crib rehashing the day's events. The brothers stood in the parking lot near the mailboxes. Bookie gave Tawayne the rundown while he sipped Tanqueray and puffed on a flavored Black & Mild. His neighbors and friends, Dre and Manuel, were supposed to be enroute with more bottles. So it was imperative Bookie "tell all" if he wanted positive feedback before his bro got "lit".

Jigga pulled up, stealing their train of thought. The three of them chopped it up about the past for a couple hours. Nuke, who lived upstairs from Tawayne in the apartment complex, disturbed the session to inform Tawayne his soon-to-be baby mama was looking for him.

"What she want?"

"That's yo girl, nigga, how I know?" the thirteen-year-old answered with a high-pitched laugh.

"Damn, I was posed to go grav her somethin to eat," Tawayne remembered.

Nuke laughed and shook his head.

"You out here fucking around and you got that lady in there pregnant, belly big, hungry and shit, you bogus."

"If she was that hungry, her ass can cook. She'll be aight. Huh, kill this."

He handed Nuke the last swig. Nuke sat his ball down and put his right foot on top of it. Took the alcohol, turned it up like a pro, wiped his lips with the back of his hand and handed Tawayne the empty bottle back. You could tell this wasn't his first rodeo.

"Tell her I'll be in there in a minute, aight?"

"Aight. What's up, Killa, you got that mufucka on you?"

Bookie smiled in response. "You know ion go nowhere without it." He raised up his shirt tail just a peep.

Smilling, Nuke responded, "I already know." He walked off dribbling his basketball to deliver his message.

Tawayne's baby mama was due around the same time as Kadaisha. Firstborns for both brothers.

It wasn't until the next day, after sleeping on it, that Tawayne told Bookie that he should inform Donnie of the ill plot formed against him. Unfortunately, Donnie was in Racine, Wisconsin, on business. The conversation would have to wait. While Bookie chose to put the conversation on ice, avoiding talking over the phone, a local hustler named B-Lo was robbed at gunpoint.

When he failed to comply with the gunman's demands in a timely fashion, gunshots rang out. Patrolmen arriving on the scene found three victims. B-Lo, his spouse and a small child were all rushed to the ER. The Chevy Boys were the prime suspects; the robbery fit their MO. By the time Donnie returned from his affairs in Wisconsin, police had a suspect in custody. One of the Chevy Boys.

Bookie and Donnie met at his mom's house in Mary Crest later that night. He spilled his guts while Donnie listened intently, asking an occassional question here and there.

"Yea, I heard about you getting some guns and shit. You know how the streets talk!" Bookie wondered if he'd heard, who else had heard – hopefully not the cops.

"For some people. Not just anybody. I ain't riding around advertising or soliciting. If I fuck with you, then yea. If not…"

"Yea! I wish you would have brought me all them mufuckas, I woulda got 'em all. But man, whoa, I appreciate you pulling my coat tail."

"It's like this," Bookie explained, using a host of hand gestures. "We went through what we went through, but you did extend yo hand. That and that alone gotta count for something. *Loyalty before royalty.* Plus, ion fuck with them niggas no way. Never did and never will. Fuck them hook-ass niggas." They stored each other's numbers and parted ways after he promised to keep Donnie abreast of any new information. In return, Donnie, this time directly, reiterated that an Entourage jersey was still available with Bookie's name on it, and he'd be glad to have him. "Nawl man, I ain't on shit. I'm out the way. If I do decide to get off the bench, though, I'll let you know."

"Aight, keep me in mind. I heard you was already

jammin with Y and Jigga. You pose to be over here. Team Entourage."

******

Back home with a very pregnant Kadaisha, life was average. A different temp service, Manpower, had found Bookie a gig at R&R Donnely making telephone books. They worked different shifts and when quality time was spent, it was either on Sunny Side or on south Lincoln at Mary's.

Mary was Kadaisha's biological grandmother and had been a grandmotherly figure to Bookie since his days in diapers. When they were just snotty-nosed kids, Mary had picked up where Benny left off teaching Tawayne and Bookie how to bait a hook on some of their very first fishing expeditions using her twelve-foot cane poles. This was way before Kadaisha.

In junior high school, when he'd began "courting" Kadaisha, as Mary would say, the solidification of his grandson status was officially initiated. A decade later, with their firstborn only months away, it was as official as a referee with a whistle.

It was late afternoon and the two lovebirds were enjoying the day off. They sat on Mary's screened-in front patio idly chatting as traffic zipped up and down Lincoln Street. A half smirking Mary sat opposite the "grandbabies," with a suspecting eye and mouth full of snuff.

"Bookie, you can't wait for that baby to come, can you, honey?" The question itself was so innocuous.

"Nope, I can't wait, Mary." To this day Bookie couldn't

be sure whether the smirk the small mulatto woman wore like mascara was a product of the snuff she dipped or her cynicism.

"Kadaisha, you bout ready too, ain't you, baby?" she asked in her southern accent.

"Mary, I was never ready, shoot..."

Kadaisha looked at the only man she truly ever loved and made a comical facial expression.

"But somebody else was thirsty so–"

"Aww, Kadaisha you leave that boy alone, you hear." Mary cut her off. "Y'all so cute together, look at y'all."

Mary was definitely sweet but not as innocent as she'd like to make out. She would always say things first, sort of like an appetizer. The main entree would follow sometimes in sixty minutes. Or sixty seconds, but you could count on it to follow. Bookie and his first love mutually agreed to tread light. Not that Bookie really cared.

A car rode past and honked the horn. Mary's brother Hank. Mary waved. "Old scound didn't even stop, now he know he betta slow down coming off River Street like that," she said to herself.

Soon as they thought they were out of the woods, Mary asked bluntly, "Y'all made that baby over here, didn't y'all!" The main course hadn't taken long at all this time. Kadaisha was stunned and attempted to answer before her better half could stop laughing and get around to it.

"Nawl, Mary, dang, why you asking us that? I told you already," she blushed in embarrassment

"Yep, yes, we did, Mary. Kadaisha, she don't care; you can tell her the truth." Bookie smiled.

In response to his words, Kadaisha dug her nails into her soon to be baby's father's forearm and whispered jokingly, "I'ma fuck you up when we get home, and I ain't giving you none tonight."

Bookie cried out in protest, feigning extreme pain.

"Mary, she don't want me to talk no more, so I'ma shut up. You see what she just did to my arm?" He held his arm up high.

"And she said she ain't givin me none." Then he turned to Kadaisha and said loudly, albeit sarcastically, "Not givin me none of what, Kadaisha, I'm confused."

"I knew it already. I don't know why she tell fibs. Now which room was it, baby? Tell granny. Was it the first room, her room?"

"I'ma tell you later, Mary, cause if I say something now I may end up bleedin," Bookie replied, still smiling.

"She ain't gonna hurt you, baby. Them just love taps is all."

"Kadaisha, you stop that now, you hear? Before you hurt that boy."

Bookie yelped out in pain again as she gave him another squeeze.

"Mary, I aint doing nothin to him, ain't nobody steadin Bookie. They call him Killa in the streets; he a Killa; he'll be aight."

Mary hit the bullseye with her assumption. It was right on the money. Their child was conceived in the first room upstairs, Kadaisha's room when she stayed at Mary's.

For a few minutes, the congregation sat silent. Fabolous' "Breathe" screaming from the Sprint broke the tranquility.

"Jigga. Wat's up?"

"Where you at, fam?"

"I'm on south Lincoln, 500 block. What's the word?"

"You tell them you at yo grandma house," Mary offered, straining an ear to be nosy.

"Yea, my grandma crib. Soon as you turn off River heading back to Court Street... aight, call me when you outside."

Fay, Kadaisha's mom, arrived just as her son-in-law was ending his call.

"Heyy there, everybody," she exclaimed cheerfully. She looked around at all three faces on the porch.

"Here you go, Mary, I played yo numbers."

She handed her mom the can of snuff, a crumpled-up dollar bill with a few coins in it and a crispy lottery ticket.

CHAPTER 14 – TEMPTATION

The application of knowledge is wisdom but to apply it you must first understand it. – Author

Jigga pulled up behind Fay's red Monte Carlo and parked. Bookie had seen him even before his ringtone alerted him to his presence.

"Bookie, who is that?" Fay inquired, "They here for you."

"Ion know, lemme go see real quick. Lemme up, Kadaisha, watch out." After the love taps, Kadaisha had flopped down on her baby daddy's lap.

Kadaisha deliberately ignored him, refusing to move.

"He do know who that is, Ma. Somebody he ain't got no business with."

"Come on, Kadaisha, don't do that, why you even get her started?"

"Bookie, now don't you go getting in no trouble when you got yo son coming now, you hear." Her forehead was wrinkled in sternness. They had recently found out it was a boy. Bookie had figured as much though.

"Yea, I *hear!*" he answered the rhetorical question with as much sarcasm as he could muster. B.G.'s "Don't Talk to Me" could be heard now. A text message.

"Now move, Kadaisha." He gave her a firm but gentle push.

"You not listening," Fay continued. "Ain't nothing cute

about them gangsters and drug dealers out there in them streets; they don't mean you no good. Don't go getting mixed up in all that stuff with them gangs and carrying on."

Boy, the apple don't fall far from the tree. They were so damn nosy, Bookie thought, walking off the porch and descending the stairs two at a time. Moments later, he was sitting shotgun inside Jigga's SUV.

"Who is all that action up there, fam?" the driver asked, craning his neck to get a better view of the three generations of women on the porch.

"Action?" Bookie scoffed. "That's my baby mama 'em."

"This yo grandma on yo mama side?"

"I know yo grandma who lived in Hillcrest, sold all the weed, where err mufucka used to gamble at? That's where Cocoa 'em stayed out there ain't it, that was yo daddy mama?"

Bookie had never met his mother's parents. An aunt and uncle that he barely remembered were about the sum of it.

"Yea, that was my daddy's mama."

"She died, didn't she?"

"Yea, her and my granddaddy died. Streetwalker, err mufucka died while I was locked up, shit crazy. This really my baby mama grandma crib, but she like my granny too."

"That shit fucked up. That's why a mufucka gotta be easy out here; these people will lock you up and throw away the key. You get out, and you the only mufucka alive."

He looked in his rearview mirror before adjusting it.

"Let's hit a couple blocks right quick."

"Hold on, let me give my BM these keys."

Bookie had the keys cause he was doing a lot more driving than Kadaisha nowadays due to the pregnancy; however, the new midnight blue Sunfire belonged to her. She was tired of driving her mother's car, so she went and got one of her own.

"We ain't going far," Jigga whispered, half-distracted, eyes still glued to the mirror. Two right turns later, they were in the alley, parked in front of Mary's garage. Reaching behind his seat, Jigga retrieved a black designer woman's bag with gold fixtures. He removed the contents, tossing a neatly wrapped square onto his passenger's lap.

"That's the shit Jeezy be talking bout, stamp still in the middle," he boasted.

******

Bookie looked at the red logo, or what was left of it anyway. There was no denying it. The single kilogram of cocaine was surprisingly light. He didn't quite have the words to explain, but his demeanor told Jigga he was confused.

"Yodi told me you had an eighth coming out that bitch. Told me don't even bust it down unless you around. I'm fina go to my mama crib, you coming or what? You know you fam, and we fuckin with you the long way."

"Nawl, I ain't fucking with it right now," Bookie responded with no hesitation. "When you get it together, you can just hit my line, or I'll have my brother link with you."

Realizing he was in an alley with enough cocaine on his lap to get him a twenty-year sentence had Bookie sweating all of a sudden. He'd seen bricks before, but that was ages ago. And he wasn't on parole then. He felt like a sitting duck.

"What you want me to do with this?" He decided against hanging on to the cocaine any longer than necessary.

"You know you fam," Jigga repeated, taking hold of the fed case like it was just another day on the job.

"We need some more real niggas on the team. We been on our knuckles lately, but we fina get this mufucka back up and running. When we do fye back up, we want you there. I'm tellin you. On my mama, we fina fye this thang back up. We around this mufucka breakin' down books and shit while clowns like Donnie 'em eatin'. A few years ago we wasn't even openin' bricks. If you ain't get them mufuckas whole, you had to go to them lil niggas like Donnie. We was serving all them clowns."

Bookie detected traces of malice in his tone. The resentment for Team Entourage and its leader was clear and present. Bookie could also hear the thud in his chest cavity as the sun went down and he sat in an SUV with 1008 grams of pure cocaine. He allowed Jigga to vent some more before wrapping up the conversation. He'd listened long enough.

"Aye, I gotta get a lining real quick, catch Norm before he close the shop, you know he be actin funny and shit. How you want me to do yo shit? You want it separated or all together?"

"You can just make two sixty-threes." Bookie didn't really want parts. He gave his brother both sixty-threes, told him to pay for just one of them. He never even saw them.

The next day was a Saturday. Some of his old buddies from the joint was having a party on Rt. 30, Lincoln Hwy. at Knockout's Bar & Grille. Bookie drove the Sunfire up there alone. The party ended prematurely, a tad after 2 a.m., and the crowd dispersed. Most partygoers departing trailed each other to an afterparty in nearby Chicago Heights.

It wasn't a full hour later, and Bookie was on 57 south doing twenty miles over the speed limit racing towards exit 312, Kankakee bound. Next to him in the passenger seat was an empty .45. The incident had taught him two valuable lessons. He'd told too many people, especially females, where he was from and his name. Second, Bookie had parked nose first, which made for a terrible position when having to get away in a dash.

After that day he never parked a car unless he could back in. Also, when people who inquired as to where he was from, he'd fabricate different locations and names. He started using Killa and other aliases. Lessons learned, but what was the price? What would he have to pay for such a lesson? His life? Freedom? Sanity?

Once home, Bookie removed his battery and tried to get some shut-eye. Sleep didn't come easy, and when it did, it was invaded by a dream. That dream evolved into a nightmare. Wide awake, he lay in bed holding his pregnant girlfriend, questioning his actions. Was something really wrong with him? Were his violent reactions normal, would he ever be regular again? Just a few months ago, he thought he was cool. There was no denying he had some issues. His responses were different, his reactions to everyday actions were just different. He saw a different picture. Leaving the nest way too early, during his developmental years, prior to the conclusion of the nurturing process may have something to do with it. Or maybe just the place he was at, the treatment he was subjected to. He traded parts of his sanity to get by, but now with parts missing... Was that the definition of insanity? That feeling of not being complete?

He woke up later than usual. Kadaisha was gone to take Mary grocery shopping. She'd called on the house phone asking if he wanted anything from Ultra Foods and was he hungry. Bookie was glad she was gone. He didn't have an appetite. He put his battery back in and held his breath. In horror, he read text message after text message. Voicemails popped up. The phone wouldn't stop ringing.

Two people in critical condition, one on life support. The one on life support wouldn't make it. Hospital administrators were waiting on spousal consent to pull the plug. Bookie had hoped it was all a dream, but that would be too much like right.

So many people had seen him. The cops would be knocking on the door any minute. He prayed aloud and asked God to deliver him from this evil. He requested the cup be passed from him, much like Jesus had done in the wilderness. This was a cup he'd rather not drink from. Then and there he made a pact with his Creator, a vow saying he would straighten up and fly right. If he was spared.

CHAPTER 15 – PRODUCT OF YOUR ENVIRONMENT

Knowledge without application is just *information.* – Bro. Dex

The Shapiro Developmental Center was a local facility that housed mentally challenged individuals for indefinite amounts of time. The pay was a meager couple grand a month on average, but it was a state facility that had decent benefits. With limited options in a poverty-stricken community, hordes of young minorities applied for positions there. It was about the best thing Kankakee had to offer when it came to jobs, so many flocked there seeking employment.

You had the occasional guy working there, putting in overtime and switching shifts every so often, but seventy percent of Shapiro's employees were female. Thus, it was a breeding ground for gossip and rumors.

A knock at the door compelled Bookie to put a clip in the .380 Taurus he'd reserved for his baby mama. He refused to go back to jail. Especially for a body! The knocking grew persistent. It was the cops. They were coming to drag him back to prison in shackles. To throw him in a cage with the rest of the savages, right where he belonged. He damn sure wouldn't go kicking and screaming, fuck that! Wouldn't be a cakewalk.

A window catty-corner to the back door revealed it wasn't police. Bookie stashed his BM's "shady eighty" in a cabinet next to the Frosted Flakes and opened the door.

******

"What you done got yo self into, Bookie?"

Those words spilling from her mouth was her greeting. He didn't know how to answer. What was she talking about? There was no way she was referring to last night; it hadn't even been twenty-four hours yet.

"What you mean?" He tried his best poker face. What other options did he have than to play stupid?

"Bookie, tell me you ain't went up there and shot all them people. Bookie... tell me you ain't shot a whole crowd of people, ten or twenty people. Bookie?"

The very few lines in her face were wrinkled with concern. The motherly affection touched Bookie. He felt guilty, bad that this had to take place. They stood in the kitchen, him and his mother-in-law, barely inside the still open door. He was barefoot and could feel liquid pooling under his toes, armpits, and lower back.

"I told you, Bookie, I told you. I told you bout being out there in them streets, Bookie; you got a baby coming."

Every time she said his name, it hit close to home. Fay was more concerned about Bookie's future and that of her grandsons' than she was angry.

"I had to come over here on my lunch break, Bookie; they talking about it all up there on the job, Bookie." She was a supervisor at Shapiro, privy to all the rumors.

She continued to scold Bookie. Almost like he was two or three, instead of twenty-three. He hadn't noticed no one from K3 last night, but it was possible someone had recognized him. There were a few missed calls from a homie at Shapiro, but Bookie had failed to return his call, thinking it was just the usual folly, him calling about another one of the "Shapiro girls." Him working different shifts, having sex on the job during graveyard shift, him sexing old employees, young employees, etc! But now Bookie wondered if the call pertained to shooting victims as opposed to sexual escapades.

Obviously, Bookie denied any involvement to all who inquired including Kadaisha, Martha and his parents. Tawayne was the only exception. It didn't take long for word to spread. Bookie stayed in for a whole week or so following the shooting. When he did come out and encounter people, he was handled differently. Those who used to speak didn't anymore, avoiding eye contact whenever possible. Some who never spoke or never noticed him now broke their neck to acknowledge Bookie. Everybody seemed to know. Rumor had it Bookie had gone "crazy" again, this time up north.

Niggas in the hood commended him; the youth from these parts saluted him in passing.

"Waddup, Killa," they'd say and be proud he spoke back or took time to shake their hands.

Weeks went past, and he was still free. So far he was in the clear but couldn't take any chances. He intended on keeping his end of the bargain with the Man upstairs. During the little time he was under the radar, he made those moves necessary to get rid of all his guns. Even handing off the bulletproof vest he'd had since he first got out. He was done! Finally he could get back on track. Back on course, follow his plans. He'd been adrift for too long. Far removed from where he should be, it was time to get back at the helm so he could drop his anchor in the desired location.

******

"The phone for you," Kadaisha handed him the house phone.

"Man, why you ain't answer yo mufucking phone?" It was Tawayne.

"Ion even know where my phone at. I just got up. Think my shit downstairs. Waddup, though?" Tawayne sounded worked up, unlike his usual calm, collected self.

"Man, these niggas over here talking about you got they brother locked up for that B-Lo shit."

"What? Who? What niggas? Where you at, you at home?"

"Yea, man, these niggas over here now. We all outside. Just slide through."

"Ten minutes." Bookie got up to get dressed.

"What's going on? Where you going?"

Kadaisha overheard the conversation and demanded some answers. From her tone of voice and body language, she smelled trouble.

The phone rang again as Bookie slipped a shirt over his head. It was Nuke.

"Man, Lo and these niggas over here; they got yo brother surrounded. It's like four of em. Lo got that seven in his hand tho, he treating they ass. U kno he ain't goin'. I think he lit too."

"What?" Bookie went from zero to sixty while a nervous Kadaisha looked on with increasing dread, blood pressure rising to the occasion.

"Who is it, Nuke, who is the niggas?" Bookie's voice was an octave higher than normal.

"The Chevy Boys." Those three words got Bookie off the bench.

"Aye, Lo, they say if you ain't talking they lingo when you get here, it's gone get ugly. Yo bro laughed and told them its definitely gonna get ugly then."

"Look, Nuke, make sure you get all the kids from outside. Clear that mufucka out, I ain't doing no talking. I'ma let this mufucka banger talk for me."

Bookie thought of all the kids from the complex, their face lighting up at the sight of Tawayne who would pass out candy or other goodies every day like it was Halloween. His apartment was also the closest to the parking lot, so every kid coming or going would most likely encounter him, either on their way to or from their destination.

"I already know you about that business, Killa; they playin' with the wrong mufucka."

Nuke was young but wise beyond his years, a lot smarter than the average cub his age. Tawayne lived directly below Nuke and his mother, so it was natural for him to take the lad under his wing, especially with them both being C.V.L's.

When Bookie was dressed and ready to go, he realized he had no gun. He was born at night but not last night. After all, he was a street dude. Even if you take the dude out the street, you can never take the street out of him.

He had to keep at least one gun. He could have bummed his baby mama's .380, but she probably would have had a stroke if he asked for her gun after hearing one end of the conversation and trying to piece together the rest, plus it was registered to her so that was definitely a no-go. She'd begged him to stay, but her cries fell on deaf ears. Bookie saw red. He'd have much preferred to stay on the bench, but if they wanted him back in the game, he'd give 'em all he had. Go hard or go home.

Bookie exceeded the speed limit getting to Mary's house just a couple miles away. His brother-in-law Irey was holding for him an FN Five-seven with two clips. When he arrived, Mary told him he had just missed Irey. "He just went to the Plaza, baby, sit down. He won't be long."

"Granny don't like to do this, but..." She offered her grandson one of the trusty revolvers from the locked closet in the cozy living room, but Bookie politely declined.

Irey was nowhere to be found. Twenty minutes and three phone calls later he was being handed a stolen high-point 9mm by two boys half his age. He thanked his two lil cousins and zipped the Sunfire up to Court Street and headed east. Enroute, he asked God if this was a test. If so, he would fail drastically! Therefore, he apologized in advance.

Alicia Keys & Usher's "My Boo" played back to back as Kadaisha's calls went unanswered. Tawayne called twice asking how long. He was thirsty for some action.

Nuke had texted, telling him Lo had another gun now, in his waist, an automatic of some sort, and was smoking a Black, waiting patiently. Bookie arrived on foot after parking at the corner store down from Taylor Dodge. He cut behind some houses and ran through the edge of a huge field that brought him to a clearing with a bird's-eye view of his would-be targets and his brother's front door. Instead of the Chevy Boys, the cops awaited his arrival. He tossed the bulky high point and got the hell out of Dodge. The Kankakee Area Metropolitan Enforcement Group, or KAMEG, gave chase, but he managed to evade capture. Foot chases used to be fun, easy too, but these new police were pretty fast. When Bookie was coming up, you had Romando, aka PacMan. He was the only one you had to worry about. Nowadays, they had an entire unit of PacMans. All of them were lightning fast or either he was turtle slow. He'd been eluding pigs since he was eleven. A decade or so later, he was losing his mojo. He got away but barely.

Later, as the pair drove to Mary Crest, Tawayne shared with his baby brother how the people had swooped earlier.

"They just came outta nowhere, damn near had me."

"You too? Shidd, they damn near had me. Prob got that burner too. I should of answered the last two times you called, but I was pulling up and was done talking."

They met Donnie at his mom's again. "You gotta be careful, homeboy, these niggas dangerous," Donnie was saying moments later, choosing his words carefully.

"Who? The Chevy Boys? Them niggas some hoes."

"They dangerous cause they'll pop that pistol if cornered but more so cause they'll get on the stand with no problem."

That was another element Bookie had failed to factor into the equation. Way back when he went away, people were telling here and there but not like this. It was prominent now. Niggas coming into the courtroom shoulders back, head up, walking to the witness box as if they'd been doing it their entire life, proud. With these new guys, the landscape of the game had changed. The generation responsible for teaching the next generation was all locked up, so they had to teach themselves. Fortunately for Bookie, he was able to get a lil fat put on his head while he was in the big house, but he had sacrificed so much in the process.

This constituted an issue. A failed attempt could mean twenty to thirty years imprisonment. Attempted murder was a very serious felony in the State of Illinois. He felt pressure exerted from all angles. At this stage in life, it was crucial you pick and choose your own battles carefully, not allow anyone else do so for you. In this situation, that's what it was beginning to feel like. Like someone else had made the bed and he was being forced to lie in it.

"What you wanna do, G? We can go do this shit tonight." Tawayne was precise and to the point in his approach, visibly disturbed by the happenings of the day involving his little brother.

"*We?*" Bookie looked at him and crinkled his unibrow. "What you mean *we*? I got this shit."

"How you got something and you ain't even got a gun?" Tawayne tilted his head to the side, twisted his mouth and gave his brother a look that said: explain that since you got all the answers.

"Aww, yea, homeboy, you say you threw yo pole?" Donnie asked sympathetically.

"I got a unit for him right here, but, G, don't fuck with

revolvers. At the crib, though, I – I got somethin' for him," Donnie interrupted before Bookie could remind them both of the FN, getting up to leave the room. He returned with a discreet small hard case and a shapeless Nike pouch hanging from his shoulder.

"Ion know why he don't want this?" Tawayne asked no one in particular, holding up a huge .357 Python.

Ignoring his brother, Bookie's eyes lit up as Donnie revealed the contents of the case he carried.

"I got something right here for him, he good."

He opened it slowly like bad guys do in movies with briefcases full of drugs and money. Two of the prettiest Taurus 9mm's Bookie ever laid eyes on were neatly wedged in thick gray foam. Three individual slots in between the weapons held three fully loaded magazines.

Before he knew it, Bookie had one of the pistols in his hand twirling it around so he could get a 360° view. The contours of the black metal, the sleekness of the semiautomatic pistol...

"These mufuckas decent. How many times they shoot?" Donnie couldn't even reply before the next question came. "They virgins too, ain't they? They ain't never been busted?"

Donnie was good at manipulating. He concocted a scheme, wrote a script and cast Bookie in the leading role. He allowed him to keep the bangers, tossed in a bag of ammo and offered him his personal vest. Bookie's individual perception of his new comrade's actions didn't allow him to see them for what they really were. He accepted the gratuities graciously, seeing no harm in the gestures. In the car, Tawayne, sipping a bottle, saw it from another angle.

"You doing this for you or for him? It's like he tryna exploit yo weakness or somethin. I fuck wit him, don't get me wrong but that lil nigga slick as hell. Think of his ulterior motives."

Bookie knew his brother's interpretation was accurate, but he refused to admit it. At first, he had just viewed the picture from one angle. Now, though, from Tawayne's perspective, the situation was as clear as a contact lens. He'd deal with Donnie later, but for now, his focal point was the Chevy Boys. It was personal.

CHAPTER 16 – FORK IN THE ROAD

Guard the heart with all diligence, for from it comes the issues of life. –
Proverbs 4:23

SOS. The tone was set. Only in this acronym, "smash" was substituted for "shoot"; thus, for the next month straight, Kankakee streets were plagued with gunfire. The small community was now ground zero. Where and whenever Bookie encountered them or known associates, he "shot on sight". No ifs, ands, or buts about it. One such incident transpired on Court Street, midday, with multiple eyewitnesses.

If it wasn't Bookie shooting, it was Donnie's henchman or members and associates of the Entourage. The Chevy Boys shot back a few times, but they did a lot more shooting with their lips than with bullets. On a weekly basis, they would stop by the station and make statements. Entourage hitter Dre Baby literally chased a couple of them into the station one day where they made yet another statement.

When the month concluded, Bookie had been pulled over, questioned, searched and interrogated more times than he could remember. Several people were in jail. A lot more people in jail than those who actually got shot or drilled. An adage of old said time heals all, and it did just that in this case. After a period of time, things died down and almost went back to normal, for a while anyway. Bookie's routine had never really changed aside from him getting canned at the new gig. It was over with, he told himself; he'd retire. No more working. Staying on a job twenty or thirty years, retiring and receiving a pension, a 401K or IRA, it wasn't for him. In the end, you may finally get a nice car or a nice house, but the downside is you'll be so old you can't enjoy it. What's the use of a Corvette and its 200 mph odometer when you're sixty-five? Why get a Bentley when you're seventy? You got a bad back, Alzheimer's, rheumatoid arthritis, going blind in one eye, senile, etc... What sense does that make?

If he was to get a Bentley, he wanted it now! While he could enjoy it. He never understood those people who live like peasants, saving every dime, depriving theirselves of luxury, only to kick the bucket, leave it to their children and it's all gone down the drain in ninety days. That wouldn't be him. He'd live like a rockstar and still leave some for the kids. Working hard for someone else, thirty long years? No way, Jose! Smart people work for checks and wages, brilliant people work for profits and shares. Therefore, if he wasn't receiving partial ownership he wouldn't give a job thirty days let alone thirty years.

******

Bookie dialed 815-939-1880 and ordered a chicken wing dinner fried hard, BBQ Sauce on everything for Donnie and a gyro plate with a cup of nacho cheese for himself. At Donnie's request, they were meeting at Poor Boys. Having beat Bookie there, Donnie paid for the food. He sat in a window seat, chirp in one hand, a wing ding in the other, watching Court Street traffic. Naturally, Bookie took the booth-style seat opposite him where his cheese was still steaming. Going back and forth with Alex about a Kobe Bryant performance, Bookie copped a squat, not paying attention.

"What the fuck?" he'd sat on an uncomfortable tube sock. Donnie diverted his attention from the i860 briefly. "That's for you," he said in between pushes of the walkie-talkie button.

"You don't owe me shit. Just get on and make sure you shop with me."

Bookie placed the lumpy tube sock next to his supper and spoke to Spiro as he showed his face. A bit curious about the sock, he started to ask, but Donnie, still multi-tasking, picked up on it.

"That's a nina. Soft! All meat, no shake. If you need me to put it togetha for you, jus let me know." So much for curiosity. Soft didn't mean soft literally. It just meant the cocaine wasn't cooked or converted to crack, at which point in time they'd refer to it as "hard". Donnie mentioning all meat was indicative that this nine ounces or "nina" hadn't been tampered with, came straight off the brick. Bookie scooted from the table and shuffled to his feet. His appetite had evaporated, but boy was he thirsty.

"Spiro... Lemme get a Sprite," he yelled behind the counter.

"Alex didn't take care you guys already?" he asked, looking genuinely apologetic. "Sprite, no ice."

On the table already was his usual cocktail, grape and lemonade mixed. He usually stayed away from soda, but the need to settle his stomach was dire. Butterflies flew about unimpeded.

"The Family talking about you behind yo back," Donnie was saying, "bird feeding you. I got a brick with yo name on it already; you just gotta tell me where you want me to drop it off at, or lemme know when you ready to come get it. Ima make sure you get some cash, some real cash! Jigga and Y, them niggas fakin like a Jamaican." Donnie stood to leave.

"Holla at me, homeboy. I gotta make this move real quick."

******

Now he was officially back in the game. Initially, he tried to deal with only Tawayne, but it didn't go so well. The nine ounces had been cooked up and turned into eighteen, but the half of brick was garbage. Tawayne was more into quality, whereas his brother, never having a half of kilo before, just wanted to know what it felt like to say he did. Bookie took the quantity approach. He thought about cooking that half up to a whole bird, but his brother told him it probably wouldn't be a good idea.

Tawayne schooled his younger sibling on how the game had changed since their teen years. "Why you don't be buying no weight, steady gettin that lil shit?" Bookie inquired.

"In the end, it's all the same thing," explained Tawayne. "Don't be no fool, just cause a nigga got weight or copping weight that don't mean he got a bankroll. I buy a ounce for $700, a ounce hard. When you do the math, I make about $100 a gram. So I spend $700 and make $2,800. You got niggas buyin a sixty-three soft for $1,400. They cook it up, put twenty-one grams on it and what they make? A sixty-three only eighteen eightballs, then you add twenty-one Gs, that's six more balls. All together you get twenty-four eightballs, 3.5 eightballs. They only go for a hunnid a pop. So you spend fourteen and make twenty-four, that's only a stack profit. Who got more money?"

"I'm making double that, plus a hunnid extra. Niggas see me and be like he only grabbin a ounce. I can get more, but since they buying sixty-threes or eighths, grabbin two and a quarter or four and a split, they think they on or somethin. Cause they sellin balls or buying weight. I'm looking at the time though. They cookin, selling balls, doing all this for a stack? Then if they get caught, they'll be in the Feds. Somewhere a thousand miles away. I get caught with a $50 piece, a gram or something, shit ain't nothing. Then I *fuck* with my people. Bond mufuckas out of jail, help pay bills if they need it, give 'em credit. They know they'll never get robbed or whooped knocking on my door."

Tawayne made good points. He had a relationship with his customers who appreciated the fact they could come to a homely environment any time of day or night and score. In a way they even paid a little extra for this. What they could get in the hood for $50 Tawayne charged $60, possibly even $70, but he also reduced the risk associated with the hood. A fair exchange wasn't a robbery.

Tawayne's method of operation, the plate he kept on his kitchen counter with the crack and safety pin on it, just wasn't going to cut it for Bookie. He had his sights set on bigger fish. Thanks to his big brother setting the record straight, he'd aim a lot higher than sixty-threes, even half or whole bricks.

Bookie and Donnie became road dogs. He knew in order to learn the business he would have to receive on-the-job training, thus he spent as much time as possible around his new mentor. Just as sure as night follows day, it started to happen. Bookie began to emulate character traits subconsciously. His persona began to undergo a noteworthy transformation. Aspirations and ambitions grew. Several perks came with living in Donnie's shadow, many pros and cons. It was a matter of mixing the bitter with the sweet.

Entourage's HNIC was getting in between fifteen and twenty-five kilograms of cocaine per month. When compared to Yodi, the amount was miniscule. Yodi *sold* people fifteen at one time, but for this particular era, Donnie was the new Yodi! The purchasing of an unorthodox contraption, a compressor or "re-rock" machine, and learning how to use it, made Donnie able to turn one kilo into two, or as he saw fit. Usually, two would be converted to three.

"Best five racks I ever spent," he mentioned to Bookie while turning on a fan to rid his storage facility of the fingernail-polish-like scent after re-rocking a couple bricks. Despite getting only twenty bricks on average, people would have sworn he was getting two hundred. A certified stunna, moving in this fashion long before Cash Money's Birdman was referred to as such. After they were inseparable for a month, people thought Bookie was getting twenty bricks, when in actuality he was receiving, on consignment, more like twenty ounces.

Everybody began to take notice. Females widely reputed

for messing with dudes who got money or dating ballers only were beginning to introduce themselves; higher-level players in the game were starting to spark conversations. Dudes were confused. "Is he a shooter or is he gettin money?" Girls too were curious. "Who is the baby-faced cutie? Some people say he a killa, some say he getting money. Sure don't look like no killa, he all little, got those deep ocean waves with that good hair."

Bookie would be picked up at 9 a.m. every morning. Donnie would drop him off around midnight. Twelve to fifteen hours together, every day. On weekends they went out. Donnie ordered drinks, Absolute and Cranberry or Grey Goose and Cranberry. Slowly Bookie came out of a shell he didn't even know he was in. Lured by an illusion, a blinding illusion.

Bookie was fully in the swing of things. Partying and turning up, hanging out, traveling up and down Hwy 57 making deliveries with Donnie. While on the road, they'd eat well, shop good, you name it. Talk about the life, frequenting strip clubs, throwing money. Club O and Cowboys on 167th, not far from Markham Courthouse were favorites. All the girls knew Donnie by name.

Hundred-dollar bills were spent like they were counterfeit. At any given time Donnie would ask a stripper, "You know my name?" If they knew it, he'd give them a $100 bill. When he wanted some action, they'd head up to Arnies on 147th, where you could disappear in the back, returning all smiles for $50.

Back in Kankakee, Bookie would leave the house with a hundred individually wrapped eightballs. Three hundred grams of crack total. Three gram balls that were sold for a mere $80 or two for $150. Shaving off that $20 was a gimmick Tawayne had taught him to boost sales, and it worked. Standard eightballs weighed out at 3.5. In an ounce, there are eight of them, thus the name. Retail is $100, even steven. An eightball distributor stands to gain $800 off every ounce sold. If he can somehow shave off a half of gram then he could get nine eightballs, make $900 plus have an extra gram. Out of ten customers, maybe four or five have the whole hundred, so due to the shorts (which is fair cause you're shorting them), he just did away with the fives on their end but told them to keep $20 of their money on his end. It all worked out. Bookie was content with seven or eight hundred bucks. It was all "blow up", mostly garbage.

He bagged them up to look bigger than they were, another trick his brother showed him. All the eightballs were flat and wide or long and skinny. If you could sell potential buyers on the idea they're getting a deal, keeping $20 or getting a bigger eightball at a cheaper rate, more people would be susceptible to shopping with you. Kind of like stores advertising buy one get one free. Nothing in life is free.

If stores were giving away free merchandise, they'd be out of business before the sun went down. Instead, when you buy the first one, the price for the second or "free" one is already included, so technically you've already paid for it. They just tell you it's free. People like to be lied to, but they won't admit it. Long as you make them feel good, you get them.

No matter how many balls he left home with in the morning, he would always return empty-handed, cash only. When it was time for him to punch the clock, ending his shift, he'd lower the prices $5, $10, or $20, or give out credit to loyal customers, who mostly paid the following day. With time, he began to hone his craft. He tweaked his operation until it ran smoothly with minimum effort.

CHAPTER 17 – SIGNS & SYMBOLS

Boredom breeds stupidity. – Author

Bookie got a call one night from Nuke.

"They just kicked in your brother's door."

"What? Who?" He felt a lump start to form in his throat.

"The Meg."

His heart sank.

"He ain't there though," Nuke added quickly.

There was hope yet. His mind raced. A couple weeks earlier, Bookie had an epiphany in the form of a dream.

He'd told his brother he'd seen his door get kicked in, and he had a strange feeling that it would come true. The vision was dismissed as him "trippin." But the feeling was too strong to ignore. Since Tawayne refused to listen, days later Bookie came up with a plan to remove his brother's guns, all five of them. Two vests and ammunition were also taken.

Three calls after hanging up with Nuke, Tawayne was on the line. He was at Gala Lanes, shooting pool with Dooda. The prepaid U.S. cellular that he used to trap on had died an hour ago, so he left it at home. There was no need to carry it until he grabbed another ounce.

Bookie tossed caution out the window, talking a bit freely on his Sprint. "So you saying only a sixteenth? That shouldn't be shit then, we could beat that or get probation. A half an eightball shouldn't be shit."

Bookie called Nuke back.

"They still in there, Lo. A couple more just pulled up too."

"Aight, lemme know if something change, im fina call Wizzle back real quick."

He dialed Dooda's number again, this time on his prepaid Boost Mobile instead of the contract Sprint registered to his name. Tawayne picked up on the first ring.

"Ain't shit in there, a 'tilla' probably."

"You sure?" the younger brother asked desperately.

"Yea, man, no more than a gram or somethin, a lil 50 piece," an intoxicated Tawayne explained. "I can't let them lock my BM up tho, G."

"What the fuck you mean, fuck that bitch!" Bookie's visceral reaction was harsh. This was his brother's baby mama after all, the future mother of *his child.* He softened a bit.

"We'll go get her out before the ink on the paperwork dry. She'll be aight," he assured Tawayne comfortingly.

"Nawl, G, she pregnant. I can't do her like that."

"What the fuck you been drinkin, dude, you gotta be drunk! I hear it in your voice. Ima call this lawyer real quick. Ima call you back, lemme see what the fuck goin on."

Donnie had an attorney he called for any and everything, no matter what or when. If Entourage was just hanging out having a debate and expert testimony was needed, he'd call. If he was pulled over or had a run-in with the law, he called. If any of his family or friends needed an attorney, he dialed Hyatt.

Donnie picked up on the first ring. "Homeboy waddup?"

"Aye, what's yo lawyer number? They raiding my brother, I need to hit buddy real quick."

"Damn, he cool? Ain't shit in there, is it?"

"I'm tryna see now. He said somethin about a half of g, some petty shit. Ima call you back after I talk to the lawyer tho."

"Aight... hold on. 791-81..."

"What's his name again?"

"Hyatt."

"Like the hotel?"

"Yea, like that. And if he go to jail, we'll go get 'em. Don't even trip."

Bookie placed the call and briefed the attorney on what he knew thus far as he raced the Sunfire towards Hillcrest. If Hyatt was bothered by the after-work hour intrusion, he didn't show it. Instead, he asked a barrage of questions that were impossible to answer from the outside looking in. At the conclusion of his twenty-one questions, Bookie was already in the parking lot, feet from Tawayne's unit.

He wanted to ask if his brother was in any trouble, should he turn himself in or what was the most time he could get. Possibly even put Tawayne on the phone with an expert in the hopes he could talk some sense into him, speak some sobering words that would hit home.

Under the guidance of legal counsel, Bookie walked up to his brother's residence and commenced to knock on the door. His objective was to gain some intel that could possibly be passed on to Hyatt who was still on the phone. A wide-eyed Nuke watched as the door to Tawayne's apartment swung open, and Killa was snatched inside, with the door slamming shut behind him with such force framed pictures fell from the wall, shattering on impact.

Bookie's phone was ripped from his grasp and haphazardly thrown to the floor. Tawayne's baby mama sat on the living room sofa crying a river, her huge belly heaving in conjunction with her sobs. Mimicking her mothers actions, a two year old, Taiana, sat indian style on the floor at her moms feet, crying as well. A heart wrenching scene. The small living quarters were crawling with KAMEG agents, ransacking every square inch.

"Aye, I was on the phone with my lawyer, and he said...."

"Fuck yo lawyer!" one agent yelled.

"Fuck you!" It came out before Bookie ever realized it.

"Oh, yea?" a tall lean agent with a crew cut snarled. His name tag read Kitwell.

"Man, you know who the fuck I am?" Bookie asked the question as if he might have friends in the White House.

"Personally I don't give a shit who you are. Put some cuffs on him and get'em outta here, I'm tired of his mouth already," Kitwell ordered.

"Man, I'll be outta jail before the ink on the paperwork dry. Y'all can't do shit to me. I got so much money I know who killed Kennedy."

Twenty minutes later, Bookie was being booked into Jerome Combs Detention Center. After the process he sat dumbfounded, trying to remember Hyatt's number by heart. The only thing came to mind was those two dumbass sayings of Donnie's he'd used to get himself there. If imitation was the sincerest form of flattery, Donnie would have truly been proud. Now Bookie silently thanked his supervisor and that dumbass lawyer of his. Still on parole, he was sure to be violated at the very least. Maybe even the feds would intervene.

This was his second time in JCDC, the county lock-up. The first had been a close call, the warning before destruction.

******

One of Tawayne's lil homies, Fred, much closer to his age than Nuke, called him out the blue, stating he needed a hammer. Bookie thought he remembered Fred growing up but couldn't be too sure. At any rate, he'd gotten acquainted with him after his release via Tawayne.

By all accounts Fred was a lame, a mama's boy, not really built for the streets. He had one guilty pleasure: underage girls. A confrontation over a sixteen-year-old had led him to contact Bookie.

Without hesitation Bookie gave him the .45 but on second thought decided to tag along, hoping to ensure all went well.

"Let's drive yo car, they know to look for my car," Fred told him at the last minute. "Plus my mom will go crazy."

Bookie was in the Sunfire. A green light from Tawayne gave them access to his Chevy Lumina since they were in Hillcrest already. With the banger on his lap, Bookie got in traffic, Fred in the passenger seat. Jeezy's *Trap or Die* CD pounded through the two twelve-inch subwoofers.

Halfway to their destination, Bookie's phone rang. It was his lil cousin. Apparently he had a situation with some "grown" dude, and he too needed a pipe.

"Okay, gimme a sec. I'm in traffic right now! Soon as I take care what's already on my desk, I'll be right with you, Ima just drop this foe-nickel off over there."

At Fred's instruction, Bookie pulled up to Hobby Hikes. Before he could park, his lil cousin and three other people ran up to the car. It took a couple seconds to register but a couple seconds too late. Both parties wanted a gun for each other. Bookie tried to grab it, but Fred was already reaching for his lap. Bookie and Fred wrestled over the Colt all of fifteen seconds. Fred's two hands vs. Bookie's one hand on the pistol prevailed.

His lil cousin, confused at what was happening, began to back away from the Lumina in disbelief. Fred was out of the car, on his feet, waving the semi-automatic like a madman. Yelling, foaming at the mouth, saying he'd kill everyone and himself. Bookie was finally able to park the car and get out. It was 2 pm. No less than thirty people were outside, kids and adults, everything in between. He knew it wouldn't end well; too many people with access to telephones had seen them. The police would be in route. Too much time had passed.

Bookie thought if he'd had another gun, how or where he would shoot the idiot. Instead, he stood by helplessly, watching as the grisly scene unfolded. Aunt Myrtis confronted the gun-wielding lunatic, telling him her son was underage, why would he go get a gun. She asked Bookie his stance. "What the hell is going on?"

"He called and asked me, said it was an emergency. I didn't know it was for family."

Their faces when they ran up to their cousin's car... and

to their horror, the person they wanted the gun for was in the front seat. Bookie decided to step in.

"Listen, man, the police coming. We gotta get outta here. Put the gun down."

"Yea, baby, put the gun down. Listen to my nephew. Bookie, give him a ride before he hurt somebody," Myrtis whispered. It took a couple more minutes, but eventually the Lumina was mobile again. Two blocks away, Bookie jumped out the driver seat, abandoning the car and its sole passenger in the middle of the street. He knew the police would be there any second. Fred pleaded and begged for him to get back in and drive. He was beating a dead horse.

Just as he said "fuck it" and raised his left leg over the console to switch to the drivers seat, Bookie heard screeching tires. KAMEG hit the block, coming straight for them. The black impala with presidential tint, trailed by an identical blue one, was speeding in their direction. Bookie, who was a hundred or so feet from the vehicle, was rushed to the pavement and searched immediately. Fred could be heard saying, "What's going on, officer? We didn't do nothing."

Soon, both men were standing, handcuffed behind their backs, at the front of the unmarked KAMEG car.

"Whose is this?" An agent came back holding the .45. Fred had somehow managed to toss it under the driver's seat. He was last seen on his way to said seat but not actually there, which left agents looking at Bookie funny.

"Fuck y'all looking at me for, ask him." He nodded toward his soon to be co-defendant who stood only inches away.

"We're asking you, whose it is?"

"Like I said, ion know shit," Bookie repeated.

Fred just looked at the ground, huffing and puffing like he'd just run a marathon, possibly hyperventilating.

Moments later, cuffed in the back of separate cars, they were back on the scene. All witnesses vindicated Bookie, kids, cousins, Aunt Myrtis, everyone.

"Ima level with you here," a sergeant told Bookie. He'd come, opened the back door and squatted down so they could be at eye level. To Bookie's astonishment, it was Kline, the cop who arrested him for the cocaine over eight years ago in school. Kankakee was so small, Bookie and Kadaisha had run into Kline weeks prior at Wal-Mart, where Kline told Kadaisha, "Keep'em outta trouble," and to Bookie, "Congratulations on the kid," referring to Kadaisha's belly.

"We know it wasn't you with the gun. All of your family here, all these witnesses made that pretty clear. A couple of the teenagers wouldn't say if it was your partner's or not either, but enough of the kids and an elderly couple fingered him."

"Well, if y'all know that, why I'm still cuffed?"

"Because if you don't make a statement right here and right now, I got orders to bring you in."

"What, so unless I tell I gotta go to jail?"

"Yea, that's the way it's looking." The sergeant sounded genuinely hurt by his lack of options.

"Hang on here, I can get you a pen and paper unless you just wanna tell me, but I'll still need your signature."

A brief moment of silence! Sergeant Kline was positive

Bookie would tell now.

"So you got something to say or what?"

"Yea, man, yea... Can you turn the radio station to Power   92.3   or   107.5?"

CHAPTER 18 – SMOOTH SAILING

You don't have to lie about anyone because the truth about everyone is bad enough. – Unknown

They both ended up in Jerome Combs. Bookie's P.O. violated him on the spot. Federal agents came two days in a row to question him about the firearm, asking if he was ready to make a statement. Threatening him with interstate commerce, a serious violation of a federal statute.

"We could prevent your P.O. from violating you, you know."

"No, thank you," was all he said both times. The second time, as he was being led back to his own living quarters, he looked in the window of every pod he passed until he spotted Fred.

"Aye, right here, I'm in here," he told the C/O frantically.

"You sure?" some young pig-farming C/O who probably didn't have a G.E.D asked.

"Yea, I'm sure, right here."

"I thought you was in E pod, but okay, hold on."

Access granted. Bookie approached Fred. "Fuck you waiting on to take yo weight, man; you betta tell them that was yo mufuckin gun. Let 'em know right now... Write a statement telling them it ain't mine. But we both gotta write statements; we both gotta say what happened." He looked back at two C/Os talking and pointing at him. Time was running out; they'd be on him in a matter of seconds.

Hands down they were dumb as a box of rock, but it was two brains vs. his one after all, so eventually they'd figure it out.

For good measure, Bookie informed a few people he knew, including Tip's nephew, Zeke.

"Aye, dude, ho'ass got me in here. Y'all stand on 'em, make sure he write his statement and take his weight or else." Zeke, who was family, guaranteed Bookie that he would make sure "that bitchass nigga" complied.

Dumb and Dumber were coming for him. An hour or so after returning to his pod, Bookie wrote a statement. At the submission of both statements, Fred owning up to the gun and Bookie denying any responsibility, he was informed his charges were dropped.

"Hey, what's going on?" he asked a CO on the next shift.

"You ain't heard? You got a hold. D.O.C enroute to get you as we speak."

After he'd written his statement, investigators read over it with a careful eye.

"You say here Joe Blo had the gun. Who's Joe Blo? Your buddy already admitted to the gun, so you write here that Joe Blo is your buddy. Write it here on this line." One of them pointed to an empty spot at the bottom of the page, but Bookie refused. Writing a name on a statement form even if agreed upon was still too close to *working* for Bookie. He couldn't do it. Maybe refusing to put down a real name was the problem.

Bookie called Kadaisha collect. "Hit my P.O. Tell her to lift the warrant and to hurry up. Let her know it was a mistake and all charges against me been dismissed."

It was a close call. Bookie was so happy to leave when he finally got the word, he left walking, with no shoes.

"Give us a few, we gotta locate your shoes."

"That's okay, y'all can keep 'em."

Now look at him. Back like he never left. This was a bad omen. Bookie took in his surroundings, noticing the correctional officers' friendly demeanor towards one another. How they interacted with transport officers, dropping off bad guys like him, the hostility they directed his way. He wondered whether or not those cocksuckers knew who his uncle was.

If they knew his dad's youngest brother was serving time in a maximum security prison for allegedly killing Jerome Combs. Bookie wanted those cowards to know he had the same blood running through his veins and he'd love to show them. Uncle Henry had been locked up since 1986. When Bookie came of age, he inquired and was told: "Yo uncle like you, he don't go for no bullshit. He got that fire in him. Those racist-ass guards was beating him, four or five of them on him and a bootlicking-ass house nigga tried to help them honkys. He'd escaped before and caused a lot of hell, so as they beating him, he's fighting back. One of those chumps was a real fat muthafucka, outta shape and bout to die anyway, they say yo uncle kicked him in the chest, and he had a heart attack. I think it was the bootlicka."

There were four or five different variations to the story, depending on who you asked and what mood they were in when you asked, but there was a common thread in them all. Inherently, Bookie resented C/Os, the system and those in authority due to this and what he'd experienced thus far in his short-lived life.

******

"Hey, get dressed, you're free to go."

"Huh?" The unibrow shot heavenward.

"Yea, we'll drop you back off where we picked you up from," a KAMEG agent declared. They weren't even done filling out the paperwork that came with handing Bookie over yet, thank God.

"He said he'd be out before the ink dried. Who the fuck does he know?"

The agents and C/Os questioned each other, puzzled beyond measure, but not more so than inmate Sharp, who was quickly changing from the pale orange back to his own clothing. Wasting no time in between.

******

Back in Hillcrest, where a crowd of spectators had gathered, Bookie learned Tawayne had promptly surrendered after hearing news of his brother's arrest, a sacrificial lamb for Bookie as he had been so many other times in life. He would sit in JCDC for quite some time, then eventually suit up, picking his twelve. He was charged with that 1,000 ft. from a school or church crap. A firm "parole hold" wouldn't allow the $100,000 (10%) bond to be posted.

He would go to trial with Hyatt representing him and subsequently be found guilty! A $50 piece of crack... he was sentenced to ten years; he'd be out in five, give or take. Shortly after he blew trial, at St. Mary's Hospital, Kadaisha gave birth to Bookie's firstborn, Kamarion L. Sharp. Exactly one week later, Tawayne's firstborn son, Nhazir, was here.

This new Bookie, fame, fortune, all the notoriety, his new persona, it proved too much for the only love he'd ever known. Kadaisha packed it up and headed to the Peach State, taking his beloved Kamarion with her. On that midnight train to Georgia, like Gladys Knight sang about. Before Donnie and his alliance with Entourage, Bookie would have been devastated. Half of him was already gone, albeit the better half. With his foundation removed, his backbone behind bars, Bookie held his head even higher. He turned full time to the streets, seeking refuge and comfort where he knew it didn't exist.

******

Kootaroo and Bookie were riding down east Court Street when Bookie saw B-Lo coming out of McDonald's. He motioned for him to pull over in Marathon gas station, across the street.

"What's up, Lo, you aight?"

This was the second time Bookie had seen and talked to him since he and his baby mama had been shot and their baby grazed.

"Yea, I'm good, waddup wit you?"

Bookie noticed his usual spunk was gone. Long gone now. He was alert, with an increased level of timidity. He spoke from behind the steering wheel of a Chrysler Pacifica with the engine running, feet on the brake and vehicle in drive. Every few seconds his eyes swept the cabin, an entire 360° sweep, looking around as if something or someone might emerge at any minute to do bodily harm.

"Still looking for them stool pigeon ass niggas. I ain't on shit, just fucking with you. You still ain't heard shit?"

A solemn headshake no.

"I ain't heard shit, I ain't even trying to hear shit. If I do though, I'll let you know. Aye, I gotta get in traffic though, Lo, and drop this food off. Stay up!"

"Who the fuck is that scary-ass nigga?" Koota asked as they pulled back onto Court, this time westbound. Bookie gave him a quick synopsis.

"So now he just laying low and playing slow, huh! He ain't doin shit about it," Koota asked.

"Nothin'," Bookie laughed. "He ain't even talking shit and swallowin spit like he used to. That nigga scared straight." They both laughed, "He ain't on shit."

Koota was just coming home from doing a decade downstate, for an attempted murder rap. It was taking him a minute to get back in the loop.

CHAPTER 19 – COMPETITION

Eighty-five percent of your character will be based on the characters of the people you keep around you. – Author

Kootaroo had two younger brothers. In Harrisburg, Bookie had been cellmates with the younger of the two who was out now and on the front lines for Team Entourage. In Danville, he'd had the middle brother put in his cell during a ninety-day stint in segregation. He was currently serving twenty-seven years.

Koota had paved the way for his baby brothers, while being a pioneer for many others as well. Born in Roseland, the "Wild 100's" not far from where lil Yummy had made national headlines, spawning a rap song from Tupac, Koota's mother had fled the high-crime area, settling just a half hour due south. Kankakee County had promising potential.

Sadly, it was quickly realized that Kankakee's potential was to emulate neighboring Chicago. By the early 90s, it had become transparent that Koota would eventually be a problem. During this era, Koota made a name for himself when a bloody war broke out on the streets of K3, headed up by a migrant thug from Chicago's Holy City. The war was waged on all Kankakeeans who opposed him and his ruthless advance to become a force to be reckoned with in the criminal underworld. He especially hated GDs, which Koota represented to the fullest.

Newspapers reported a drug kingpin from Chicago,

chief of the Vice Lord street organization, was hellbent on taking over Kankakee, all from his HQ, the Maple Street car wash. Bookie remembered those days like yesterday. He was GD; the car wash was only a block from his home. The war alone claimed a stunning seventeen lives in total over its time span, mostly in Kankakee County. These statistics would catapult the county to the forefront of a movement, however, surpassing by a milestone the other 101 counties of the state, and areas like Gary, Indiana, Little Rock, Arkansas, and Chicago in a race for Murder Capital of the country, a title handed out to one unfortunate city every year.

Prior to the war, Koota was getting money. When Bookie was in junior high school, Koota should have been graduating high school. Instead, he was graduating from the block. His company car was the cleanest Parisienne Bookie'd seen to date, purple with triple gold Daytons and a diamond in the back when everyone else was doing box Chevys. Koota raised the bar with his Parisienne. After the feds raided the car wash, nabbed the warlord, and did their sweeps dismantling his crew, they shifted attention to the other side, picking up a few GDs. Koota, having eluded authorities, got right back to the money. From putting in work with the pistol to putting in work with the pack, wasting no time in between.

But like they say: If they don't get you in the wash, they'll get you in the rinse. And that's where they got him. He was sentenced to twenty years, did fifty percent, and now he was back at it like a crack addict. Ten years later, back up to his old tricks.

"Donnie just text me. Im fina turn around." Bookie was still reading the text when he checked his rearview and busted a wide illegal U-turn.

"Fuck you doing, you got lights on top of this mufucka or somethin'," Koota inquired jokingly.

This was high noon on the busiest street in Kankakee Illinois.

"Man, fuck the police. I'm rich!"

"Yea, aight," Koota laughed. "Keep talking that millionaire shit listening to Donnie if you want. Feds don't care about no money, see what they did to Rayful."

Bookie laughed to his eyes watered.

"Donnie talking all that Bill Gates shit, yea, aight. Them people'll take err mufucka thing, have yo ass eatin out the garbage. And give you a hunnid years."

Bookie viewed the feds like he viewed city police, sheriffs or state police... They all as a collective group could blow him!

"Where he at though, what he say, come get him?"

They were passing McDonald's and if the next two traffic lights permitted it, would be on exit 312 in less than thirty seconds.

"Yea, he in Hidden Glen. I'm fina get on the e-way real quick, you say you hungry... We can go right there to Denny's."

"Man, drop me off at the shop first. Fuck that, I can go to Bozo's and grab a Italian beef. I got three heads waiting on me."

A quick glance at traffic going west and Bookie was about to bust another U when Koota stopped him.

"Come on, man, I got this shit on me, you fina do that goofy ass shit again. You got that banger on you *and* some yams, and we both on parole!"

Bookie hit his right signal instead, turning into Shells.

"Stop crying, man, I got L's. The only thing they can do is get us for being on parole and hanging out. They can't search us."

"Yea, aight, keep thinking that. They don't honor that license and insurance shit. You know they gon search."

"Man, quit crying, just be ready to line me up," Bookie told him, pulling back onto Court in the opposite direction.

"Damn again? I just cut you up."

"This a linin, not a cut."

"Fuck you think you is, Usher, Nelly or some mufucka?"

"My hoes like it when I look like money," Bookie shot back with a crooked-tooth smile, giving him the "you feel me." tap.

"Yea, you right. Get the fuck outta here," Koota added sarcastically.

******

Donnie got in, then got right back out of the passenger seat. "Watch out, man, I'll drive."

They played a bad version of musical chairs.

"Man, you not gonna believe this shit," he sighed as they exited the Hidden Glen Apartments Complex and snaked around the maze, taking them through Olivet Nazarene University, home of NFL's Chicago Bears practice field.

"What happen?" Bookie wasn't as enthused as the driver

would have liked. His mind was elsewhere. He could care less, to be honest; he figured it was about a thot or Donnie being his usual dramatic self.

Bookie adjusted the volume on the CD player, increasing it just a hair. Jeezy was saying how he used to hit the kitchen lights, and cockroaches was err where, now when he hit the lights it's marble floors err where.

Donnie reversed the gesture and asked, "Homeboy, you ain't heard? Homeboy, you mean to tell me you ain't heard for real?"

Donnie slammed on the brakes and looked at his passenger as if he'd just discovered fire.

"Heard what?" Bookie smirked. "What happen now?"

Behind them angry commuters honked horns. Without another word, Donnie raced to Kennedy Drive where he picked up a newspaper from Phillip's 66.

A new spree of robberies had been underway. The culprits had been quite busy, bringing in the New Year with a bang. Headlines read: "Masked gunmen held up a Commonwealth Credit Union on Washington Street and made off with approximately $400,000." Anyone remotely associated with the streets knew who was responsible for the heist.

******

Team Entourage was the heartbeat of the streets. Not only did they know the culprits, but Bookie and Donnie were actually in Fresh Gear fucking with Cho when the masks used in the crime had been purchased. Less than forty-eight hours ago, the idiots had discussed their plans openly, even tried on their new ski masks in the countertop mirrors at the clothing store.

This new crew was nothing like those bums calling themselves Chevy Boys. They stuck up business establishments, hotels, stores, currency exchanges. Their assaults were a lot more brazen. Even so, no one in their wildest dreams thought they'd ever get away with 400 racks at one time. *The line between bravery and stupidity becomes so thin at times that it's invisible.* Jumping in front of a bullet for say, the pope or the president... Many would consider you brave. A saint even, maybe a patriot. In the hood, you'd be a damn fool. But in the hood, you selling ounces of crack with a pistol in your waistband, knowing if you get caught, you'll do ten to twenty years with mandatory sentencing guidelines. Whites consider you dumb or stupid. People in the hood say you a real street dude, say you a get-money nigga; you got balls.

To Bookie, the culprits were fools; to Donnie they were competition. No matter how Entourage felt individually, they were heroes in the hood.

"Man, I been in the streets hustling all my life, now just like that, in one move, them niggas...."

Donnie was visibly pissed, appearing defeated. It was Bookie's first time ever seeing him like this.

Later, at the shop, they both took turns in Koota chair, Bookie first. The Washington Street heist was the talk of the town. Grown men gossiping like Girl Scouts.

"We seen it." "It was five people." "It was three." "We heard gunshots." "It was a million dollars, a hundred thousand." In walks Fat Boy.

"Killa, check it out," he yelled from just inside the foyer.

"What?" Bookie looked up.

"Bitch, c'mere, you heard me. You can't come without asking your boss first? Donnie, tell that lil bitch he can come see what I want."

Classic Fat Boy. Everybody laughed. Including Bookie.

"Man, what's up, fuck your fat bitch ass want?" The childhood buddies were outside the shop. Fat Boy's custom Brougham was still running. 24's shining, paint spotless.

"Bitch, how much money you got on you?" His expression was serious now, on the verge of desperation. Fat Boy kept looking side to side, toward Bozo then Burger King like someone might be watching. Bookie never had under 5K in his pocket. It was his badge of honor, and it wasn't a secret.

"How much you want? You gotta give me some slow head for it too. I want my head from the back—"

"Bitch, stop playing," Fat Boy snapped. "I ain't got time to play with you. Gimme the mufuckin money."

This was unusual for Fat Boy, so Bookie enjoyed the moment.

"Just gimme what you got." He held out his hand, eyes glued to Bookie's pockets for what he knew was there.

He was like a crackhead. Bookie removed a bankroll of smaller bills from his right pocket. He counted out one hundred fifty $20 bills, then another thirty-five $100 bills from a back pocket. $6,500 in total. They went back inside.

"Aye, Koota, you and Killa was fucking them monsters the otha night, huh?"

Bookie and Kootaroo looked at each conspiratorially. The way Fat Boy came back in, making his announcement without preamble, it would appear Bookie had divulged classified information to him. Truth told, Bookie too was caught off guard, just as shocked as Koota.

"Was she hollarn, Killa, that's all Ima ask, G, tell the truth. Did that bitch make any noise? Y'all was at the 6, wasn't y'all? Beds right next to each other?"

Bookie was having sex with two or three girls a day, so it was hard to remember.

"Aye, you fat bitch, stop playing with me." This was a conversation Koota wasn't fond of, especially in front of an audience.

"That's what that bitch said she told you when you put that lil ass worm in her."

The entire barbershop erupted in laughter. Koota hated to be the butt of a joke. This hit a nerve. Fat Boy continued.

"He got a worm don't he, G, tell the truth, G, you know that bitch ain't make no noise. On the BOS, she said she ain't even feel that nigga in her, all them damn muscles and you got a worm."

Fat Boy was doing stand up; Koota and his family jewels was his material, the barbershop his stage.

"Koota, pull that mufucka out, I can't take it, lemme see that lil mufucka... Killa, tell him let us see that worm."

Koota had become infused with anger, making Fat Boy's antics much funnier than they should have been. Koota, the only one not laughing out of fifteen or twenty people, set his clippers down. Fat Boy kept at it, revealing details and embellishing the truth until Koota chased him out the shop, trying to use the muscles he acquired during his decade-long stint in the clink to do physical harm.

"Bitch, it ain't my fault you got a worm," Fat Boy joked. "Why you wanna fight me?"

From that day forward, the term — "worm" was a household name.

Bookie didn't know until the next day when Fat Boy picked him up to pay him that he went to go shoot dice with the robbers. He paid him his $6,500 plus an extra stack.

"They had so much money they couldn't even count it. Them bitches rich, on the BOS, they had to have a million dollars," he said in mock admiration. On *GGGGGGD!*

"You know I had to throw the thangs on me a bitch." The beads on the ends of the micro-sized neatly parted French braids rattled.

Fat Boy said that he won ten racks, but people who bore witness said it was more like twenty. Had the game not ended prematurely due to Ick's request, Bookie didn't doubt Fat Boy would have won the whole 400K with his special trick dice called the Big Man's.

Before he dropped Bookie off, they rode past one of the Chevy Boys, the ringleader, walking in the jets. Fat Boy rolled down his window and slowed down to a crawl. When he was right next to him, he said, "Shit, grab yo seatbelt, G." He feigned seeing the police and trying to hurry up fastening his seatbelt. Bookie was weak with laughter.

CHAPTER 20 – THE BRIDGE

Be not curious in unnecessary matters, for more things are showed unto thee than man understands. – Apocrypha 3:23

Dee, another childhood buddy, contacted him requesting a face-to-face meeting. Bookie rarely discussed business over the phone without using standardized coding, agreed to and understood by both parties. His presence being demanded told him the subject matter was money or some form of illegal activity. Dee didn't sell cocaine, though, so Bookie was perplexed as he drove into the Great Wall Parking Lot on west Court.

"That's you," Bookie asked, checking out Dee's transportation. They shook hands.

"Might as well say it is. I'm in this mufucka err day and paying for it, but nawl. I got that green Lincoln I saw you in last time, this my granny shit." The eggshell-white 300M looked to be showroom floor material.

"What's up, G, what's the word?"

Dee wasn't flashy, more of a laidback guy. Everything was plain, but clean and neat. His cars, clothes, even his French braids. When everyone else did Iverson's or designs, he did straight to the backs. Mild-mannered and humble, Dee seldom even raised his voice an octave higher than a conversational tone.

He represented that rare breed of street guys who made it in this profession. They knew their lane and stayed in it, never venturing outside of their comfort zone or getting in anyone else's way.

"Shit for real, just wanted to holla at you. I hear you fuckin wit the Entourage, doin yo thang."

"A lil some-some, nothin' major," Bookie gave his best impression at modesty.

"On the G, I hear yo name so much in the streets, err bitch I talk to or try to talk to say they either fucking with you or used to fuck wit you. The niggas... well, you know how that go... they be hatin and shit. Most of 'em scared of you. I just had to check this nigga at the ATM the other day."

The ATM was the Old Show & Tell, a local dive not worth riding past let alone going in, but in K3, it stayed packed wall to wall. Located on Kankakee's north Side, it was the same spot where a previous incident involving an assault on Tawayne had transpired, allegedly involving Fat Boy.

"Yea, you had slid through there one night, but you ain't stop. You know ion be fucking wit that club shit. I was outside in the cut on some parking lot pimpin shit tryna "catch" and makin a few dumps here and there.

"A nigga next to me was gettin out his car, saw you riding past and said some slick shit to the bitch he was wit."

Bookie was smiling but inquisitive. "What he say? Who was it?"

"Ion know, something about you being a worker and driving otha niggas' cars or some hatin-ass shit."

"Who was it?"

"I forget the clown name. I think he went to school with you, though, he a year or two younger than me. Think he

got a baby by that lil bitch that used to stay in the Harbors."
Dee gave the French braids a couple pats.

"Yo shit itching, G?" Bookie was humored.

"Hell yea, I be hating that shit."

"Why you don't be getting no designs and shit? Err time
I see you, you got them straight to the backs, them
mufuckas older than me."

He wore his hair identical to Fat Boy's minus the beads.
Bookie was tickled.

"Fuck them hatin-ass niggas. Tell me who his BM is,
I'ma go fuck her on camera, that's how I pay them type of
niggas back. Even if she not my type, fuck it."

"Hell yea, on some real shit. Ion blame you." They both
laughed and extended their hands simultaneously. After
shaking up, Dee added, "You know that shit come with the
territory, next they'll be saying you got AIDs or herpes.
Say you smoking the pipe... all type of shit."

"Shid, if that mean I'm rich they can say all that.. Throw
in I'm gay or I'm the police, ion care, fuck it. Just bet not
let me hear 'em though. I just told this fat-ass bitch I was
gay; bitch gone say 'umm you fine'. Told that bitch I'm
gay too, just did seven years and can't wait to go back."

Dee was doubled over with laughter, holding his
stomach, leaning on the 300 for support. A couple more
handshakes and ten minutes of small talk later, Dee cut to
the chase.

"I meant to ask you... a mufucka said you had some
smoke, some decent shit for the low."

"A thumpa? A burner... What you mean, 'smoke?'"

"Nawl, nigga, some green, some tree, say you had

blocks of that shit."

"Damn, I did. I ain't even think to hit yo line."

Bookie bit his bottom lip and slammed his right fist into his left palm.

"A few pounds had come across my desk; they gone now. I had bout twenty of them bitches. You know ion really fuck with 'em though fo real, fo real, so I dumped that shit for the l-o."

"Yea, I know, I had bought two of them mufuckas from JD. Called right back to get two mo, and they was gone already. Let me know if you get some mo or if some mufucka you know get on deck."

"What JD charge you per bow?"

"He wanted eleven an elbow. I gave him twenty-one for two."

"My man Black got them bitches right now as we speak for the even steven!"

"A rack?" Dee's eyes lit up like a Christmas tree on December 25th.

"Right now?"

"Right now!" Bookie confirmed with a head nod.

"How many he got?"

"How many you want?"

"I got a stang right now for three. They say they got thirty-five, I charge them twelve a pop. Then that nigga Quick probably get three or four?"

"What you charging him?"

"Aww, ion charge Quick shit. Any otha nigga I'll tax, but you know, Quick like my bro. You remember Quick used to live by Ced'em on that corner, back in the Harbor days?"

Dee smiled, reminiscing on the good ol days.

"Yea, I remember Quick; he had a lil brother too. I went to go pick my baby mama up a while back and seen that nigga at Baker & Taylor. I was asking him about this fake-ass Muslim Thomas X, a supervisor up there, tryna get my BM to work overtime so he can stay wit her. Then I asked how he get them big-ass rims under that lil-ass car."

Dee was already shaking his head, grinning. "On the G, I told that nigga the exact same shit."

"Aye, I heard about Bunkie too; where that shit happen at, in the Harbors?"

"Nawl, ion think that was in the Harbors."

"I was in the county, though, I forgot. They say folks swallowed some work and choked, but I think the police killed 'em. Shit crazy."

"When they told me the story, it definitely didn't add up, same shit with Terrance Springer, them was C/Os though, but that shit didn't sound right either. Fuck that shit though." Bookie patted his hip. "That shit make me wanna up this bitch and shoot the first police I see in his face. I be hatin shit like that. Racist-ass devils."

Dee looked uncertain of his buddy's sincerity. He'd heard Bookie was crazy, and he'd "pull it"; he knew he was a shooter, so it was possible. The last thing Dee wanted to do was egg him on, so he got back on track with the issue at hand.

"Let me see, though; if Quick get three for a rack a pop, that's sixty-five." Dee was adding numbers in his head.

Bookie aided and assisted him in his righteous endeavor.

"How many you want? Cuz if you put up thirty-five cent, he'll give y'all eleven for the sawbuck. If he don't give it to y'all for the ten 'even steven.' I'm a hunnid percent sho he'll give it to you for the 10.5. Either way, even if you have to put up a extra $500 –" Bookie did the math as he spoke – "you still ain't losin. You getting five blocks!"

"Well, shidd... you ain't lyin', either way I'm winning. When can he be ready?"

"How long will it take y'all to get the money together and shit?"

"I can be ready in twenty minutes. I'ma just pay for everything out my pocket... You sure it's the same shit I got from JD, right?"

"Positive."

"Aight, I'ma just pay for it all then double back on them."

This became a weekly ritual. It lasted a couple months until Black's well ran dry. The next batch was a lower grade, so Dee and Co took their $10,500 elsewhere. It didn't matter to Bookie. Black was well-established and had an extensive clientele base so he didn't miss it. Bookie never made a single dollar off these transactions; he sold cocaine, not marijuana. Dee had offered him a few hundred on more than one occasion. Black told him he had a couple pounds for him as a token of his appreciation, but Bookie was adamant in declining both offers. This fortified his individual bonds with both men.

******

Donnie texted Bookie a name, one he didn't recognize.

"What's that? Who is that?"

"That's Tyrone name. Go put $200 on his books for me. You gotta go there for yo brother today anyway, don't you, or is that tomorrow?"

"I posed to did it yesterday, but I'm gon do it today."

"Aight, he just hit me, said they get commissary today, so make sure you do it asap."

Bookie drove to JCDC and put $200 on Tyrone books and $250 on his brother's. He didn't know Tyrone but had talked to him on the phone a couple times, did a few favors here and there. He knew he was Team Entourage and when asked, Donnie would just say he was a "good lil nigga."

In the hood, Bookie had a million customers. He could pull up to a dice game on Rosewood outside Mrs. Rabbit's and sell 20 eightballs. Hit a block or two, come back, and people would be screaming his name, flagging him down, Killa, Killa, aye, Killa, and he'd stop and do it again. Get out on foot, walk to the back of Mrs. Rabbit's crib and sell five or ten more to the Alleyoops. Everything was sold in balls. You wanted half an ounce, you got four eightballs. A quarter ounce, two balls. On the first of the month, in one stop, Bookie would sell a hundred grams in eightballs. When a customer purchased an ounce or more, he gave it to them whole, weighing its proper twenty-eight grams, whereas if you got an ounce in balls, with each one being 3.0, you came up short four grams. He sold a lot of crack, despite an occasional sixty-three or eighth move; all his work was sold in balls.

If he took a loss, had to pay a debt, or just wanted to for no reason, Bookie would take a few ounces hard and melt them back down. Add the necessary ingredients to double the quantity, and voilà. Donnie was an expert in this field, so his protégé relied on him heavily when it came to "goin in the kitchen".

Bookie did this more often than he probably should have. People sometimes complained or demanded their money back. Several times he wanted to return certain individuals' money, dudes he knew rather well, but with Donnie coaching him, stamping anything he did and condemning actions he perceived as signs of weakness, it was always "fuck'em." After all, who wanted trouble with a "reputed" Killa?

When he was released from prison, he didn't even tell lies. For what reason? To who? Why would he? He didn't know no other way; he was straight up and down, 6 o'clock. Being the picture of honesty got you nowhere fast in the criminal world. However, being joined at the hip with Donnie for a considerable amount of time shed some much-needed light on the situation.

They were up north shopping one weekend around the first, and Bookie got a call for a zip. Quite a few people had called already, but this particular call was overheard by Donnie.

"Nawl, not right now. I'm up north," he told the caller.

"You can rock and roll one time to get the hex off you then run into me when I touch..." a pause... "Probably a couple hours."

From the driver seat, Donnie snatched the prepaid U.S. Cellular out of Bookie's hand and pressed the red "end" button. "Homeboy, don't never tell no mufucka 'you'll be a couple hours' and 'go to somebody else'! Never!

Especially not for a whole ounce! Tell them you around the corner, the police hot but give you a few minutes, tell them you waiting on yo bitch to bring you the car back, waiting on yo sister to come watch the kids, you just put the shit together and waiting on it to lock or dry or something, anything! It's a rat-race out here. A dog fight! A tight fight, a gun fight and *err* mufucka got guns. Here you come with a knife. How long you think you gonna last? You gotta get a gun too if you wanna survive. You gotta lie too; they lie, so what the fuck you telling the truth for?"

Bookie didn't quite agree, but Donnie had a valid point. This wasn't the first or the last of many such lessons, but it was the first time Bookie began to see that despite his lack of academic intellectuality, Donnie wasn't a fool by a longshot.

They got back to Killa Kees just as the sun was making its descent. Bookie made $5,000 in forty minutes. Took a shower, changed clothes, then Donnie was calling.

"I'm pulling up now, whoa."

Usually Bookie picked out his own clothes, but this time Donnie had chosen for him an Akademiks outfit off the mannequin for some reason and covered the $289 tab.

When his pupil got in the car, Donnie looked at him from head to toe. "Damn, homeboy, you shitting on me. I shoulda picked that mufucka for myself," he teased with a broad grin.

"I make the clothes; the clothes don't make me. This shit in me, not on me. I just make it look easy," Bookie shot back, spraying his wrists and neck with Issey Miyake.

That was music to Donnie's ears. His hard work was

finally paying off. "I'm fina go pick up Eyes; we fina go up the way."

Now it all made sense. "You know all them niggas jealous of you and be hating and shit. I really just wanted you to shit on them."

"Man, fuck them niggas."

"They hate you with the Entourage, that I fuck with you the way I do. They know you next up."

Bookie had so much money in his right front pocket that his thigh was sweating. He couldn't wait to pull it out and watch people faces.

Eyes was a petty hustler whom Bookie sold work to at times but who'd much rather cop from Donnie. Since he was the same age as Bookie, went to school with him, etc.... there was a latent competition. Bookie didn't see or feel none of the jealousy or envy; he didn't share such sentiments. Either Bookie was too green to pick up on it, or he simply ignored it. Whenever he or his crew said something slick, Donnie instructed Bookie to flash a roll taking aim at their pride and ego in the worst way. And the latest addition to Entourage was always happy to oblige.

His crew would buy an ounce apiece, pitching in together on an eighth or so. In Bookie's eyes, they weren't really factors. For the past few months, they'd been asking Donnie to party with him, to go up north, let them hang out with him. Check out a strip club or two. Donnie finally caved in.

"Them niggas can't dress anyway, all they wear is big ass white t-shirts, and them bogus-ass Girbeaus. Ion even know if they gon let them in wit them fake-ass airforce ones they be wearing."

They both laughed, knowing it to be true.

"Aye, when we get to the Junction to pick them up you can drive."

"I gotta stop right there anyway to drop off this half to DeeTee."

CHAPTER 21 – HUMAN NATURE

There are but two guarantees in life: human stupidity and death. –
Author

During this era, Bookie had a steady girlfriend. He'd met her on a fluke at the Subway on west Court while he was still with Kadaisha, but Honey didn't become his main squeeze until long after Kadaisha left. An action that almost broke him. Leaving him angry and confused, second-guessing whether or not love was actually real. Via Honey, he was able to find his bearings.

Honey was eighteen years old, far removed from the hood and the etiquette of the hood, not to mention she was quite a looker with a body to die for. She became his escape from it all. She represented something Bookie had forgotten could exist. In addition to an escape, the young beauty was an investment. She certainly had the means and support to go places in life.

It was almost a sure thing when and where she went, Bookie would be with her. On the side, there were two other prospects. Nisha and Monique. Both had one child who over time Bookie bonded with as he possessed a natural affinity for kids. He played a dad while someone else was playing a father to Kamarion hundreds of miles away.

Nisha had a home that Bookie had keys to; same thing

for Monique and her apartment. They came second and third to Honey respectively, and knew their places.

Nisha was a hard-working girl who wanted nothing more than her slice of the American pie. Not much younger than Bookie, a couple of years at best, through unscrupulous actions she'd become stable financially. Her day job as a care tech at Shapiro paid the bills. Other funds, most noticeably those rendered from her part-time gig, executed under the cloak of darkness, went to her savings. She was an excellent cook and cared a great deal about her new beau.

Nisha was unsually quiet, and most took her for anti-social due to her introversion. Extremely dedicated and determined to please Bookie, she was a real freak, with more piercings than she had senses.

Monique lived in Hidden Glen; her abode was convenient when Bookie needed to be close to Donnie, who often slept at his baby mama's crib, only a few doors down from Monique in the same complex. Although Donnie paid rent at several residences and had a ring of keys larger than that of Floyd the janitor, for some reason, he'd always end up in the Glen. Bookie was not sure if it was due to his daughter being the apple of his eye or him not being able to resist putting his "apple" in his baby mama's "eye", but that was the case.

Monique (she liked to be called Mo) was related to the 400K heist-pulling bandits on her mom's side. She was barely twenty years old. A sweet girl with a huge heart. She wasn't freaky as Nisha nor as young and pure as Honey, but she had her benefits.

One would think these three might satisfy Bookie's appetite for sex, but one would be sadly mistaken. As a matter of fact, an argument could be made for the exact opposite. In a seven-day period, he would spend two nights with Honey in a hotel, one night apiece with Monique and Nisha, and the rest with random females. One such random, stored in his phone as my lil freak (MLF), did what she did so well she became a regular. She even took the name to heart, showing up at the Super 8 with a fresh tattoo on her chest reading *HLF* (His Lil Freak).

During daylight hours, if he had sex, it would be with MLF, Honey, Monique or Nisha. A night owl when it came to getting naked, Bookie was nocturnal in his pursuit for a number of reasons. Mainly, though, he too was part of the worm club, and unless he was comfortable with you or you were seeing it from your knees, he'd rather not show it to anyone while there was light. At night he didn't so much as give it a second thought. Kadaisha had created a monster. Bookie averaged twenty orgasms a week; he put the "S" in sexually active.

That was his life. He'd been free from prison going on eighteen months and was so far off his mark that you would have never known he had a mark to begin with. The more cocaine he sold, the more girls he took down, the more triggers he squeezed, the easier it all became. *Perception isn't reality, but when it's unchallenged and allowed to flow unimpeded, it can and will become a reality.* Therefore, this was his reality.

His lifestyle was very demanding. Bookie barely had time for family, or anyone else for that matter; the streets were where his energy went. Whenever he ran into his mom or dad he would mingle, have a few words, then he was back in traffic. Martha, his only sister, was just graduating high school. He shared with her the significance of doing so, instructed her not to stop there, and that was it. Back to the streets he went.

There were so many younger cousins up and coming, all of whom looked up to Bookie. Teens and preteens idolizing their big cousin. He dealt with them individually, at times collectively looking out, giving them the game as it was given to him. They were the future, soldiers in the making. He was their role model, their example, father figure to many of them, the only one they had. Not quite old enough to be any of their biological fathers and with prison practically being his father, Bookie did his best. Being that he was a primary figure, a "tangible" example, he was sure to tell them all do as he said, not as he did. It went in one ear and out the other. They did exactly what he did. Many even aspired to do it better.

What was supposed to be merely an affiliation with Entourage evolved into Bookie becoming Entourage, eventually becoming a flagship member of the crew. The previous year, Team Entourage had been dealt a devastating blow. Donnie's business partner and co-founder of Entourage, TG, and members Sog and Reece-One were all gone. Gone fed! Apparently there was some finger-pointing amongst the crew as the ship sank, but the paperwork was yet to be seen. Entourage consisted of Bookie and Donnie now; their other two part-time members were obsolete.

He was delegated to handle day-to-day activities by default while Donnie acted as overseer. A role not new to Bookie. It was just like when he was in the joint, Supreme Captain for the Nation, with Brother X overseeing.

Dee had been bugging Bookie to "fuck with him" for almost two months since the last time he got them eleven elbows from Black.

A party was coming up, rumored to be the party of the year. It was to be held at Market Hall, hosted by some hot shot from Chicago for his sister's twenty-first birthright.

Rumor was the host spared no expense. This would certainly attract quite a crowd, but with the word "free" on flyers in bold print, the entire K3 populace would be in attendance. Everything was free! Including drinks and admission. In party sectors, this was unheard of. Bookie couldn't miss it. Even Dee, who wasn't big on partying, agreed that it was "must attend."

Bookie was a social drinker by now, courtesy of Donnie. They got a pint of Remy VSOP and hit the e-way. 57 north via exit 312. Jeezy's "Thug Motivation" was the only sound as Bookie accelerated the vehicle to over 100 miles per hour. Passing up exit 315, Bradley/Bourbonnais, Dee turned down the radio.

"Where the fuck you going? You missed the exit. Don't tell me you drunk already?"

"No, I didn't, I ain't pass it up by accident. I wasn't going to Bradley. I ain't fuckin with them racist-ass honkeys out there; we gotta shoot up north real quick. I got some hoes on deck, decent lil hoes; they ready too."

Bookie maintained contact with and took care of a few

guys still locked down. He sent about twelve money orders or Western Unions every month. On occasion, he'd execute extracurricular tasks, sending cocaine, weed or heroin to the joint for them.

One of these guys, BD from the Calumet, reached out asking for assistance. He needed to borrow $1,500 specifically until income tax time. He gave a sob story about his baby mama needing money; she had received an eviction notice. As if that wasn't enough, his mother lived with her too. His mother *and* three small kids! It was urgent. How could Bookie tell him no? Zakat al-Fitr was one of the five pillars, wasn't it?

Donnie gave him an income tax lesson. "It's a time to come up." Whenever he gave these lessons, he'd be whispering, looking around as if he was sneaking or sharing a valuable secret. "Everybody got money. I mean everybody! The dumbest of niggas got racks, free bands! Then all the bitches in the hood so stupid they give they whole check to a nigga. Give'em two stacks here and there until that shit all gone. Some hoes so sweet they give it all up at one time. Bitches saying they want some furniture or a car, end up with nothing. Some mufuckas get furniture from Rent-A-Center, and ninety days later they taking it back, big-ass T.V.s and shit they know they can't afford. They buy cars; in a month, motor gone, transmission fucked up. Shit sad. Every year the same shit.

"Anybody who got somethin to sell, income tax time is the perfect time. Clothes, cars, cocaine. You name it. Bitches end up giving all they cash to a nigga who trick it off, lose it gamblin or give it to another bitch. Lyin to his bitch, tellin her he'll flip it. Lyin to another bitch, sayin he ballin. Lame-ass niggas trying to kick it with real niggas or trying to fit in, you can sell them anything and they'll buy it. This the time to come up!"

Donnie said every year he got niggas. He cooked up garbage crack just for this time of year. So even if Bookie didn't get his $1,500, he wasn't tripping; he had a huge payday coming up. Tax time was around the corner. Days away. Donnie told him how he'd cooked up a brick, thirty-six ounces, converting it to a hundred ounces last year. Bookie planned to follow suit. He was all too eager to cash in, to capitalize off human stupidity.

"Man, you ain't tryna turn up? Fuck we stoppin' for?"

"You the one ain't tryna party, and I know you ain't wearing that, is you? Man, I know you ain't wearing that, just tell me you ain't wearing that shit, you got on church clothes. Dee was dressed like he was going Morning Star or Shiloh."

"Look at that bullshit you got on."

Bookie had a one-bedroom apartment on Sangamon in the wild 100s, 121st. and Sangamon. The outside didn't amount to much, but the inside was lavish. He was killing two birds with one stone. He would stop and pick up his Sean John leather from the apartment. It was his first $1,000 coat ever, although he'd purchased it for $800 due to Donnie buying two of them, same exact coats but in different colors.

Aside from Donnie, no one in the Kees had one of these coats. With a dookie brown Sean John and coordinating Timbos, Bookie didn't really need an outfit. He dialed up

Erica's number.

"Can you go to the crib real quick? Where you at? Aight. How long? Nawl, I need you to grab that Sean John leather and them boots I just bought. Meet me on 119th at the gas station. Huh? What you mean? I'm going to a party. Nawl. In Kankakee. Yea ... Nawl, I don't know. With yo nosy ass." Bookie smiled. "I guess, man, ion care. Wait, who wit you? I got one of the guys wit me. Okay. Twenty-five minutes."

Turning to Dee, he said, "That was my bitch, G. She talkin bout she wanna go now. Instead of them otha 'eaters,' I guess they gonna come. I told them otha hoes meet us at Loews Theater on 167th. Fuck it now. We was gonna just grab'em on our way back but...but fuck it now. She got a lil decent buddy wit her too. I wanted to hit that bitch too!"

Had Bookie lived in Chicago, or on Sangamon, Erica would have been his girlfriend. But he didn't, and she wasn't. They were close though and had sex about once a month. The crib was her aunt's, the sister of a guy he left in Danville CC. Now she was in jail, charged with theft. After her ninth collar for larceny, the judge was fed up. He sent her to a state prison for women in Dwight, Illinois.

When it came across Bookie's desk initially, he didn't exactly dive on it, but since it was Section 8 or low-income and rent was only $86 a month, Bookie paid it up for the twelve months she was supposed to serve and got the keys.

Twenty-seven seconds and thirty-three minutes after they got on exit 312, Bookie and Dee pulled into the gas station on 119th. BD's baby mama was already waiting. He cashed her out and called Erica. He took a shower before he left; he was planning on keeping on his pants, changing his shoes and grabbing the coat. In less than sixty seconds, they could be on their merry way. Pull a Clark Kent with Citgo acting as his phone booth. It didn't come to fruition.

Life never went according to plan. Erica wasn't ready. Her or her buddy. So Bookie drove to his spot on Sangamon. A whole hour later he and Dee were back on I57, going in the opposite direction with two of what would probably be the best-looking girls at the party. They made it back to exit 312 in thirty-six minutes flat. Excellent timing. Their first stop was Marathon.

Bookie couldn't function without chewing gum. Fat Boy told him the significance of keeping gum and cologne in your car at all times. His preferred combo was Winter Fresh and Issey Miyake.

"Fuck you do, waste that shit or something?" Bookie asked him one time.

"Bitch, I'm fat, I gotta spray a lot, what you expect?" he asked, holding up his hands in defense.

The aroma was so strong Bookie couldn't breathe. Fat Boy had gained even more weight since their reunion, so Bookie saw his logic, but Jesus, when was enough enough?

Smiling and chewing his Winter Fresh, he said, "See, bitch, you ain't no player. If you a player, you gotta keep what? What you gotta keep in you car at all times, cologne and what?"

"Cologne and gum," Donnie answered for his protégé without giving it any thought.

"See, bitch, you ain't a player. Donnie a player, you a

killa, so you don't know shit."

It made sense. Since that day, Bookie kept them both. His intention was to be anything but a killer, so if he could be a player then so be it. Whenever he ran out of either, he'd make a pit stop, filling back up like people did when their gas lights were activated.

"Aye, y'all want somethin outta here?" Inside, Bookie grabbed three Mistics and a Sprite, the gum and put $20 on pump #4. He was almost where he wanted to be thanks to VSOP. Another sip or two and ... Bookie looked up just in time to see one of the Chevy Boys enter the gas station. One look at a Sean-John-clad, gold-chain-wearing, Issey-smelling Bookie and off he goes.

"Man, mufuckas got my brother locked up, I'm telling you, if he go to the joint ... I'm telling you ... on my momma, jo, on the fin."

The words were spoken indirectly but loud enough to be heard. They were the only patrons present, so Bookie couldn't ignore it if he wanted. Which he didn't want to, even though this dude was obviously a coward. It was their first encounter since their month of playing Cowboys & Indians. His brother was on trial so what he was basically saying is if he lost, it would get ugly. He was too much of a chump to put an address on it, but Bookie snatched it out the air anyway.

"Fuck the fin, nigga, fuck you mean? I told you I ain't got nothing to do wit that shit, it's whatever, what you tryna do?" Bookie wasn't ducking no "rec". He tucked his chain and hiked up his pants.

"Yea, aight, nigga, we a see. I'm done talking." The

yellow belly coward left without making a single purchase. On his way out, he said, "I'm telling you –"

"You telling me what? I ain't tryna hear that shit, nigga, fuck you and yo brother!" Now Bookie was getting out his body.

An Arab behind the window was laughing.

"Don't do it, Killa, let him make it. What pump you say you on?"

Bookie finished paying for his items and walked out a minute or two behind his adversary. A herd of Chevy Boys awaited him. He stepped directly into a huddle of four, and they closed in.

"Man, I just told you in there what the fuck you wanna do. It was me and you and you ain't want no smoke. Now all y'all wanna surround me. Man, get the fuck outta here." Bookie was more angry that they was fuckin up his night, and more annoyed than he was afraid.

Marathon be cracking so hard, traffic so heavy, him trying to be discreet about what he was driving led him to park out of view of the entrance. A grave mistake. Dee was probably chatting up one or both girls right now while he was outnumbered, four to one, staring potential danger right in the face.

"What you wanna do? Bitch-ass nigga, you act like you tryna box or something." An unknown Chevy Boy called him out.

Taller than the rest, he was a dude Bookie had never seen before. Looked to be in pretty good shape. He might give me a run for my money, Bookie thought. Had they really been about that life, really with the shits, Bookie would have been a bit concerned, but he knew they lacked heart, thus no worries. He was by far the smallest in the crowd of five, but he possessed more brawn than all them put together. He was sure of it; he was also sure you should never underestimate any man. This was the first time in Bookie's life he had ever been talked to that way. He wouldn't forget it.

Gently, he sat down the double-bagged Mistics, careful not to break the glass bottles. Someone took a step forward; he took a step back but threw up his guard and pulled up his pants all in one quick motion. He was on Court Street of all streets, on parole with a loaded gun on his person, at a well-lit gas station equipped with multiple security cameras. Even if he won the battle, it was very possible he could lose the war.

He had to think. He would shoot every one of them in their face on camera before he allowed them to beat him to a bloody pulp. Although disastrous, essentially he'd be trading his life for theirs; in that sense, he'd be getting robbed. Bookie could look in all eight pupils and see confidence growing. They were becoming infused right before his eyes. They probably didn't think he had it on him. Everyone knew Bookie went by Marcus Garvey's motto: *"If you stay ready you ain't gotta get ready."* They figured if he had it, he would *have used it* by now or at least flashed it as a defense mechanism.

With each fleeting second, their certainty of him not having the great equalizer increased. Soon they'd be on his ass, and he'd *have* to use it. The tallest one didn't know him from a bump on a log. That explained why he was the toughest. In all actuality, the most foolish. The three wisemen in the crew knew better, but once they cast out those wise thoughts and substituted them with folly, thinking he didn't have it on him, Bookie would have to kill one or two of them. He felt it. He didn't mind killing, especially them, but not on video or on the front street. Twelve months ago they would've been on the ground bleeding by now. A car full of girls pulled in, then another. Finally, he pointed to them. Peter Paul said try them all.

"Man, look, all you niggas some bitches. Y'all tryna jump me, that's some hoe shit. I'll fight anyone of y'all one on one right now. Not right here, though. Y'all tryna get some help, want the police to save y'all. We can go around the corner though, right now."

Bookie wasn't scared to fight. Years ago when a Four Corner Hustler called him a bitch and invited him to his cell, Bookie went in there and took care of his business. The Four Corner Hustler, which is basically a Vice Lord, being twice his size didn't matter. He didn't see size. Later, addressing a deep gash over his right eye, the Institutional Coordinator (IC) for the Folks told him, "You already won the fight when you went in the room with a mufucka twice yo size. No matter what happened in the room, even if you would've died, you would've died a winner. A man who demanded his respect and didn't just go for *anything.*"

But the present was a different agenda. They had fallen for the banana in the tailpipe. These dummies actually agreed and drove out of Marathon, making a left onto Court Street, driving west then turning left on the first street going into Mary Crest. After pumping the gas he followed them. It happened so quick Dee or the girls never even noticed. They all bobbed their head to Jeezy talking about trunks full of white and how he was from the bottom of the map. Nor did they recognize the driver's mood change. Maybe it was because his mood never really changed.

Bookie hopped behind the wheel, untucked the gold key medallion, removed the Ruger from his waist and cranked the volume. "Aye, where we going, G?"

"The party that way," Dee yelled over the music as the sedan glided into Mary Crest.

"Gotta handle something real quick. It won't take long," Bookie replied matter-of-factly.

Bookie calmly took a sip of his Remy as he pulled up to park behind his victims. Dee noticed the hammer but kept silent. The Chevy Boys had just parked off to the side of the street. They were thirsty for some action, and Bookie was thirsty to give it to them.

Headlights shined bright on the back of the huge black Chevy Tahoe before Bookie clicked them off. Dee's reaction time had been slowed due to his alcohol intake, but he put two and two together, more than four seconds too late. Bookie hadn't said a word, yet he was parking behind his enemies' truck, turning off his lights, leaving the car running with the music full blast.

Gun in hand, Bookie exited the vehicle. As if on cue, both rear passenger doors to the Tahoe opened in perfect synchronization. Bookie left approximately fifteen feet of space in between both cars intentionally to minimize difficulty with the inevitable getaway. As an intoxicated Bookie rounded the hood of his car, the same tall dude who called him a bitch slammed his door with aggression and started toward Bookie from the right rear side of the SUV.

CHAPTER 22 – POKING A BEAR WITH A STICK

The ink of a scholar is more precious than the blood of a martyr. –
Prophet Muhammad (May peace be upon him)

Bookie leveled the P95 Ruger. Bang Bang! The tough guy yelped in pain, clutching at his neck. He fell like a Mike Tyson victim in the first round into the bumper of the Chevy before collapsing to the pavement motionless. Attention was shifted to the clown who said what he'd do if his brother were found guilty. He'd taken his sweet time getting out; now, he wasted no time getting back in. "Go, go…go, man, he got a gun!"

A door opened behind Bookie. He ignored it, hoping it was Dee and not one of the girls. Running up to the truck's driverside window, Bookie was confused when he didn't see anyone. Where had the driver disappeared to that quick? He wasn't that drunk. In the passenger seat, a horrified cohort opened the door and took off on foot but not before disclosing his cousin's location by glancing down.

The truck was making that grinding sound cars make when you try to crank them, and the engine's already running. Just as Bookie pulled the door free, the truck began to roll forward, knocking him off balance.

More shots rang out. Dee was behind him by then, and

he emptied his clip. Bookie, from his position on the ground, saw the tail of the Tahoe shrinking as it picked up speed. There appeared to be a foot or leg sticking out its rear door. Well, at least he got one of them, he thought, picking up the .45 and stumbling to his feet.

A car turned off Court, and headlights swept over the scene briefly. Instead of putting another bullet in Luke Longley, who wasn't moving or didn't appear to be breathing, both shooters rushed back to their only cover as the passersby drew nearer, slowing down to view a bloody man laying spreadeagled in the street. Bookie couldn't believe it.

Neither could his pretty passengers. Erica's friend kept screaming, "Oh my God" and asking is he dead? Erica just said angrily, "Take me home." Behind the wheel, Bookie was calm, cool, and collected; he was notorious for maintaining his composure under pressure. He was definitely still "Killa," just in case there was ever any doubt. The leathers, gold chains and watches, his youthful appearance, fresh linings and pretty-boy swag made them think he'd gone soft. He was the exception to the rule. Most pretty boys were wimps. A majority of people who talked shit were cowards, and majority of cowards talked shit. Not Bookie though; he'd talk it and back it up. There was a saying, *those who know, don't talk, and those who talk, don't know.* Bookie would talk, but he knew, and he had no problem showing anyone that didn't know.

They thought he'd lost it; boy, were they wrong. Had the girls not been offended, Bookie would have attended the party even after the shooting. But now, that was all over with. Even Erica wanted to go home. He reluctantly obliged them, getting right back on exit 312. Good thing he'd gotten $20 petrol.

An hour and a half later, Bookie was back in K3, dropping Dee off at his car. The getaway ride had been left with Erica along with both weapons used. He'd get them back when things died down. Meanwhile he had Erica's whip; no one would recognize it or him. He had to tie up a few loose ends then go back to the city where he would lay low. He'd camp out on Sangamon until he found out what was what.

"Aye, G, holla at me. You trippin, did that shit in front of them hoes. Ol girl kept hollarn 'O my God!' Bitch was scared to death." They laughed and shook hands. "Fuck them niggas, though. Lemme know if you need me."

At the party they should have been at, Donnie wore his leather. The black version of his protégé's brown Sean John. At some point, Donnie commandeered a mic and made an announcement to all partygoers. His message was regarding him giving away $10,000 to some lucky female in exchange for a particular service.

Donnie wasn't a buffoon who made scenes at venues on the regular, nor was he the type that got drunk and stumbled over his own two feet. He lived to be the center of attention but not this kind of attention; this was his first time ever speaking to an entire club while on stage via microphone.

The following day things went back to normal. People gossiped about the party and went on with their lives. There were no immediate consequences related to the shooting.

Not that Bookie gave a flying bird's ass. Actually, he'd come to K3 daily looking to finish the job he started, but as the prey stayed invisible, the urge eventually died down. Two weeks later he was back to regular scheduled programming. Riding around Killa Kees in the getaway car like nothing never happened. Had to get back to the money.

******

One month and three days after Donnie made his debut stage performance, he called Bookie with another announcement.

"Them bitch-ass niggas called my phone talkin bout give 'em ten racks, or I'm going down. Homeboy, I'm not giving them niggas $10, fuck 'em! On my mama, that shit dead."

"What the fuck...are you serious?" Bookie's mind was racing.

"They say since I got ten grand to give to a bitch at a party, give it to them or I'm going to jail." He paused then added, "For that shit in Mary Crest."

"Man, I been looking carefully for them niggas. Call 'em and tell 'em OK, have 'em meet you. You know where they at right now?"

Bookie was happier than a sissy with a bag of dicks; he couldn't contain himself.

"You trippin, homeboy, talking reckless on this jack. Fuck them niggas, though. Keep getting to the money like you been doing. Leave them broke-ass niggas alone. You know they eatin out the garbage, they tryna run up a check on some blackmail shit, where they do that at? Hollerin we know who did it, but since you his big homie and you

186

talkin that money shit ... fuck them niggas, though. I meant to tell you too, we should be decent today or tomorrow."

Bookie was pissed that Donnie didn't want to eradicate the problem once and for all. Much to his dismay, he stood down. Least there was some good news. "Decent" meant bricks were enroute. They had been dry without work for over a week. Bookie was down to his last three zips.

These demands on behalf of the Chevy Boys persisted for two more days. They refused to throw in the towel and vowed to move forward if not paid in full. They made good on their threat. "We know it was Killa," they told anyone who would listen, "but since this bitch-ass nigga talking this rich shit and tryna stunt, we gonna say it's him unless he check in." It was that simple.

At the conclusion of those forty-eight hours, Donnie contacted Bookie again. Some detective wanted to speak with him. He was laughing like it was all a joke, enjoying the spotlight as he usually did. For Donnie, it wasn't about a shooting case or the Chevy Boys. This image he played up, the name he'd chosen for himself "Bino," that's what it was all about. This teflon Don, John Gotti "Gambino" image.

KPD was well aware of his exploits and dreamed of the day he was placed in a jail cell. Donnie knew this, of course. He seized every opportunity to taunt them, to mock the entire force, no matter the department. With Donnie, it was about walking into the station, behind enemy lines (opposition turf), accompanied by his attorney, wanted for a Class X felony, and walking back out a free man with a huge smile on his face. Class X's were the most serious of felonies, punishable by a six- to thirty-year mandatory prison sentence. Ultimately giving credence to the legend: he was untouchable. There can only be one victor; *whoever wasn't a victor was a victim.* Donnie was determined not to be the victim.

"Them niggas, the police anyway, fuck them. I'm fina call Hyatt, and we fina go down there."

CHAPTER 23 – NO MATTER HOW HIGH THE BUZZARD FLY, HE MUST ALWAYS COME DOWN TO EAT

All we are is a result of what we thought. – Buddha

The first shock came when his lawyer called Bookie instead of him calling. Donnie had been arrested.

"What's the charge?" Bookie asked in disbelief. "What the bond gone be?"

"They don't know yet," Hyatt answered calmly. "He has to go in front of a judge. As you know, there is no preliminary hearing here, so there's a good chance I'll have to file a motion, but we'll have a bond tomorrow. He's charged with attempted murder."

"You know what courtroom?"

"It'll be at 1:30. I think Elliot's doing custodies."

Bookie asked a couple more questions before ending the call. KPD got the last laugh this time. Donnie was the victim.

He went to court, the charge was established and a bond issued, $1,000,000! Ten percent would be a hundred racks. 100k to walk. Attempted murder! The Entourage shot caller didn't look worried, so Bookie didn't panic. One hundred thousand wasn't no money. Bookie alone had run through that amount several times. In fact, Bookie wasn't into saving. What he had at any given time was just what he happened to have.

He blew money every day, on nothing. Hotels, motels, food, women, gambling. When he got to his bankroll and did inventory, he had just under 30K. Including the $3,900 in his pocket, Bookie didn't even have $35,000. But if he had this much, Donnie had to have ten or twenty times what he had. Here was a man who was the captain of his yacht, quarterback *and* owner of his own team; surely he saved, planned and set goals. Bookie was just on the boat with thirty-something odd grand so he could imagine what the H.N.I.C had. Donnie will be out in no time flat, he told himself.

It took the sole member of Entourage a week to decipher coded messages issued by his fallen teacher. There was no money. Bookie knew a substantial amount of cocaine was being held by the Plug, but he didn't know why.

Prior to Donnie's apprehension, they hadn't had any coke. Every day Donnie would update him. "We should be decent," he said, "probably Monday," "for sho Thursday," "Homeboy, we gon be good next week."

Bookie was more than familiar with the operation and how it ran. He already knew the Plug had the money but not all of it! What sense would that make? Apparently, Donnie only had about a hundred and fifty grand more than Bookie, virtually "peanuts" compared to what he should have. Bookie spoke to the Plug first by phone then face to face in Chicago, downtown in an executive suite at the Sax.

It turned out the money being held totaled 180k, and yes, it was Donnie's. But that depended on what angle the picture was viewed from. Donnie had a credit line of $250,000.

Without going into intricate detail, it was explained to Bookie that ever since he'd met the Entourage founder, Donnie'd been in debt. It was okay cause he usually paid. With Donnie being on the ropes though, and owning $169,000, the Plug explained he was between a rock and a hard place.

Bookie kept looking at a stocky, dark-skinned dude who had his face in his phone during the meeting, sitting close by on a cozy-looking sofa, never looking up once.

"I had my people there in the courtroom." The Plug spoke clear strong words, carefully selected. One could surmise precision was on his list of priorities. He motioned towards the phone tech. "He said he heard the proffer, the synopsis of what allegedly transpired."

Bookie knew he looked familiar. He had been front row at Donnie's hearing, only he was in a well-fitted suit, and another guy was with him, much older, wearing a suit and tie too.

"We don't think it's looking good."

What Bookie couldn't know at the time was that the mild-mannered guy in front of him, dressed in a soiled dark blue auto mechanic outfit with the name "AL" over his chest, was a distributor for the Twins. The Twins' main hub was Chicago and "AL" was their number one go-to guy.

In fact, one of the Twins was on his way upstairs now, having just finished a call with his boss in Mexico, El Chapo Guzman.

Bookie had no way of knowing the person that sat in the

first aisle at Donnie's hearing was Al's nephew who was currently in law school, and the man next to him a partner at a prominent law firm, Al's brother.

"It wasn't him," Bookie tried optimistically. "He gonna get out."

"We know it was you. But we also know Donnie's reputation too, especially down there. He's history. If he bonds out, the feds will intervene.

"He won't get out. They won't let that happen." The words were spoken so definitively Bookie didn't dare try to refute them.

"We know about you too." Bookie looked at the nephew who sunk his nose deeper into his BlackBerry. "We know you'll run through the units, but we know you like to shoot people. You don't care who, where, when, or why. I'ma give you some game. Everybody in the world got a reputation. Everyone! Some people even got a reputation for not having a reputation. Is that hard to wrap your head around?" he asked in reply to the puzzled expression at his last revelation.

"Nawl."

"Girls, cars, gambling, fighting, shooting. What's your reputation? What do the streets know or recognize you for the most?"

A Mexican about the age and size of Bookie walked into the room using his own key. Aside from the thick gold Cuban link, bald fade, and Air Max, he was just another Mexican. He came in, spoke and shook everyone's hand, starting with Bookie, then busied himself in another section of the suite out of view.

"If I give you his money, ya'll both will probably end up in federal custody. You will try to get him out and ... that will be it. If I bond him out, the feds will follow the money trail back to me. Even if they don't, if he got out scot-free, he'd be watched day and night, in the end everybody, would all go down, me, you, him and everybody else would be targets."

The Plug kept talking, but Bookie had heard enough. He knew right then and there, Entourage as he once knew it was no more. A teacher's illustrious career was ended prematurely on account of the student.

In Donnie's absence, he tried to step up to the plate, but with limited resources, his efforts were thwarted. Those shoes left behind to fill would have been too big for Shaq, let alone Bookie's size 8 ½ feet. He met with attorneys, went to court dates, accepted calls, went to visits. Helped out with his daughter, was in the Ob/Gyn ward when Donnie Jr. was born, offering up balloons, flowers and his physical support where needed. It was rumored he had another son much older, but the issues surrounding that specific conception forced Bookie to keep his distance.

Everyone in the streets watched Bookie closely. Monitoring his actions with a microscope. Would he sink or swim? Odds were not in his favor, so the streets awaited his sinking. Could he really survive on his own or had Donnie been the driving force behind his success? Bookie even wondered himself at times and experienced periods of trepidation.

In the game, you only went as far as your plug allowed you to go. If he was only giving you an ounce, how would you get past that? Rob him, rob someone else? Where will you spend the money? How would you get more product? You could have a million bucks, but if he bird feeding you ounces only, then that's your cap. You could always get another plug, but if that's all he's willing to give or that's all he's got, that's as far as you'll go.

Donnie was Bookie's plug, Al was his plug. Al's plug was the Twins, and their plug headed up the most lucrative Mexican drug cartel in the world, Sinaloa. Bookie wasn't plugged into the socket anymore, so he had no power (source). With no power, you were basically dead.

CHAPTER 24 – SINK OR SWIM

Nothing in existence precedes thought. – KeKe (G.I.)

In a short period he had developed a costly lifestyle, acquiring a number of expensive habits. With looking out for Donnie, sending Kadaisha a few hundred here and there, hitting Tawayne's books, and making sure his offspring was cool at the same time, Bookie's bankroll began to dwindle. He still sent other guys money as well. It would have been completely depleted except for collecting some of Donnie's cash off the streets. He had $60,000 out, but with each passing day of the Entourage leader being a no-show, people became more defiant and reluctant to pay. More than one incident required the use of a firearm as a tool of persuasion.

Although had he been a legitimate entity, he would have filed chapter 7, 11, or 13 by now, Bookie's number one priority wasn't to generate revenue. Instead his objective was to do away with the Chevy Boys once and for all. If he didn't, there was no telling what would happen to Donnie or even himself for that matter. Whenever he got close, they would slip between a crack or crevice, disappear courtesy of a nook or cranny. It never failed. God was truly with them.

CapBall, a K3 trapstar who sold crack like McDonald's sold Big Macs, owed Donnie $7,000. He told Bookie he had the money, and he was welcome to it.

"If you wait til after the first, though, I could probably put somethin with it, at least a couple grand. I know y'all need it, probably can give you like a sawback."

Before Bookie could say no, he continued "...and I know where dude 'em at. You know my cousin got a baby by one of them niggas. I think they living in a motel or somewhere right now, but on the first they posed to be moving in this crib."

Forget about the $7,000 or even the $10,000; the other info, if furnished, was priceless. All Cap cared about was fucking young hoes and playing video games for money. And selling cocaine of course. He was amongst the elite in these categories. "Let's just hope he keep his word," Bookie thought, before inquiring about possibly embarking on a business venture with him.

"You still be fucking with that nigga Breed or what? If not, we could do something probably on the 2nd or the 3rd." Bookie didn't want to step on Breeds' toes.

"We'll see what's up," Cap said, dividing his attention between Bookie and John Madden.

Bookie was confident the majority of his financial woes would be solved if he could lock in CapBall as a partner.

Ten days later, the first of the month came and went. Not only did Cap renege on the prearranged plans, but he failed to fork over the ten grand as well. He handed Bookie $5,000 and kept saying something about "that bitchass nigga lil C got me raided." On top of that, the address that he did provide proved to be futile. Bookie heard through the grapevine that CapBall's door had been kicked in so he was out the loop for the last couple weeks.

******

Running out of options, Bookie got in touch with his old comrade. He bought five pounds from Black, and Black fronted him five. "When you come back, I'ma just let you get 'em for the price I get 'em," Black told him.

Black and anyone else with five senses knew Bookie had fallen from grace. Black hated to see him like that while everyone else, mostly cause of his incarcerated CEO, loved it. With the ten blocks, Bookie got on the bandwagon with Dee. Remembering what Bookie had done for him, Dee agreed to alternate his sells. When an order came in he would fill it, and the next one went to Bookie.

Bookie was grateful to finally have a revenue stream that was low risk. If only it weren't so slow. Quarter ounces, half and whole ounces, quarter pounds, it didn't matter, the money still came at a fucking snail's pace. They'd spend all day together, sometimes eating breakfast, lunch and dinner. Riding around making moves waiting for the sun's descent. Then it was time for the Remy and to find some thots.

If or when Bookie got a room for him and Honey or any female, maybe some food, an occasional dice game, then he was set back. Waking up with a $100 profit wasn't going to cut it. Something had to give. He was thinking he needed some "yams." This weed thing wasn't for him.

******

A minor traffic violation landed him in the courthouse one early morning where he encountered his sworn enemies. The tri-level courthouse was packed, wall to wall, crawling with cops and robbers. He came within arm's reach of the three bums. After all the intense chases, shootings, searches, looking high and low, here he was.

Face to face with three of the Chevy Boys.

He took in their appearance: pants too big, shirt collars stretched out, hoodies wrinkled, the $40 Air Force Ones people sold out their trunks, the ones FatBoy referred to as "biscuits," the bottoms dingy yellow instead of off-white. No haircuts or linings. They looked homeless. With a bright, but fictitious smile, Bookie greeted them.

"Good morning, officers. Been looking for you guys. Y'all hard to catch in the streets, but ... I knew I'd find you here amongst colleagues. Where y'all been, Salvation Army? Soup line? Been in the city, Lower Wacker Drive, maybe? Wanted to ask too ... that dude I shot, he must didn't die, been wondering about that, wondering why he wasn't in the paper with you." Bookie had been talking with hand gestures to emphasize sarcasm, now he pointed his middle finger toward the runt of the litter, the one who had Donnie locked up. He'd been shot in the leg as the truck fled.

Truth be told, Bookie was surprised to see them, period, but apparently not as surprised as they were to see him. Due to lack of education, it took them a minute-plus to pick up on the insults.

"Fuck out our face." The eldest of the trio mouthed the words with such hate and disgust, it's a wonder he didn't scream each syllable. Just so happened, the courthouse was the one place Bookie was certain not to have a pole on him. God was with these boys.

Disdain was shared equally by both sides. In a place like

this, full of peace officers and the like, there was nothing that could be done. Bookie enjoyed the moment while it lasted.

With his index finger an inch from their faces, he began to sing "Eeny meeny miney moe." When he stopped, he was at the runt again.

His mouth was fixed, like he was conjuring up saliva to spit in Bookie's face.

What many people didn't know was that Bookie would swing a punch just as quick as he would shoot a gun, probably even quicker. He just preferred the gun over the fist because his intent was to kill, not injure or assault. Bookie swung without thinking. The runt went down hard, flopping like a shorter version of Vlade Divac when he played for the Maloof Brothers.

He was laughing and shouting simultaneously, "I told y'all he work for Donnie, I told y'all, do y'all believe me now, he Donnie hit man, I told y'all." He spat blood onto the polished floor and told Bookie, "I got yo ass now."

Bookie too laughed at his own stupidity as a handful of county sheriffs pounced on him, one or two standing back, guns drawn. He was arrested and whisked off to jail, misdemeanor assault.

Three weeks later in the same building on the third floor outside Judge Erickson's courtroom, Bookie sat on a bench awaiting Donnie's 10:30 am appearance. The Chevy Boys, two of them at least, sat opposite Bookie and Donnie's baby mama. They occupied the bench directly next to the state's attorney's office. One of them looked at Bookie, more like stared. He nodded his head up and down, up and down, sending Bookie some type of unspoken message or warning. It was the same one he'd hit a couple weeks back. Bookie came off the bench like it was made of springs. Donnie's baby mama reached for his arm. "Bookie, no." Vlade Divac ran into the office next to him, emerging fifteen minutes later, with company.

"Excuse me ... Mr. Sharp," a state's attorney named Pinnawit, wearing a cheap suit that didn't fit and thick glasses, approached Bookie, smiling from ear to red ear. The rat stood behind him. A woman secretary was also present.

"This is a state witness. Any threats or intimidation tactics on your behalf will result in a felony and—"

"This fucking rat," Bookie said to himself half aloud.

Bookie left before he allowed his self to be tricked off the streets again. It was too easy.

When he had asked, "So you saying I can't even look at him?" the district attorney, who looked like the daddy from *Honey I Shrunk the Kids* with even larger, thicker bifocals than those worn by Rick Moranis, replied, "You can look at the ground. If he feels threatened by your glare, you're history."

Not long after, during another one of Donnie's many court dates, a hearing on some petty motion, Koota and Bookie sat in the audience. They quietly discussed who was the thickest between two sisters whom they'd both had the pleasure of seeing naked. Neither Koota or Bookie paid much attention to the court proceedings until Pinnawit's voice boomed, "And do you see the gentleman in this courtroom?"

They both froze. From the witness stand, "Yes, sir."

He pointed to Bookie in ET-like fashion.

"Let the record reflect the witness is referring to..."

Bookie and Koota sunk in their seats. These dudes were unbelievable. The cheese-eating rat was testifying on a motion the State had filed saying Bookie intimidated and even assaulted him on Donnie's behalf.

The very next day, on a hunch, Bookie tried another approach. Always more than one way to skin a cat. Niccolò Machiavelli, in his masterpiece *The Prince,* wrote, *"Where force fails cunning may succeed."* An acquaintance of theirs, a second cousin, had been in Harrisburg at the same time as Bookie. Early on, Bookie had caught him down bad. Having the "ups" on him, he was spared due to their rapport, established years ago while on the inside.

Their cousin made it abundantly clear he had nothing to do with his family; he remained neutral; he didn't condone or promote their behavior in any way, shape, or fashion. Bookie believed him to be sincere. Out of all them, he was the only one really trying to get some money, a real hustler that stuck to the script. Bookie rode past his block and just as he expected, there he was outside, trappin' like a fool.

Bookie parked and jumped out, leaving his Dodge Stratus running. The cousin appeared to be considering whether or not to flee. He didn't.

"Tell them bitch-ass niggas I got that sawbuck for 'em."

Hours later, he'd taken D-Wren's mom Rachel to JCDC to see her only son. He too was locked up, charged with shooting one of the Chevy Boys. One of the four people they currently had in jail fighting for their life. He'd convinced his long-time homie that he should offer up some cash.

"Ten stacks ain't shit. See if they bite the bait. I got somethin on it. You can kill two birds with one stone, get me and yo boy Bino out."

Bookie's intention was to offer the initial 10k they'd requested. In exchange, he'd request two signed affidavits, one for Donnie, one for D-Wren. A nearby parked car door opened before he could get a response. His thumper was left behind in the still-running Dodge Stratus he'd borrowed from Monique. What a dummy!

The ghost of Kankakee emerged. The same guy Bookie had shot and left for dead in Mary Crest now looked at him with eyes as cold as Antarctica ice in the heart of winter. If his looks conveyed his demeanor, he was as mean as a rattlesnake. His expression, due to some nerve damage caused by the shooting, was a permanent snarl. "What the fuck you want?" His words were venom. Bookie showed his hands in defense the way Fat Boy always did, palms up.

"I ain't on shit, fam. I'm tryna come holla at y'all, I got them ten racks for y'all."

What else could he say, sorry for trying to kill you? He had to say something.

"For what?" he scoffed. "Not to come to court? You bitch-ass nigga, y'all had y'all chance ... Matter of fact, I'm fina call the police right now and tell them you over here and ....."

Bookie just turned and ran back to the car. From his rearview, he saw him on the phone trying to get a good look at the license plate to the Strat-dog. It's a good thing he didn't have a gun or wasn't a killer; Bookie would be a dead man.

******

It was during these times Bookie first heard the rumor. The word circulating was that Donnie was trying to emulate Eddie Murphy. Emulate him by trading places with Bookie. By any means necessary. As his situation intensified, he realized he was in grave danger. Bookie dismissed these allegations, claiming they were unsubstantiated, thus false. He still visited, still did what he did on the streets to keep Entourage alive, although he knew the plug had been pulled long ago.

So many who hated Donnie now hated Bookie. Those years of shitting on people, stunting and causing multitudes of dudes to envy him were like energy. It couldn't be destroyed. Instead, it changed host sites; Bookie inherited it. They hated anything and everything Donnie stood for, whatever or whoever he was associated or affiliated with. In addition to haters of Donnie and the Entourage, Bookie managed to acquire a few enemies of his own.

All the guys he'd sold to, pulled out bankrolls on, talked slick to, they all were glad Donnie was where he was, elated Bookie's electricity had been cut off. Glad he was eating out the garbage. Smack dab in the middle of dealing with all this, now Bookie had to address these accusations. He went to go see his former supervisor at county lockup. Before the visit even got underway, Donnie brought up some skeletons long since buried. What the fuck, was this intentional or had he lost his noodles? Was it an innocent mistake? A smirk on his face and that glint in his eye told his former subordinate he was probably aware of his actions.

Tawayne, when asked on the following day, told him through the same monitor Donnie was on that he'd been hearing things. Things that corroborated what his brother insinuated. He promised to confront Donnie at his earliest convenience, once again coming to his lil brother's aid. Immediately after the visit, Bookie's phone rang. Tawayne and Donnie had got "into it." Tawayne wasn't sure or couldn't give a definitive answer but either way Bookie should "be careful" in his dealings with Gambino.

Bookie took the advice with a grain of salt. He reevaluated the entire situation and decided he'd tread light, with extreme caution. His presence was felt but not the way it used to be felt. Donnie noticed the change and inquired, not one to hold his tongue. When Bookie first heard the rat rumors, he asked Donnie what the fuck. Donnie vehemently denied any such action. A fair exchange wasn't a robbery. Bookie wasn't tucking his tail, he would take his weight in a heartbeat, but no one ever asked him; everyone knew. Including investigators, the victim and the streets. It didn't even fit Donnie's MO; he wasn't a shooter. Things already known need no further explanation, so what was there to explain? Donnie's arrest was bigger than him. Speaking on Donnie's innocence would be preaching to the choir; after all, the "victim" had fingered him, so what could Bookie do or say?

Bookie's money got so funny he consulted Icky, who was still living the life of a rockstar off the 400k heist. Icky, or Ick as Bookie called him, was a good buddy of

Tawayne's ever since the Progler days when all fifth-graders in Kankakee went to the same school located on the 700 block of north Chicago Avenue, across from Benny.

He was the brains behind the Credit Union robbery and the other string of hold-ups in Kankakee County. It was hardly a secret. Mink coats, eight or nine gold chains, three bright orange box Chevys, all on 24's, the buying of cases of Don P and Cristal, passing out hundred-dollar bills .... he was a pioneer in his profession, a true Robin Hood.

"When y'all next lick, man? I'm fucked up, I gotta do somethin."

Bookie had never robbed anyone or anything, but it couldn't be that complicated if Ick had gotten away with over a half ticket in his short tenure.

"We linin it up now. Long as you got your own ratchet, then you good. Ion care who go, but you at yo own risk."

Bookie knew Ick from his Eastside Bulldog days where he earned the moniker Icky Woods, scoring touchdown after touchdown on rival Azzarelli Colts. Ick never cared for Donnie. He didn't necessarily have a problem with Bookie; whenever he saw him, he spoke. Because of Donnie, he didn't fraternize too often, but he was willing to overlook that on the strength of Tawayne and a dufflebag full of money. Ick had two teenagers riding along in his Chevy. His knockoff designer Chanel shades didn't fit his face; combined with the chains and the mink coat with no undershirt, Ick appeared to be a "hood nigga" from a parody or SNL skit.

An AR15 assault rifle across his front seat told you, though, that nothing was funny about this scene.

"Ick, you don't even have L's and you riding like that?" Bookie snuck a peek at the two eagle-eyed admirers occupying the back seat of the Caprice.

"What the fuck you doing? You trippin!"

"Hell, nawl, I'm going out with a bang though. You don't need a license to do what I'ma do. Holding court in the street. Fuck the police," he replied, smiling, slobbing on a mouthful of Now and Laters.

Bookie declined the invite but loaned one of the shorties his slammer at Ick's behest in exchange for a promise to give him $5,000 and the same gun back upon their safe return. As Bookie left, Debo was pulling up, Donnie's baby brother. Bookie thought nothing of it.

While Ick plotted, the feds plotted. They followed him and kept tabs on his every move. Receipts to the purchases of Don P and cases of Cristal were handed over to them by Ray at Plaza. Ick and Co. shopped up north daily, and each time the feds were there snapping pictures. Obviously, he wasn't a rocket scientist, and it showed.

Their next takedown was scheduled in Champaign, not far from the Greyhound Bus Depot Bookie was dropped off at when he got out the joint. Their entire crew was nabbed. So much for going out with a "bang." Newspapers read, "taken into custody without incident." Not a single bullet fired. Debo, those two shorties, Ick's brother and a couple more bandits were all captured. When all was said and done, mostly everyone told on the mastermind and received lighter sentences. His brother, Moan, and Debo took theirs on the chin, refusing to cooperate with the government. The judge viewing this as buckin' the court, handed them their ass holes. Ick though, Ick got a letter, the Big L!

Long after Ick was serving his life sentence behind bars, people were still enjoying the fruits of his labor. At his granny's, Mrs. Rabbit's on north Rosewood, amongst Alleyoops, he was a legend. In the hood, he was revered. Them "Ick Licks" had the streets in a frenzy. Tip, Fat Boy and a few others had sold vehicles to Ick and Co. for exorbitant amounts of cash. Tip had even got one of his cars back by default, for free (courtesy of KPD)! Fat Boy sold his Chevy and went and bought a Cadillac truck. Females had in their possession money, clothes, jewelry, etc., essentially they were glad he was gone.

Ick should have learned from those who came before him. He traded his life for the fame. He could have gone to any state, possibly to another country, got him a drop top, been riding foreign under palm trees with beautiful women throwing themselves at him. Like the TV show *Cheers*, he wanted to be where everyone knew his name, now the rabbit had the gun. Guys like Donnie had shitted on him his whole life. He stuck around to get his lick back, to rub it in, have his way with the girls who had rebuked him for years. Bookie learned a lot from Ick.

******

Days were now spent with Dee or Koota, sometimes both. When it came to hustling, Bookie rocked out with Dee on the pounds every so often and would pitch in with Koota, grab a half of brick and run through it. He couldn't get ahead, though, with his daily expenses and the occasional loss, if Bookie didn't find his lane soon he'd be in serious trouble.

Bookie was in traffic, him and Dee working off their phones. Having turned off Court Street, they traveled south on Albert. Up ahead they could see DQ. A car rode past going west on east Hickory. The passenger of the vehicle was bobbing his head up and down, in a mocking gesture, just as he'd done in the courthouse.

Bookie, already braking the Chrysler he'd borrowed from Nisha in accordance with the octagonal red sign, now hit the gas. There was no state's attorney to save him now. Finally Bookie had his man.

CHAPTER 25 – MIRAGE

Ignorance does a man more harm than a cancer in the body. – Khalil Gibran

Dee hadn't seen what the driver did, but when a stop sign had been run, he tuned in. The car containing the bobble-head was trapped. Maple was a busy intersection and traffic wouldn't allow the car to go any further. Bookie's pistol was on his lap. He was so thirsty he began to salivate, so anxious he began to perspire. Slamming on the brakes after turning right and coming within two feet of the enemies car, he yelled, "Put it in park!"

Bookie jumped out of the still-rolling vehicle, twisting his ankle in the process. A sharp pain reverberating from his ankle upward was outbid by a surge of adrenaline. Bang Bang! From his position just behind the sedan, he aimed the Heckler & Koch and went to work. The back window imploded with a loud thud after the secon bullet penetrated the glass. Closing the distance between him and the car, still firing his weapon when, to his surprise, the Impala jerked forward. Directly into oncoming traffic. Aiming at their heads only, he kept shooting. Even as the sound of cars colliding on impact, metal on plastic, followed by tires screeching and horns honking, hit his ears, he kept shooting.

When there were no more bullets, and he was satisfied

his mission was complete, he turned to run back to the Chrysler and went down hard. His ankle was busted. Dee was out the car, on his feet, pistol in hand. "Come on." He helped Bookie back to the car. The entire episode lasted seventeen seconds. Good thing DQ wasn't open, Bookie thought, leaning the passenger seat back, trying not to wince in pain as Dee put the pedal to the metal.

Word was sent. The Chevy Boys were arrested. Not in the hospital or the morgue unfortunately, but at least in police custody. No license, no insurance, fleeing the scene of an accident and a host of other charges. Apparently, they'd driven home instead of waiting on the police. Bookie was shocked no one was hit or dead, but since they were in JCDC then .... fuck them. When he found out they'd made statements only and been released an hour later, he was furious. To add insult to injury, the bullet holes in their car had been attributed to Bookie, so said an investigator who questioned Bookie and Dee days later.

"That's it," Bookie said aloud. Maybe he was barking up the wrong tree? The real Teflon Don Gambino crew was the Chevy Boys!

******

"Man, this nigga got me fucked up. On the BOS, I can't go like that. I can't go, fuck that!" Dee wasn't himself. He seemed to be coming unhinged.

"What happen, G, what's going on?"

"That nigga Quick," he ranted. They were in Nisha's living room.

Bookie was babysitting while she went to pay some bills. When Dee came in huffing, which was highly unusual, attention shifted to him. "That nigga tryna get me...I know what he on ..."

Bookie listened to the whole story before rendering judgment. Quick was doing a favor for Dee similar to what Dee would do for him back when he was dealing with Black. Only Quick had to travel an hour north to Chicago and get the blocks of reggie, dealing with his new crew's people. First time or two with him by his lonesome, things went swell, allegedly.

Soon as Dee got involved and put some money up ... Quick said state troopers got on his line. He had to toss out the pounds of weed on the expressway. Sounded like the banana in a tailpipe, the oldest trick in the book.

Sure it sounded fishy, but Bookie dared not tell his homie who was clearly on edge already. Instead Bookie added, "Ion think he tryna get you." The last thing he wanted was to send him overboard. Dee was seething and wasn't convinced in the slightest. Bookie was well aware that *any man who lived life on the edge would eventually fall off.*

"Would you go for some shit like that? Come on, man, get the fuck outta here," he said bluntly. "I know you wouldn't."

Dee was a hundred percent accurate in his assertion, but his friend didn't want to put the cables on him.

"Ion know. If it was my man, a hunnid grand, if we was ninety-eight and two...if I was like his brother, godfather to his baby... ain't no tellin like Jack told Helen."

"Man, I ain't tryna hear all that slick-ass shit, get the fuck outta here. That nigga playin games with my mufuckin bread." Dee was pissed, and his friend wasn't helping the situation.

Bookie wouldn't have gone for it, and Dee knew it, but what other option was there? Especially with someone being family. What should he tell him?

The loss came at a bad time, as Dee was already hurting financially. Nobody had had good blocks of regular for over a month. This forced Dee to venture outside his comfort zone. He purchased some lime-green shit from his cousin's baby daddy, but it was compressed and wasn't really smokin'. Days afterward, a shipment of that fluff came through. His phone stopped ringing, and he was stuck with everything he bought.

Quick came along with promises of popcorn for the "lo lo." As of late, Quick had been running with a couple dudes from up north. Under their influence and with peer pressure exerted, the pair of out-of-towners had Quick outside his element doing things he normally didn't do. Like popping pills and possibly turning on his family, his "Day One's."

"It's them niggas, them niggas got him on that. I'm telling you. I already know what the fuck going on. Watch. Matter of fact I'm fina go over there."

Dee's mind was already made up.

"I'm already fucked up, damn near broke!"

Bookie told him, like his homie KeKe from Gary Indiana used to tell him, "Broke is a circumstance. It could change any minute. Long as you're not poor, see, that's a condition." This philosophical perspective upset Dee even more. He didn't want to hear none of that bullshit.

"You coming?"

"Nawl, I told you I'm babysitting. I gotta fix this food real quick and then help out with some homework. Nisha'll be back in probably bout forty-five minutes. I can go then. If it's just you and Quick though, for real, for real, ion need to go. It ain't like he gonna bring you a move. Y'all can talk that shit out like brothers. If them other niggas there though, if they want some smoke shiddd ... You know I'm wit the shits." Bookie shrugged his shoulders. "Or if you just want me to, then lemme know."

Dee thought for a minute.

"Nawl, it's cool! He told me to come holla at him like five, so I'ma go ova there and see what he talkin about. He gonna have to do somethin though, I can't go like that." He stormed out the house, and seconds later Bookie heard rubber burning.

******

Bookie glanced at his Joe Rodeo. It was barely 4:00 p.m. An hour passed and Dee was back, looking disheveled.

"Bitch-ass nigga tried to steal on me."

"*What?* Steal on you?" Bookie got to his feet. "What you mean, steal on you?"

Dee was fuming.

"Yeah, on the G, the nigga tried to snake me. We was over there and this nigga got to talking slick in front of them niggas...we ended up boxin'."

Now, Bookie was starting to worry. This wasn't only an assault on Dee; it was an assault on him. This was an assault on him and his reputation. Dee ran with him; they were together 40 north, tight as ten toes in two tube socks.

Because this was Quick, and he didn't really want to take it there, this made Bookie look bad, even weak perhaps. Once Bookie got involved, it probably wouldn't be a lot of talking, probably no fighting either. Hopefully, before it went that far, the two brothers could reconcile their differences. Everybody in the streets, including Dee, knew what Bookie's involvement could potentially lead to and it wasn't worth someone losing their life over.

Bookie needed to know for sure if this was what his friend wanted, and if so, he needed to know he was of sound mind, not speaking out of anger. "So what's up, they didn't jump you or shit, did they?" He wanted to talk him out of it, offer an alternative solution.

All of this over a couple grand. *Peanuts!*

Right or wrong, Bookie was riding with Dee. Obviously, he didn't want to get down on Quick then end up regretting it down the road, nor did he want Dee to get down on him if it wasn't necessary. Bookie stood down. He reached out to Quick personally. Quick's response, "Fuck Dee!" And he wasn't talking or working shit out! "What happen was what happen, just how I said it. I went up north to grab the shit, police got on me; I threw it out. My shit gone too. It is what it is. Whoever don't believe it then fuck 'em; ion got nothing for no mufucka. "

Bookie still did nothing. An extreme case of sibling rivalry at worst. Quick seemed high on something, speaking irrationally and making gestures not consistent with his character. His lips were ashen, eyes wider than usual, veins on his forehead and in his neck protruding. He was a totally different person.

Bookie never been the type to let beef exist. If or when it showed its face, he immediately sought to resolve it peacefully or otherwise. Riding around with pistols all day every day had been the norm for him before. He was in another lane now. Attempting to achieve what most in this lane who came before him didn't...longevity. Like Al explained, everyone has a reputation for something. When you think about it, this guy has lots of cars, people like Tip. That's what he's known for. Donnie sold bricks. Dee weed.

Some people fought at the club; others danced. Females sucked cock good; some had a good "shot". These were all reputations. "Knockout artist", "twerker", "fye head", "bomb pussy". There are good reps and bad reps; body odor, stink breath, broke, dirty, etc. Many embrace their reputations, even adopting names and the likeness of them. Others, obviously in denial, vehemently reject them. To sum it up, Bookie liked the rep of getting and having money as opposed to shooting and killing people. Living in a small town with enemies wasn't good. You could be in McDonald's with your kid picking up a Happy Meal and see the person you're beefing with. Then what? Such close proximity guaranteed an encounter eventually. If your enemy was serious, really with the shits, then you and your kid would be in serious danger.

CHAPTER 26 – KILLING HOPE

Everyone must die, but do you want to go walking or crawling? –
Author

Bookie recalled the 25/50 lesson Donnie broke down one day while they were on I94 headed to Wisconsin.

"Niggas wit a bag don't want no problems. That's why most mufuckas who got money, people call them punks or view 'em as lames. Niggas say I'ma hoe, or a bitch-ass nigga all the time. They just don't say it to my face. Otha mufuckas, they say it to their face though. If you in a club and you step on a nigga feet, if them niggas gettin money, a real bag, like really really got that sack, I'm talking bout got a real check, they'll probably apologize to you!

"It's only 24 hours in a day, ain't it? All 24 of those gotta count. You can't spend one or two hours worried about $50 or $500, when you got $550,000. If you do, then you'll be neglecting yo half a ticket. Think about it. It's like you being able to bust three nuts a day. You got Beyonce at home, what you gonna do? Go waste one or two of them nuts on a crack head or a hoodrat bitch? How the queen B gonna get satisfied?

"That's why niggas who runnin' it up, that's why they quick to apologize. Why wouldn't they? They got twenty-five stacks in they pockets, anotha twenty-five bands on their wrist or neck. A fifty rack foreign outside. Twenty-five hoes in the club tryna ride shotgun in that foreign, fifty more on the phone tryna ride his shotgun. He got twenty-five moves to make, fifty grand to pick up in the street. The plug callin him sayin he got anotha fifty pack in; he has twenty-five minutes to come get it. Whips to drive, boats, motorcycles. Throw all that out the window for you and a pair of shoes? Let's be serious. A person with nothing has nothing to lose. They're dangerous people. Even if they're wearing $2,000 Louis Vuitton shoes...and? Is it worth it? People with money know the answer to that question. A broke dude don't have a clue. Being broke will have you looking at it like 'I treated that nigga' or punked him out. Don't get me wrong, sometimes people wit money might get high off something or wasted and you step on they shoes and...or people act like they got it, but really they broke. Step on they shoes and they shoot the whole club up. You saying to yoself, damn, I thought he had money, why would he do that? Occasionally, you might find a nigga who got money, like real money, but he doing crazy shit. If you look close enough you'll see the reason, but it's definitely a reason. White people do crazy shit all the time. Mufuckas like Charlie Sheen. You'll find out ten years from now that he got AIDS and you'll be like, 'Aw, ok.' That's why he was doing all that stupid shit. What's that movie star white bitch name, the klepto bitch?" he snapped his fingers two times in concentration.

Fortunately, Bookie was at the point where he didn't want any problems anymore, with anybody. He would still give you problems, though, if you rubbed him the wrong way. He hadn't quite "arrived" yet. In the meantime, he didn't want to interrupt the edification process either. He was well on his way.

Well aware of his environment, when Bookie wanted to go out, he hit Highway 57 in order to avoid drama. Up north he didn't have to worry about police or existing beefs.

"Aye you tryna hit the e-way? My man say it's a party tonight, unlimited action."

Dee was all for it. Bookie was told it would be a "lock-down" so there wasn't a need for fancy attire. Stopping at the Plaza to fill up on the Remy, the boys set out on their mission, exit 312 northbound.

"Damn, Killa, slow this mufucka down. You know we got these missiles in here."

"Fuck the police. Pull us over they gonna get their mufuckin issue. Betta us kill them then let them kill us. They just killed a mufucka on the e-way the other day. I seen that shit before. I can't go, fuck that."

Since the incident with Quick, Dee had been riding dirty like UGK; he refused to put up his hammer. In K3 Bookie rode with his, on the freeway; anywhere he went, it went.

Dee used to keep his within city limits; when he left Killa Kees, he'd leave his protection. But since beefing with his bro, he kept it on him, even going to the city. He was adamant Quick was the aggressor and up to no good. Seeking to bring him harm. Putting safety first, he said he'd rather be safe than sorry. Bookie begged to differ. He didn't see Quick as a threat or he would've already eliminated it/him personally. Nevertheless, Dee stayed strapped nowadays.

"Fuck the police, like I said though, turn that Jeezy back up." *Thug Motivation* gave Bookie a lot of the motivation he possessed these days. When it came to that trap shit, that cocaine talk, street life, nobody could deliver like Jeezy. He was the voice for authentic street dudes. They knew he really lived the life by the way he said what he said; thus, they identified with him, and Bookie wasn't exempt.

"You don't even know where we going, or where we gettin off at. What exit? Did you call and see?"

"Damn, you ain't lyin, cut that shit down real quick, lemme call Clip."

Full Clip was an old school gangsta. He'd run with the *Old Man* personally. Bookie got acquainted with him while he was executing a sixty-year sentence for his role in a triple murder. Those twenty-nine years and six months behind bars had preserved Clip's youth.

Ever since their release, they maintained contact. In Chicago's criminal world, Clip was well-connected and equally respected. Revered by people from all walks of life.

Upon first glance, he might be mistaken for mid to late thirties. Surely, he was as energetic as a twenty-one-year-old (and loved to party with them whenever an opportunity was afforded). He was in shape, better shape than Bookie perhaps. Those couple of decades locked down had been kind to him. Being a half-century-plus came with a well of knowledge, wisdom and understanding, which came in handy more often than not. Passing up Volmer Road, Bookie ended his call.

"He told me get off on 79th." Remy Martin VSOP was distributed equally before the dark green bottle was tossed out the window around 167th. Bookie sent a text message with his right hand, sipped the contents of the smoke-clear

8oz plastic cup with his left, and guided the vehicle past 147th with his knees. Young Jeezy's cocaine-laced lyrics blared through the custom JVL Audios with the perfect amount of bass vibrating outwards from the massive subwoofers strategically placed in the trunk of the car.

Cups were running low by the time the boys got off the Dan Ryan on 79th. The Remy was starting to have its desired effect when Bookie's phone rang.

"Turn that shit down, G, this Clip right here." Bookie put the Sprint to his ear.

"Hello! Hello." He stayed the phone with his shoulder, indexed a mute button on an expensive TV-radio with his now-free hand, and looked up just as an enormous pot hole came into view. He dodged it with his knee, then took hold of the wheel at the last second with his right hand. The left hand, the hand holding his cup, was still doing its job perfectly.

"Yea, Killa, go head."

Clip had one of them nonchalant drawls that made a listener think all would be well in the middle of a tornado. With a natural smoothness uncanny to some, he reserved a super-syrupy tone as a persuasion tool for a particular female audience. Even in Bookie's quasi-intoxicated state, he could detect it.

"Who you wit, fool? You must got some action wit you."

"Aww, you met her already, that ain't nobody but Renee. Where y'all at, though, y'all got off the e-way yet? Y'all can go right there on 79th, just wait on me at that Shell when you get off."

"We here now."

"Damn, Killa, that's my fault. I'm walking out the door now. I'm still in the hunnids, you must be in one of them Lambos or somethin." He laughed, an old-school player laugh. "I'ma stop around the corner, grab my belt and I'm on my way. You want the address, or you wanna meet me at the Glass House?"

"Ion know, how long before you pull up, you think?"

"I'ma hop on the e-way right here, probably 119th or 111th. Be there in five or ten minutes. I'm walking out now."

"We fina go to the liquor store then we'll meet you at the Glass House and follow you."

Dee looking around nervously and clutched his .40 cal.

"Where that nigga at?"

"He in the hunnids, by Ada Park. He fina pull up. By the time we grab another bottle, he'll be here."

This time the boys got a fifth. Twenty-five minutes later, trailing Clip, they arrived at their destination. A two-story white house with maroon trimming and a mangled porch railing, on 74th and Parnell. The side street was a one way. Music could be heard coming from inside the crib as they got out of the car on Chicago's southside.

******

Inside, Clip and crew were greeted warmly, introduced to men and women alike. A combo of VSOP and lack of lighting made it difficult for Bookie to fully grasp his surroundings. What he could see, though, were hosts of scantily clad women milling about. Thongs, corsets, garter belts, stilettos and see-through heels upwards of five inches seem to be the standard uniform. Men of all ages and even a few women drooled at the smorgasbord while others loitered unfazed, obviously with different agendas.

The music was deafening, shaking the home's foundation to the core. A vibrating floor, courtesy of mega bass lines sent vibrations outward. As a Gucci Mane track played at its maximum output, Bookie felt the onset of a migraine. The stench of cigarettes and excessive secondhand smoke didn't help.

The peculiarity of the "no weapons" clause played over in an intoxicated Bookie's mind. He had agreed reluctantly on the strength of Clip. Soon as they got out their car, Clip asked them to leave all guns outside.

"They don't want no guns in there, but y'all good, y'all with me," Clip pleaded.

For one, it wasn't necessary, but number two and most important of all, it was a security measure.

Still sipping Remy, Bookie commented, "Ion fuck wit no house parties so ... ion know. Since it's you, though ..."

"Calm down, Killa," he said with a disarming smile, literally. "It's a lockdown, a lil different than a house party." Aside from the naked women, Bookie couldn't tell. They enjoyed the show for an hour before the remainder of their mind-altering intoxicant was clumsily kicked by a wayward dancer. On a badly restored hardwood floor, the bottle toppled over, its entire contents going to waste. They sought out Clip to let him know they were out of Remy and would be heading back to Fairplay, Kenwood or some shit, wherever they sold Remy Martin.

Inside the sedan, firearms were removed from

designated stash compartments and relocated to laps and waistbands.

Bookie first put the Nina on his waist, but it was cool to the touch and uncomfortable, so he retired it to his lap instead. Which was a better place for it considering their location.

Armed to the teeth and heavily intoxicated seemed to be the way of life in Englewood. According to recent statistics, it was the single most crime-influxed area in all of Chicago. This was the etiquette of The Windy City, so the boys blended in perfectly fine.

Whereas some people became hazardous or detrimental to themselves and others while under the influence, Bookie's paranoia and mild schizophrenia heightened his awareness. Alcohol had the opposite effect on him. As opposed to dulling his senses, rendering him a snoozer, it made him more nervous. The residual effect increased his alertness.

Hence when Clip approached the tinted window as Bookie pulled off, it rolled down prior to him announcing his presence. "Y'all coming back?" he asked with the combination of charm and coolness that garnered him a spot in many a woman's bed.

"Fina go grab a refill right quick, tryna ride or you want us to grab you something." The street was a one way and the boys were facing north, with Full Clip standing in the grass, bending down to speak through Dee's window.

"We'll be back in a hot second."

"Step out real quick before you go; somebody wanna meet you," the OG spoke with authority.

"We'll be right back—"

"It won't take long," Clip countered.

"Who is it?" Bookie inquired, puzzled at his friend's persistence. Behind his buddy on the sidewalk, Bookie noticed a small gathering of people out of his peripheral.

"Just come on, lemme introduce you."

He reset the gear shift to park, left the car running and got out, simultaneously tucking his burner under his shirt. A semi-circle awaited him and Clip, consisting of approximately eight men. All complete strangers. Bookie entered into the mouth of the horseshoe and stood face to face with its lone occupant.

Not much taller than Bookie himself, he was slim, with salt and pepper French braids. Brown-skinned with minimal facial hair. A tiny gold rope dangled from his neck, a sparkling six-pointed star medallion on the end of it. Had Bookie ever met his mom's brothers they'd probably resemble this fellow.

The "man in the middle" exuded an aura that said he was lion of this jungle. Due to Bookie's inebriated state, he found this amusing. Had he been sober he might have cared. His instincts, however, prevented him from laughing or even speaking for that matter. He turned and looked for Clip, who remained just outside the opening of the structure.

"This him here, Clip?" the "middle man" asked with confidence, seeming to already know the answer.

He made a hand gesture that coincided with the head nod directed towards Bookie.

"Yea, that's him there," Clip responded in a voice that

had lost a dash of its coolness. Middle man was definitely the alpha male.

Facing his host, Bookie asked, "What's going on here?" as casually as he could muster.

He maintained his composure, but his cheek muscle was twitching here and there in an amused smirk at this charade.

"JR Hope. You can call me J-R."

Bookie grasped the extended hand and replied stiffly, "Killa."

"Killa?" JR chuckled unabashedly. "Killa, huh? Killa," he let the word roll around on his tongue a few times. Scanning faces in his small but very attentive audience, he went on. "Everybody wanna be a killa. Ain't that crazy? How everybody say they a killa?"

Bookie didn't know if it was a question or a statement. From his perspective, J-R only asked questions he already knew the answer to, so he'd wait and see where it went.

"Before I left, it was only a few of us."

This was allowed to linger for dramatic effect. Once he was sure everyone had it, he pressed on.

"Now every mufucka a killa."

The tables turned. Now he was the one amused, smirking while engaging the crowd. With his fancy tickled, he switched gears, and his mood took on a darker hue. Bookie felt insulted, like he was being made a mockery of, but he kept his cool.

"They say you earned it, though. I been hearing about you. Good things too, all good things. I heard you with the business, with keeping the 'vision' alive." He held his finger at chest level and made quotation symbols.

Within the mock session, there was just a few feet for JR Hope to move about unimpeded. He made the best of it. Pacing a couple steps, turning, stopping, then repeating it all over again but talking while doing so.

Every opportunity he got, he looked Bookie in his eye. He asked, "So you making a lil noise down in Kankakee, huh? That's yo town?" he asked, patronizing the lad. At this, Bookie laughed louder than he would have normally done under similar circumstances. He refrained after noticing no one around joined in on the fun. Bookie wanted to leave. He wasn't with this shit, dude ass was crazy. Something wet came in contact with his forehead, a rain drop? He looked up at the sky instinctively, then back at Clip to make sure he was still there.

"They say you know a thing or two about that girl." Another rhetorical inquiry. Bookie turned back to face JR.

"Just like you run yo city… I run this mothafucka." His forefinger stabbing the air.

"What you paying for a T-shirt?"

This guy was switching gears like Jeff Gordon on a last lap. He spoke with such authority that one was compelled to respond.

"Twenty bucks," Bookie replied without hesitation.

"I can beat that number. We can get it down to nineteen, 19.5. We gonna sit down at the table. Not this Sunday. Lemme see…what day that fall on… okay, yea, next Sunday, not this Sunday. Me, you and Clip. We gonna come down there, hit I57 and come yo way. Not this Sunday but next Sunday. Mark it down in yo calendar. I definitely got something for you, but we gotta sit down, make it all make sense."

He had to be forty or fifty years old calling bricks T-shirts. That lingo was from the early 90s when crackheads were called cluckas, dope fiends, junkies, or plain ol' crackheads. Now you had fiends, geeks, hypes, smokers, jay, swerve, etc. They called kilos bricks, books, and Bs. Times had changed but not for this guy apparently.

"Me, you and Clip, not this Sunday but next," he said again prior to all of them going their separate ways. "Aye, Killa ... you know I got the keys to the city, right?"

Bookie initiated eye contact this time. His unibrow arched, questioning just a hint, but he nodded affirmatively. Alone, walking back to the car, Bookie called out to Clip. His old comrade escorted him the few feet while lending an ear.

"What was that all about? What was he implyin, got the keys? I know he not talking about ..."

"He ain't lyin," Clip interjected with a very straight face. "He a senior board member and he got the city. That came from all the way up top. You know he just got out."

"State or feds?"

"He was in the feds. He probably been gone since you was five or six years old. You should know his rappy Durk."

Bookie had heard of them but didn't know them personally.

"He been standin on the business since he been out, getting shit in order. They say he shook a couple niggas down, ion kno bout all that but what I do kno and can vouch for is he's a man of his word. Like I vouched for you. I told him about you after you took care of that last business for folks 'em on the low end. See, he really tryna lay his hair down, but he building his team. He can't do shit without a team of good men.

"He only as strong as the niggas behind him, but that's true with every mob. He makin it his business to start wit all them lil small towns, Kankakee, Joliet, Champaign, Decatur, Springfield ... he tryna post up. So be ready next Sunday. He got a lot of shit now. I think he just hit Killa Bone 'em in Joliet. He asked me who I got and trusted outta town. I told him you. He been hearin about you; he just thought you was from the city. He was gon give you one at first, just on the strength of me. But he like you. He say you remind him of him at yo age. He'll probably bring you a couple of em and give 'em to you for eighteen or nineteen G's apiece."

At the car now, Dee was standing outside, banger slightly on display, at the ready. It was starting to make sense. Bookie had heard about JR or some recently released board member putting the press on niggas. All over the city.

"So he serious?"

"As serious as a heart attack and twice as deadly!"

When they returned from the liquor store on Halsted, Dee brought in his "blower."

"Fuck that, they ain't searching anyway, ion know these niggas like that. We might have to fan one of these niggas or anything."

"Ion know, they probably said that cause that dude in

there, or it was probably even him who said he ain't want no pipes in the party."

"We ain't honoring that shit; fuck all that. Now when he give us them bricks ... now that's a different story."

Inside they took up their positions and commenced to pour up. Bookie was left alone. Dee disappeared with a girl taller than him wearing a postage-stamp-size pair of underwear.

Bookie would talk, every blue moon, touch, but he never had sex with strippers. Never. It was a cardinal rule of his. Anyone who showed their nipples or lips of their vagina for three or four measly quarters (literally) would do a lot more for three or four Washingtons. You toss in a Franklin, and there's nothing they *wouldn't* do. Ultimately, they're slaves to a dollar. Where was their moral compass?

Bookie kept a pocket full of hundreds, so much money sometimes he couldn't even fold it. Bills stuck together. If a stripper would allow you to examine her as if you were a licensed OB/GYN, poke or fondle her cavities, all for a single dollar bill, what would she do for 10,000 of them? Just being him and having a reputation flashing copius amounts of cash, he couldn't trust strippers.

Then there was the disease factor. Most dancers for the right price will perform sexual favors, and condoms didn't protect you from everything. A pit stop at Arnie's one night revealed an empty box of lambskin condoms on the floor of the john. The irony of finding such in a strip club was that someone was probably walking around with an STD from the encounter. Lambskin condoms don't prevent venereal diseases, only against pregnancy. No rubber, no matter what kind could stop herpes or infections passed on via two pubic areas being in contact. So his rule of thumb was no strippers. Period.

Yes, he would support their hustle, party or hang out with them, but no sex. After all he'd stoop low for the right price but that one, or whatever the front number was would have to have a few zeros behind it. Even then he'd only pull a trigger, but not pull his pants down in front of strangers.

Half an hour had passed when a very loud bang was heard over the music.

A gunshot.

It was no mistaking that sound. Partygoers' body language told him he wasn't hearing things. Dee found his way to his homie about the time Lil Wayne's "Go DJ" had stopped. People came from every room, even from upstairs trying to see what was going on. Naked girls huddled in a corner, frightened. Two middle-aged men, both dressed in black, made a vain attempt at crowd control!

"Nothing's going on…"

Convinced, Dee told Bookie, "I'll be right back."

"Fuck you mean, you'll be right back? You drunk, G, something ain't right. We outta here. Come on." Jay-Z's "99 Problems" came on.

"Gimme like ten minutes, man. I gotta get my hat anyway. I'll be right back."

"Aight, man, I ain't fina wrestle wit you. I'm fina go to the car though, just hurry up."

His head was pounding, smoke suffocating him. He needed fresh air. Apparently, he wasn't the only one in need of oxygen. Other party poopers agreed obviously, hovering around the entrance trying to find their coats to leave. Bookie shouldered his way through the coagulated group inhaling the night's cool air. A small cluster of bodies refused to go any further than the tiny porch due to a light drizzle that threatened to pick up.

"Who is that?" some curious woman asked nosily.

To the left, Bookie saw a figure standing on the corner oblivious to the light rainfall. That's odd, he thought. He must be drunk or something, probably waiting on a ride. Fuck him. Bookie quickly descended the stairs two at a time. Too much funny shit going on; he needed his banger. "Fuck, no keys."

He was back on the porch in a matter of seconds. Stragglers left, went to cars, walked off disappearing into the night. He could smell rain now, moisture in the air. Bookie called Dee's phone. No answer. He called again. Same thing. To make matters worse, his phone was dying. More patrons split, leaving in groups. Not caring to go back inside, he kept the porch company along with a few cigarette smokers and those awaiting someone to pick them up.

"Who is that, Killa?" JR flashed a self-assured smile. "Scuse me, Killa." He bumped into the younger version of himself intentionally as he started down the steps, being sarcastic and sporting a friendly smirk.

Bookie wasn't offended in the least. He actually liked this JR guy. When he reached the bottom he turned and looked up at Bookie. "Not this Sunday but next Sunday."

They both laughed after simultaneously repeating the

line. Despite the rain in his face, JR made it his business to tell Killa bye. He turned and hurried to his car.

Bookie shifted his attention to a fellow porch dweller who apparently had had a little too much alcohol. The snaggled-toothed gentleman was attired in a pinstripe zoot suit, an outfit more appropriate for a costume party than the current social event.

Bookie asked if he'd seen Full Clip.

"Whaya say, Lil Flip?" The man was out of it.

Bookie was too, but sobering moment after sobering moment combined with an intense headache was working a number on him, clearing up blurred lines.

Frustrated, he answered, "Clip, man. I said Clip. I saw you talking to him in there. You know Full Clip, right?"

Eyes half open, half closed, the drunk looked at Bookie questioningly. A still-lit Newport short dangled from his lip. One of the Garfield-like eyelids was lower than its mate due to the trail of thin white smoke coming from the end of his cigarette.

"I'm tryna have you tell 'em c'mere, or jus tell my man to c'mon," Bookie said.

Ashes almost as long as the stick of nicotine itself threatened to fall any moment. It was obvious he couldn't be much help to anyone including himself in his current condition. He leaned to one side in a matrix-like stance, drunk off something other than liquor.

Frustrated, Bookie turned to someone else for assistance. This time, it was a female with way too much makeup, reeking of cheap perfume. Her eyebrows had been shaved bald and replacements horribly drawn in a perpetual arch with eyeliner. Her expression made Bookie ask her, "Huh?" He thought she had asked him a question. Ten or so years older than him, he could tell she used to have it, but time hadn't been on her side. She smiled a radiant smile at the younger eye candy. When he didn't return the gesture, she turned to costume man and asked for a "short."

Bookie rudely interrupted. Eight people were on the porch, including Bookie, everyone talking, smoking, drinking, all at the same time. When someone left the porch, another person came out the house to take their spot. Bookie needed to find Dee so they could move around. He couldn't take it anymore. He would send for Clip, then Clip could either get Dee or the car keys from him. At this point, it didn't matter.

He reached out and gently tapped Eyebrows' shoulder. She was already smiling when she turned to face him. Zoot Suit frowned instantly and mumbled something about a "young mufuckin punk." Eyebrows blew a cloud of secondhand smoke in Bookie face.

"What's up cutie pie?" Now Bookie too was masked up and looking crazy, but he couldn't treat her; after all, he needed her.

"Aye, you know Clip." Her eyes said she did, so Bookie got to the point. "Can you do me a favor? Can you go tell him—"

The explosion was so loud Bookie jumped and tried to duck at the same time. It sounded like someone on the porch had shot a .50 Desert Eagle. Silence followed. He realized it really wasn't a silence, it was just his ears adjusting.

Bookie turned to see what the hell was going on. People were running outside to see what was happening but got nowhere. They ran into men running over women on the porch, trying to get back in the house. The figure from the corner was standing over a body in the street, at the end of the block. JR! Next to his car, JR Hope lay in a motionless heap, a lone gunman looking down at him. Bookie stood and watched from the porch as he was killed in cold blood. The gun in the assailant's hand came to life again. He was killing Hope! Gunshots echoed, sounding near and far. Bookie reached for his banger instinctively, but even as his hand touched his naked waist, he knew it was already too late.

"Damn, man, he already dead," he yelled at the shooter unconsciously, who held his position over JR, still squeezing off rounds. When he was sure his mission was completed, he turned nonchalantly and walked in the opposite direction, careful to take his time.

When Dee finally found him on the porch, Bookie was sober as a gopher. Dee had his pole in his hand.

"What's up, you good, G? Who was that shooting?"

Bookie noticed how Clip was nowhere in sight. All of the relevant faces were MIA.

He pointed, "Man, they just got down on JR!"

Dee looked confused.

"Who, who got down on 'em?"

His eyes were wide with shock. He didn't have to ask. Bookie knew what he was thinking.

"Who would get down on him? On the BM, at a party for all the guys, and no one was around?"

It was a cold game. Although Bookie was too far from

the shooter to see his face, the darkness and rain further obscuring his vision, he wondered what the shooter might have looked like. A voice in his head told him he looked the way Bookie had looked to so many unfortunate people he'd visited over the years, like the Reaper!

Hours later he caught a brief segment on WGN covering JR Hope's murder. In a dream, he saw JR put his keys in his car door, the killer sneak up behind him and with the gun to his head fire the single shot. Honey told him in his sleep he'd mentioned something about "next Sunday."

CHAPTER 27 – COME WITH THE TERRITORY

To go north, you must first leave south. – Author

Trouble seem to follow him wherever he went. He couldn't shake it. On the land he went all in like a last hand of Texas Hold 'Em with Koota. Playtime was over. He needed to get back on track. This detour was taking a toll; he had more gray hair than Grandma Mary. Things went smooth for a while. Bookie served time with a Titanic Stone named Bread from Chicago. Bread, after seeing his picture on the screensaver of a P-Y-T's smartphone requested his number. The girl dialed up Bookie from the Kennedy King classroom and handed Bread the phone.

Bread was from over east, heavily affiliated with Bump J and that whole GoonSquad Movement. Sly Polaroid was his family. Bread HQ was located on Drexel, seconds away from Illinois Senator Barack Obama's Hyde Park residence, a stash house with an unlimited supply of the product Bookie demanded. They bridged the gap. Every other day he bought an eighth. The four and a half ounces would be cooked up, converted to seven, eight, or nine ounces of crack. Bookie was just starting to see progress when things went south again.

******

Koota bought a clean Suburban already on 24's from Whiteboy Joey. The truck became the company vehicle.

Everyone was at GameKeeper's barbershop shooting dice one afternoon when CapBall, not having a valid driver's license due to unpaid child support, asked Bookie to run him to Poor Boy's. Bookie had won $1,200 and quit. He was waiting on Koota to get a lining.

Koota was down a few grand. Cutting hair was the last thing on his mind. Blood Brothers Trick and Spud were working a number on him, tag-team action. Slugger and Spank was aiming at Slick Dan. Dan was shooting at Koota, Koota was trying to just break even. Someone yelled out, "Gangsta Hank & Boomer on their way." Dice games like this could go on for hours. There was probably a hundred thousand dollars in the room at any given time.

"Come on, fuck it." Bookie agreed to give him a ride before he ended up back on his knees losing his free $1,200. Since it was nice out, he passed on the car he'd come in and the rental Cap drove. Instead, he took the company vehicle.

Kankakee was so small that you could take the scenic route, viewing the entire K3 populace in just a few short minutes. Taking the long way, they came down Chestnut by Plaza, setting off car alarms as they passed. Bass pounded as Jeezy rapped about liking to drink and smoke then mix Arm & Hammer with his coke. When they made it to Court Street, Chris was there on the corner selling Final Calls.

Bookie hadn't spoken with him in months. He'd developed a strong dislike for the N.O.I member, almost a hate. This held true for anyone playing with the Deen. He used God to hide behind while he did the devil's work. He was a fraud in the worst way. Bookie had long suspected but had no proof. Late night he'd run into Chris and ask, "What you doing here this time of night?"

It was during one of these nights that Bookie ran into him parked at a club setting, in the company of a female. She told Bookie, "Ugh, he always tryna talk to me, tell him you my boyfriend." Bookie waved her off, thinking she must be joking or mistaken somehow. But she was adamant, so he complied, even telling Chris he was going to sleep at her house and wouldn't go home to Kadaisha until the next day. The same night Kadaisha called her baby daddy, telling him Chris came over at midnight asking if he was there and could he use the bathroom? If he already told Chris he wouldn't be there, why would he go there intentionally, knocking on the door asking for him?

When confronted, he offered a lame excuse. Bookie was skeptical but gave him the benefit of the doubt. Who wouldn't? He was an N.O.I. registered member, wore suits, was polite and respectable. He was married with a wife and kids. Bookie remembered the saying about, *"He who sees with the eyes only was easily deceived."* One has to see with more than the eyes. On the outside looking in, a person can only see so much.

Paper Girl helped Bookie come to a more definitive decision. She worked at the beauty supply on Court and Hunter, and she was highly desired by both men and women alike. She and Bookie became good friends. She would tell him stories of the daily offers and propositions she received until his ears ached. Chris had been amongst a few diehards practically stalking her for years, ever since she delivered *Daily Journals* on her Huffy, ergo the name.

Paper Girl would talk to Bookie for hours. She told him how Chris tried to first get close to her by sparking a convo about the N.O.I. When that didn't work, he offered to perform cunnilingus on her. Still getting nowhere, he asked, "How much?" He even bought her gifts and presents. He wasn't just a regular dude trying to hit a pretty young thang; he was offering to do some really freaky stuff. His method of approach was that of a creep. The weirdo had been exposed.

He knew Bookie knew. This was a guy Bookie had let into his home, hold his son, meet his baby mama and family, had at family gatherings during the holidays, etc. Even Mary liked him and welcomed him back anytime. He was lucky Bookie didn't shoot him in the head.

As they came up on the intersection, Cap muted Jeezy and let his window down. Instantly, he smiled and sat up in his seat. Bookie heaved a sigh. He knew where this was going.

"Bitch, gimme one of them papers!" Chris walked calmly to the passenger side of the Suburban, to two waiting smiles.

Bookie directed traffic to go around them. The busy intersection quickly became congested as Chris started his rant.

"Man, I told you quit playin wit me, Cap; I'm not one of yo lil flunkies," he spat.

Bookie knew that was meant for him, but he just laughed. He knew he wasn't a flunkie. Chris put it out there intending to wipe Bookie's smile off his face, but it had the opposite effect. Cap laughed, too.

"I'm just fuckin wit you." In a show of good faith. "I'ma get a couple of them papers then, man, since you crying and shit." CapBall leaned back in his seat, forced his hand into his designer jeans and pulled out a DopeBoy knot. He peeled off a $20 bill. Chris didn't accept it.

"Nawl I'm saying, I told you bout that shit; you talk to these otha niggas like that, not me. Ion call you out yo name, do I?" His face was stone.

He stole a quick glance at the driver, who was now shaking his head at the way Chris was disrespecting the bowtie. How can one serve the people talking like that? This further confirmed he was a fake.

Cap replied smoothly, "You right, man, my fault. I was just fucking wit you." The residual effect of his smile slowly started to evaporate.

Chris, not seeming to notice, plowed on.

"I ain't gonna keep tellin you niggas—."

Cap cut him off.

"Bitch-ass nigga, I told you I'm gone from it, fuck you keep talking for? You tryna box or somethin?" The smile on Ball's face had all but vanished, replaced by a very nasty frown.

Chris first looked to make sure Cap was serious, then proceeded with caution. "I'm just saying, man ..." all the bass was gone from his voice now.

Cap interrupted again, berating the fraudulent N.O.I. member. He repeatedly shouted obscenities, at the end of which he invited a bowtie-clad coward to a duel. Bookie watched, not surprised in the least. He stifled laughs, not wanting to incite this debacle any further, but when Chris did what all punks with no heart do, the levee broke. Both men looked at the driver when they heard his cackle. Bookie's head was back, and he was laughing out loud. Chris standing down and tucking his tail was comical.

"Y'all leave that shit alone," Bookie pulled himself together. "You know yo bitch-ass got warrants and shit." Cap had a warrant in Kentucky for child support and a possible warrant in K3, failure to appear. Bookie was still shaking his head from side to side at the pathetic nature of the situation.

"Fuck this bitch-ass nigga," Cap said to Chris's face. This time the only reply was silence. "Come on, you right!" He put his custom New Era Fitted back on his bald head.

The name Bizzal was emblazoned on the temple, courtesy of Lids. He hit play on the remote, and Jeezy came back to life. Bookie cranked the volume manually and eased off the brake leaving Chris standing there, mouth agape.

Poor Boy's was just across Court Street. Chris beat them there almost; he wasn't done. Before they could park, he was pleading his case, trying to save face. The radio had been powered off due to a heavy police presence inside of the small diner. Poor Boy's wasn't only a favorite amongst residents of Kankakee but law enforcement agencies as well, especially county sheriffs and state police who received discounts for their service and protection of the public.

"I ain't tryna hear that shit," Cap was saying through his open window. He took the Kush out his pockets and placed it in the glove compartment. "You a bitch nigga, talkin like you tough. On my mama, I'll beat yo ass ... Told you I was gone from it, you steady talkin and shit, wolfin."

Bookie laughed again, but this time it struck a nerve with the victim.

"Fuck so funny, nigga?"

"Yo fight right there, slick homie. Fuck you barking up this tree for? He the one treatin yo ass," Bookie told him in between giggles.

"That's my man, he can say that, but you — man, this ain't what you want. I'll beat yo ass, though." The emphasis on "yo" made it clear he wanted no smoke with Cap and already had in his mind he couldn't win with him.

In his mind he was already mentally defeated, telling himself he didn't have a chance.

Instead, Chris chose the smaller opponent. Bookie. Cap was maybe 5'10", 240 lbs, he had a little gut but was strong as an ox. Chris was roughly the same height and fifty or so pounds lighter. Bookie was a featherweight in comparison to both Chris and Cap.

"You don't scare me. All that Killa shit, nigga, you ain't tough." Bookie noticed his voice raising a decibel.

As Chris got closer to the truck, Bookie suspended the parking process, not wanting to run the man over while he spoke his piece. Now he commenced to finish the job.

Initially, he had trouble backing the huge SUV in. Chris walked to the driver's side. After two tries, Bookie got it. Not caring for Chris's demeanor and knowing cowards, he attempted to put the Suburban in park and get out to better address the situation, but it was too late. Somewhere in between the fraction of a second it took to switch the gearshift from R to P and kill the engine, a fist came through the open window. Bookie slammed the truck in park and jumped out. Chris took two steps back and threw up his guard. Bookie attacked like a pitbull on a cat burglar. A wild punch landed but not in its intended destination. He aimed for a jaw bone and got a neck and part of an ear instead. Chris charged toward him, driving him against the truck, grabbing at him frantically. Bookie tried to break free, but Chris had him as they tussled.

"Fight with yo fist, hoe-ass nigga," Bookie panted.

Chris went to lift him. Bookie was prepared. He locked his leg around his opponent's. Outweighed by fifty or so pounds, Bookie knew he couldn't win wrestling. A significant height advantage with much longer reach wasn't exactly in his favor either.

He stood a much better chance standing apart, looking in his eyes and having a chance to react to his actions. He would have to fight this fight defensively; he was outmanned from an offensive standpoint. When the opportunity came, he'd switch to offense, but he had to be careful. One wrong move and it could get ugly.

During one of his few fights in the joint, the IC had told him even if you lost you won cause you stood up, you fought for what you believed in. You demanded yo respect, you didn't jus go for *any* ol thing. Bookie had decided then and there that he would never *not* stand up; thus, he'd win any and all fights that ever came his way whether in the form of a physical confrontation or a mental obstacle.

After countering his move with a ferocious leg lock,

Bookie squirmed to break free. He threw three or four wild punches, but his main focus was getting loose. Chris's energy was put into trying to lift the much smaller Bookie to slam him. Suddenly a team of uniformed officers was there, and they were pulled apart. Bookie felt his eye swelling.

"Hey, what's going on here? Would you like to press charges, pal? What's your name?" Question after question.

"Nawl, that won't be necessary," Bookie told the trooper coolly. "Thanks anyway, officer. This my buddy though, he just a lil upset ova a ballgame."

"He don't look like a buddy the way he sucker-punched you through that window there. You sure you don't wanna press charges?" another officer inquired, wiping crumbs from his mouth with an already soiled napkin.

"Yea, I'm positive," Bookie told the top brass on the scene.

The sergeant looked a bit hesitant but eventually directed his men back inside to finish their meals. Chris was definitely guilty; the crime in question, though, was punishable by death, not some misdemeanor fine or citation, and Bookie wouldn't rest until the sentence was handed down.

One of his younger cousins, Lil Ron, walked up.

"What's up, man? Dude did that shit to yo face, what's up? What you wanna do?"

"Hold on." Bookie looked around for Cap who was coming out of Convenient.

"Damnn, on my soul, yo eye fucked up," Lil Ron was saying.

Martha had pulled up. One glance and her eyes became moist. Without thinking, she reached in her purse. Lil Ron was sill asking, "What's up?" Just barely a teenager, he was trained to go.

"Hold on, you see all them police in there?" Bookie warned his sister. He looked toward the cops. A couple of them watched with a weary eye in between bites of their lunch. Had Martha pulled out the .25 automatic, the situation would have gone from bad to worse. A lone policeman wrapped up a conversation with Chris on the west side of the diner before seeing him off. He closed up a small notepad and placed it in his breast pocket as he rejoined his colleagues.

Cap was back on the scene.

"Man, that nigga fucked yo eye up, on my life ..."

"Them bitch-ass warrants, I wanted to fuck that nigga up."

Bookie went to the Suburban, adjusting the driverside mirror best he could to survey the damage. He nodded his head up and down, affirming Cap's words. Martha asked if he needed the great equalizer again.

"Thanks anyway. I'm good though. I gotta bake a special cake for him; that lil pea shooter ain't gonna cut it," he smiled, but the humor was lost on his sister.

When night fell, an anxious Bookie immediately sprang into action. His eye had swollen pretty bad. Fortunately, it wasn't black. Nothing a dark pair of Chanels couldn't fix. Chris would not be as lucky, though. Hours were spent outside his residence.

No sign of anyone wearing a bowtie. Bookie was so

bold as to casually knock on his south Chicago Street apartment door. Nothing. Back inside the car, he watched for any sign of life, any activity whatsoever. There was none! He couldn't take it.

Agitated, he jumped out of the passenger seat, walked to the door again and abruptly kicked it open. Already deviating from the plan, Bookie dashed back to Taj and the idling sedan for cover. He could watch from a safe distance. If the coward showed his face to close the door, or even if police came... Bookie sipped his drink directly out the bottle.

"Why yon ain't go in there and operate?" the driver asked curiously.

"Man, it's some mufuckin stairs, a lot of 'em leading up to another door."

"This wasn't part of the plan anyway. It's probably kids and shit in there. This a sign, bro, come on. Let's just come back tomorrow."

Bookie wasn't in agreement with Taj, but they'd been staking out the area for hours now. Not so much as a light had come on. He knew no one was there but he didn't want to accept it.

CHAPTER 28 – REVENGE

The line between bravery and stupidity is so thin, more often times than not it goes unnoticed. – Author

Bookie hardly slept. The next day, when night was approaching again, Choppa called.

"Aye, G, it's a party tonight at Jaguars, y'all fuckin wit it? Meet us right there at McDonald's on 147th when you get off the e-way on Sibley."

Bookie, in his response, briefed him on his eye and the situation involving Chris. He couldn't turn up until Chris was put down.

"What? I'm on my way!"

"Naw, I got this. This shit personal, fool. When it's done though, I'ma be that way." Bookie took the phone from his ear and looked at it when he heard no rebuttal. The LCD screen read, "Call Ended."

Choppa was one of the guys from "out west" originally, K-Town. Recently he'd sought refuge in the south suburbs. Bookie first met him in IDOC. Their bond had grown over time, becoming finalized when Choppa had gone against his own people, New Breed Black Gangsters, for Bookie. Nowadays when an operation was needed in or around Cook County, Choppa reached out to Killa if he couldn't do it himself.

It was common practice for Bookie to contact him for assistance in Kankakee or even Chicago for that matter. As of late, however, Bookie had been gravitating in another direction, which was fine with his buddy, long as when he called or needed him, Bookie came. In total, Choppa had visited Kankakee five times, four of which were official business. On the flip side, Bookie had doubled that number returning the favor. At least three of the times, Choppa was on the frontlines with him.

Two hours after the phone call, Bookie, Dee and Choppa were patrolling the streets of Kankakee, looking for Chris or anyone who even resembled him. He was at the top of Bookie's most wanted list, even surpassing the Chevy Boys. God forgave, he didn't, nor would he forget those actions perpetrated by the coward in the bowtie. Revenge was a dish best served cold, and Bookie's veins were ice. He was so determined that it's possible he would have sent a message by a family member. He was so driven he sought out women and kids, going against the golden rule. He was out for blood.

Choppa just rode in silence. Smoking blunts and sipping Remy continually, as if those intoxicants were his fuel. Dee kept an eye out for Quick or his new running mates. A couple of incidents had transpired in the last week or so that had pushed them to the top of the food chain, right along with Quick.

Ten-minute intervals were spent riding past south Chicago Street. Still no sign of life from Chris or his family. An hour later, still no opps had been spotted. Choppa was told about Quick and why Dee was on his bumper during this downtime.

"Yea, so I'm riding past and I hear a shot. All the time the radio and shit was on so ... I knew it was a shot, but I wasn't a hunnid percent sho. I come back and tell Killa I rode past them niggas' area and heard a shot, he talk me out of it, sayin, 'Was you sure? Did you or the car get hit? Did you see 'em? —and all this goofy ass shit." ...

"Man, I ain't say all that clown shit," Bookie interrupted, trying to convey the message properly to Choppa who remained expressionless. "I just asked you was you sure it was a gunshot and did you see them shoot at you. You ain't know for sho, so—"

"Like I was sayin, this nigga talkin bout they prob shot in the air or some bullshit. I think it was the same day or the next day..."

Dee told Choppa about Quick and Co. tryna get down on them. Bookie was behind the wheel of the 300M when he turned off Court Street onto Chestnut Ave. His burner was on his lap but a nosy semi-truck driver looking down in the Chrysler made him put it on the floor under his seat. As the car turned, the gun slid further underneath him.

Bookie reached under him to retrieve it but scraped his hand on some jagged metal. He kept driving. Coming up on a party or some type of gathering a few houses behind Plaza, Bookie slowed down, eyes scanning the crowd. People were in the middle of the street. This particular section of Chestnut wasn't busy, so pedestrians obstructing traffic wasn't abnormal in a sense.

As Dee and Bookie neared the host site of the event, they scanned faces for recognition. There was movement. Dee was looking for Quick or his cohorts, Bookie for Chevy Boys. Out his peripheral, he noticed some strange movement. Two people ran from the streets back towards the house. Bookie looked up to the rearview just as the Chrysler cleared the crowd. "Aye, this nigga Quick chasing us."

"Where ... Where? Where he at? I told you that nigga was on some other shit!" Dee clutched his pistol and twisted in his seat. They came up on a stop sign. Bookie obeyed it, turned left and ignored Quick. "Man, that nigga crazy; you ain't lying!" Bookie agreed.

In the small rearview mirror, he saw an image of Quick running full speed with a black object in his hand. He had a few yards on his companions, but there were apparently two more people joining the chase—the two dudes who had run to the porch. On Chestnut and Hunter, there was another stop sign. Again Bookie stopped. Just then a gunshot echoed in the distance. Fuck that mirror. Bookie turned to look. Just as sure as the English alphabet starts with an A and ends with a Z, there was Quick, arm extended and shooting at them. His crew was by his side now. They were shooting too.

From a half block away, all three of them fired shots repeatedly. Bookie put the car in park then reached so far under his seat that his hand was cut to the white meat. He wasn't thinking clearly at all. He got out. Dee was out too, shooting back.

"Man, shoot them niggas," Bookie yelled. It was like a scene from a Movie, Dodge City ... an old Western. Except there was no one yelling "cut."

Bookie had never seen or met these new guys but had known Quick since junior high school. He'd hoped for a more peaceful resolution, but with that single act, Quick's fate was sealed. Bookie was reluctant to get off the bench in this particular instance, but when forced, Bookie had no problem playing the game. The 300, now at Tip's autobody shop getting painted, was the only victim in the intense broad-day gun battle. One of the best autobody mechanics in town, Will Napoleon, had texted that morning and said primer was currently being applied. He'd have it sprayed after lunch, and it'd be ready in forty-eight hours. Hence the rental.

Chevy Boys had slipped a notch or two below, losing their top spot to Chris. That slot for Dee belonged to Quick and his two partners in crime. Choppa didn't know Chris, but he was present, willing to aid and assist through all endeavors, no matter how righteous. That's all he knew.
It was the weekend, and Kankakee was turned up. Someone had a party at Lee's Lounge on Court Street, the word was around midnight it should be cracking. Everywhere the boys drove, there were crowds of females, Plaza Liquors, BP Gas Station, the Chicken Shack...and females attracted males; they were never too far behind. Everybody was eventually gonna end up at Lee's. They rode in circles. Bookie fantasized about where he'd shoot "Chris the Coward" when he finally ran into him. Everyone was in their own world. Talking was at a minimum as the midsize sedan glided around the small town, seeking its prey. Even the audio was off. A silent tune of murder was the only sound to be heard. They drove past Plaza again; it was packed. Cars everywhere. Both entrances were clogged with vehicles coming and going. Droves of females were on location, many of whom wore clothing that revealed more than it concealed. Flocks of both sexes loitered in the

parking lot of the popular liquor store.

It was a festive scene. Music was being played, drug transactions made, blunts rolled, and smoke was in the air. There was even a dice game. Only thing missing was a DJ booth and dance floor.

"Aye, there go Koota." Bookie saw his truck but didn't see him.

"Goosenecking," Dee added. "Fuck Koota, there go them niggas."

"What niggas?" Bookie's palm began to moisten.

"Them niggas that was wit Quick."

Bookie's fangs came out.

"Ion see 'em. Where? How they look?"

The rental car had turned around and was riding back past the targets.

"Right there. The light-skinned nigga, you see the one next to him with them braids?"

"Braids to the back?"

"Nawl, the braids going down. He got a white tee on."

Both Bookie and Dee were excited. There was finally some action.

"Oh, yea, I see 'em ... and buddy wit the black fitted on next to him, right?"

"Yea, that's them hoe-ass niggas right there."

The car made a right turn on Gordon, ending up in Walgreen's parking lot.

"What's up?" A cold edge had crept into Dee's voice.

"You know what time it is," Bookie answered.

He was hoping everyone in the car knew what time it

was. For him there wouldn't be a lot of chit-chat; his banger would say all that was needed to be said.

"I'm ready...been ready," Choppa stated in a voice that might have been used when explaining to a waiter he wanted soup instead of salad.

Breathing hard, Dee commanded, "Lemme out, I'ma..."

Bookie laughed a dry laugh. "Be cool, G, you thirsty. I'ma go back around the corner. When I hit the block, I'ma let y'all out."

"You wouldn't be saying that shit if it was Chris. I ain't tryna hear that shit. Hurry up before them bitch-ass niggas move around."

"If it was Chris, I would have drove right in the parking lot and popped his goofy ass, fanned him in front of err muhfucka." No one laughed.

Had Choppa known his way around Killa Kees, it would have been Bookie and Dee operating. Since Dee was the only other person who knew the lay of the land and it was personal for him, Bookie would sit this one out. He was better needed behind the wheel.

******

Loose gravel that had somehow found its way onto the uneven pavement made the only sound as the two unmasked gunmen approached their destination. The chorus the rocks sang was a symphony of death. Their strides were brisk, their movements swift and expertly executed. The shortest of the pair assumed the lead, ultimately dictating the pace of the assault.

An idling Ford Taurus with New Jersey tags waited patiently, its driver listening to Gucci Mane rap about how he was So Icy. Any second his passengers would return, albeit in a rush. He positioned the rental car to make their getaway as uncomplicated as possible.

The shooters walked to the edge of the parking lot in front of thirty or so preoccupied witnesses. Without a hint of hesitation, they both took aim. Bang! Bang! Out the corner of his eye, the intended target saw fire escape a chrome barrel. He saw the flash, hearing a simultaneous explosion even before he felt the bullet. The fitted cap fell to the ground. Another blast, another victim crashing to concrete like an unsupported sack of potatoes, his white tee now splattered a violent red. A series of shots followed in rapid succession.

Plaza was more than just an alcohol dispensary. It was a meeting ground for all walks of life that shared a common goal. On weekends, particularly at night, the liquor store became a scene from a conventional rap video.

Flashy cars, guys behind the wheels in their Sunday best. Girls half naked. Everyone either on their way, or just leaving the club. Hordes of people fraternizing. Tonight, however, that fun had been interrupted. A hail of bullets had rained on their parade. There was a stampede underway. Complete chaos. Panic. Men and women screamed. Bodies dropped, cars collided in a rush to flee, horns sounded off, car alarms came to life.

In the wake of the melee, there were three gunshot victims, seven reported injuries, and five fender benders.

******

"Go right," Bookie told the driver. "Turn left." They were back on Court Street. Left turns were prohibited but so was murder, what the hell. They turned left. Originally, he'd planned to let Dee and Choppa go, but at the last minute, Bookie had to get a piece of the action.

Half an hour later, in Choppa's car, they drove past the scene to assess damages. The rapid discharges had emitted a small cloud of acrid gray-blue smoke. The smoke had singed hairs in Bookie's nostrils, and now he had trouble inhaling without interference from the scent of gunpowder. He cracked his window.

Plaza was a beehive of activity. Yellow caution tape formed a perimeter protecting the crime scene. Emergency personnel were everywhere. Ambulance, fire trucks, you name it. Patrol units, state troopers, unmarked cars, detectives, KAMEGs, sheriffs were all parked haphazardly, silent sirens with lights flashing blue and red.

"Damn, I wish Chris was ova there," Bookie mumbled to himself. He knew he hit his target; he just hoped he wouldn't live to talk about it. They rode past Chris's house one more time before looking for somewhere to park.

"Man, let's go to Lee's," Dee suggested. There was no protest from Choppa, so the boys headed for the lounge on Court, only two miles from Plaza. No sense in riding around when police were hot.

In the parking lot of Lee's in between Oak and Court, they posted up and cracked another bottle. A very familiar group of women were one car over from them. Bookie got out to engage them. It wasn't just any group of girls, it was a group he was well acquainted with.

CHAPTER 29 – SENSELESS

He who is kind to the cruel is cruel to the kind. – Unknown

Donnie and his little brother Debo's baby mamas had two friends with them.

"Heyyy, Bookie, gimme a hug," Debo's BM got out.

"What's up, Ciara, you want some of this drank? You heard from Debo?"

"Yea, I talk to him damn near every day. I'm tired of putting money on my phone for that shit. Yeah, pour us up, y'all got cups?"

"What they talking bout with that case?"

"Ion know. They say Ick 'em the only ones who went in the bank, so he probably won't get that much time."

"When you coming to see the kids?" Donnie's baby mama asked from behind the wheel.

Bookie went back to the 745LIi to get his cup. Ciara followed him over to speak to Dee and Choppa. Bookie, with Ciara, walked back to the girls' car and poured them all shots from the huge bottle. Returning to the Beemer, he handed them the liter of Remy and his Smith and Wesson .40 cal.

"Hold this. This mufucka keep slippin."

He decided to hang out with the girls. Donnie's baby mama was showing him on her i870 pictures of lil Donnie.

"He gettin so big, lookin like a lil man, look at him," Bookie smiled as he chatted up Ciara and company. His eyes scanned the crowd every sixty seconds. The more he drank, the more he scanned, becoming more paranoid.

Now it was forty-five seconds, his eyes swept the crowd, from east to west. Then thirty seconds, north to south. As Bookie laughed, carrying on in his usual manner, his dilated pupils zeroed in on what appeared to be Quick. He stopped everything and squinted. This couldn't be Quick. Bookie couldn't believe his eyes. Approximately thirty yards from them and headed in their direction was a stumbling Quick.

Maybe the Remy was getting the best of him. He wasn't certain, so he said nothing. Choppa and Dee had joined in on the conversation with the girls but remained in the BMW, a few feet away. Bookie and Ciara were the only ones outside the cars. The car that was parked in between them had left, so their interaction was now unimpeded. Ciara followed Bookie's gaze.

"Aye, there go Quick! Ain't y'all into it wit Quick?"

"Yea, look alive, look alive! Three o'clock."

Bookie spoke the words, but his eyes never left the approaching trouble. Quick was closing in fast, oblivious to imminent danger. Bookie heard a door open then close. Another door opened. Dee was on his feet. Choppa was readying his weapon. So many people were in the parking lot that Dee and Choppa both had trouble locating Quick's position.

He saw Bookie first but never broke his stride. Their eyes locked yet he continued to close the distance. Quick started fumbling for something all of a sudden. Aside from this, he didn't really react to Bookie's presence. Bookie could see him clear now. He looked to be as wasted as Bookie if not more so; he was making confused facial expressions, patting his pockets, a veteran smoker searching desperately for a missing Zippo to light the Newport short he held between his forefinger and thumb.

"Which one is Quick?" Choppa asked in a flat tone.

"The one with the red hoodie and red and white Mike's right there walking this way," one of the girls answered.

Bookie saw Quick's eyebrows began to dance up and down in confusion, he finally began to understand what Bookie's presence could potentially mean for him.

He desperately looked to see if Dee was in the vicinity. Bookie heard a gun cock.

"Damn Quick," Bookie said to himself. Those other guys at Plaza he didn't know, thus could care less about. Quick, on the other hand, Bookie had a rapport with; he knew him. Sure he'd gone off the deep end, but now Bookie didn't really want to see him go out like this. If only he'd turn back, run...retreat. But Quick just kept coming, much more slowly now.

His eyebrows were completely arched in a question-like form when all of a sudden he stopped walking. He wrinkled his nose, eyes still on Bookie. He opened them wide, narrowed them to slits, tilted his head a bit and started reaching. He'd abandoned the search for a lighter; he was going for his waistline now.

Bookie looked back. Quick was no longer focusing on Bookie. He had found and made his focal point, Dee ... he had his man. Quick reached for his burner, but Dee and Choppa had the ups on him. Now Bookie thought, "What if?" What if he got off a shot or a whole clip before…Then Bookie thought "damn, the girls"…Now he wished he hadn't put his gun up. He didn't really wanna kill Quick, but if it was his life or Quick's life…every man for his self, God for us all, he thought.

Frantically, Bookie looked at Dee and Choppa. His face begged them "Please shoot first and hurry!" With Bookie's Smith & Wesson already in hand, Dee raised it and closed one eyelid like he was in a James Cagney Western shooting a six-shooter. Eight of the longest seconds of Bookie's life passed and nothing happened. "Safety, safety!" Bookie yelled. "Take off the safety!" Bookie was worried. If Quick was allowed to get off the first shot, there was nothing separating him and seven or eight easy targets. Even an intoxicated person could hit a bullseye from a few feet away if he had ten or twenty tries.

Bookie saw Dee fumbling with the safety mechanism, cursing under his breath. He turned back to Quick. Quick was pulling out his gun then stopped. Like he wasn't sure or undecided, like he was finally understanding Dee was his brother, his family. He went to pull it out again and that's when Bookie heard the shot. Just one single shot. Although Bookie had been holding his breath, waiting for and expecting the shot, it caught him off guard.

Bookie thought, *Damn, why didn't Quick shoot first? He let us make it.* That split second of indecisiveness had cost him dearly. After the shot was fired, Bookie saw both men he came with holding guns. Who had pulled the trigger was a mystery, and there was no time for questions.

Quick didn't go down like the dramatic scenes

fabricated in Universal Studios by professional stunt coordinators. He actually kind of sat down, then fell backwards like an exhausted graveyard shift worker coming home to his own bed after a twelve-hour shift. Lee's had three parking lots, and for the most part, they were all filled to capacity. The scene from Plaza repeated, but times two. Sheer pandemonium. "Man that nigga fakin." Bookie grabbed Choppa's rocket from him and ran over to where Quick lay to get a better view. Dee tuned in, staying at the ready. Bookie stood over Quick and looked down at the bloody past. He was on his back staring straight at Bookie, eyes wide open. Quick was dead.

CHAPTER 30 – SAY LESS

Those who talk don't know and those who know don't talk. – Unknown

"I'm not sure if you have the right person here." He opened his hands sympathetically. Although the man in the uncomfortable fold-up aluminum chair was by far the youngest and smallest person in the building, he had an air about himself. He spoke as though he might be in charge, in a position of authority. Clad in his classic black attire, Bookie wore black Levis, a black track jacket over a black V-neck with huge dark Chanel frames. The twenty-four-year-old didn't quite look the way he sounded. His sarcastic wordplay might have been more suitable for a college professor of Caucasian descent as opposed to a "mid-twenty something" drug dealer in the hot seat for a homicide.

With each hand gesture, a diamond bezeled gold wrist watch gleamed in the dim lighting of the small room used for interrogations. What was even more insulting to investigators was the fact that each syllable was delivered with a slight hint of an accent. An Austrailian accent at that!

"First, I would like to thank you for coming." As if I had an option, Bookie thought. "My name is Detective Passwarder."

When Bookie offered no response, he continued, "And

you are...?"

"Leonard."

"Okay, Leonard, would you like anything to drink? Coffee? A soda?"

"No thanks."

"Smoking is prohibited, but we make exceptions every now and then. So if you like—"

"Don't smoke."

"'A Newport,' I was gonna say."

But Bookie noticed the bright red pack of Marlboros in the detective's breast pocket. They must have a special pack or even a carton of Newports for rats.

"So much for that," the detective feigned a smile. "Can you start by removing the sunglasses, please?" the question was polite but firm, "Not a lot of sun in here, case you haven't noticed."

"Is it necessary?" Bookie was tempted to add 'mate' but caught himself.

For some reason, the lead investigator reminded him of the Crocodile Hunter.

"I was under the impression I was here voluntarily, so with that said, I'd prefer the shades stay on. I apologize, but I had a very long night. By the way, they are prescription if it's any consolation."

With a look that said, "And my grandmother is the tooth fairy," Passwarder spoke up.

"This is all a game to you, huh, son?"

"Wow." That didn't take long, Bookie thought to himself. "Son?"

With his eyes hidden behind designer frames, he

scrutinized the veteran detective. Chanel shades followed his every move as he paced back and forth. The investigator consulted a mountain of papers stacked on the makeshift table while Bookie sat motionless. Under the papers was a thick manila envelope. From said envelope, Passwarder removed enlarged photos of a crime scene. Several closeups of a deceased Quick were placed on the table directly in front of Bookie, strategically positioned so he could view pieces of every picture without moving a muscle.

Surveying the carnage nonchalantly, Bookie asked, "What's this?"

Passwarder ignored his question, presenting one of his own. "On the night in question, excuse me, the morning, do you recall your whereabouts?"

"What morning? Unfortunately I suffer from short-term memory loss. Then there's the senility aspect in my old age. You see all this gray hair up here?" He pointed to his lightly speckled ocean waves. Since he'd been a delinquent, lighter pigmental follicles were noticeable, but as of late they had sprouted like wild weeds in a domestic garden.

The investigator never mentioned a date or a time or even a name for that matter. Bookie had to be careful. Sure, he was told before the interview that he was wanted for questioning in relation to a murder investigation, but whose murder or when it happened had yet to be mentioned. If he were to start blurting out names, dates, alibis, or times, he'd he digging his own grave.

A white-knuckled fist came slamming down onto the table, sending photos flying to the floor.

"You listen here, you fucking punk, I don't have time for this bullshit, you hear me!"

This guy went from zero to sixty in under a second. Talk about breaking the ice. His face was beet red, and he wore a snarl that could have been used to scare off trick-or-treaters. Bookie knew the game, though. He was a veteran himself, sort of a young O.G.... He'd been around.

Men sharpened men like steel sharpened steel, and he'd been sharpened by the best of them. This bozo had probably conducted twenty such homicide investigations throughout his career. Bookie, while behind the wall, had heard twenty such stories via his peers who'd sat in the same seat he currently occupied. That was in a month's time! He'd served a total of eighty-four months, so in a way, he might have been even more experienced than this idiot investigator. Bookie had always paid close attention to convicted killers, even taking notes. He knew one day it would all come in handy. He read their paperwork, dissecting transcripts, cross-referencing with the law statutes. He knew a little more than the basics.

There was a common routine interrogations usually followed. Levels. The first person normally didn't have a lot of experience or game. He was just a rooty-poot. Number two, if you made it to him, would be more crafty. He was the person who made most guys break, made suspects crazy after hours of applied pressure. Sometimes it would even be the same cop with a second "act" or approach. Bookie was hip though; he knew the score. This guy was a joke, they may as well brought out number three.

"Punk?" Bookie asked calmly as if the word was

farfetched.

"You heard me! What the fuck are you gonna do about it? Huh? Kill me? Like you and your buddy killed Quick?" The detective squatted down, grasped a random photo and put it an inch from the Chanels.

"I resent your implication, Detective." Bookie's expression never altered. "In addition to said resentment, I'd very much appreciate it if you were to remove this picture. It's obstructing my magnificent panoramic view. Please and thank you."

Neither person present spoke or moved for a full sixty seconds. Slowly the photo retracted.

"Are you familiar with enhanced interrogation techniques by any chance, Mr. Smart Guy?"

Bookie didn't comment.

"No smart-aleck remarks, no wise guy answers? Or is it that you don't understand me?"

"Actually, I *overstand* you, but I am underwhelmed. I'm familiar with my strawman too." If looks could kill, Bookie would already be a feet deeper than the standard six.

"Why would you want to torture me?" he continued. "Pull my fingernails with pliers, electrical shock therapy? Waterboard me? Maybe I should give my attorney a ring after all. Prior to my dismissing him, he informed me if there was anything I didn't agree with or quite understand that I should contact him immediately. You could explain it to him; he'll put it in layman's terms for me." Bookie smirked and winked despite his eyes not being visible.

Casual requests to speak with Bookie had been consistently denied for over a month. Each denial ruffled more feathers. Garnering more attention from the wrong people. When superiors, insulted by Bookie's response to their requests, gave the green light, his listed address was raided. The address was only a ruse. He knew if he were ever in hot water, the search would begin there, granting him a head start when he got wind of it.

Bookie dialed Hyatt, who agreed to sit with him through any interview that might be conducted. Although he was calling for legal advice, this was the last thing he wanted to hear. He had no such intentions of agreeing to any interview, absolutely none. Police were the enemy.

KPD gained an edge by contacting Springfield, the HQ for the parole division. A supervisor there, in turn, directed his P.O. to cooperate with KPD in their endeavor to bring in a murder suspect. He was given an ultimatum: surrender or go AWOL. Meaning violate parole, which translated to a mandatory trip back to prison. A trip Bookie had dreaded ever since his release. Another legal opinion was acquired. Both lawyers told him it was a sixty/forty chance he wouldn't be arrested. Hyatt even went as far as to say seventy/thirty during a later conversation.

In the end Bookie, complied and submitted to an interview. He was a gambler after all.

Hyatt had escorted Bookie to the station, but after laying down the terms and conditions and informing Bookie he didn't need him, he had split. Before he left, he assured his client that both detectives together had the brain capacity of a toddler. "Surely you can talk to them without me," he'd contended, further reassuring his client he had nothing to fear.

Passwarder was on the verge of exploding. He wanted to rip this punk's head off and use his skull as a drinking mug! He took a step toward Bookie. Then another step. Just as he was in arm's reach, the door flew open and in walked Detective Milla, his ferocious partner. Milla was black, twice the size of his partner, and as mean as a rattlesnake. He made Passwarder look like a schoolgirl.

"Hey, good evening there, Mr. Sharp, I'm Detective Milla. How the hell are you?"

"So far so good, thanks for askin. How about yo self?"

"Can I get you anything?"

"I'm good."

Both men who'd been in the room before Milla came in watched each other intently, trying to read one another's mind. Only one was breathing hard. And it wasn't the lad.

"Three is a crowd," Milla acknowledged. "How about you let me wrap this one up?"

"We were just about finished, huh, Leonard?" Passwarder asked innocently.

"Not a good idea," Milla replied cheerfully. "I think I'ma take over from here." Hang on here, lemme get my notepad." When Detective Milla left the room, he made sure the door was wide open.

Passwarder kept his distance.

"You won't get away with this you know, you or your buddy. You can sit here with those stupid fuckin sunglasses, smirk and play these little games with your European accent, but you won't get away. Who the fuck do you think you are?"

Milla walked back in and the room fell silent. Again.

"Now, where were we?" Milla asked, holding a yellow legal pad with a dull no. 2 pencil hanging in limbo.

"He was just asking who did I think I was?" Bookie said sarcastically. "I know who I am. The Asiatic Black man from the lost tribe of Shabazz." Bookie flashed a patronizing smile towards Passwarder, who just shook his head in disbelief.

"What the fuck is that, your gang?"

But before the investigator could become unglued again, his partner interjected.

"Mind if I have a word with you...in private." To Bookie, he said, "Excuse us for a moment."

Left alone, Bookie tried to not look at the pictures, but curiosity got the best of him. "Damn Quick." He closed his eyes and saw a crimson sea of blood beneath Quick's body, growing larger by the second. The dark liquid spewed from his open mouth. A combination of shock, pain, and regret was eternally etched into his expression. Bookie shuddered.

The detectives were back. Milla apologized for his colleague's behavior. "I'm sorry, but he's passionate about his work. Sometimes he flies into a rage when frustrated. On behalf of the KPD, we'd like to sincerely apologize for Detective Passwarder's behavior this afternoon." Bookie listened tentatively, giving the impression he was appreciative of the efforts.

"Can you help me pick up these photos, Mr. Sharp? Do you prefer Mr. Sharp, Bookie, Killa, or Leonard?"

"Whatever suits your fancy." Bookie asked himself how in the hell does he know all those names and what else does he know? This was probably another tactic to get me to think they know more than they do, he thought.

Diamond earrings and a matching pinky caught and dispensed light with each of the suspect's movements, forcing the investigators to squint from time to time. Passwarder removed himself from the equation slamming the door behind him.

Milla took his time writing on the notepad. He sat the notepad down face up, but then thought better of it at the last second and flipped it over on the small table at the last second. Bookie knew of Milla's reputation. He was an animal when it came to investigations. Anything but the nice guy image he currently projected. He was good, though. Real good, able to switch lanes, do an about face, and put forth the image of a reasonable man, as he was presently doing... It took real skills. You had to be a pro. That he was. But he wasn't that good nor smart if he was hanging his hat on Bookie bumping his gums about a body.

It was classic good cop/bad cop. On top of the good/bad approach, it was black cop/white cop. Bookie could never go for that. A nice black investigator and a lunatic Caucasian one. They were playing the race card.

"As I was saying, I, or rather the department, apologize. We've all been under a lot of stress, especially with this particular case. Frankly you're the only lead we got, Leonard. Can I be frank with you, Leonard?" He paused. "Do you mind?"

"Shoot!"

"Every shred of paperwork in this case points to you and an accomplice...this Dee character. Soon it'll be time to pay the piper. SBS—familiar with the term? The acronym? Sinking by the second. I made it up," he said, not bothering to await an answer. "It's one I like to use in these situations. There's a hole in the boat. Soon we'll punch another and another. Larger this time. Hopefully—but even the small ones add up if you know what I mean? It's going under. Sooner or later, there's no doubt in my mind about that. Nobody's on the boat but you and your buddy. Actually, you're on it alone right now. Help us help you or go down with the boat. We're the lifeguards. The rescue team. We're offering you a preserver, and we only have one."

He let that register before continuing.

"I don't make many promises, Leonard. When you been doing this shit long as I have you learn anything is possible ...the shit I've seen...So I try not to promise when I'm not sure if I can deliver, but I promise you this: either you or Dee is going down for the murder of Quick. Save yourself. The first law of nature is self-preservation, and you should think about following it. Don't throw yo life away on this stupid *street code* bullshit. No snitching or stop snitching," he scoffed. "Let me ask you this. If the shoe was on the other foot, you think your buddy would do the same for you? Stick to the 'code' as y'all put it? This silly street honor garbage. You got a son, don't you, Leonard? You love that boy? How old is he?"

Bookie had muted Investigator Milla way back when he was talking about the boat. He refused to process the words this Uncle Tom, bootlicking-ass house nigga was saying.

"Hey, nice watch."

It was more of an accusation than a compliment. Bookie had drowned out so much he hadn't heard the door open or close. Passwarder was back in the game. Milla took to the bench after giving it his best shot and coming up empty-handed.

"We know you were there. We just need you to fill in a few blanks, and you can be on your way."

"Think," Bookie interrupted.

"What was that?"

"You *think* I was there?"

Passwarder picked up a piece of paper and commenced to read aloud. Then another. And another. All statements taken at Lee's Lounge during the night in question. Each person's recollection of events had placed Bookie on the scene. Passwarder stopped at the fourth, but there had to be thirty more at least. He tossed them back on the table. Kankakee County was definitely rat-infested.

"Every one of these witness accounts places you in the general vicinity of our victim here. We don't 'think,'" he mocked Bookie, putting emphasis on the think, "we *know* you were there! We're positive. He was shot at home base. Had you admitted to being on first or second base, with no knowledge of the shooting, we might buy that. Even the dugout. Here you are telling us you wasn't even in the outfield. Not even the fucking ballpark?"

His voice was starting to rise.

"Who the fuck do you think we are? You can try blow smoke up our ass all you want. Blow until your face turns blue and your tongue is hanging from yo fucking lips! Cause when you go to state prison, it won't be smoke going

271

up your ass...ohhhh no...that will be too much like right."

For the first time since his rant, he smiled, showing perfectly lined coffee-stained teeth. An evil, wicked smile. "And that tongue...those lips...I'm sure they'll be put to good use as well." He ended his sermon with a wink.

The disrespect and the threats, vulgarities, obscenities, the assumptions...it all went on for a couple more hours. Allegations and insinuations, one after another. Eventually, Bookie tired of the bullshit and invited both investigators, the black and white one, to his phallus. Specifically, directing them to suck it.

******

At the conclusion of his four-hour-plus meeting with Milla and Passwarder, he was a marked man. His days in K3 were numbered. Since his interview, his picture had come across the desk of every detective on the force. Multiple times. Around the office his was a common name. It had actually been that way already, but now they had a face to put with the name. Even the tape from the interview was viewed dozens of times for "training purposes." There were several other active investigations—shootings, kidnappings, murders. They all had a common thread. Leonard Sharp or one of his various aliases.

As of late, his name was even coming up in drug-related investigations. Confidential informants were reluctant to entangle the young shooter they referred to as "Killa." And for good reason. But Bookie wasn't a dummy; he knew a storm was brewing. Still on parole, he had to take his show on the road like the Ringling Brothers or suffer dire consequences. He'd be another statistic of the high recidivism rate. Walls were closing in. Fast! There was no telling how much longer he could remain on the ropes.

Anytime he was spotted in traffic, police harassed him. Traffic stops, illegal search and temporary seizures were all commonalities. Those who were known associates of Bookie's weren't safe either.

******

Taj called out the blue, a couple of weeks after Bookie told the interviewers to blow him.

"They just jammed up Jigga."

"On what? When, what happen?"

"We don't know yet. They say yo name came up cause they saw you in his truck earlier."

"Fuck outta here ... you serious?"

"Yea, ion know, that's what a mufucka told me."

"Didn't Jigga get a call? What he say? What's his bond? He should be out by now."

"A weak-ass traffic violation, his L's fucked up or somethin'. We called the county; they say they don't got 'em."

"They don't got 'em?" Bookie repeated. "What the fuck that mean? I'm fina hit Y and see what's going on."

"The feds got Yodi last week."

"*What!*" Bookie removed the phone from his car, stunned.

Taj was saying, "You keep switching numbers..." but he was talking to his self.

It was time to tell his story walking. But where to? Dee was painting a picture of money, hoes and a jolly ol' time down south. Every time Bookie talked to him, he was telling him about a different thot, a different club, a different rapper he'd met or hung out with. His latest turn-up was with a local trapper turned rapper named Yo Gotti, who had traveled from Memphis to Columbia, TN, where Dee was currently holed up. That wasn't Dee's MO. Not for real. Bookie saw through the layers of insulation. It was all a facade. A smoke screen. Dee was covering up his true feelings. Being sought after for killing your brother from another mother, missing your family, parents, baby mama, kid ... he wasn't himself. Circumstances were taking a toll on his psyche. The picture was whole, but emotions cropped it.

Going down south could be dangerous for Bookie. He could lead cops right to his buddy's doorstep. He knew they were watching him like a hawk does its prey. Or .. God forbid, Dee got nabbed. Bookie didn't want to be nowhere near the scene. Any horse that run fast can't run long. Soon you have to rest. When you do, the pursuers will be waiting. The minute your guard came down, they'd be there. Dee wasn't getting away, he was merely getting by. The cops had reiterated that it was just a matter of time before he got sloppy and make a bad decision that would cost him. That had been the deciding factor. Bookie had wanted to go on the run himself initially. His buddy talked him out of it.

"You could talk to 'em, see what they got."

"Maybe I should tell 'em who did it, just tell 'em it was self-defense," Bookie offered.

"Fuck outta here, maybe we should say you did it. Man, don't put my name in that shit."

Dee wouldn't hear it.

Bookie figured at worse they could get a self-defense or "man one" based on actual facts.

"Or I could tell 'em you did it. At trial time become the star witness. Once I sign up, I'll be the foundation of their case. They'll put their all into me. Once I get on the stand in open court, I'll swear under oath that they coerced me to lie. Or I'll get amnesia all of a sudden, recant my statement. I seen a murder case beat like that before."

Dee wouldn't hear any of it. Instead, he'd asked Bookie to play with fire and hope not to get burnt..."Talk to 'em, see what they got."

While he hadn't gotten burnt yet, the flames still flickered. Flames strong as ever. At any time he could be a victim, and if he didn't move around, it would be a lot sooner than later. Smoke inhalation was already getting to him. Anyone with half a brain knew wherever there was smoke, there was fire. To stick around would be suicide.

A tremendous amount of discipline was required to execute his next move. Bookie had to shut down, stop all illegal activities cold turkey if he was to survive. If he wanted to stay free, he had no choice. He was under heavy scrutiny.

CHAPTER 31 – RINGLING BROTHERS

Luck is when opportunity meets preparation. – Unknown

He occupied his days shooting craps. In the hood, Bookie could be found getting it on strong for hours on end. He preferred indoors but didn't exactly oppose alleyways, street corners or gangways. Police interference and robberies impeded "good gambles," however. Although he wasn't worried about being a victim of a stick-up, running from patrol cars every half hour wasn't his ideal leisure time activity. And an encounter with police was the last thing he needed.

Bookie gambled anywhere. He followed the money. If it was there, so was he. During these times he saw so many people get poked at gunpoint or simply strong-armed, which made him realize that it was just a matter of time until the inevitable took place. He cringed at the thought of being apprehended for a botched robbery where someone was murdered, even as a witness. They may just lock him up for the hell of it. Inside, he tried to restrict his urge to gamble to Ronnie and Melissa's crib, Ninny and Big Al's or "the shop." Outdoors he would still gamble on north Rosewood, at Mrs. Rabbit's, but not often, and not unless Thirty Two was "housing" the games.

When up for it, he'd grace with his presence Harrah's or Emperor's Casinos in Joliet or even the Majestic or

Horseshoe in Indiana. Downtown Joliet, Harrah's Casino and Hotel, was his favorite of the four. He was more enamored with the atmosphere than the art of gambling, but Bookie didn't mind frequenting blackjack, craps or roulette tables. Craps was by far his pick of poison.

Fat Boy spent more time at Casino's than anyone Bookie knew, so it wasn't surprising when Bookie ran into him at the buffet during the dinner hour at Harrah's. As the cashier handed Bookie his receipt, Fat Boy walked past with a plate of orange chicken. "Bitch, what you doin here? Who you here wit?"

"I ain't on shit. Where you get that chicken from, they don't got no otha kind of Asian chicken?"

"Yea, it's over there," he pointed with his head, hands occupied with a tray of food and a soft drink.

"Yea? Man, I ain't on shit. Tryna stay the fuck away from Kankakee," Bookie told him as Fat Boy led him back to his table.

Bookie had been ready to go for the last hour, standing around crap tables bored, betting $5 chips on "the field" every other roll. His buddy was supposed to meet him forty-five minutes ago.

"Who you here wit, G?"

"Come on now, man, yo nosy ass."

"Bitch, you here wit somebody. Tell me who you here wit before I grab yo ass in public." Fat Boy smiled and reached like he might make good on his threat. Bookie twisted away from him so as to protect his glutes and swatted down his friends hand at the same time.

"Stop playin wit me, Fat Dog. Yo bitch ass askin questions like you workin."

"Nawl, for real, G, who you here wit?" Fat Boy was notoriously nosy.

"Yo bitch ass nosy. My man Rokilla picked me up yesterday; my bitch taking me back when she get off though. I been at her crib."

"Rokilla? Who is that? Bitch, you lying." He was laughing, looking like a big-ass Curious George. "I think I know Ro."

"Ro-Ro?" Bookie asked. "You don't know 'em. He from Joliet.

"What's his real name? Bitch, I know Ro."

"Corey bitch, you don't know him. You don't know no mufucka but niggas who shoot dice on Rosewood and Alleyoops. That shit sickenin, yo police ass, I know you was workin! What type of rat ass shit is that 'whats his real name' on the gang c'mere, I gotta pat yo ass down."

"Yea, aight, bitch," Fat Boy laughed.

Bookie went to grab fruit, turkey, chicken, pasta, cheese pizza, fried rice and drinks. He hated going back and forth at buffets; he liked to get everything at one time, even if he just wanted to taste it. When he came back, Fat Boy said, "Bitch I just thought about it, you know Monique; she a mufuckin Alleyoop too."

"She told me you tried to get her number too, I meant to tell you that. Tell the truth G, why you tryna hit my bitch?"

"Fuck outta here. Aye, you ain't grab none of that steak?"

"Bitch you know ion eat no beef or pork. I ain't like yo

278

fat ass, eat anything go down easy."

After their meals, they entered the Casino section.

"Bitch, gimme a rack, I got knocked."

"That shit ova wit."

"I shoulda stayed in the hood. They say they gettin it on strong in the hood, say that bitch Trick winnin good. I'ma clean that bitch up soon as I get back. I keep hittin his line, bitch sendin me to voicemail."

"Where they at in the hood?"

"Bitch, you know where they at, on Rosewood."

The Mecca of all street gambling was on nNorth Rosewood, 354 to be exact. The Alleyoops had run the infamous "basement" since the 80s. Bookie seldom won in the hood; too much going on. He could never focus. People shooting, fighting, dealing drugs, robbers taking money out the pot, pulling guns, everything under the sun. None of the fishy business was ever directed toward Bookie, but his state of mind would never allow him to let down his guard or relax. Too much going on. This, in turn, affected his concentration.

On Rosewood, there might be three dice games going on simultaneously. One in the basement, one outside the back door leading to the basement and another game on the side of the house. All ages welcome. One game they're shooting dollars, another $10 and $20. In the basement, though, you shoot whatever you get faded for. It wasn't unusual for a person to be in the dollar game, come up on ten bucks, leave and head to the basement. An hour later, they're winning $5,000. Kids, crackheads, grandparents and anyone was welcome in "the basement." Like Birdman and

Lil Wayne, the only thing that mattered down there was cash money.

The lady Bookie had been waiting for was handing a watered-down gin and tonic to a disgruntled customer who was on a two-hour losing streak. His failure to tip garnered a roll of the pretty brown eyes before Keysha turned in Bookie's direction.

"You gonna spend another night wit me or what?"

"Nawl, I gotta get back to Kankakee."

"This yo ride right here?" Keysha pointed to a gawking Fat Boy.

"Hell, nawl, I ain't his ride. I ain't wit this bitch, he gay."

Keysha laughed. "You a Barfield."

"A Barfield? My name Fat Boy! And I got more money than this broke bitch. He got herpes too."

Keysha looked at him. "OMG." She smiled.

Bookie had told her his buddy from the joint Frank was picking him up. They were going to hang out until she got off, so she could take him back. Frank was a Barfield, one of the most notorious families in Joliet. Similar to the McNeil's out west and the Benders in Kankakee. Bookie and Frank would hang out in Joliet until she got off. So far he was a no-show though.

Minutes later, Bookie said, "What the hell." He ended up leaving with Fat Boy. Keysha didn't want to take him back without another shot of the worm.

"Bitch, I'm still hungry, let's go out to eat."

"What?" Bookie said, shocked that his buddy was still hungry. "Dude, your fat ass just ate all that shit, now you wanna eat again?"

"Bitch, I'm hungry. That nasty-ass senior citizen ass food in there."

"Where you tryna eat at? That's crazy, though." Bookie was still shaking his head in disbelief.

"Ion know, where you wanna go? Bitch don't shake yo head either, you know I'm fat."

"You driving too." He tossed Bookie the keys. Bookie had just stopped shaking his head in time to look up and catch the key ring. He started the process all over. "How long you been fucking that lil red bone bitch in there? That lil bow-legged bitch gave me her number before."

"You bullshittin, what's the number?"

Fat Boy went through his T-Mobile Razor and ran off seven digits.

"Yea, that's definitely the number. Why you ain't hit the bitch?"

"Bitch ain't answer when I called."

Laughing out loud, "She don't want no fat mufucka... a fat bitch with a worm, come on now."

"On my momma, my dick bigger than yours."

"Man, I'm not fina talk about no dicks and the size and shit wit yo faggot ass."

Bookie drove back to Kankakee, the back roads 45/52 route. Fat Boy told him it was an emergency; he had to get back to Hidden Glen real quick, his baby mama was locked out. A half hour later, as they pulled into the Bourbonnais, Bookie discovered it was a ruse.

"Bitch, cook that shit for me." Fat Boy retrieved a Kroger shopping bag from his trunk. Inside were key ingredients to make a dip—or "that shit" as Fat Boy referred to it.

Ramen noodles, Hormel chili in a can, summer sausage, jalapeno squeeze cheese, instant Spanish rice, Doritos, and a couple other items.

"Bitch, make that shit for me, I can't take it."

"That's crazy! Yo bitch ass got me way over here just to cook this jail shit? You ain't gonna be satisfied until yo ass back in there eating this same shit. Fat ass wanna make dips and shit."

"Bitch, just hurry up so we can get it on." He removed his shoes and shirt, getting comfortable, getting ready.

"You ain't tryna do nothing. What we shooting, yo bitch ass ain't even got no roll, you broke!"

Fat Boy went and his pocket and pulled out fifty new $100 bills. "Who broke? Bitch, I ain't you. These all pineapples," he boasted, fanning them so Bookie could get a better view.

That week alone they ate three of them dips, first two times Bookie and Fat Boy, the last time Icholis and Murda showed up with some flour tortillas and dug in. It was the start of a camaraderie.

Fat Boy, Mook, and Icholis sold cocaine. They didn't stand on corners and chase down cars though; they worked off their phones. Countless customers would contact them throughout the day for "pieces."

A fifty piece, hundred piece, two hundred piece, etc. Most of their clientele was from Bradley and Bourbonnais, therefore white. Icholis' and Mook's anyway. Ninety-nine percent of Fat Boy's people were white. If you combine

Bradley and Bourbonnais together, they are just as big as Kankakee, if not bigger, with as many residents. Seventy-five percent being white of course. Drug dealers who didn't mind going the extra mile, literally and figuratively, would have a field day selling drugs in these areas.

******

Bookie was buying eights and nines, blowing them up and making his rounds in the hood still, but not nearly as much as he used to. He stayed more behind the scenes these days. Rocking with Koota here and there, seeing Dee every blue moon. He had took a couple months off but he was sinking quick so he had to do something. Same destination but a different avenue or route. Over a short period of time, Bookie and his new crew became very close. He'd always known them, but he'd never really got in bed with them at this level.

Fat Boy and Icholis, who were cousins, had been friends with Bookie since middle school. Mook was around too, but he was a Vice Lord and had gone to jail for an accidental murder when the rest of them were in junior high. After that, Bookie had gone to jail, and he didn't see Mook again until now.

Things went on this way for a couple months. Everybody sort of did their own thing but came together when needed. If Bookie didn't tell you himself, or you weren't a customer, you wouldn't really know he was doing anything. As far as customers go, he only had a handful. Fat Boy, having the most money, was the unofficial boss of this crew. It was basically already his crew, but they had let Bookie in because they all rocked with him. They'd get the new Jordans, buy Pelle's and fitted Caps every week. Bookie was more of a jeans, a custom t-shirt and Air Max type guy. The need to reduce spending habits had been imminent since his Entourage days. There were many aspects of life where he could downsize or slow down on dispensing cash, but he started with clothes. He was sort of a pretty boy and he was articulate, so getting girls was not a problem. Spending a fortune on wardrobe wasn't as necessary as it was for others. Occasionally, he got outfits and dressed up but with some jeans, a t-shirt, a track jacket and a diamond watch he was good to go.

Things continued on this way for ninety days or so before Fat Boy's court date. The four of them drove to court in Fat Boy's yayo-colored Dodge Hemi listening to his favorite rapper, the SnoMan. His box Chevy was sold for double its worth. Ick cashed him out, 500 crispy twenty-dollar bills still wrapped in bank wrapping. With proceeds from the sell and a few grand extra, he went and got a Lac truck.

At the end of 2006, Fat Boy traded in the Escalade, grabbed a bankroll out the stash again and headed to the Magnum lot. Instead of the wagon, he left with a spanking new 2007 Charger. He was the first person in the hood with the Charger. Now he was out on ten percent of a $100,000 bond.

******

The case stemmed from Fat Boy being greedy. He decided to cheat JC by throwing the thangs on him. JC, the recipient of a recent cash settlement, was in the streets but not of the streets. To sharks like Fat Boy, he was food, i.e., fish food. For hours Fat Boy had JC in the Harbors at his other BM's crib throwing the Bic Mans on him. JC was down $11,000 when his phone rang. Some white guy wanted a gram and a half.

Fat Boy tried to talk him out of making the sale. "Bitch, you got all that mufuckin money, fuck you chasin that lil ass hunnid dollars for?" JC was losing so bad he felt his opponent just had to be cheating, though he could hardly prove it. He could care less about the $120 on his phone, but for now he had to get away from Fat Boy. Peer pressure wouldn't allow him to quit outright. He needed an excuse and this was it.

Maybe Fat Boy wasn't cheating. He was known for being fortunate and winning on the dice. If he could only leave, take a break, then he could possibly return, and his luck might change by then. "Huh, bitch, here you go." Fat Boy slang a c-note across the living room floor. "There go a hunnid dollars right there, fuck that dump."

JC was adamant, though, about leaving and now adamant about Fat Boy cheating him with loaded dice. Why would he pay him not to leave? Ever the pro, however, Fat Boy wasn't easy to catch in the act. When JC stood to leave, he stood. Put on his shoes, found his shirt and grabbed his keys.

"Bitch, I'm taking you then. Come on, can't let you get away, I'm tryna knock you." What JC couldn't know at that time was the $120 he was going to pick up was OAF (official advanced funds) belonging to KAMEG, and the caller was a confidential informant, (CI). Christmas came early for authorities, two for the price of one.

They made the sale, and the MEG closed in on their suspects. A vain attempt was made by the driver to flee, take them on a high-speed chase, but it fell short.

******

Out on bail for basically the $10k he finessed JC out of, Fat Boy hired arguably the best if not most expensive attorney in Kankakee County: Sacks. Now he was going to face the music.

At his 10:30 a.m. hearing it was made clear an offer was on the table. Five years behind bars. In Illinois, for a nonviolent offender, that translated to two and a half years, roughly two if he were to get six months good time conduct credit. Sacks got a continuance until 1:30. "Take what's on the table or go to trial." In less than three hours Fat Boy had a decision to make.

Walking out of the courthouse, Fat Boy said, "Damn my bitch-ass chasing. I should of jus let that bitch leave, being thirsty. Already had over a sawbuck. I should of just let that bitch leave. Now I done bonded out for that sawbuck and gave Sack's bitch ass another sawbuck. They still tryna nail me." At the initial custody hearing, JC had tried to vindicate Fat Boy.

"Your Honor, I just wanna say Shawn had nothing to do with this case; he was just giving me a ride."

Judge Elliot rudely cut him off.

"This is only a custody hearing where I hear the facts, get a proffer and appoint bond. Please be mindful of what you say; it can and will probably be used against you at a later date. Right now, it can't help you anyway, not at this point. Can't help you or Shawn. Save it for your attorney."

Unfortunately, JC couldn't post his $15,000 bond. Instead, he remained in JCDC fighting the case. While there, he heard through the grapevine about the Bic Mans. Fat Boy bragged to a crowd full of peasants what he'd done to JC at a dice game in the basement when he bonded out. Word spread quick in the hood. The streets talk. JC's baby mama's little cousin's baby daddy was actually present and heard the news firsthand. He told his baby mama after she jumped down his throat for being out all night, possibly cheating on her. He utilized the information he came across as a deflection or diversion tactic to keep her off his case. She told her cousin, and the next day when JC called he got the scoop.

Guys who never cared for Fat Boy, despised him, wished him nothing but bad for always talking shit and stunting on them, calling them broke and plain ol' being disrespectful, got wind of his actions. A couple of them were in county lockup with JC. They got in his ear and told him what he should do as payback.

When his next court date came, JC was singing a different song. To the tune of fuck Fat Boy; he on his own. *Every man for himself, God for us all.*

To Bookie it sounded as if Sacks had sold out his buddy. But, what did he know, after all he was just a common criminal and Sacks was an expert. "Best lawyer my ass," Bookie told Fat Boy, "I could've done what he done."

Before they left the courthouse, Fat Boy offered more money, to no avail. "I can't get 'em to come down. Either go to trial (the irony) or bring your toothbrush at 1:30."

This, after verbalizing he couldn't beat the case at trial. Fat Boy was out of options; allegedly the best lawyer in town telling you to your face he can't beat the case, after he got your money in his pocket. What were you to do? Go to trial and get ten years? Fat Boy wasn't a genius, but you didn't need to be one to figure this out.

******

Bookie's recently upgraded Sprint rang. The contact name "Henry Work" flashed across the LCD Screen, 815-802-7220 under it. Jerome Combs Detention Center, named after the person his Uncle Henry was in prison for killing. Who could this be calling from the county jail? Someone, a new arrestee, was calling him with their courtesy call.

"Man, you ain't gonna believe this shit."

It was Kootaroo. The sound of defeat in his voice as clear as Swarovski crystal. With his background, and still being on parole ... his life hung in the balance.

"What happened, what's yo bond?"

Bookie's words were rushed, knowing time was of the essence.

"It's over with, dog," came an exasperated reply from Koota.

"This goofy mufuckin nigga Fred. We coming from the shop, the people get on us; I tell 'em bust a right and let me out this silly mufucka go left then ..." Bookie couldn't believe it. Fred again? Deja vu.

"What? Man, that's some police-ass shit, Jo."

"Nawl, he ain't the police; he just a fuckin goofy. But, on my deceased mama, you told me."

"Yea, I definitely told you. It is what it is now, no sense

in cryin ova spilled milk. What they get? I mean, umm, what they *say* they get..." Bookie stammered, emphasizing "say."

"Jus a few bags, some lil shit. It's all bad though. Aye, look do me a favor. I need you."

At the conclusion of their brief conversation, Bookie had complete instructions. The heavily coded convo revealed a hidden location containing five zips of hard, 140 grams of cocaine. Koota had a family member who worked at a pizza joint. According to Koota, it was on south Schuyler Avenue, a couple doors down from Lavonna's shop.

This situation was a product of Koota's bad habits. Bookie would be on him about selling bags and pieces. They argued back and forth all the time. Why get half or whole bricks if you gonna sell that lil shit, Bookie always said. Both had agreed to sell weight, but Koota spent so much money, gambled so much and just blew through his check recklessly, he'd always find himself in the hood trying make up for his losses. Trying to get the best bang for his buck or the most money for his product, breaking it down to the smallest denominator.

Why sell an eightball for $80 or $90 when I can make $250? That was his argument. And a good one it was. "Cause you gotta sell a ten-dolla bag, you gotta sell twenty-five dimes to get $250, that's twenty-five chances or risks you gotta take dummy," Bookie would reply. You got to get caught. Bookie's point was just as valid. Koota was now asking Bookie to grab the few ounces he had and dump it for him. Give the money to his baby mama.

Bookie, like a good friend, came through in the clutch.

Twenty-four hours later he handed a bankroll to a tall attractive women with an unorthodox mole on her face. Koota called from E-Pod.

"Man, Jo, I appreciate that, real nigga shit." He asked Bookie if he had seen Fred.

"Yea, I ain't talk to him yet, though. He ain't been coming around." Fred had only been out a few months from that case where he almost took Bookie down with him. He too was still on parole.

"I hope he don't never come around, though. He ain't got a fuckin clue."

"He ain't have a clue before he went in from what I hear. That's kinda yo fault even bringin me around that goofy."

"Ain't no mufucka tell you to try and use that lame-ass nigga as a taxi. You got him driving you around makin moves and shit."

"It's too late now, fuck that shit. Aye, guess who in here with me?"

"Who?"

"That fat bitch."

"Fat Dog?"

"Yea, when they put me in here, he gonna fall down on his knees and cry thank you Jesus." Koota laughed.

"Fat Bitch say he prayed I came to jail and Jesus answered." Bookie laughed out loud. "He telling err mufucka in here bout that shit at Lincoln Mall."

Months prior, Bookie, Koota, and Fat Boy ran into R. Kelly at Lincoln Mall on Lincoln Hwy. First outside in a gray Maybach, then inside walking with a couple buddies.

"Waddup, Kells, let a mufucka hold something," Bookie joked.

"Yea, let a mufucka hold something," Koota added. By now they all were shaking hands. Kells said something slick about a mufucka can hold his nuts.

Bookie went there, letting the multi-platinum recording artist know that if he liked making music, he betta recant his statement. Koota backed him up. There was a standoffish discussion in which the veteran R & B singer apologized, saying he meant no harm. Bookie was strapped and was eager to earn some more points.

******

The news that JD was murdered woke Bookie out of his sleep. Murdered and possibly robbed. After Bookie chose cocaine for his hustle, JD didn't really trip, but he said he was only rocking with the weed. They would still see each other, greet each other, talk shit and swallow spit but not really get money together despite JD hitting Bookie with weed and money on three separate occasions. Now this! He was dead. "JD? What, JD? You sure?" Bookie turned on a bedside light. "What the fuck happened? How? Who got down on 'em?"

The caller insinuated some Junctionites might be involved, but he wasn't certain. Something about some deal with some people from the next state over, it went bad and .... He promised to keep Bookie up to date. Bookie lay awake until birds chirped. "A Girls Gone Wild" infomercial came on back to back, all these girls and this guy on a yacht. Bookie thought how could he be having all this fun and JD was dead, as if the stories were interconnected or they knew each other? He never met the guy but didn't like him, his girls, his boat or his infomercial, just because. At the first sign of a rising sun, Bookie got up, killed the T.V and offered up his first salat since 2005. He didn't bother making wudu.

Days later the *Daily Journal* reported a fugitive from justice had been nabbed. Dee had been captured in Tennessee, arrested for killing Quick.

******

Since he was already in the game, he figured may as well play a full quarter. Bookie got back into the swing of things. He sat at the table with Icholis and Mook. They all had the same destination, so why not ride in the same car to get there.

Icholis sold anything under an eightball to white people, mostly in Bradley or Bourbonnais. Working strictly off the phone. Mook sold eightballs and up. They still possessed Fat Boy's phone and shared all his sales, no matter what they were. Bookie sold anything from eightballs to ounces.

Bread was the plug. Like Eyes and his lil crew used to do, they bought an eighth every day, five or six days a week. Mook cooked it up at his baby mama Blade's crib on Chestnut, stretching it to seven, eight, or nine zips. The cocaine would then be divided three ways.

When Icholis and Mook wanted to buy more, Bookie convinced them they should only get what they could move in a day or so. Why hoard crack, let it pile up and just keep fed cases lying around? If they were all selling weight, maybe, but in and out of the spot, dumping bags and eightballs, too much traffic. Reluctantly, they both agreed.

Eventually, they would hone their craft, make sort of an adventure out of the daily trips to see Bread.

They kept a couple rental cars circulating at all times. Fat Boy's baby mama, Chica, still had the hemi, seeing as how legally she was the owner. Bookie, Mook and Icholis all had full access. Whenever they saw fit they'd toss her a "pineapple" and get the keys for a few hours. Although they did their fair share of joyriding, the Charger was mostly used when tearing down Highway 57. In between exit 312 and Bread's usual meeting location on Garfield Blvd (55th), there were a million other exits and two million things to do. Shop, eat, visit girls, etc.

They would pay $2,800 for four and a half ounces. Icholis put up $300 while Mook and Bookie coughed up $1,250 apiece. It didn't seem like much but, on average, Icholis grossed upwards of $2,000 off his half zip. Essentially, he'd receive the half, while Bookie and Mook got two ounces a piece. Most of the time the microwave beeped to indicate completion, like magic the grams would be doubled.

Bookie would sell his 112 grams any way he could, in half and whole zips, quarters, eightballs, anyway he could. Typically he'd rake in $800 per twenty-eight grams. He made $3,200, subtracted the $1,250 he paid, and came out with $1,950. That was his profit, per day, minus expenses. Mook's profit was somewhere in the vicinity, but his profit exceeded Bookie's; it had to. Not only was he cooking all the work, he was the most advanced. In addition to these factors, Mook didn't mind going under the eightball.

Under the eightball was where the money was.

Maximum revenue for Bookie was $100 when selling balls. Mook usually got $300. There were a lot more risks associated with going under the eightball, but those who did were highly compensated. Instead of making an additional twenty transactions for $200 bucks, Bookie would rather just make one, selling the ball whole.

Even then he was willing to take a further pay cut. Bookie would pay another individual $10 or $20 to deliver each eightball. He was all about minimizing risks. That was his philosophy: maximize pay and minimize risk. To him it wasn't about who could make the most money, but who could spend the most, and in order to spend your money, have fun and enjoy your bankroll, you had to be free. Icholis and Mook, sometimes with pockets full of money, accepted tens or twenties to deliver balls for Bookie. If you had five or six thousand in your pocket, why would you accept ten bucks to make an illegal drug transaction? For three and a half grams of crack within a thousand feet of a school or church? Pure greed.

Bookie was starting to get smart, seeing more than just dollar signs. All they saw was the money, which was a blinding character trait in and of itself. Bookie wasn't desperate or thirsty, thus he thought about prevention.

It all balanced out in the end. They were doing numbers. Making thousands of dollars a day. They had money to burn. Literally. Mook held a birthday bash at the Elks Lounge for his 27th birthday. He and Icholis must have burned thirty 100-dollar bills. At the picture booth the photographer Robert Dillion didn't know whether to snap a photo or look for a fire extinguisher.

Things continued like this for a few months. The entire crew were dice shooters and gambled on a daily basis, but Mook and Icholis were diehard. Bookie was more of a recreational gambler; it was sort of a leisure time activity, a way to pass time. He won a little, he'd quit, talk a little shit and get out the way. He lost, the same thing. He could do this because he never lost it all. Icholis and Mook, on the other hand, would either lose it all or win it all. Do or die! That was their mission.

Any vice or affliction one suffers from that becomes stronger than that individual is extremely dangerous. You're no longer in control. Bookie noticed this about both Icholis and Mook. They were cool, got money, were both great hustlers, had a good time turning up, but he dreaded that moment he knew was always right around the corner. They would get broke in a dice game and need Bookie. He didn't mind, this was his crew, but when it became a habit, when it was redundant, it started to impose on him and his future plans.

Their imposing left him no choice but to impart to them how they were hustling for nothing. Get five steps ahead in one week, next week one dice game set you back six steps. It was an obstacle neither Icholis nor Mook could overcome.

At this time, Bookie's financial burden was as heavy as it had ever been. Tawayne, Koota, and Fat Boy were all locked up. He took care of his brother and "looked out" for many more, including Donnie, despite accusations. His assistance wasn't limited to only their books or commissary. It included this, but on the other side of the fence their children, baby mamas, households, families, etc ... Guys from lockdown called continuously throughout the day with requests. Calls alone reached $25 any given day.

Kadaisha was becoming more spiteful and bitter by the day. She refused to let Bookie see Kamarion when they were in Kankakee visiting. She would make statements sayin, "He isn't your child" and lash out in general whenever she got the chance, out of jealousy. Bookie still reached for him and tried to bridge the gap despite her actions. Kamarion's aunt Lavetta, his grandma Fay, and his great granny Mary, were all instrumental in assisting him in this process.

It was mandatory he keep three cell phones. Monthly rental car fees along with the phone bills totaled $1,000 plus tax. Keeping a bankroll was essential. He couldn't afford his crew's gambling habits and his lifestyle. He was going under fast. His only flaws or habits were girls. Multiple females could become very expensive. Traveling, eating, splurging, hotels, drinks, shopping ... The slope was becoming more slippery with all his profits going to saving Icholis or Mook or his lifestyle; he couldn't put up or stack any money. In the streets you always had to save money because you never knew when that money will have to save you.

On top of this, every week people told him, "Aye, police tried to get me to set you up," or "The MEG asked bout you." It was too much. He could feel it in the air like Phil Collins said in 1981. Bookie threw in the towel. He notified his colleagues that he was flying the coop Monday. Mook had ten racks, Icholis five or six...by Wednesday, they both flat broke! Still a bit indecisive about leaving, and not really wanting to exit his comfort zone, Bookie got on the e-way at 8am that Thursday.

******

His first cousin Pelow, a decade his senior, offered him a way out. Pelow caught a murder rap in Wisconsin and did his time like a man. He was to be released any day now. In the early 90s, growing up, Bookie's older cousins were his idols. Pelow had two brothers who was with the shits, Vincent and Pankey. There were two other brothers, much younger, who had grown up in a different atmosphere, a different setting, but Anthony and Malcolm were Brittons nevertheless.

Bookie could remember early on coming up in the projects when Vince and Jeff Dickerson beat some unfortunate fellow to a pulp right in front of him as he left Jeff's mom's house, the candy store with his freeze cup, and iced oatmeal cookies. He was there when Pankey was arrested for the murder of the bootlegger by the party house that Pankey, Ru-Ru, Tom-Tom and Reggie went down for.

Pelow, the eldest of the brothers, had set the tone with violence. He and O-money had been accused of gunning down some guy named Tyson in cold blood in front of a parade of witnesses. Much like the Lee's incident, only this one took place inside Red's, a hot nightspot on south Schuyler Avenue. For reasons unknown, O-money was never charged, but Pelow was. Bookie was just a pup but had sat in the courtroom staring in awe as the huge .357 used in the slaying was held up for all to see. It was determined that the killers had used not one but two weapons, an Uzi and a .357. Which bullet had actually ended Tyson's life? Well ... The jury was still out on that, and it was almost twenty years ago. Pelow walked scot-free. Not thirty days later Bookie had a front seat to the "Pete Show" again when he shot his own father in the leg, in front of Dre Jones mother Charlene's house in the projects, as a warning.

In a way, Bookie had formed a perception of life based on these early incidents. His way of thinking was being shaped and molded without his knowing. He knew back then, much as he did presently, that he would never go for just *anything*. He had his cousins to thank. When Pelow was released after doing well over a decade, he woke his little cousin with an early morning phone call.

"I been hearing about you ...You know I'm on my ass, cuz."

He hadn't seen his cousin in over ten years. He was elated. He got on the e-way an hour later with $7,500 cash. He stopped to see Bread at his Hyde Park distribution center to pickup a nina. The 9-ounce purchase set him back 5k. Four hours and fifty-one minutes after he contacted him, Pelow was riding shotgun in the rental with Bookie and the quarter kilo.

They hung out in Wisconsin for a week. Back and forth from Milwaukee to Cheboygan. Bookie had an account with TCF, so he withdrew funds as needed. The $2500 was more or less for Pelow. He wasn't high maintenance, just requiring the bare essentials. Bookie ended up spending more of it than he did. After the second consistent day of withdrawing $400 from an ATM, he decided to open the nina. No sense in keep making withdrawals when he could make deposits. There was no need to cook it all up; if he was going to get caught, he'd rather it be soft than hard. With a hundred-to-one ratio and all.

In Cheboygan, he cooked up one ounce of "straight drop" and made so much money so fast he got scared. When night fell, they were on the e-way again, heading further north to Minnesota where all of Pelow's immediate family was. Bookie was sleep-deprived, so he allowed his older cousin to take over the wheel, bad idea. He woke up two times. The first time Pelow'd hit something, and the second time they were in Michigan, somewhere lost at a gas station. Fresh out of prison, not driving for over ten years. Bummer. No more sleep for Bookie.

Bookie had to get them there and get them there he did! Upon their arrival, they were greeted warmly by all. Everyone was eager to see Pelow, waiting patiently at his mom's house on 36th and Emerson, northside Minneapolis. Bookie paid homage, then quickly found a hotel room in Brooklyn Center off Shingle Creek. He was beat and had a long day ahead of him.

Early the next morning, Bookie found a Target down the street from the Crowne Plaza and picked up a few items. A three-speed hand held cake mixer for $9.99. Three different size pyrexes in a set for $5.43. A utensil set that included spoon, fork and knife, 89¢. Five boxes of baking soda, 59¢ apiece, and one box of heavy-duty sandwich bags, $1.19. The clerk looked at him like she might have wanted to call Crime Stoppers. Bookie just laughed.

Pelow called. "Cuz, what's up, man, you woke yet, you

up, man?"

"I been up. What's the move?"

"Ain't no moves, cuz," he laughed. "Let's eat some, man, you already ate?"

"Nawl, but I'm cooking breakfast right now."

The waffles, fresh fruit and cereal in the lobby had nothing on the meal he was preparing. The phone was on speaker while he worked the blender settings from high to medium and eventually low, as the contents of the largest thick glass measuring jar began to harden. He converted the eight ounces of coke into twenty-four ounces of crack. It was pure garbage and chalk white, but he didn't care.

"Cuz, let me call you back when I get done."

Bookie disconnected the call. He had to dial up the two contacts that would more than likely buy the majority of his freshly prepared product.

As long as it was hard, it was good to go. He knew this far north people would really be affected by the ongoing drought, so they'd buy anything. He wasn't from Minnesota, nor was he planning on returning. He dialed up Bread just for good measure. "Man, I told you I wanted all meat."

"That was meat, chollie."

"Charley, my ass, that wasn't meat. That shit was shaky as the Four-Corner Hustler nigga name Shawn."

Bread laughed. "What you do to it, chollie, you probably took it to the moon. If you don't like it, bring it back, I'll swap you out."

It was Bookie's turn to laugh. "I took it past the moon! Fuck, you mean I'm in Minnesota, though. I told you bout that Minnesota operation."

"Yea, I'ma holla at you bout that next time I see you. I'm with it, though. My man ready too."

Bookie had heard about the Sotas from friends and family already. He'd been trying to get Bread to pay a visit for the last month or so, bring the pack while they worked it. Bread even told him it was a goldmine; he had been here before. And one of his people had got money there on and off.

"Where that Gee at you and Mook owe?"

"Mook ain't bring you that shit yet?"

From the last time Bookie and Mook had shopped, they owed Bread $500 apiece. A week ago, Bookie had informed him that Mook would be coming the next day to get him squared away. When Bookie left Kankakee, Mook and Icholis were flat broke. Icholis didn't know Bread, but Mook did. Mook knew him just as well as Bookie did. Bookie gave them thirty eightballs. "Sell fifteen or twenty of these mufuckas and go get a Halsted or somethin."

The instructions were simple but specific. "Whatever you do, pay Bread first, then y'all do what y'all do. Get a sixty-three or whatever y'all can afford." They were so happy seeing the thirty balls, he didn't think they even heard him.

"Man, I'm fina call Mook right now and see what's up."

"Aight, G, holla at me."

He called Mook from the trap phone he'd talked to Bread on, the one he trashed every thirty-day cycle and replaced.

"Man, why yo bitch ass ain't go holla at Bread yet?"

"I'm fina go up there today."

"Mook, don't be fucking around. Take care of that shit, Murda. I'm telling you, you making us look bad."

Bookie called him Murda sometimes after the legendary freestyle battle rapper Murda Mook. The the only physical trait they had in common with was complexion.

"Killa, I'm going up there today, on my momma. Fat Boy just called too, did he call you?"

"Nawl, not yet. What's up with him?"

"Somebody gotta send him $200."

"That's crazy. Aight, I'ma take care of that, you take care Bread."

He hung up and called Icholis.

"He got cleaned up last night in the basement. That bitch eating out the garbage. On the BOS, he can't buy a cheeseburger from Burger King," Icholis laughed, "The man just called me talkin about he ordered some shit from Five Star wings and wanted me to pay for it, I hung up on his bitch ass."

"I just talk to him. The man lying and shit, putting it on the fin, on Mafia, on his momma, on KT, all type of goofy-ass shit." According to Icholis, Murda got broke in a dice game and barely had money for a meal, let alone a grand to pay their debt. That's the shit that had Bookie in Minnesota in the first place.

He was in Minnesota for two weeks and a half, almost three. Off the two dozen ounces, he made 21k, give or take. He spent ten partying like a rockstar and picking up any tab he came in contact with. Visage, Karma and Cream were favorite night spots, real clubs, not that K3 crap. He handed

Pelow a couple racks and got down the road. Ironically, Bookie went back to Illinois with $7,500 on the head. I'm no better than Murda and Icholis, he thought as he stopped to see Bread.

******

He left his car at the McDonald's on 47th and Cottage Grove. Across the street at Save-A-Lot, he slid into the back of the CL 550 with peanut butter guts. The car turned left onto Cottage Grove heading south. At 51st it entered into the parking lot of Walgreens. He was about $300 short, so he was hoping Bread was drinking. Bookie knew there was no need to try him if he was sober, but he figured he'd be drunk, so he removed three Franklins from the pile prior to entering the late-model Mercedes. When Bread was off the Hennessy, he never counted the bankroll; he'd just hold it in his hand and say if it felt "light" or not. This was so funny that Bookie actually looked forward to it so he could get a good laugh. A couple times Bread had been drinking and still counted the money out, catching him in the act and they both had a good laugh. Turns out Bread was in fact drinking this particular night, but his passenger wasn't.

"This who I was telling you about, Killa, this Vino. We bout to put together some in the Sotas on the first. You still be fuckin around up there?" an intoxicated Bread asked from behind the wheel of the high-end sedan. Bread had mentioned this before, but Bookie thought he was just talking. "Champaign, too. I told him you was getting money down there or something you was telling me."

Bread was referring to the extra ninas he'd get back to back. He knew Bookie had a customer in Champaign who used to buy eighteen ounces hard for $18,000. If Bookie copped an eighth every day or a nine and he was with Murda, two days in a row during the beginning of the month, that was normal.

When he came by himself or one day with Murda, and got nine ounces, then the next day he came for a half of brick, to the connect, that was abnormal. Bread, being curious, had long since questioned the inconsistencies.

"Who you was down there fucking with, fool? What's the nigga name?"

"I got this nigga, G-Unit, who be buying eighteens hard. Dollar for dollar, get off on Market Street. Meet him at the mall."

"*G-Unit*? That nigga the police!" the passenger shouted enthusiastically. Bookie's train of thought was cut short. There could only be one person with such a name. Deep down, Bookie felt he was the "people" anyway. He always had. His money would be so perfect and so neat. One time Bookie had told him the price went up. He didn't even argue. This was, in itself a hint, that he was working. Niggas from the hood always complained about prices, *especially* when you raised them. Their money was never neat. Lots of small bills, some crumpled, ripped, discolored, damaged to the point you could barely tell if it was a ten or twenty-dollar bill. Last but not least, the product itself being all trash would normally incur protests. But not with G-unit. Bookie didn't want it to be over, the money was so good. But in his heart of hearts, he knew it was curtains. Vino went on to tell him all he knew about the situation and even made a few calls on speaker phone to validate the revelations. "You better hope them alphabet boys don't come grab you. They already booked like seven niggas down there and got warrants for five more. All of em was serving buddy ass."

Bookie was only selling him nine ounces in all actuality. He'd take a quarter brick and cook it up to a half. No wonder he bought it every time, never complaining, he was working with "twelve."

******

In Kankakee, Smoke had been jumped by some Chicago niggas, some breeds from the Village. Smoke was like family. He told Bookie about what had taken place while they stood out in the projects one afternoon. Bookie had inquired about the remnants of what looked to be an old *pumpkin* head. "What the fuck happened to your face, Jo?" "You got into it wit some mufuckas?" Bookie was appalled. Smoke reluctantly narrated the story. *"What?* Who you say? Who is these niggas? Matter of fact where they at? How they look?" Bookie asked so many questions that Smoke felt like he was getting beat again. At least one time he even flinched.

Across the street stood a group of three. Icholis, who was with Bookie, listening to the incredible tale being told, asked and pointed to the trio loitering a couple hundred feet away. To Bookie's surprise, they began to approach them.

"Fuck y'all pointing at us for?"

Nobody spoke so Bookie volunteered.

"Y'all jumped my man?"

"Ain't nobody jump that nigga; stop lying to yo homies, Smoke," one of them said. "Tell them what really happened."

Bookie didn't care for the tone of voice being used.

"Smoke, did they jump you or what?" he asked.

Smoke was noncommittal. People didn't just stand around in the "jets." Those who did were more than likely selling something, trying to get off a pack. Taking into consideration they weren't from Kankakee, standing out like this and talking sassy, they had to have a gun on them. Probably more than one.

"Fuck we gotta jump him for?" another one added. "On the G, we ain't jump that nigga." This from the French braided Breed, "And if he feel like he ain't get a fair shake, we can do it again right here right now."

"Smoke, you wanna shoot the fair one?"

It was three of them and three of Bookie's crew. Not including Smoke, it was three on two. Bookie didn't like the way this they was talking. Icholis was mugging one of them with his good eye. Bookie looked at Smoke. He remained silent, but his body language shouted that he didn't want a one-on-one. He had the wrong name because he didn't want no "smoke" whatsoever.

"Ain't no mo' of that shit going on, ain't no mo' fighting, that shit dead."

"So what you sayin' then?" one of the Breeds questioned with contempt.

Bookie looked him right in the eye as he said, "You know what the fuck I'm sayin."

In all honesty, he didn't know what he was saying, but something had to be said, and someone had to say it.

"So it's pistol play from here on out?" French Braids

asked.

Bookie had a cannon on him, and if that was really how he felt, he would have shot him in his face at point-blank range. Bookie's reply was stern, "It is what it is, homie."

Not a full twenty-four hours later, Bookie got a call that Icholis had been shot. By the Breeds. It wasn't life-threatening, but it was enough to get Bookie off the bench. He went to the hospital to see Icholis, emptied two clips an hour later and hightailed it to Minnesota. He didn't have to buy no work; Vino was already there with it. Bread sent him ahead with eight bricks. Pelow, whom he'd left behind on his previous trip to Minnesota, was flourishing in the drug market by now. The discipline he'd acquired while in prison, along with a few basic skills, guaranteed him success.

This was relatively easy, considering he had brothers who sold, cousins, friends and a host of other relatives who indulged in the distribution of cocaine. All he really had to do was direct traffic.

The same day Bookie arrived, he met Vino on Broadway at Twin Towers. Per Bread's orders, he was given a whole brick. Immediately, he went to work. Back in Brooklyn Center, he first tried the Crowne Plaza but didn't care for the room, so he ended up in a whirlpool suite at a different hotel next door. The same Target, the same utensils. He set up shop while the war between his side and the Breeds was going on back home.

He was living the life and Blowing Money Fast in the Sotas. Selling more cocaine than the law allowed, turnin' up at Cancun in St. Paul. Cream, Karma, Visage, and Aqua in Minneapolis. When he didn't want to club, he could be found in the 4th Street Saloon where he did a lot of business, Gabby's, *the 200*, or on weekends, Augie's. These experiences were his first with real clubs, and he was hooked.

A female he ran into at Brookdale Mall one night near closing had to remind him of how she knew him. He was on his way to being wasted and couldn't put a face with the name. She was Nikki's friend and used to live behind the bricks. Nikki was like his sister; he had keys to her apartment and practically lived there at times.

Her name was Diamond. Diamond and Nikki had driven him to meet G-Unit before in Champaign, she reminded him. "We got that room at Red Roof Inn, and you cooked that stanking stuff up in that microwave, then we met that boy at the mall, remember?"...The two of them being aliens in the state, they gradually began to spend time together. Mall of America in Bloomington, NBA City downtown. Pizza Luce's for lunch. He had another girl, Mia, a local, but there was something about this Diamond.

Diamond's parents also lived in Minnesota. In Brooklyn Center, to be exact. Bookie met them and found out her father-in-law was in the streets, a trapper. In a matter of days, he was Bookie's number one customer. Overall, operation Sota Pop was a success. He had Pelow who brought other guys with him whenever he scored. JuBoy and Tito shopped on a daily basis. Both family. Malcolm ran into Bookie twice a week.

Bookie monitored the war closely, following it by phone. Giving advice often and calling plays from hundreds of miles away. Icholis's refusal to attend therapy had restricted full lateral movement in his arm, but aside from this, he was doing great. The Breeds were in a war with the whole K3, it seemed, which wasn't new in Kankakee. The town itself had been killing natives of Chicago for years. Guys coming from the city, trying to lay down their lick. Thinking Kankakee was sweet. Fool's gold. But by the time they find out it's too late, the coroner'll be zippin' up a body bag.

Every now and then Bookie went back to Illinois, either with Vino or his security Mitch, to see family. He hated driving long distances and riding dolo made it even worse. No passengers meant no one present to hold the gun or anything else illegal if stopped by a highway patrolman. He had to do the speed limit, which seemed to take forever. Rarely did he take a six- to seven-hour drive by his lonesome. Driving south from Minnesota, through Wisconsin, once he got to Cook County, there were endless options of rest areas in the form of females' cribs to choose from. Intending to go on to Kankakee, at times he became distracted and never made it. Throughout the Chicagoland he had unlimited girls all vying for his time, attention and affection.

If Chiraq, Drillinois, was crazy with females, the south suburbs were insane! You might catch Bookie out west shopping on Madison or eating at MacArthur's, on Jackson & California, shooting the breeze with lil Walt or Meech. On Drexel or over east, fucking with Bread. On the Pole or up north, in traffic with St. Nick.

Seventy percent of the time he was in the city though, he

would be in Moe Town where a number of his relatives resided. From Racine to Halsted, 51st Street to 55th. Aberdeen or May aka "the YAM" where the FollyBoys Ent and family had a stronghold. And across the Blvd, in "No Love" with Slim, one of the original Bogus Boys.

In the south suburbs, though, it was a different story altogether. South Holland, Sauk Village, Lansing, Chicago Heights, Matteson, Richton Park, Country Club Hills, Hazelcrest, Park Forest, University Park ..in these areas he frequented the most, there were more females than one could dream of. Not just any females. Decent females, the cream of the crop. He was extremely picky at that time. The burbs offered him what Kankakee or Chicago didn't. It was the liaison between the two, and he spent a lot of time there.

The last quarter of 2007 crept up on him unexpectedly. Being all over the place, spreading himself thin, came with a steep price. In Kankakee, the burbs, Chicago, or Minnesota, every other day was taking a toll on his body. Some days he visited all four within twenty-four hours; fatigue and exhaustion were starting to get the best of him. The constant diminishment of his testosterone resources didn't help the situation.

The debacle in Kankakee with the Breeds had calmed down. At least one person was dead. He followed it closely, keeping in tune with Murda and Icholis, who were both maintaining financially and physically. Monique and Nisha were both seeing other people by now, in his absence, but when he called, they came. Honey remained loyal; her only pastimes were college studies and CNA work. Bookie was seldom seen in Kankakee due to the whole G-Unit thing. Kankakee was in such close proximity to Champaign, he didn't feel safe. The feds might come get him any minute; local police still had him on their radar as well. In the twin cities, his relationship with Vino had blossomed into more than that of business or a working relationship. They were like a family. Now the two of them and Mitch spent eighteen to twenty hours of the day together. They went everywhere and did everything as a team.

One weekend they met four blond-haired, blue-eyed models at the Mall of America. The girls were some type of foreign-exchange students, moonlighting as models, living and attending school in Canada but here in the States for some huge contest involving a photo shoot. Each university had sponsors who chose four girls from that school to represent them. The roundtrip flights, room and board were all expenses paid. This meant the models had to pay for all of their own leisure-time activities, and they didn't have the funds to pay for almost anything. Together the four of them had seventy-something dollars. That was to last them five days and four nights.

Smitten by the athletically built light, bright Vino with the designer jeans and the custom $40,000 diamond watch, the freshmen gave him their ear while he gave them huge slices of pizza and smoothies. He found Bookie in Nordstrom buying a pair of white Gucci Aviators and some Issey Miyake cologne at the counter. "Look what I found," he smiled conspiratorially. Bookie looked around like they were in the 50s and his last name was Till. He had never interacted with white girls, so initially he felt skeptical. The girls saw him pull out his bank roll and almost fainted. One of them asked if it was fake. They had a good time, Bookie and Vino. Mitch didn't want any part of it. It took him a week and a trip to Canada to find out all their eyes weren't exactly blue. Returning to the States, they were red-flagged in Minnesota, apprehended, and questioned at length.

While they were being interrogated, their passports were confiscated due to an ongoing conspiracy investigation. The "nature" of their trip was put under intense scrutiny by TSA airport security personnel and a morbidly obese gentleman with a bad haircut and off-the rack suit. Simultaneously, another set of questions was being asked back in Chicago. The only answer Bread gave was, "I want to call my lawyer."

CHAPTER 32 – END OF THE ROAD

There is always a price to pay when you back the wrong horse in a race. – Unknown

"So what you gonna do? If you don't do nothing, I'ma do something." Honey's bottom lip quivered and her eyes watered. Bookie was on the road all the time, which compelled him to get some shut-eye soon as he stopped, no matter where. Usually, he stopped at a female house. While he rested up a female would get in the bed next to him, one thing would lead to another, and he'd have sex. Still tired, he'd lie up. Once he'd leave, he'd be more tired than when he came. Hit the road and repeat the process all over again. This would result in him lying up only to have sex and lie up even more. Then get up, hit the road and repeat the process all over in a different geographical locale. With a different female, there was multiple women. So many. Now it was all blowing up in his face.

Diamond was back in Kankakee and pregnant! Honey was also pregnant, and the cat had just been let out of the bag.

"Either she get an abortion, or I get one. And if I get one, the baby won't be the only thing that's dead!"

What was there to say? He didn't believe in nor condone abortions. He would never force anyone to kill their child. As far as Bookie was concerned, that was murder. He hated to see Honey go. A part of him would be going with her.

That was his investment. His future. His heart. Instead of trying to stop her, he turned the other cheek while she walked away.

In October of '07, he completed parole, beating the odds. Was it luck? Bookie wasn't big on luck; he knew it to mean "when opportunity meets preparation," but what he had prepared to do was a world away from what he was actually doing. What he was doing was squandering opportunities as opposed to taking what was needed to get back on track. This was imperative, essential to his survival. He couldn't carry on like this. He'd gone from five salats a day to no salats. The prostration mark, permanently displayed on his forehead, was a testament to the prayers he'd offered in the past, but even that was fading, along with his route to the ultimate destination. God watched over fools and babies. Bookie was not sure which one he was, but divine intervention was the only explanation for his presence, cause Lord knows he'd been through some things. Was he getting away or just getting by?

His zodiac sign was Aries, not that he cared or even acknowledged that crap. He could care less; as far as he was concerned, signs and symbols were for the conscious minded and that bologna was for idiots, some type of devil worship or propaganda distributed to the masses for a purpose unrelated to God. He never went near it. Close to his birthday, which he didn't celebrate due to his religious preference, he received a text message. He was under the impression that it was related to him being an Aries. The message read, *A small flame was attempting to be extinguished, but the powers that be wouldn't allow it. One day this flame would grow into a raging inferno that would be considered a great beacon for many a moon. Legendary for generations to come, this fire!!!*

He thought of Honey and the baby she still bore. This had to be an omen. Weeks had passed since she gave him that ultimatum. They hadn't spoken. He reached out and convinced her to dine with him at Olive Garden on Lincoln Highway. Honey told him her appetite hadn't been the same as of late, and she didn't really care to see him. It took some persuasion, but she agreed to listen more than she talked and eat more than she listened if he would pay and tell "all," giving her much needed closure. The terms and conditions agreed to, he was thirty minutes early, ordering a tour of Italy for both of them. They also both had lemonades with grenadine adding extra flavor. He worked on his soup and the oven-fresh breadsticks while waiting. She was an hour behind schedule. He called. No answer. Then a text message from her number came in. Honey was on the side of Highway 57 bawling her eyes out. She said she couldn't do it. He called and called but no answer. He got on 57 south, drove all the way to the Peotone exit, got off and came back north. Passing Manhattan-Monee, at exit 327, a car was on the side, but it wasn't her. He kept north and got back off on Route 30.

He knew then that it was over.

Fred called as he exited I57.

"What's up, man, you aight, you sound like you dead or something."

"I'm alive. I am dead without my banger. Where the

fuck my shit at?"

He had called a couple weeks ago asking to borrow a gun cause some people were trying to rob him. Bookie gave him a garbage-ass high point after a week straight of begging and pleading.

"That's why I was calling you. Might as well gone sell it to me."

"Man, I don't sell guns. I probably can find you one though. Gimme a few days."

"Aight, man, I need a couple balls too."

"Yo police ass love talkin reckless... you trippin', Jo." Bookie needed his ass kicked for giving him another gun after the last incident, but he didn't want to see the dude get killed. Maybe he had learned his lesson.

He navigated the rental car east down Route 30 until a sign read Chicago Heights. He had nowhere to be. He drove aimlessly, thinking how could he fix what had been broken. Emotionally, he was drained. Despite the life and all the girls, he was a sucker for love, and love Honey he did. He felt like he should be doing something more but didn't know what. Another sign said Harvey. Was he lost? Locating 147th. He drove west. Stopping at the Huddle, he went inside the liquor store and bought a bottle of false courage.

"You going to the party too?"

"Huh?" Confused, Bookie looked behind him.

The clerk, a middle-aged black woman with thick glasses and in need of a perm asked again, "I said, you going to the party too?"

"What party?" he asked, bewildered.

"You must not be from around here."

"Not really. What party though?" He was curious.

"Huh, baby, here you go. Take this with you."

She handed Bookie a flyer from a stack on the counter next to the bubble gum and single magnums.

Bookie was no stranger to Harvey. After Donnie got booked, he never stopped turnin up. Every weekend it was Mannheim Rd. and Nitro. On 147th, he would attend the Lick, Mr. Rickey's, or Secrets in neighboring Dalton. Jaguar too before it succumbed was a favorite. However, on the flyer, this was something new.

A club he hadn't heard of. The cashier saw him reading it and offered her assistance just as a group of gang bangers entered.

"Listen, baby, you know where Kenny's at, don't you? All you have to do..." Bookie didn't let her finish.

"I know where it's at." She looked surprised.

His gun was in the trunk, and the last thing he needed was these young street punks sizing him up, looking at his watch, thinking he was a "stang." A lamer from desplainer. Outside the liquor store, he peeled off his upper clothing in the car. Tossing the beater onto the passenger side, he quickly put his shirt back on. Pressing the trunk release, he threw the tank top over the pistol as he fished it from the confines of the trunk. With it right where it should be, on his lap, easily accessible, he set out to locate this new club. Bookie's objective was to just peep the scene, maybe sit in the parking lot and try to catch him something, what they call a "parking lot pimp". Sipping his bottle, he went through his phone to find some action. It was almost 10:00

p.m.

Driving back to Minnesota tonight was out of the question. When he did drive back, Vino and ten squares of the white would be with him to keep him company, and he wasn't ready. Kankakee wasn't in the cards. The options were the city or suburbs. Since he was already in the burbs ... Dionna called him, stealing his train of thought.

"Where you at? Did you get my message?"

"Yea, I got it, all that zodiac bullshit!"

"Boy, that ain't no zodiac bullshit. Why you say that; that ain't where that came from. I got that from Star. She went—"

"Well, that's where her lil black ass got it then. I know zodiac shit when I see it."

"Whateva. Trying to see me or what?"

"Not right now."

"Damn, you don't wanna see me?" She feigned hurt.

"Dionna, stop it, knock it off, Slim, actin all dramatic and shit," Bookie laughed. "You funny as hell. I'm not saying it like that. I'm just not around right now." Had he been close he would have loved to "see" Dionna. They shared chemistry, a connection unparalleled by any.

"You comin to Kankakee; where you at?"

"Nawl, it ain't looking good." Suspiciously, he added, "But why yo lil slick ass keep asking me where I'm at? You and Star together ... y'all must be out hoeing and blowing, it's the best thing going, huh?"

This tickled her fancy. Snickering, she replied, "Boy, you crazy. I ain't on shit. We bored."

"Yea, I bet. Tryna see if I'ma pop up on you and—"

"Boy, please."

"Yea, aight," Bookie smirked, "Yo slick ass. Damn, hold on."

He had taken a wrong turn. The flyer fell under the passenger seat, so he pulled over in some Mexican spot that had a name he couldn't pronounce. "Dionna, let me call you back real quick." With the flyer in hand, he tried to determine his exact location. Leaving the car running, he got out to ask a bouncer for directions.

He handed him the plugger. "You know where this at?" The beefy bouncer stood just at the entrance of the night club, smokin a cigarette and eyeing him warily as he approached.

"Hey, why're going here? We have a better spot here," he said exhaling the nicotine while jerking his thumb over his huge shoulder to indicate the building to his back. He could have played one of those no-neck security guys in a B-rated mob movie.

"Yea? This a Mexican place, ain't it? I can't even pronounce that shit." Bookie pointed towards the sign.

"Mexican..." he tilted his head back, revealing a tree-trunk neck and let out a throaty cackle that sounded as if it weren't authentic. "Do I look Mexican? I'm Italian, but the owner here just...just take a look inside." He opened the door.

It wasn't full to capacity, but from Bookie's angle, it looked like the place to be. Rick Ross screamed how he don't steal cars, he just deal hard, how everyday he was *Hustlin'*.

"How long this been here?"

He checked a couple fake IDs and allowed some underage girls to enter before focusing his attention back on Bookie.

"I don't know. A couple months maybe. Mr. Flores bought it. He hasn't changed the name yet though. Well, not the name but the sign."

"You talking about the Flores who had the spots in Dalton?"

"Yea, Mr. Flores!"

He'd awoken a sleeping giant. He smiled a lopsided grin.

"You know him?"

"Is he in there? I been looking for him."

"Aww yea, you know Mr. Flores." He was a lil kid in a candy store.

"Not really, but he knows me."

"Well, I tell you what, you can wait inside. He'll be here in bout an hour. There's a two-drink minimum."

"I gotta make a couple phone calls but gimme a second and I'll be back."

Text messages, phone calls, and VSOP for twenty minutes. Not to females though but to a guy. Omar Zamora was one of the guys he left in Danville. They stayed in contact with each other. He was Dominican and at least thirty years older than Bookie. Originally from NYC, Omar had come to Chicago in the 70s. Instead of getting his slice, Omar had got the entire (American) pie. Then it was all gone just as quick as it had come. Left with a forty-year sentence, he was to do twenty straight years for his kingpin role as a wholesale heroin distributor.

Omar called Bookie his son, and Bookie affectionately referred to him as Papito. Initially, he'd helped Papito with his English in addition to his schoolwork. When he had an issue with the Hispanics, Omar was there to mediate. Every time the Latinos cooked their gourmet cultural dishes, which was often, he made sure Bookie ate. Bookie wasn't sure if they hated him or Omar more for these actions, but he was positive it didn't sit well with them as a whole. Papito taught him how to play chess on and off the board, and as a token of his appreciation, Bookie assisted him in receiving his associate's degree, tutoring him for an hour a day. A devout Christian, Papito wanted no part of any illegal activities, for Bookie or himself. The old man was adamant about going legit upon his release. He was completely rehabilitated and had changed his life. When Bookie met him, he was doing his fourteenth year in state prison.

He knew Bookie though and knew that with his lifestyle, he might need some assistance at some point in time. With this in mind, he furnished him with the phone number of his best friend Flores, also the ex-husband of his younger sister. This was in 2004. Bookie had used the number once in 2005 and hadn't even thought of it since. Papito had told him in 2006 or maybe 2007 that Flores was getting sued, thus having financial troubles. Then he got a divorce from his second wife. It was rumored that he had five or ten different clubs, nice upscale joints. Looking at this place, Bookie thought it had to be a downgrade.

Flores arrived in a discreet Chevy Impala that had seen better days. He looked more like a cabbie than a successful small business owner. The one time Bookie did meet him was so brief that he had forgotten what he looked like, but with "no neck" pointing in his direction, he figured it had to be him. Bookie got out and introduced himself. Instant recognition! Flores was Mexican, Bookie assumed, but he could pass for white if he didn't speak. The unlit cigar between his lips bobbed up and down as he spoke. He looked like the guy who trained Balboa in all the Rocky movies.

"Omar talks about you all the time. Come on in, what're you drinkin?" he asked enthusiastically.

Flores patted Bookie on the back, rubbed a couple of times, then wrapped his arm around his shoulders as if he were a long-lost relative. Over a drink, Bookie told him a little about his life. When asked what he did for a living, Bookie replied, "I'm in the streets." It didn't take a scholar to figure out what that consisted of. By looking at him, you could tell.

Flores explained that he was still doing okay financially but not nearly as well as he'd done in the past. A series of lawsuits brought him back to reality. "I've been sued as many times as the years I've been on this earth," he said. "I only lost two. Practically at the same time. Those two was enough, though; they brought me to my knees." He went on to elaborate how the city had sued him as well as the family of a victim who was paralyzed by a rival gang's bullet while on the premises of his establishment. An underage victim!

They talked and took shots for two hours. Bookie drank Remy, Flores some kind of tequila. Bookie promised to

come back but told him he had a prior engagement so he
had to run. Flores understood. Bookie wanted to come
back! Friday and Saturday nights belonged to blacks.
Hispanics Sunday. Monday was some amateur stripper
night, and Tuesday, Wednesday and Thursday were Poker
Nights. Doors opened at 8 p.m., no matter what night. "I'll
tell yo old man you stopped by. He's always worrying and
talking bout you." His English wasn't the best. If Bookie
strained his ears and gave him his undivided attention, he
could barely make out the heavily accented words Flores
spoke.

Bookie phoned some nearby "action" and called it a
night. Early the next morning, with Vino riding shotgun,
they headed for the 10,000 lakes. Enroute, Vino warned
how their next trip they might get only five bricks. It was
supposed to be twenty, but now something was going on
with the plug, so it was looking more like five if anything.
Not the news Bookie wanted to hear. Bread was in the
MCC facing ten years to life. Some female in Rockford had
set him up for a few ounces of hard. Bookie never
understood why he was still selling crack anyway when he
didn't have to. He said the first plea they offered, he was
jumping on it. No need to play. Feds weren't people you
wanted to play with, he explained.

In Minnesota, they had girls now. Keys to their cars and
cribs. They still used hotels but not as many. These girls
caused them to spend less time with each other than they
did before, and more time with them. They used to spend
nearly twenty-four hours of the day together; now, it was
more like a fourth of that. When they first started this

operation, they'd get two rooms at decent hotels rooms, one with twin beds. Three-star or better. Sleep in one and keep the work in the other.

Mitch stayed there sometimes, on the couch, but his sister lived in Minnesota on the northside; he always had options as did Bookie with all of his family who lived there. Vino even had some relatives there as well that they visited but for some unknown reason he would always sleep at the hotel.

******

The money went back in increments of a hundred grand or per request and only by Greyhound or Megabus. Strapped to a female passenger's abdomen. Once in Chiraq, the courier would be intercepted by a runner named Biscuit. Biscuit or Biscola would then count and organize the bundles of cash, making sure everything was right. Once the inventory was complete, he'd pass the package off to Bread, who would run it into the end zone.

With Bread now locked up and no longer on the other end to receive, apparently this was a dilemma. The plug didn't wish to be taking a huge risk nor did he want to associate with random females every other day regarding business. This presented a conflict of interest. Either Vino would wait until all the work was gone and take the proceeds back personally, or he would take a trip (a few times weekly) back to Chicago. From Minnesota ... through Wisconsin? With all or the majority of your eggs in one basket? Not a bright idea for anyone, but especially not the Prince of the Corleone BD's, a successful faction of the Black Disciples street organization. One check of his name and troopers of the Highway Patrol would automatically dismantle the vehicle.

Vino contemplated going into business for himself. Only bringing a couple bricks a few hundred miles then turning right back around—it just wasn't worth the hassle.

Fact was the Minnesota operation had all but run its course, but not for Bookie. He remained there, bringing nines, eighteens and even whole bricks. Working his number, he couldn't get enough of the Sotas. What other options did he have? Kankakee? He posted up and sold anything from eightballs to sixty-threes, all hard.

Bookie had upgraded from being on the road seven hours. He would purchase an Amtrak ticket, a sleeping car. Then he would pay some lucky female to make the journey for him with the yams. Immediately after depositing her downtown on Canal, he would take a cab to Midway or O'Hare from Union Station. Business class all the way.

He posted up in a crib off Freemont, northside Minneapolis, and was getting to the money the best way he knew how. Living the life. Every night he was turning up at different clubs, with different girls. The majority of daylight hours in between trapping were spent at Mystic Lake Casino, or the University of Minnesota, where he had a P-Y-T from Pennsylvania named Ciara who worshipped him, along with a few other random "eaters." Bookie was on the road to riches, well on his way. A destination in sight ... then it happened.

First, Bookie and his cousin Pankey punished an intoxicated or delusional middle-aged white guy outside of Sex World. Downtown amidst all the activity, all the people, this idiot waltzed up to Bookie and asked if he could "taste his cock?"

When they fled the scene, the Caucasian with the blond ponytail and tiny gold stud piercing his left earlobe was unconscious and would soon be in dire need of a blood transfusion. The lightly sprinkled salt in his five o'clock shadow was saturated with a very dark, rich ruby red liquid that looked black in the pale glow of the neon pink lighting outlining Sex World's huge windows. The right eye protruded from its socket a fraction of an inch.

Grainy footage of the brutality caught by security cameras was shown on the local news channels for a full month straight. The police needed the public's help in caging the two animals responsible for the comatose homosexual's condition. It was deemed a "hate crime." With no audio, the twenty-three-second video clip had been edited to show only the attack. The brief conversation, the approach, facial expressions and hand gestures that took place prior to the assault had all been omitted. Social engineering at its best.

With that situation still hanging in the balance, Zay, a guy from the neighborhood, tried his hand. Not long after coming to the Sotas, Bookie met Zay and ever since, he'd been one of his best customers. Not being able to keep his pants up led his girlfriend one day to flushing his life savings down the porcelain facility.

Prior to going into business with Bookie, Zay was a nickel and dimer who only bought eightballs and quarter ounces. Bookie gave him the game and a golden opportunity that he ran with. At the pinnacle of his career, he had nine ounces of soft and a couple racks. His response? Domestic Battery. Minnesota is a women and children's state. You could be cited for yelling at a woman in public, but do what he did and you'd go down quicker than the Titanic. Down he went.

The female judge, a conservative Republican, had stressed that no violence in the State of Minnesota would be tolerated, but that of a domestic nature was especially frowned upon. Bail was set. The three grand didn't quite cover it, so Bookie had to put up the remaining 2k to help get him out that jam. After he made repeated apologies for his infidelity, the girlfriend would eventually renege on the courts and drop the charges, but the process was a lengthy and costly one.

Bookie would go on to cover almost half of this overall tab. After all, he was a damn good customer, so why not? In addition to him doing his part by being a client, he also doubled as a partner by acting as a conduit to the streets. Bookie sold a couple zips a day to Zay's associates, giving him a small commission off all transactions he facilitated.

He was broke for a period, so Bookie fronted him sixty threes hard. This was summertime, and the heat was ferocious. In the summer, you would never believe it got as cold as it did in the winter. Around the corner from Bookie was an Arab-owned Quick Mart. Despite the refrigerator full of soft drinks in the kitchen, he would still get bored and walk the four-minute trek to the convenient store to purchase a cold Mistic or a Snapple.

Across the street from the store was a huge oak tree that offered a respite from the scorching sun. In this shade was where Zay and company "trapped," peddling their dope. Bookie had to walk up the block and turn left to pass under the tree on his way to the store unless he went out of his way to go around. He followed the sidewalk's path under the tree directly through the crack dealers on the bright sunny day. Bookie was street-bred, so he peeped the play long before it played out. Zay had set him up to be robbed from the looks of things.

It was broad daylight outside. Maybe Bookie was jumping to conclusions? He always kept racks on him. It was widely reputed, not a secret. Today he had a little more than usual. Zay had phoned to tell Bookie he had a band for him and he could come get it.

Zay called out to Bookie as he approached. The base of the massive shade tree was just a spit from the front door of the trap house they were hustling out of. He was requesting that Bookie step to the side of the house so he could count the money out.

******

Soon as Bookie had stepped out of his crib, he noticed their lookout, who could view traffic coming and going in all directions from his post. He looked directly at Bookie as he faced south; to the right, he could see the Quick Mart. It was weird because it was so obvious. Police would spot this guy from a mile away. Here, like Chiraq, cops hated lookouts. In Chicago, though, they'd just beat you senseless. But here in the Sotas they'd beat you and trump up some charges so they could beat you in a court of law as well. No one in their right mind would risk their necks on the chopping block like that. Unless he wasn't looking out for pigs, but looking out for people.

Lil Lord, a fourteen-year-old who bought an eightball or two every day, was on his bike, blocking the sidewalk, forcing Bookie to walk around him. His eyes were trained on an invisible spot in the grass. There wasn't a time when the youngster hadn't been enthused to see Bookie. Anxious to hear him talk, see what lingo he used, peep the clothes or shoes he was wearing. Swipe a lil of his etiquette. Looking forward to Bookie's opinions and input, hanging on to his every word. Happily discussing all of his dreams and aspirations, cars, watches or the latest video on 106 & Park.

But not today. Today he wouldn't even look Bookie in his eye. Another telltale sign was the huge pistol print in the pocket of Zay's cousin, who Bookie had beat out of $2,500 a week ago on the dice "pad" rolling. He had been bitter about Bookie quitting. Now his failure to acknowledge Bookie after he spoke cordially, with the constant flexing of his jaw muscle as he gritted his teeth, told Bookie that nothing had changed.

Zay's head moved side to side as he looked around nervously. "Aye, check it out right quick, Killa, I got a lil of that paper I owe you," he said while taking down the last of his French braids as he walked.

Transactions were conducted on the side of the single-story trap house or in the backyard of the dilapidated residence, long since abandoned.

Zay hobbled his short, 250-pound frame along the cobblestoned walkway leading to the rear of the house, expecting Bookie to follow. Instead, Bookie followed his gut instinct, continuing to the Quick Mart.

"Hold on, Jo, I'm fina come right back."

"Nawl, check it out real quick," Zay insisted.

Bookie stole a look at his cousin's face and knew that would not be a good idea. Internally, there was something boiling, building up inside the ex-con, recently paroled from Stillwater State Penitentiary. Soon it would surface, and his body language told Bookie he wouldn't want to be around to witness it when it did.

Crossing the street, he yelled back over his shoulder, "Gimme a second."

Inside the mart, he called his cousins. His heart was pumping faster than usual, and he wasn't sure if the sweat came from the high temperature or the heated circumstances that he was in. None of his family were available. In forty-five minutes or so, but not at present. Bookie dialed Tito. No answer. Yodi had told him that when he was getting money in Minnesota, whenever he had an issue he got Tito on the line. Bookie was seething in anger, but he knew he had to use his head. Being upset would get him nowhere fast, possibly even killed.

Lil Lord came in to buy an orange Faygo and hot Cheetos, still avoiding eye contact. Bookie watched as he paid for his purchase, exited, straddled the dyno with GT mags and headed back towards the tree twenty or so yards away. The sophomore who should have been in school reported directly to Zay's cousin. He was quarterbacking the play just as Bookie figured. More than likely Zay didn't want to participate, but surely his cousin came before the out-of-towner with the slick mouth. It was absurd to think he'd side with a non-native over his own flesh and blood.

Not to mention Bookie was a walking "lick."

Lil Lord definitely wasn't with it, but his loyalty lay with them, not Bookie, some flashy GD who they'd just met this year and wasn't even from the Sotas. There was also the lookout and two other bystanders, anything but innocent. Six people in total and at least one gun. Their intent was malicious. It didn't help that the ringleader, the person dictating the pace, already on parole for an armed robbery, viewed Bookie as an object of contempt.

What was he to do? Twelve eyes were glued to the entrance of the store, versus his single pair of eyes peering back at them.

Looking up at Bookie, over an open newspaper from his perch on a stool behind the cash register, the nervous Arab clerk asked if everything was okay. He sensed tension. Bookie assured him that all's well that ends well and that the reason he was drenched in sweat was due to the inclement weather conditions as opposed to the transpiring of some unforeseen situation. This seemed to relax him a bit, and he went back to his paper, printed in some Middle Eastern language. Bookie had to improvise. If not, he would become a victim of a midday robbery or worse. It was hotter in the store than it was outside. The only fan blew on the clerk.

Eight minutes that felt more like 800 minutes passed. Bookie bought a couple of candy bars, a push-up ice cream and some generic duct tape. A bathroom not normally open to the general public facilitated his next course of action. Bookie thanked, then "salaamed" the cashier for his hospitality, left out the door and headed straight toward the boys.

"Fuck you was doing in there, boy? I was waiting on yo ass for an hour damn near. Check it out right quick ..."

Now he was picking out his fro, removing dead hair from the pic. A wad of cash was already in his hand. He pretended to count it over after hiding the pic in the fro, freeing up his other hand.

Bookie looked at Lil Lord. He was counting the laces in his 95 Air Max sneakers. The lookout had disappeared along with the print of the pistol in the jeans pocket of his cousin. Bookie took three steps in Zay's direction and halted, raising his shirt tail a few inches. He flashed what appeared to be the duct-taped handle to a "throw-away."

"I gotta put this mufucka up real quick, them people riding. I'll be right back."

Bookie's t-shirt, shorts, and even the low-top Air Force Ones he wore were all a birthday gift from Honey he'd never worn. He thanked God the outfit was a size too big.

The sweltering heat was melting Bookie's "gun" by the millisecond, so he quickened his pace. Once back inside the crib, he was furious. He couldn't allow that to slide. Almost two hours later, accompanied by Tito, Bookie was back. No sign of Zay or his cousin. The only familiar face present was that of Lil Lord's. His youthful eyes pleaded with Bookie's deadly glare, begging for mercy without having to open his mouth. The connection was detected.

Tito was Bookie's cousin through marriage, and he was riding with Bookie as if he were Yodi or one of his other blood relatives.

"What's up, Shorty?" he asked angrily while tightening

his grip on the exposed Glock 40. "He was with them niggas, cuz?"

In these situations, Tito did more acting than thinking. Any suggestion that Lil Lord knew or was with the opps was sure to result in his death. Tito waited impatiently for an answer.

"Nawl, ion know Shorty ... never seen him."

Like the scene from Scarface, when Tony killed the pig who didn't fly straight, and Manny asked what was up with Ernie .... that brief moment before Tony offered him a job, Bookie chose to let the kid make it. He knew the youngster wasn't with the move they'd tried to bring him. Had he been with it, like really with it, *Killa* would have blasted his ass way before Tito even knew who he was.

Bookie hit Zay's line twenty times. Voicemail. He chirped him and got nothing. The last few times it said something about how the Nextel subscriber couldn't be reached. Nightfall came and he was still M.I.A. Bookie said fuck him, it was time to turn up. He would deal with him later.

In the V.I.P. section of Cream, Bookie stood chatting with the manager, a cool white dude named T.J., when his Sprint vibrated. Ignoring the call and focusing his attention back on the $350 bottle of fake Remy, that clear bottle Remy Cruze garbage, Bookie demanded that it be swapped out for V.S.O.P., or he receive a full refund. Then he received a text message.

The police had responded to a disturbance call made just after 2 a.m. at his residence. They found the back door kicked open and the place turned upside down. Bookie's vehicle was parked in front of the house, and a kitchen light had been left on, giving the impression that he was home. The intent was clear. This was not a random burglary. A neighbor reported that there were two unmasked men in dark clothing. No masks! One of the intruders was a bit overweight with a bushy afro.

Thirteen hours later, at a little before 3 p.m., Bookie paid the trap a visit and left a permanent mark in the shade tree. Bookie guessed Lil Lord was a long distance relative of Miss Cleo cause he was nowhere to be found, probably in school where he should be knowing what was in store for Zay. He found the fat piece of shit copping a squat on a parked car rolling a blunt with some freshly twisted French braids. Bookie had his man!

BANG! BANG! BANG! Bookie operated with utter finality and was back with Flores taking shots before he sold his first Corona of the night.

CHAPTER 33 – HARD FACTS

There is no such thing as partial freedom. – Nelson Mandela

Back in Kankakee, things were a little different. Seeing the picture in passing was one thing, even slowing down to get a better glimpse, but when Bookie completely stopped and took in the scene, he noticed a significant contrast. A year or two on the road, not really paying attention, made him notice, now, significant change.

His first eye-opener occurred when he visited Mrs. Tate in the hospital. She had all of a sudden taken ill and had to be hospitalized indefinitely. Something related to her diabetes. They laughed and talked, joked and teased with each other, but when he left the medical ward, he had a strange feeling that something was drastically wrong, something serious.

Close to home, the change was even more noticeable. All of Bookie's little cousins were growing up at a rapid pace and were making names for themselves in the streets. Despite their age range being from fourteen to twenty-one years old, they still, for the most part, jumped off the porch about the same time. If you had four brothers who were close—fourteen, fifteen, sixteen, seventeen—when certain things like weed get introduced to the seventeen-year-old, most likely the fourteen-year-old will smoke it too. On a smaller scale, their hands were in a mixture of everything: girls, gambling, weapons, drugs, gangs. Sadly, it was typical adolescent behavior that went on in poverty-stricken communities or inner-city hoods where you had limited resources.

One of them, who looked as if he not too long ago experienced puberty and was otherwise anti-social, had not only pulled a gun, but had used it recently when some Mexican or white dude, or white "looking" Mexican dude, named Jay or Jay-Dog attempted to manipulate him out of his penis. Bookie wasn't homophobic, but as he listened to this tale of deception, he wanted to kill this faggot personally.

"Okay, start from the top again." This was the second time hearing the story, but Bookie wanted to be absolutely certain before rendering judgment or making a decision that could potentially be life or death. He felt like a mob boss as two of his little cousins and one of their friends sought his permission and partial assistance to "whack" someone.

"Aight, look, I seen the dude and spoke to him once or twice."

"When and where?"

A look of frustration washed over the baby face, his peach fuzz mustache crinkled in a puzzled frown.

"Man, ion remember. I don't know. But the last time was at Shell's on Court at bout one in the morning. I was walking out and he pulled up in some type of lil truck, beating."

"He had sounds?"

"Not sounds, like banging. Just some factory shit, but it was turned all the way up and it was loud. Playing some type of Lil Wayne song, lollipop or some shit. So when he got out first, I thought he was white, so I kept looking at him. Then, when he got close, I could see he was Mexican or some shit. He had on a couple lil gold chains and a couple gold rings."

"Okay."

"He asked me bout some trees. I told him I don't got none, but could get it. He looked like a fag or was kinda acting like a fag, but you could tell he was trying to play hard like he was supa tough."

"Aight, then what happened?"

"Say his name was Jay or Jay Dog. He told me he wasn't trying to get weed, that he had weed, he sold weed and he had whatever. Told me I could call him if I wanted some. I was like this nigga a lick, so I took his number and gave him mine."

"You wanted to poke him?"

"Yea, I was gonna slide later on, me and Lo and make'em get nekkid. He a lil short chubby dude, look like that one comedian dude who play in ... in ... I forgot the name of that movie, but you know it if I say it. I think his name is John Levitts or something."

"Aight, then what happened?"

"I had forgot, then he ended up calling me."

"What he say?" Bookie was asking questions almost before the sentences even concluded.

"Said he had got some new green in, a lot of it. Said if I wanted some let him know. Then asked what I was on? Said he had some hoes and they wanted to kick it."

"Aight."

"It was on a weekend, so I tell him what's up?"

"Okay. So what happened?"

"I'm thinking he got some bad white hoes or some Mexicans or some shit—"

"What he have?" Bookie inquired.

"Hold on, man, damn, slow down," he looked at Bookie, frustrated and made a face. "So he pick me up later. In the doe I bring my banga. So he riding around like he on something. Playing rap music, driving fast, selling lil bags of weed, telling me to roll up here and there. Keep giving me weed. I'm thinking bout poking him, he thinking bout poking me."

Bookie had to stifle a laugh, not wanting to interrupt him.

"So he send me in the store one time to grab a box of cigarellos. He give me a hunnid-dolla bill. When I come out, he tell me to keep the change. A couple hours later we get gas and he give me a fifty-dolla bill. He tell me to put $10 in his tank. I pay while he pump. He didn't even need gas cause I looked and his shit was over half full. I tried to give him the $40; he told me to keep it. He asked if I drink, I said nawl. He kept asking me, you sure you don't want nothing to drink? Then after bout another hour he said the hoes said tomorrow. He said he was busy and had to drop me off. I was trying to find out where he live and see how many elbows he had in that mufucka and— "

"Man, what happened the next day?"

"The next day he called again. I had got almost $140 yesterday, so I told him to come pick me up. He said the hoes would definitely be ready today. It was a Saturday too. When I get in the car I see a Finish Line bag on the back seat. He tell me it's some new Jordans in the bag. Somebody stole them, a hype, and sold them to him. Said he can't fit 'em. Asked what size I wear."

Damn, Bookie was shaking his head; this dude was something else.

"Now, the day before he'd asked me what size I wear, and I told him. So I grabbed the Mike's, they just my size. Fit perfect. He tell me I can have them if I want. I see the receipt in the bag and the time they was purchased was at the top, so I know a mufucka didn't steal 'em. Plus they was in a bag, so c'mon man. He had just bought 'em before he picked me up."

"He think you a dummy."

"On my soul," he agreed, grateful his big cousin finished the sentence this time.

He licked his chapped lips, took a deep breath and continued. "Aight, lemme see... long story short. We go to his crib. He say he had to go to the crib for a second and we could chill and call ol girl 'em. I'm still tryna case the joint out and I guess he was casing me out. He said he had some Kush and we ain't have to keep smoking that reggie. He kept offering me drinks and pills. So while we there, he keep asking me what kind of girl I want or prefer, skinny or thick. Black hoes or white hoes, Mexican and all this otha goofy ass shit. He asking me how many can I handle and what I'ma do? When he don't hear what he wanna hear, he ask flat-out 'you ain't gonna let none of them give you head? You don't like that?' I was like, hell yea. He talked for like another minute then said, 'If you want, I can do that for you'."

Still not believing his ears, Bookie asked, "What you say his name was?"

"Jay or Jay-Dog or some shit."

Just barely old enough to buy alcohol, Tre was often carded when purchasing tobacco products. But he was nobody's fool, having done time in juvenile and been around the block a few times.

Again, Bookie didn't have anything against homosexuality, but this here deception, in the black community amongst the youth ... this fag should be slaughtered. Literally. Bookie had seen people, young men with him. This same guy riding, smoking, drinking, with new clothes on and new shoes. He been getting lil boys all this time, less fortunate individuals who would sell their souls for a couple hundred bucks. Think of how many people he'd gotten to. Tricked. Suffice it to say, Bookie assisted in the righteous endeavor to exterminate this pest, but the plan backfired and Bookie almost ended up back behind "the wall."

******

Bookie had no girlfriend nor was he committed to anyone. Honey was just a memory. Nisha had recently been spotted sporting an engagement ring, and Monique was involved with someone a lot older than she. Bookie took the occasional "fly by" but most of his time was spent with a very pregnant Diamond, who had an apartment behind the bricks. She was due in October. Sometimes he chilled with Dionna who was just returning from school. It was time that Bookie re-acclimated to the K3 life until he could find somewhere else to go; thus, he went to the drawing board.

It's been said *one should think before he act*. Bookie thought long and hard, once again weighing his options in the streets. In his absence, a handful of hustlers had risen to the occasion and now laid claim to the top spots Kankakee had to offer those of this profession. Tyrone was out, picking up where he'd left off. Eyes was doing well for himself; DeeTee wasn't far behind.

******

The Killa Kees, at this time, was in a sad state. Maybe it was just happening or maybe it'd always been this way, but Bookie was beginning to take notice of specific elements regarding the psychological structuring of Kankakee, Illinois, its residents and their pessimistic view of life. A contagious attitude that permeated the hearts of all the K3 citizens.

Tawayne had a saying, "If you trick 'em, you can beat 'em." People in K3 were being tricked. Duped. Bamboozled. Hoodwinked. Bookie had no intentions of perpetuating this behavior. Breaking the mold and getting back on course, aligning back up with the route, was imperative. Essential to his survival, if he intended to arrive at the destination.

The small town consisted of classes, like so many other communities. Upper, middle and lower. These "levels" were based on your ability. The ability to acquire or obtain certain material possessions. To make idle purchases. You were categorized by where you lived or the car you drove. Often by the quality, or in some cases, the quantity, of females you had sex with. Based on these criteria, and using this scale, Bookie was considered a major thread in the social fabric of the Killa Kees. A heavy weight!

Guys from his age bracket were soaring to heights foreign to them. It was their turn. They were in their mid-twenties and very much pertinent. Generations prior to them were gone, "has-beens," washed up. The statistics weren't good. Each generation of street figures would yield only a 20% return as far as those individuals who made it out. No bullet, no loss of freedom, life or limb. But they'd have to quit while they were ahead and sometimes that meant with little to no money. No Social Security pension, IRA or 401k. Less than 10% would live long if they continued their criminal enterprises indefinitely. The remaining seventy-plus plus percent ... may God be with them. Anybody's guess was as good as Bookie's. Concrete or pine box for most of them.

The objective wasn't who could make the most or get the most money. It was about who could stay free, spend and enjoy the most money! With the implementation of movies like *The Mack*, leading up to, during and especially after that specific era, the shame and the glory had been misplaced. What should be glorified is shamed, and what should be shamed *is* glorified. In the 50s and 60s, black communities were united as one. Mass incarceration didn't exist.. there was no need for the prison industrial complex. Then you introduce this heroin, these pimp movies ... all these soldiers come home from Vietnam worse off than when they left. You erect some project buildings and things take a turn for the worse. Then later with crack and gangs. You build more detention centers, jails, lockups and prisons than any other country in the world.

In the hood, people don't realize this until it's too late. The classic banana in the tailpipe or carrot on the stick. We were told or showed the "game" but no exit strategy. We know how to get the money, but we don't have a clue what to do with it. So we end up stuck. Fool's gold. Bookie was taught better than this. He knew better. Those who came before him were all dead or serving long prison sentences, the "standup" ones. The other ones, those that squat down to urinate, they turned rat, obviously.

During the Clinton administration, the prison population tripled. How? In the 50s and 60s how many jails or prisons were there? How many are there now? The Clinton administration locked up so many browns and blacks, but unconscious minorities only remember him getting some head in the Oval Office. According to them, he was the first black president. What was the greatest trick the devil played? **Voilà**! While he was convincing the people that he didn't exist or the evil *in him* didn't exist rather, he was signing the '94 crime bill. You heard about the fellatio, you heard about him smoking weed, but you didn't hear about his plan to mold mass incarceration.

The Killa Kees, living up to its namesake, had literally killed so many dreams and aspirations. It was to the point young black men didn't dream anymore. They had nightmares. Financial nightmares—thus, they aspired to be drug dealers. An occupation that's tangible. The only solution obtainable in their eyes. He couldn't remember if it was the Honorable Elijah Muhammad or W.E.B Dubois, but one of them said, *"He who prescribes the diameter of your knowledge (or thinking) will then control the circumference of your actions."*

Are there really no other options out there? Or are people just being led to believe none exist or that selling poison to their own people was the only way? Who're the determinants? You or someone who's thinking for you, the social engineers behind the scenes? How many Goldies were there in the hood before the *Mack*? DeBos before *Friday*? J-rocs before *South Central*? Ninos and G-moneys, *New Jack City*? O'Dogs before *Menace to Society*? These all fictional characters created by people with an interest at stake. They gave us these characters and made them so appealing that everyday people wanted to be like them. Wanted to be drug dealers, pimps, killers, gang members. What did the kids want to be before these characters existed? Who were the role models prior to Nino and O'Dog?

Coming up, Bookie watched the street figures before him. Buck, Tyree, Fonz, Frog... the list was endless. He didn't just watch; he was a part of their agenda. He jammed with Buck, bought weight from Tyree, gambled with Fonz and fucked with Frog all before he had pubic hair.

Long before the Advanced Auto on Court Street and Hobbie were there, it was Better's Chicken. Tyree lived across the street in the Burrell apartments. A stone's throw from Bookie's bedroom window, Tyree's crib was the hangout. Bookie and Tawayne were there every day, along with all the hustlers. Whether they were gambling, buying yams, playing the game or whatever else they did, it was done there. These were the people to be like, to emulate. They didn't want to be anywhere else. After all, it ain't like much was going on in the house they lived in anyway.

Tyree's house practically became home.

It's been said that all of these guys cooperated with law enforcement later in life. Not that Bookie ever saw any paperwork personally and didn't care to see it, but many people swear it exists. Bookie could vividly recall riding with Frog in his sky blue Park Avenue on 30 & Vogues, to attend the funeral of Tyrone (who was killed in Minnesota). Services were held in Hobbie Hikes. Frog passing him the White Owl, saying how he swore on his soul he'd never snitch. Now people were swearing on their soul he *did* snitch. These were the people, all a decade or more older than Bookie, that he looked up to. The group they looked up to, 20 yrs older than Bookie minimum. He'd been in their presence as well.

The Clays, Lil Harrys, Reggie Reynolds, Baby Boys, Lay Low, Bo Scott – Bookie saw them too. Despite being almost twenty years younger than Lil Harry, it was Bookie who started him back to smoking weed after he got out the joint. They went and ate at an apartment he had on Sunnyside. Bookie was impressed with the all-white decor. Even more impressed by the pictures hanging on the wall of the "decent lil red bone" Harry called, wifey.

Bookie fought dogs with Baby Boy, bet big with Double R and Lay Lo, rocked with Clay tough and drove Bo Scott's cars to school as a 6th grader, using pillows to see over the dashboard. He saw the glitz, the glamour, the fame, and all the fortune. He was also privy to the flipside of that same coin, such a disgrace. A very sad ending to an otherwise happy story. These were the pioneers, the figures who made Kankakee or the Killa Kees what it was. They were all ten, twenty, some even thirty years older, (like Party

House Andy). Bookie bore witness to the destinations and new routes they'd taken to get there. He knew better, he really did. But if he really knew better, wouldn't he do better? After seeing generations of trailblazers, after bearing witness to their rise and fall, how could he follow the same footsteps?

CHAPTER 34 – THE SOCKET

God watch over fools and babies. – Unknown

In mid-2008, Tip pulled up riding a purple and yellow CBR 900. Bookie stood on the corner of Osborn and Hickory entertaining Juice and Vick.

"This mufucka for sale, so if y'all know anybody want a bike, lemme know," Tip declared while planting both feet and revving up the engine.

"Killa trying to buy a bike," a voice called out from the doorway. It was Baby Joe, Vick's uncle and Yodi's baby brother.

"Bookie don' know how to ride no damn motorcycle. Killa gonna fuck around and get killed," Tip teased. His eyes asked another question.

"Or do you?"

"You ain't gotta know how to ride when you got money! I'm rich. I might just buy this mufucka and park it if I need to, shidd. I'll pay a mufucka to ride me. Joe, what's up?"

"Man, you betta gone wit that faggot shit. They already saying you gay." This tickled everybody's funny bone.

This tumultuous time was actually one of the lows of Bookie's career. His funds had been diminishing gradually over the past couple of months. A lot of withdrawals and no deposits. Coming back to town, Bookie had gotten back in rotation with his old crew. Murda was eating out the garbage, and both of them were shaken a bit due to Icholis catching a secret indictment. Until they found out who the CS (confidential source) was, or until Marcus got his "discovery," they were flying under the radar. Half of Bookie's life savings was in his pockets, and Diamond would be giving birth to his second son in approximately four months. Normal parents would be saving up for college tuition, but Bookie was anything but normal.

Bookie's lifestyle demanded that he keep cash on his person at all times. The saying about a fool and his money was the epitome of how he lived, he and his money parted ways daily.

"I'm outta here, y'all ain't tryna do shit." The words stipulated conveyed that Tip was only eighty-five percent sure. It was true. Bookie didn't know how to ride a bike, nor was he even thinking about buying a bike until Tip showed up on a shiny new CBR. Yet Bookie took advantage of the remaining fifteen percent. Seeing an opportunity, he lept through the window.

"What you want for it?"

"It's a six-grand bike, easy. Ion want shit but five. From you I'll take forty-five hunnid right now."

"Get up real quick, lemme see this mufucka."

"I'm tellin you, man. On my mama, Bookie, if you drop it."

"Man, jus get yo broke ass up, and lemme see what it do. I ain't tryna hear all that cryin and shit, nigga. If I drop it, I bought it," Bookie said with a touch of finality.

Tip reluctantly swapped spots with Bookie with the motor still running.

"Aight, what do I do from here?" Bookie asked quickly.

Tip was already looking at Bookie curiously, not knowing whether he should take him serious or not. He reached over and fumbled with a button on the handlebars, immediately the engine died.

"Man get up, dude, you fina hurt yo self."

"Joe, check it out." Bookie ignored Tip.

"Tip, watch out, Killa know how to ride better than you." Turning to Vick, Juice added, "He think he the only mufucka know how to ride."

"Bookie, on my mama ... I'm telling you!"

With Tip, his protests of concern could have been for Bookie or the CBR; it was hard to tell at this point. Leaning to one side, Bookie pulled out his trademark bankroll.

"Huh, man," Bookie said, handing it over to Tip. "Count this lil shit."

"And shut the fuck up," Juice included for good measure. No argument from Tip.

Joey Boy showed Bookie what to do while Vick and Juice looked on optimistically.

Sorting the Federal Reserve notes with a half-assed smirk, Tip said, "Now when yo ass fall," he paused for emphasis, "first thing I'ma do is follow the sound of the crash. All yo lil change gonna be on the ground cause I know you got some more in yo otha pocket. It's gonna be a long trail of blood, diamonds, skin, and money. Yo watch, earrings..." Now he was smiling.

Bookie's phone rang.

"What's up, man ... fuck yo broke ass calling me for?" It was Fred.

"Bitch, where you at? I need you. It sound like you on a

motorcycle or some shit."

"I am, just bought it and I'm fina go pick yo bitch up."

"Fuck outta here." Tip had the boys laughing in the background, talking about calling 911 for the bike and not Bookie cause he was hard-headed.

"Aye, I need to grab a couple balls."

"Whoa, whoa man, what the fuck is you talking bout?" This dude was reckless on the phone.

"My fault, I mean biscuits or ... man, my fault." He sounded sorry, but ...

"Aight, man. I told you I ain't have that shit. Stop calling my phone talking reckless. I'ma send a mufucka yo way to look out. Man, don't call me no more with that goofy-ass shit."

It was as if every time Bookie came back to K3, this dude was calling him for drugs or a gun. He ran with Tyrone, Eyes, T Dub and all these other dudes who were into that, so why call him? Even then, he changed his number, his phones, etc. So how did he keep getting his new info? Bookie made a mental note to look into that later. For now his attention shifted to the crotch rocket.

While the younger pair of spectators laughed uncontrollably, Joe showed Bookie what to do. He instructed Bookie to squeeze what appeared to be a brake lever on the handle bars. "That's the clutch!" Bookie had never ridden a motorcycle before, so this was all new to him.

With his toe, he kicked the gear shift down once. "Now ease off the clutch and—" The bike jerked hard, the front wheel coming off the ground an inch or so, then the engine died.

Bookie was already on his tippy toes, and the bike would have fallen had Joe not steadied it. They got it running again. "Now ease off ... Not too quick and don't give it too much gas or –"

He was talking to himself. Bookie was already gone.

******

With the state of 10,000 lakes behind him, and his well running dry in Kankakee, Bookie found himself exploring other options. On impulse he rode to Texas with a female friend and discovered that every thing was bigger in the Lonestar State just like his dreams. Initially Bookie made his presence felt in the Dallas suburb of Carrolton.

Carrolton was where the Blood Brother Trick's old man, Rick, resided. Bookie reached out to Trick and his twin Stelly, and they bridged the gap from the Kees.

"I don't fuck around personally," the old-timer had said when asked about a plug. It was as dry as the Sahara in K3 and had been for some time. "I'm too old for that shit, but I could point you in the right direction."

The same day Bookie was introduced to a slick-talking well-dressed Mexican about his age. Noah was his handle. They hit it off immediately and made plans for the very near future. The conversation alone enthused the humorous Mexican, who was fluent in English. Hopeful about the potential of their dealings, Noah insisted that the new partners celebrate. Truthfully, Bookie's money was funny. He was on his last leg and in no position to discuss any move worth making. Yet he apparently had sounded convincing when speaking, like he had megamillions despite only possessing a few grand. Why not act like it?

Bookie had a plan, though. Utilizing his street acumen, he tapped into his resources. Black reigned supreme and was hailed as the undisputed champ in the ring of marijuana, a real Kush Cowboy. Bookie was happy to hear his voice when he answered his line.

"Hello."

"Aye, what's the word, boy?" Black asked.

He was adamant bout not answering numbers he didn't recognize. Therefore, regardless of how many times Bookie switched his phone, every thirty days, Black had to see that 815-549-8896 (Bookie's personal number).

"Shit, I'm coolin, down here where J-Prince 'em at fuckin around," Bookie answered.

"Tryna get it together, huh? How long you been down there?"

"Shidd, not long. Hang up real quick, I'm fina hit yo line from the trap phone." Seconds later, he was back on the phone.

"Hello, yea. You stay switchin these mufuckas up, don't you?"

"Err thirty days like clockwork. No exceptions. Can't let the feds wash me up."

"I hear you. I hear you. When you coming back this way? Wish you woulda told me, I needed to be down there wit you."

"You know I got some room for you, if nobody else. That's why I was calling you though for real, for real. I had run into yo boy Corn."

This translated to "I ran across some of that good green,

the weed people called Popcorn." Although Black sold a lot of Kush, he'd got on by peddling reggie and still indulged whenever possible; reggie was his true passion. Black was hip. "Aww, yea, what that nigga was on?"

"Man, on my life, that nigga A-1."

"Damn, I need to check him out asap."

"He said you was suppose to call him tomar, what time you usually call him?" Bookie said, meaning, "How much was Black currently paying per pound?"

"I usually call around 6:30. It just depends. And lately it ain't even been Corn answering the phone." He usually paid six and a half or $650 and it wasn't corn.

"Look, I'm fina get up wit the nigga right now. He had told me I could call around five, so if you want, you can hit him then."

"Hell, yea, that's love. Make sure it's Corn, though, cause if somebody else answer I'm hanging up."

"Aww, it's definitely gonna be him. I already talked to the nigga and seen him face to face."

"Well, shidd ..."

"Aye, look, my baby mama tryna pay her lil Sprint bill. If she don't pay it by the first they gonna clip her," Bookie was freestyling now.

"How much is it?"

"A mufucka gotta at least pay a few hundred to keep it on, but what can you stand?" Black caught on quick.

"I got $250 for her. Tell her I'm ready whenever she ready."

The coded conversation resulted in Bookie locking him in for a 250-pound purchase. Noah wanted $450 per pound,

Bookie told Black $500. He stood to gain $50 times 250 and he still wasn't content. Noah and Bookie went back to the table. In this case, the (table) was a partially nude strip club downtown of Dallas. By sunrise and a $3,800 tab later, Bookie and Noah agreed on $400 per pound, with the understanding the next purchase would be done at the original $500, the standard market value. The exchange would be made in a week. In the meantime, the female Bookie had come with headed back north, and he decided to stay behind.

Bookie was like a little kid in a candy store. Killeen, the military town, welcomed him with open arms. He even put down a deposit on a 1975 Monte Carlo from Deonte's brother, Harlan, at KB Customs. When Bookie became tired of the soldiers and their girls, he took the four-hour commute to Prairie View A&M University where he had hung out before with Baby Joe and a few female friends who he maintained contact with. It would have been quicker had he not made a wrong turn once or twice.

Bookie shopped at Sharpstown and ate lunch with T.V. Johnny in the food court. Bookie was surprised at just how small he was in person. He partied downtown at The Vault and had a great time while in H-Town. The day came for the deal to go through, and Bookie barely had $1,000 to his name. However in the next twenty-four hours he was sitting on 25K cash and was headed back to K3 after making a promise to see Noah two or three times a month minimum.

Once the transaction had been completed, and all parties were happy, Bookie, flush with cash, was back on the hunt for cocaine. The original conversation with Noah had been about cocaine but had somehow led to marijuana. A product Bookie had no interest in. He was almost happy that it did. Once the bird landed, Black gave him five pounds and a couple grand cash for brokering the deal. Once he dumped the five blocks, he had brick money.

Bookie was a cocaine cowboy; that was his forte. In all of America, the powdery white substance was becoming rarer by the day. The drought was in full force. When it was located, the price was so high that potential consumers were discouraged from buying it.

A little over a week later, Black was done with the pounds and wanted more. Noah had an unlimited supply but had firmly explained the price would be $500 this time. He was standing on it.

"Come on, man, where in Texas could you get popcorn for the prices I'm giving them to you?" he whined. "This not Arizona."

Bookie had already agreed on $500, so there was really no point in going back and forth. He gave Black the phone number and got out the way. Black assured him that he would give him either ten elbows of reggie or two blocks of "loud" everytime he copped from Noah, out of appreciation.

******

Bookie hadn't seen Flores in a month or more. From stopping by weekly to going M.I.A. for months, the senior Flores feared the worse. He'd grown fond of Bookie. When Bookie stopped in, he was behind the bar doing inventory on some cheap imported vodka. A hot Latina bartender with curly black hair and light brown eyes handed Bookie a bottle of Remy Martin and his personal tumbler from its designated spot just below the register. Flores raised his arms as if asking, "What's up?" before rapidly releasing a series of Spanish words that ended with "mijo."

He asked if Bookie had spoken with Papito. He hadn't.

"Stick around, aye ... I need to have a word with you private, no."

It didn't take long for the place to fill up. Hordes of patrons, both male and female, flooded the small establishment in the hopes of having a great time and maybe hooking up. When the night was well under way, Flores directed Bookie to a tiny office in the bowels of the 5,400 square-foot building.

"Have a seat," Flores said when they entered the room housing mismatched chairs. They sat on opposite sides of his unkempt desk.

"Omar would kill me if he knew we were having this conversation," he said, breaking the ice with his broken English.

The mind-altering intoxicant in the bottle Bookie was drinking from—he'd rid himself of the tumbler—wouldn't allow his expression to change. Bookie was a duck, calm on the surface, but the part you couldn't see was moving 1,000,000 rpms a minute. He was thinking, "What the hell?"

"I need some help. Financially. I need money. I could lose my place here," he swept his arm around the small cubicle. "Both of my properties are in foreclosure. I filed bankruptcy with the lawsuits; it hasn't been seven years yet. Another one would, how they say... ruin me." He took a shot of tequila from a private bottle that doubled as a paperweight on the cluttered desk he sat behind.

"How much you need, or what you need?" Bookie asked this question as though he might have had the solution to the man's problems in his back pocket.

He poured himself another drink and took a swig, with his eyes trained intently on the contents of the miniature shot glass. Bookie's eyes were trained on Flores as he spoke slowly.

"I know what it is that you do, no?"

It sounded like a question and an answer. Bookie was confused and kept silent. Where was this conversation going, Bookie wondered.

"Your papito wouldn't approve, but my hands are tied here." Still confused, Bookie turned the bottle up and heard something about libras as the room-temperature cognac swooshed down his esophagus, leaving a trail of heat in its wake.

"My people. They get good one in Moca. Cost, though. Cost money." His thumb and index finger connected and began to massage each other. "You know the type?"

Bookie didn't answer. He didn't understand. It was like he had been asked a question only to have the questioner answer it. When Bookie didn't speak, he asked again.

"No?"

"Yea, I know the type. What they want? How much they hollarin?"

"Cinco." He held up a palm, extending all fingers and the thumb.

"I can get them off, but I'd prefer cocaine. Cocaina, Ya-

Yo, blanco," Bookie said, poorly imitating a Latino accent. Flores' eyes smiled before his lips did.

******

Bookie was connected, business was good. He finally had a real plug. Summer 2008 came to a long and drawn-out end, but Bookie was just getting started. It didn't take a metric ton of cocaine to sew up Kankakee. The retail value of a kilogram during this time was 27-29k all throughout the Chicagoland area. Flores provided Bookie on average with ten at a time. The ticket 240k. This was a fraction below standard, giving Bookie a little wiggle room.

Prior to Bookie receiving the first ten bricks, Flores had given him twenty self-serve tubs of high-grade marijuana. The tubs were all labeled with different names but fell under one universal umbrella. Kush. Later he offered Bookie meth, super-meth, and even black tar, which Bookie declined. His only true interest was the 2.2lb squares of flaky fish scales with the stamp in the middle.

Bookie would get the ten bricks before the first of the month. Between the first and the third, he would sell three or four bricks to a couple people who sat at the table with him. He sold them for the same price he got them, 24k. One or two were sold in halves or whole to outsiders whom he taxed. The remaining four or five Bookie would break down to all sixty-threes.

In each brick, there was a total of thirty-six ounces, totaling 1008 grams. Divide this by sixty-three. The math was simple. You get sixteen. Some people referred to them as "babies," or two and a quarter, or a "tre" and so forth. In the hood, dealers who had bricks were considered

"Bricklayers." Their distribution scale started with sixty-threes and ended with bricks. After a sixty-three, it went like this: a four and a split (which translated to four and a half ounces or two sixty-threes), a nina, (quarter key), nine ounces or four sixty-threes, a half (eighteen ounces), then thirty-six. Everything doubled all the way up until a brick.

Most bricklayers sold soft and refused to sell anything less than a sixty-three. Asking for an eightball or a half ounce was blasphemous. Those purchasing sixty-threes and up almost always requested that the substance be in powder form. These were just unofficial rules to the game. With hard or crack you can blow it up and play with it too much. Plus it gets you the most time, so it's always cheaper. The wise ones stay away from it even though you can make more money. So when Bookie opened bricks, he would make sixteen individual piles of cocaine, weighing sixty-three grams each. Bagged, they were sold for two racks apiece, netting $32,000. Subtract the twenty-four grand owed to Flores and the remaining $8,000 was all profit. All his. Bookie, the "Brick Layer"!

Everybody in K3 bought work from him. From a dime bag up to an ounce. If you bought it out the hood or from someone from the hood, there was a sixty percent chance it had gone through Bookie's hands first. Unless you bought a whole kilogram, your order was always filled in sixty-threes. Just like when he used to sell eight balls. You wanted nine ounces, you got four sixty-threes. A half a brick, Bookie gave it to you in eight sixty-threes. He was getting to the money.

Bookie's sister lived on the southside of town, in the

historical district of Kankakee, in a two flat. When she notified him that the apartment above her was available for rent, he dived on the opportunity. A quick phone call to the landlord authorized him to do some reconstruction of his own. Days later Vizio flat screens were mounted on every wall in the residence, including the bathroom and kitchen.

The interior of the second-story dwelling was finished in upscale decor. He finished the decorating with a statue of a black panther that stood almost as tall as him and doubled as a safe. His closet looked like the mall. Bookie lived in Ford City, Evergreen Plaza, and River Oaks shopping centers. Frequenting Jimmy Jazz, DTLR, J-Bees, and Express. Madison and Pulaski, 47th and Indiana, and Roseland were popular also.

A local jeweler, Ali of the Gold and Diamond Depot, located inside River Oaks, gave Bookie great deals on watches, earrings and any other items he wanted from the store, whether it was custom or in stock.

Joe found Bookie another bike after Tip didn't give him the title for the CBR in time, leading him to return it. He laid down all hundred-dollar bills for the GSXR. Not even a full week after he had purchased the Suzuki, he bought two vehicles, a box Chevy and a truck. The 84 Impala was to be painted orange, a full ostrich top and ostrich upholstery added after twenty-six-inch rims was put on it. Immediately Bookie paid the necessary deposits, getting the ball officially rolling on all his ideas. Despite the vehicles he had the title to, he only drove rental cars for the time being.

Money was being spent like it was December 31, 1999.

Partying and gambling. After one or two dice games at Bookie's new crib, where the stakes were in excess of $100,000, word got around. He began hosting more dice games. Gradually, he started an operation cutting or housing these games, extracting $2 per point. When the shooter would get the dice, he automatically took two bucks out the pot. No matter if the outcome was a crap or a natural, he caught a point or fell off. Every time there was a new shooter or new point, "the house" got $2.

A person down on their luck or someone who had gone broke, Bookie would allow to cut. At the end of the night they'd split the proceeds down the middle 50/50. A good hustle, but counterproductive when Bookie was losing $2,500 and at the conclusion of the game split $1,100 with someone, but that was how things turned out most of the time.

From the few bricks Bookie was left with after swapping out his partners, the 8k profit just wasn't enough anymore. Thirty to forty grand a month wasn't doing the job after a while. It was no longer sufficient.

A tactician wasn't needed to come up with a solution. Remove five grams from each sixty-three and replace it with isotol, benzocaine or Arm & Hammer. That equaled a free eighty grams every time Bookie bagged up a kilo. It worked for a minute but eventually proved to be inadequate as well. Necessity led him to take out seven grams and later ten. His pockets were like tapeworms; he had to keep feeding them. Instead of the eighty, now Bookie was getting a free 160 grams. He'd add an ounce of his special recipe and end up with 3 sixty-threes. Another $6,000 added to his already 8k profit bringing the total to $14,000 profit every brick he sold.

On occasion Bookie would request fifteen kilos, having to pay $360,000 by month's end. Sometimes when he had special orders, he even got twenty. On the outside looking in, it would appear that Bookie was on course. The right path. The money route! There was never a time he didn't have at least 10k on his person. It wasn't unusual to catch Bookie with forty or fifty large in his pockets. The money couldn't miss him. It came hand over fist. He used to misplace 10k, find it three months later and blow it on a pinky ring or some crazy trinket for his amusement.

According to the streets, there was a drought. On *The Recession* album, Jeezy was saying, "Ain't no work, ain't no jobs" and "It's a recession, err'body broke" – but Bookie couldn't tell. If everybody was broke, it was everybody *but* him. He was not affected in the least. Sure, the prices fluctuated upwards continually, but that was only because the demand escalated first.

And when his costs increased, he simply passed it on to the customer, increasing his price or "ticket." Sixty-threes went all the way up to $2,500 a pop.

CHAPTER 35 – BOYS II MEN

Sometimes you gotta go through hell to get to heaven. – Author

Bookie's younger cousins, having endured individual rites of passage, were now of age. They were infatuated with their big cousin and the lifestyle he led, so they attempted to stick to him like bees to honey. At every opportunity they were by Bookie's side, and when none naturally came, they wouldn't hesitate to create one. None more willing than Juice.

Juice had been Bookie's shadow since the age of sixteen. It was just hard to keep up since Bookie stayed on the go, and he had to attend school. With this new crib being in Kankakee, it wouldn't be as much of an obstacle. The only thing that could keep them apart was distance. And soon Juice would be heading off to school on a partial ride.

If anyone knew the lifestyle or the expectations therein, it was Juice. He was well aware of the etiquette that came with the territory, having witnessed it firsthand for years. He was to Bookie what Jigga was to Yodi in their heyday, with the exception of selling drugs. Juice had packed and popped pistols. He'd met everybody Bookie dealt with throughout his tenure and had a rapport with most of them. He was well acquainted with Donnie and knew Black on a first-name basis. Juice had shot dice with and rode shotgun in the Benz with Bread, talked sports and cocaine with Vino and for some reason had Flores' home number stored in his Boost Mobile. The latter was a feat that puzzled Bookie tremendously, seeing as how he had to get in contact with the old-timer through Juice one day.

Juice had even slapped Monique on the ass per Bookie's request. A chance encounter resulted in him seeing Nisha butt naked, and he often teased that one day he'd have a bitch "badder" than Honey. He saw Bookie at his best and worst, ups and downs. In honor of Bookie, he initiated a riot during his senior year of high school during a basketball game against Bloom.

A six-foot guard on the opposing team had murmured, "Fuck you" to Bookie as he booed him on the sidelines. Immediately after scoring the game-winning shot, Juice addressed the issue. A fight ensued.

When the first punch was thrown, Bookie was already on his feet. The entire bleachers followed, including Spank, who came to Bookie's aid after he found himself in serious trouble. The debacle made headlines in the *Daily Journal*. Since Juice was sixteen, popping bottles in clubs with Bookie was normal. Locally and otherwise. He came from a hustling family: Jim, Big Ron, Babe, his dad Wap. These guys were legendary from the westside of Chicago all the way to K3. He was always a street-savvy kid, but it was Bookie who presented the launching pad for him to spread his wings. Much to Bookie's dismay.

Contrary to popular belief, Bookie never encouraged negative behavior from Juice or any of his other little cousins. He facilitated it, yes. What other options did he have? Every day Bookie reminded Juice to do as he said, not as he was doing. He elaborated on why he had to do what it was that he was doing and the fact that he wished he didn't have to do it. The agreement was Juice would stay in school while Bookie stayed in the trap, and in the end they would meet in the middle. Juice would go off to college and get a particular skillset. Once he came back, Bookie would have the bankroll. They'd then bridge the gap. Meanwhile, he'd afford Juice all the luxuries without the teenager ever having to roll up his sleeves.

Bookie saw Juice off to college and made sure he had a little more than the essentials. The first break he got, Peoria's ICC wasn't too far, so he came back running. He and Bookie had a great time. They had had sex with more girls than they could count on both hands and blew as many racks in the process.

The crib was only a two-bedroom, Bookie's room and the guest room. When it was time to go, Juice had so much stuff they had bought during his visit that he had to leave some of it behind. There was another break that produced the same results. Third time was a charm. That's when Juice said fuck school and was back to stay. Of course, Bookie had objected, but the damage was already done.

******

Fat Boy was released from prison and couldn't believe how the tables had turned. Bookie tossed a book on his lap and told him what Jigga had told him in that alley three and a half years ago. "That's the shit Jeezy be talking bout ... stamp in the middle." Grabbing another brick for himself, Bookie retrieved his "opening" utensils.

"Aye, help me bag this shit up real quick."

They busted two books down.

"Hand me them sandwich bags and that big scale that say OfficeMax on the box."

Cutting through the layers of various gray and brown duct tape and rubber inner tubes in an attempt to mimic Bookie's actions, Fat Boy nipped his thumb with a boxcutter and soon the brown tape was partially smeared red. He kept shaking his head mumbling, "Bitch, you rich. On GGGGGGGD, you rich."

They bagged up the cocaine in record time. Every two minutes he would quote Jeezy, then reiterate that Bookie was rich. "You owe me too, bitch. I done cut myself. I fuck around and need stitches fucking wit you."

When they completed the task, Bookie gave Fat Boy sixty-three grams.

"Just shop wit me; you don't owe me shit."

"Bitch, what I'ma do wit this? I need a whole brick."

The very next night Fat Boy lost $7,500 shooting dice on Bookie's living room floor. Bookie gave him another sixty-three.

It wasn't uncommon for girls to hang out at these dice games. Free food and liquor brought the best of them out. Throw in some Kush or the potential to make a dollar, and Bookie damn near had to pull a gun on them to make them leave.

They'd pour drinks or pass out the pizza Bookie had ordered compliments of the house. Prancing around, looking cute, the girls got to act as hostesses. In a room of intoxicated men with hands, pockets, and bags full of money, their presence was always much appreciated. Most guys showed up for the money. To gamble. Some for the girls. The girls showed up for the freebies and a chance. Overall, the motivating factors were similar. Bookie benefited from both parties, either way.

Many of the girls served other purposes, doing whatever Bookie told them. They were referred to simply as the "crew," and by now the new crib was officially "Head Quarters".

******

On October 22, 2008, Diamond gave birth to his second son, Laneir. At Provena St. Mary's, watching the magic unfold, Bookie thought about the news he just received from Dionna; she too was "expecting." The abortion Honey had endured invaded his thought process. Via text message, she'd informed him that his *would-be* baby had, in fact, had a twin. Why she felt compelled to point this out, he had no idea, but as he held his son, he couldn't help but think about the "twins." He handed Lanier back to his sister Martha and walked out the hospital. Diamond, sweaty and fatigued, asked where was he going. Bookie ignored her.

******

A lot of time was spent on the GSXR even when weather didn't quite fully permit it. Bookie had that rider's high, that new bike owner's experience during their first season riding. Inadvertently, he began riding in an unofficial bike club. Actually two of them. Eyes, Tyrone, DeeTee and those in his age group and line of business all had bikes. They formed sort of an alliance. There was another group of guys who were a few years older and mostly all legit; they weren't with the shits in any way, shape, form, or fashion.

Any given day you could see Bookie riding on a bike or in a rental car. If he was in the rental, nine times out of ten, he was ridin "dirty." You could catch him gambling at the casino or on the streets. That and selling cocaine was his life. Always out, on the go, being seen, the hustler was conspicuously flashy and flamboyant. Donnie would really have been proud. Police hated Bookie.

He was harassed daily. Bookie intentionally made a mockery of the force. Had they been a reputable police department, doing real police work, he would have been in trouble long ago. But those idiots couldn't think their way out of a paper bag. Passwarder wasn't the only bozo in uniform. Just plain stupid. Especially the KAMEG. That unit consisted of a bunch of fake, uneducated, inbred, "wannabe" task force agents. One month they're in a patrol car responding to purse snatching and vandalism calls, the next minute they're in an unmarked cruiser with a beard and a semi-automatic pistol strapped to their leg. A baseball cap to the back and a vest on the outside of their clothes, doing their best to look intimidating. What a bunch of dimwits. Get real. To Bookie, they were a fucking joke.

Each time Bookie encountered them, he was in possession of a bankroll, drugs and a handgun. Yet his illegal goods were never found. Never! Talk about not being qualified. If it wasn't for stool pigeons, confidential informants squealing, the Kankakee police department wouldn't make any arrests. Even their dogs were incompetent. They were sad excuses for officers of the law who took an oath swearing to protect and serve.

******

Now officially living with Bookie, Juice came out of his shell. Bookie wouldn't sell him any drugs, so his enterprising younger cousin went out and found someone who would. What he bought happened to be Grade A garbage. Bookie wasn't having it. He contacted the seller and demanded the money back in full, or else. Bookie was in between a rock and a hard place. Juice was young and ambitious. One could see in the boy's hazel-brown eyes that there wasn't much he feared, including Bookie. Therefore, it was almost guaranteed that the college dropout would try his hand again getting mediocre work from an outsider if Bookie didn't oblige him. His hands were tied. After hours of lecturing, Bookie relented and gave Juice his first sixty-three.

The cousins cooked up the grams together right in the kitchen on south Chicago. Juice had seen the process done a thousand times before but was never allowed to participate in it.

Bookie could turn soft powder into hard cookies with his eyes closed.

"Just watch me first, then you do it next."

"Aight," Juice responded.

"We gonna need a Pyrex. Get the medium size one. Get the big scale. Grab some baking soda and sandwich bags."

Those materials had to be retrieved from the stash spot in the basement that Bookie had professionally installed. Inside the crib, if he wasn't caught in the act, he'd never be caught. Unless Juice gave him up and that was impossible. The youngin' took pride in, *Death Before Dishonor.*

"Okay, you want me to blow it up or what?"

"Yea, but not too much. I'ma sell all eightballs."

He knew the game, alright. If you blew the work up too much you could possibly sell it whole if you had a buyer. But if you were selling eightballs, after you sell one, no matter what price, chances are that customer wouldn't come back, and you'd run the risk of being stuck with a million balls. Even selling it whole, you run the risk of the buyer demanding his money back unless you had a name or reputation that protected you from such demands. You could get hurt playing games like that.

"Just make me four zips. I can sell 3.0s for $100. It's ugly out here right now."

"Aight, do the math. You got sixty-three, right?"

"Right."

"Four times twenty-eight is what?"

"One hundred twelve. So you need forty-nine more grams."

"That's what it come out to," Bookie said, acknowledging that he was good with numbers, offering up the correct math without thinking. "Aight, put that sandwich bag on the scale, then start it over so it say zero. Aight...now pour forty-nine grams of soda in the bag."

He poured it out slow, using precision. At the last minute, a chunk fell out the box. "It's 50.7. Hold on, let me—"

"Don't worry about it," Bookie told him. "It's cool...pick up the bag slow and dump it in the Pyrex."

"I thought you supposed to do it while I watch?"

"Man, you worried bout the wrong shit. Just pay attention cause you up next. Dolo."

"Fuck outta here."

"I ain't playing. Now watch what I do here."

"I already know how to cook..."

"Man, listen. Look at what the fuck I'm doing. You gonna get yo chance next. You heard a couple songs from Yo Gotti and Jeezy, now you know how to cook?" Bookie laughed.

"Don't forget Gucci," he added.

"Whatever, pay attention. The soda go first, then the yams," Bookie instructed dumping the sixty-three grams of cocaine into the glass jar before taking a fork and smashing up the chunks of crystalline powder. He added three teaspoons of water and set the Pyrex down to adjust the settings of the microwave, reducing the intensity.

"It sound like it's already cooking. You hear that fizzing?" Juice asked, picking up the jar to get a better view.

"That's cause it is, but come on, put it in here." Bookie opened the microwave. With the cocaine already in its quasi-crack stage, Bookie set the timer for two minutes and pressed start. The product circled at a 360° angle for a full fifty-two seconds before the substance threatened to spill over the top of the jar.

Bookie removed it and worked the fork. "It's oiling down. Shit look good, don't it?" The cocaine had turned into a golden oil while the soda was still its original color. The fork was used to blend it all together.

After thirty more seconds of the low-frequency radio activity, the contents of the jar were completely liquified. Bookie put the fork to work, and not a minute later the surface was starting to harden. Bookie ran the cold water in the sink and let it fall over the bottom of the jar to expedite the cooling process. When he was sure it had locked up and was hard through and through, he took a butter knife and popped the cocoa-butter-colored cookie out. He set it on the scale and it was 112.9 grams. The whole process took about seven minutes.

"Now, it's yo turn."

"You got another sixty-three?"

"Hell nawl, for what? You think I'm fina keep cooking sixty-threes and be stuck with a hundred ounces of hard? Where they do that at? You tryna get me a hundred years. Melt that one back down."

"How?" Juice looked confused.

"That's why yo ass shoulda been tuned in instead of all that mufucking talkin. If you want, I can drop it, cook all the soda off of it, and you can splash it again or you can just…matter fact, just put it back in there and press start."

Bookie left to go make a move. DeeTee wanted a sixty-three.

When he returned, Juice had a cookie, but it was damaged. Cracked and chipped on the side where he'd tried to take it out the jar. It wasn't blended as good; you could still see the white and tan swirls.

"Take a sharper knife and cut a line down the middle like you cutting it in half, then pop it out like that. Grab a paper towel or some newspaper or something you can put it on so it can dry."

CHAPTER 36 – REALIZATION

Sometimes you gotta get your hands dirty in order to clean things up. –
Author

Juice used his key to come in while Bookie sat at the table paying some bills. Bookie had just sold almost ten pounds of cocaine and was in the dining room busting down another brick. The two kilos had gone to Pete in Minnesota, nine ounces went to a nigga in Hopkins, Cap Ball came for an eighth right after Murda picked up a sixty-three, and Cap was picking up a nina in another hour. Sixteen sixty-threes were in individual bags on the table.

Bookie removed the ten grams from each bag and added another twenty-nine grams of his special recipe. Placed it on the huge digital scale: 189g. Three sixty-threes. He was still in the process of counting the money he just made. A fully loaded Heckler and Koch lay on the table. Juice had company.

"Aye, we gotta take a shower; we just got done hooping at Pioneer. He going with us to the mall. He might have to spend a night too." The plan was they'd go to the mall with Deangelo then later hit the club.

Not wanting to miscount, Bookie's eyes washed over the lad briefly. Bookie nodded his head up then down and continued the task at hand.

"Here, you want a Gatorade?"

Bookie heard the fridge open. From the kitchen, Juice said, "You told me to remind you to go on 159th to grab some more chalk, too." He was referring to the benzocaine that Bookie got from Trendsetters on Halsted. "You forgot, didn't you? I just seen Richie Rich too. He told me you said come get $40 to pay his phone bill. I gave him the forty cent and dropped him off at River Street. I told him I'd get it back from you so he ain't have to come all the way down here."

When Bookie failed to respond, he called out a little louder. "You heard what I said bout lil Richard?"

Bookie could hear Juice in the other room.

"I told you he don't care, man. He ain't tripping. You need a towel, its soap in the bathroom."

The young man was Cortez Peden, a star basketball player for St. Anne High School who had recently graduated after winning a state championship. Bookie had attended most of their home games and some of their away games when they didn't conflict with Juice's schedule. Bookie had seen him in passing, spoke to him once or twice, but had never interacted with him outside of that. Cortez tried to be cool about it and act normal as if the various mountains of white powder, the gun, the scale and all the money he saw on that table were an everyday occurrence in his life, but Bookie knew they weren't. He picked up on the forced bravado. Cortez probably was in shock. The look on his face, which he most likely wasn't aware of, had betrayed him, telling Bookie that this was his first real glance at the underworld. Bookie would see to it that it was his last!

******

Bookie was at the top of his game. He was the head

honcho, El Jefe ... The King! Being worthy of said title was an understatement. Over the years he had come a long way. He had been through the fire and made it out. So many others had aspired to be in the position that he found himself in, putting forth countless efforts he bore witness to firsthand. But they all had come up short. If anyone was duly worthy of the crown, it was Bookie.

He reflected on the past by unlocking the door taking a huge gulp of Remy Martin and peering inside his closet of many skeletons. The brief trip down memory lane caused his tear ducts to swell instantly. The realization of his circumstances was mind-boggling.

Slamming the door shut, he put the lock back in its place with his head moving from side to side in disgust. So many lives lost to the game. Years of freedom traded for that illusive achievement of street fame.

Bookie's own brother, Tawayne, was doing a ten-year bid for a measly $50 piece of crack! He'd be out in a few years with good time. Koota was locked up and Icholis was gone. In Stateville, the Entourage boss, Donnie, was doing thirty years-plus. Dee was in Menard, serving forty-five, a half a century almost. Bread was in the feds. TK and Bam were gone, both brothers incarcerated. IDOC and FBOP. The Family was a thing of the past with the two co-founders both fighting separate federal indictments.

Bookie thought about all the violence. The shootings, the bloodshed, the murders. Quick was dead. He had a family, children. Bookie remembered JR Hope ... How he had been shot down in the street like a stray dog. The rain washing his blood down the sewer. The robbery of JD, where he was shot and wounded in the process, ultimately succumbing to his injuries. Gone forever, never to come back ...

Bookie struggled to see the picture from another angle. He tried to see the whole forest, not just the trees. Envision himself on the receiving end of violence. An end unfamiliar to him. He had never been robbed or shot. Up until now it was difficult for him to empathize, having never endured that level of victimization. He had never even been shot at intentionally. The situation with Quick and Icholis was meant for him, not Bookie. He had just been at the wrong place at the wrong time.

Being on the giving end was always easy. Bookie wondered now if he'd fare as well on the receiving end. Character was not forged through sunshine and roses, when all was peaches and cream. When things were easy or a walk in the park. Instead, character was forged through the fire and tumultuous times, and gauged by your reaction to day-to-day hardship. When trial and tribulations assailed you, when you had to struggle. When the storm blew over, whether or not you were still standing on your feet, that's what counted. How you handled misfortune or dealt with adversity. It wasn't the fall that mattered most, it was the "get up." Would he get back up?

Bookie wasn't himself when his money got low. When he was only shot "at" by accident, his visceral reaction had been one of extreme violence. When he was only sucker-punched, he saw red. If he was ever actually shot .... he could only imagine.

He wasn't naive enough to think it would never happen.

When you make your bed, you have to lie in it. Anytime you wear the crown, anytime you're the king, the day will come when you'll have to defend that crown. Or your kingdom will be jeopardized, possibly even taken. While you watch on from exile or burn at the stake. Bookie knew it would come ... he just didn't know when.

AUTHOR'S NOTE

I could have saturated the pages of this novel with fancy words in an effort to boost my own morale and maybe impress the readers, but I chose not to. My target audience isn't Rhodes Scholars. In fact, I'd go so far as to say my target audience is the exact opposite. Those who never heard of Cecil Rhodes.

I have a story to tell and this is part of it. If this book deters just one person from the street life, prevents one person from being "detoured," turning from the path of righteousness, then my goal is complete.

Keep in mind, too, if this is not a bestseller, I had no access to professors or experts. There was no research team or people to consult with. No browsing of the World Wide Web at my disposal. *Exit 312* was written in a security housing unit (SHU) prison cell. I had nothing to go off but my memory and the horrible conditions that ultimately motivated me to try and prevent you—the reader—from following in my footsteps. Do what I did ... nine times out of ten, you'll get what I got. Possibly worse.

Decade : A period not to exceed ten years.

Detour: A temporary turning aside from a usual or regular route, course or procedure. Temporary road or a longer road in temporary use because of an obstruction or state of disrepair on a regularly used road.

Lane Change will be in stores soon! Complete with photos of characters.

Also coming soon(er) than later: *HisStory*, a documentary-style film based on the life & times of the author.

Lane Change

The Detour series Part II

Any horse that runs fast don't run long. – Unknown

A small but sufficient oil burner from Bath and Body Works filled the atmosphere with a mango scent of sex. R. Kelly's Pandora station facilitated Usher pushing his vocals to the max via the tiny Bose embedded inside the headboard of the Ashley queen set.

"Did you miss me?" The question, rhetorical in nature, was asked in a tone more inviting than inquisitive.

Lying on his back with his forearm behind his head, Bookie looked up first at the ample breasts then the face of the voluptuous woman standing over him, the epitome of eye candy. He knew it was wrong, but it felt so right.

"What you think?" he answered with a question of his own. "You know I did, girl; stop playing."

Normally known for a sarcastic albeit flirtatious demeanor, his eyes told her he was as serious as Ebola in Africa. She was off-limits, but the twenty-six-year-old Bookie was addicted. After all, that's what addiction means, doesn't it, a lack of self control? Being helpless.

There wasn't enough lighting from the remote-controlled lamp to admire the full nudity of his twenty-three-year-old companion's physique. The contours he could see were a treat to the naked eye. The closest thing to perfection since Jesus in the flesh. If only this erotic indulgence was his to keep. But that was wishful thinking because she was already "spoken for," and the individual who spoke for her was more than an associate to Bookie.

"Well stand up and show me, give me a hug or something." As he rose off the bed, his worm followed suit.

"You know I missed you, right?" Her words were innocuous, her voice sultry.

Upset with himself for being so weak, Bookie mumbled a barely audible, "Yea."

The wicked smile telegraphed to Bookie that she knew he was at her mercy. Obediently, he attempted to embrace Mrs. Perfect, but she had plans of her own.

Positioning herself on her knees, a recently manicured hand with a French finish grasped his erection. The worm fit into her grip like a glove. *Perfecto!* Ever so gently she guided him to the destination. Looking down just in time to see the magic show, Mrs. Perfect looked up defiantly, holding his gaze while doing the best disappearing act known to man. When the MAC lip gloss came in contact with pubes, Bookie gasped and looked heavenward. Mere seconds later with his eyes wide shut and standing on his tippy toes, he clenched his teeth before starting to retreat.

He couldn't take it. She had him running. Hands as soft as medicated cotton were now gripping both buttocks firmly to ensure he didn't escape prior to her completing her obligatory duties. Clearly in control, Mrs. Perfect would just pull forward or push backwards to her liking. This was the no-hands segment of the performance. The labored breathing through the nostrils subsided as the expert movements were retracted slowly, leaving an excessive trail of moisture alongside the length of the shaft. For a brief moment, the tip of his manhood swam solo. Just as he neared climax a wet popping sound freed him.

Another smile, even more welcoming than the previous, was displayed on the face of the harlot as she got to her feet. Running water could be heard in the distance and a faint waft of lavender body wash detected, intermingled with steam. Now at eye level, the small flame from the candle danced in the dark pools of her pupils as she licked her lips, anticipating what was to come. Realizing he'd been holding his breath, Bookie exhaled deeply then followed up with the opposite gesture as his lungs filled with much needed oxygen.

Breasts pressed aggressively against a heaving chest as the same dirty mouth was now pressed against his own, and the experienced tongue searching for its mate. Coming up for air, "Bae, lay down, hurry up, bae, lay down."

Bookie did as he was told. Without further ado, she climbed atop and—

"Y'all got started without me?" A female's voice asked from the doorway.

Bookie had almost forgotten they had company. He was so preoccupied that he hadn't noticed the shower stop running.

******

Across the street, a nosy neighbor watched from a second-story window as members of a joint task force surrounded Headquarters. Their caravan had consisted of seven vehicles. Three went to the back while the remaining four covered the front. A total of twenty-three heavily armed agents descended upon the residence located in the historical district of K3, weapons drawn and at the ready. The special agent in charge ordered his men to fan out, establishing a perimeter, careful to flank the sides, ending all possible escape routes. This was a long time corning; they couldn't let him get away. Stubbing out his Camel with a well-worn boot, Agent Nickols remembered his encounters with the target as he switched off the safety on his weapon. He also recalled the dreams he had of putting cuffs on the arrogant bastard. Not sure if he'd taken more lives with a gun or the little glass jar he cooked crack in, one thing was for sure; he had definitely lived up to his name, "Killer." Leonard Sharp was exactly the type of criminal that men of the badge loathed.

The confidential informant provided intricate details. There was already enough evidence to put the pompous piece of shit away, but not for long. 10.8 grams and a firearm from earlier in the year. But, that wasn't sufficient. The objective was to end his career! This would be many of the agents' biggest score to date. Due to tonight's expected seizure, the federal government was involved, and their involvement would almost guarantee a conviction according to Special Agent Marsholl of the ATF. There was an excellent chance that the suspect would be locked behind bars for the remainder of his natural life. If all went according to plan and the info checked out.

"Wishful thinking," another agent thought, not daring to verbalize this to his superior. He flicked his Marlboro to the ground. Passwarder knew Bookie well. "Bookie," "Killa,"

"Leonard," or whatever fucking name you wanted to call the son-of-a-bitch, he wasn't like the average street punk selling nickel bags in the park. Eighty percent of dealers who got pinched in the tri-city area of K3 County would squeal if pressed. In a matter of minutes if pressure was applied properly. Fifteen percent could be manipulated or deceived into blowing the whistle when they otherwise refused to do so. And we're talking for a gram or two of crack cocaine!

But not this one. Bookie represented that rare five percent. He was under the gun for a murder and wouldn't even give so much as a hint to who the perp might have been. Even after he discovered that half of Kankakee had written statements on him, his life was threatened, and his freedom hung in the balance. Surely he wouldn't bump his gums over a dope case. Nor could he be tricked into cooperating. He wasn't a fool; he made it past every level investigators had to offer. Bookie was unlike others of his caliber in that he talked a lot, but he also backed it up. Loud, flashy, flamboyant, obnoxious, cocky, disrespectful to the uniform and whatever else you wanted to throw in there.

Usually, these types wouldn't last thirty days. Once in the crosshairs, it was over. Fish in a barrel. Not Killa. His approach was peculiar. As a result, it took some deep digging into the bag of tricks, even some unorthodox and possibly illegal tactics, to get him in the net. And he still wasn't "got" per se. Either one of the luckiest men this side of the Mason/Dixon or what you see was the precise opposite of what you got, and Bookie was largely underestimated. Tonight would tell the difference. Once and for all.

Photo by Pete, of Christie Photography

ABOUT THE AUTHOR

Leonard Sharp

An outdoorsman at heart, the author enjoys horseback riding, most water sports and hunting various game. When not spending time with his children, he looks forward to writing, watching world news or *The History Channel* and dining on Italian cuisine. A favorite pastime is traveling, where he constantly seeks innovative ways to give back to the homeless and the youth who've found themselves disenfranchised. No stranger to adversity, the author spent his formative years in the trenches, affiliated with street gangs and selling crack.

Prison was his rite of passage. He sympathizes with those who represent the struggle, especially adolescents whose voice have been muffled by institutions of authoritative systems. He is a voice, their voice... a voice for the voiceless! The dedication, determination and tremendous amount of discipline he once used to be a part of the problem are now being used to create solutions. He's worked hand in hand with the Chicago branch of CeaseFire since 2012, integrating himself into the community in a visible attempt to make a difference. In 2017 he found B.M.F. (Brothers Moving Forward), a community-based organization that focuses on steering young minorities in a positive direction. He divides his time evenly between Chicago and Kankakee, Illinois, during the majority of the year. At the break of winter he escapes to Scottsdale, Arizona, where he resides until spring.

As an adolescent he was exposed to the game.
At 15, he had a #NUMBER instead of a name.
By 30, he conquered fame.
At 31, ball & chain.
#STORYOFMYLIFE

"90% of learning is done outside the classroom." When it comes to the streets, he's done it all. If asked, he'll admit that, yes; experience is the best teacher. Having been locked up in seven different states, served a decade behind bars, spent three years on house arrest, six years on probation / parole, unfortunately like many others he had to learn the hard way. But, in the end it wasn't worth it. Never has been, never will be. With that being said, the author has a wealth of knowledge to offer, bringing to any podium he may grace, first-hand experiences he's acquired throughout his tenure. He's a walking, living, breathing WARNING to any and all who think the street way is the right way.

Follow @

Facebook: Tawayne Sharp
Instagram: freeme_2016
Snapchat: Exit312

Contact information for booking / speaking engagements:
Email: wizzlesharp@gmail.com
Phone: 312-843-8823

Made in the USA
Coppell, TX
01 September 2021

61609169R00236